REBORN
virtues constellation

ALSO BY JUSTIN WILLIAMS

Traitmarker Books | Franklin, TN

Edited by: Robbie W. Grayson III
Interior Layout: Robbie W. Grayson III
Cover Design by: Robbie W. Grayson III

Published by Traitmarker Books
www.traitmarkerbooks.com
traitmarker@gmail.com

Dedication

I would like to thank everybody who was part of my exciting and dramatic life in India. This includes my colleagues at the Kirloskar and former Mannesmann Demag factories and offices and the suppliers and clients too numerous to mention by name who each played an outsized role in making my stay in India a true adventure. Friends, neighbors, and acquaintances from Pune showered me with their hospitality and taught me all the little and big tricks to master life in India.

I tried to do justice to as many people as possible who were part of my adventure: the good and the bad. Many of them feature prominently in this book, and I apologize to the people I either left out or merely sketched as part of my literary license. Nevertheless, they each are essential to me.

India or Bharat itself deserves enormous credit for providing a fantastic backdrop for the life lessons I received. Only India could excel in history, art, business, language, culture, cuisine, spirituality, and philosophies. I am forever grateful.

TRAITMARKER BOOKS

Record of Events

INTRODUCTION
About Virtues Constellation

Virtues Constellation is a spicy tale of a modern-day Marco Polo, the famous trader and explorer who traveled to Asia 751 years ago. His book Il Milione [1] means "The Million" in English because of the million tales he could tell his readers about his travels to China. Like Marco Polo, I set out from Europe in the 1990s to find opportunity and found Asia just as intriguing. I feel that I have just as many stories to tell.

Although set in India's many regions which includes people from all religions and walks of life, Virtues Constellation is more than a travel journal. It is a tale of drama, intrigue, politics, love, and adventure in an India that opened itself to the West just as Colonialism and the Cold War were ending.

India is one of the world's oldest and most influential cultures that dates as far back as five millennia ago. With an extensive history of trade and contact with other people, India's contributions to religion, philosophy, technology, and science are understated but equally important. Southeast Asians, Sumers, Greeks, Romans, Persians, Chinese, Moguls, and modern-day Europeans each beat a path to India. The very name India was enough to send fleets of ships, hordes of traders, and numerous armies to loot its wealth.

Despite her grand tradition, science, and ancient culture, India is only now regaining the prominent role she once had in the world after shaking off post-Colonialism. Bharat, as India calls itself once again, is an exciting new frontier of modern life, and exerts her magical, colorful attraction to the outside world. People of South Asian origin now live in many countries around the globe and contribute to significant roles among those populations.

Despite India's manifold contacts with the outside world, few foreigners deeply understand what India stands for and how interaction with the Western world has been changing India for better or worse. I believe this factor to be critical. Many Indians who have embraced the West have lost touch with her ancient values and achievements.

To understand India, it is not enough for tourists to vacation on a beach in Goa. It also is not enough for businesspersons to jet around the country to its beautiful cities or to teleconference from its five-star hotels. Anyone seeking salvation in an ashram cannot uncover the complex and colorful layers of Indian culture. Most visitors live off a stereotypical image of India which primarily consists of crowds, slums, dusty pot-holed roads, and run-down office buildings. While these features do indeed exist, India is much more than that.

When the modern economy in India was liberalized in the 1990s, it was an exciting time of change. It is fascinating to see how that unfolded and to compare it with how India has changed since then. Just as necessary are the significant and timeless insights of Indian and European culture that ought still be relevant today as it was in the past.

Myriad cultures, castes, and religions make up a colorful and vibrant fountain of humanity in India. I have roped into my mural a number of Indian personalities from all walks of life as well as a few foreigners. I intentionally have written an autobiographical memoir that includes travel adventure, conflict, history, drama, culture, spirituality, and love that, I believe, will fascinate the everyday reader.

Being a professional engineer, I present key economic and engineering terms in an easy-to-understand fashion, providing just enough basic details for the reader to understand and appreciate the central crisis of the story plot.

The intricate inner workings of family-managed, Indian companies and publicly traded, multinational corporations that I share also provide plenty of suspense to answer the questions of the central plot, What happens when foreign and indigenous business cultures clash? It is the story of living and working with people who bring to the table different personal skills and ambitions. I describe the joys and frustrations of challenges and the many ethical dangers that lurk behind it all.

Virtues Constellation is also an exciting travel guide in which I share both historical and cultural highlights, breathtaking monuments, landscapes, flora, and fauna. It is sure to be a treat for the novice with a budding interest in India as well as the expert Indologist. Everywhere in India is an adventure.

All events are true and have happened as described. If I had tried, I could not have invented the stories you will read. As the brilliant science fiction author, Arthur C. Clarke, who retired to Sri Lanka just off the coast of India stated, "Reality can be stranger than fiction." He must have known what he was talking about, because I have found his statement to be true in my interactions with India.

The names of most people, places, politicians, industrialists, and public figures have been unchanged to ensure credibility. I have endeavored to use people's names and titles per their usual cultural, social, and ethnic contexts. Anglo Saxons and Americans use their given names. Indians use their last names unless you're a close friend in which case you can use the given name. In Germany, the use of the family name, academic titles, and titles of nobility dominate unless you are, likewise, a close friend or relative. When languages and cultures cross over, a mixed use is appropriate. The situational response for each is also reflected in the book.

Just after my stay in India in the 1990s, the government of India changed several place names from English to more Indianized spellings and phonetics. Bombay becomes Mumbai, and Chennai comes from Madras. Vadodara replaced Baroda. Calcutta warped into Kolkata. People often use both place names even today. My guest town turned from Poona (English) to Pune (Marathi). Poonites turned into Punekars. But the street connecting Pune to its megalopolis neighbor is still called the Bombay Poona Road! A new expressway, called the Mumbai Pune Expressway, parallels the old road. I used the modern, official names of cities and places as far as I could and as was reasonable.

The foreign language that I use is a mixture of British, US English, Indlish, and even German, depending on the context. I have researched all facts and sources as befitting the serious scholar. I apologize in advance for any remaining inaccuracies or errors.

Join me on a fantastic journey to India where West met East.

JUSTIN WILLIAMS | HOUSTON, TX

Chapter 1

Now You Face a Power

It was faint, but Christian Belvedere heard the word reverberating from the other side of the glass.

Ascend.

Sitting on the edge of an overstuffed chair, Christian Belvedere leaned forward on the five-paneled mosaic star The casement took up the entire wall.

While several wooden shelves full of books flanked the window, Christian focused intently on each prong of the star clockwise for several rotations until his eye caught a title mid-cycle: Poems and Fragments.

Momentarily distracted, his green eyes flitted from one spine to another. The Oresteia, The Poor Man of Nippur, and The Clouds: an Old Comedy all shared the same shelf. He had expected to see titles on contemporary psychology. Instead, these were about ancient religion and mythology. Carl Jung might have been proud of this crossover. But the gods would have been angry.

Ascend… The voice was louder this time. And agitated.

Suddenly, Christian remembered why he was sitting on the edge of this chair in this office. His fists tightened and his jaws tensed. He had struggled one time too many to pull himself back from the brink of what doctors had been

13

calling "psychosis." For Christian, this manifested as an obsession with the esoteric. And for the last two weeks of the several he had been an inpatient at Angelfire Psychiatric, he had finally submitted to the treatment, allowing for the possibility that there was no voice in the forest tempting him to ascend the Ladder of Enlightenment in lieu of a boring existence.

Christian's thoughts were interrupted at the sound of footsteps outside the office door and down the hall, approaching with staccatoed intention. The doctor was usually in her chair before Christian entered the office. Those appointments had always correlated with her not approving his release. Now it was two days away from September 3rd, the last day he needed to register on campus if he were to have a senior year at all. But he held out hope. Because this time, the doctor had kept him waiting.

The hurried click clack of high heels abruptly stopped at the door. Christian's eyes watched the door handle descend in one swift motion. The door opened, and the doctor walked in.

Dr. Aceso was a beautiful woman and an exception to her profession. She was a psychiatrist who had been working with some of the most complicated dissociation cases on the East Coast for the past seventeen years.

She downplayed it today with pleated, loosely fitted, pin-striped pants that stopped short of open-toed, black stilettos. Her muscled thighs and athletic calves appeared and disappeared as the clothing swished as she walked. and an equally loose-fitting blouse ornamented with a generous amount of lace along the collar, her muscled thighs and athletic calves were highlighted by the drapery of fabric. And even though her dark hair was in a messy bun on the top of her head, it wasn't too hard to imagine her hair down, seductively revealing the hints of high cheekbones, a hint of amber-colored mascara above her almond-shaped eyes, and the attractive simplicity of her petite nose.

She took Christian's breath away each time he met with her which was hardly professional of her, he thought. The fact of the matter was that after meeting with her a dozen times, he hadn't yet convinced her that he was better. That he no longer heard voices.

ASCEND!

The voice was almost a shout this time, and it startled Christian out of his thoughts. He snatched a brief look at Dr. Aceso to see if she heard it. But Dr. Aceso was busily shuffling through a pile of paperwork. Nervously, Christian thought.

Shh, Christian whispered under his breath to the forest. But he disguised it as a sigh. He couldn't afford to be hearing voices now. Right now, he needed to convince the doctor that he no longer heard... no, no longer believed in... the voices.

In truth, this remote and rustic hospital had done the trick. After attending its inpatient program for a few weeks now, Christian didn't care whether or not the voices he had been hearing were the result of psychosis. The origin of the voices didn't concern him like it had before because it had gotten him where he was right now.

What he couldn't shake, however, was the feeling that he got from hearing them. The excitement of a grand calling, the honor of being chosen, the chills of uncertainty, and the thrill of discovery. That was all that mattered to him. He couldn't give that up.

"Good morning, Mr. Belvedere," Aceso finally offered

15

Christian a brief smile. "I apologize for keeping you wait-ing."

That's a smile of concession, Christian thought. Satisfied that he might have the upper hand, he dared to allow him-self a little comfort and leaned back into the chair.

"What is the forest saying to you today?" Aceso asked, knowingly. Christian froze. How did she know?

"What?" Christian muttered, trying to deflect. "Last night? That was a bad dream. Maybe even a bad reaction to the meds. Forests don't talk. And even if they did," he added for effect, "I wouldn't listen."

Aceso pursed her lips, and her cheeks flushed.

"Mr. Belvedere... Christian, if I can call you that," her voice softened. "Most doctors would be happy with that answer. Especially if they underestimated the great intelli-gence of their patient." There was that knowing look in her eye again, and it made Christian squirm.

"But I know just how brilliant you are. You could be tricking me with your 'truth.'" She paused. "You could be tricking yourself with your 'truth.'" She glanced at the door and then looked back to Christian. Leaning slightly for-ward and lowering her voice conspiratorially, she tapped her right index finger for emphasis on the stack of paper-work in front of her. "And wouldn't that be a pity?"

Christian shrugged his shoulders uncomfortably, not sure if that question was a trap.

Aceso suddenly sat up with a new energy, pulled a brown accordion file out of her desk drawer and slid the stack of paperwork on her desk into it, tying it up with a thick rub-ber band.

"Well, all I have to go on are your words. I'll assume that you're aware of the consequences to your person should you be lying to me." Placing the folder back into her desk, she added with the condescending tone that accompanied Christian's previous appointments, "Of course, if you're not ready to leave, then you should want to stay here. To get better. To put your health first. The world isn't going anywhere, so why rush?"

But Christian wasn't sick. Led astray? Maybe.

"I just want to be normal," Christian said in a small voice, looking down at his hands.

That was all it took.

"Then today is your day." Christian looked up, surprised.

"Meaning...?" He asked.

"Yes, I'm releasing you today, Mr. Belvedere." Almost on cue, someone knocked raptly at the office door.

"Come in," Aceso answered. In walked a hospital orderly wheeling Christian's suitcase behind him with his red duffel bag balanced on top. Per hospital protocol, each patient at Angelsfire was required to pack up their bags before their weekly appointments. The hospital's reasoning was that it encouraged the patients to engage compliantly, if not eagerly, in their treatments as well as gave them hope in the possibility of being released, thereby reducing the number of negative incidents.

"Room 305 is checked out. Sign here." The orderly who looked too old to be doing this job and too ragged-looking to even be considered for this profession, handed Aceso a clipboard. Christian couldn't believe his luck.

"Are you serious?" He asked unbelievingly. Aceso finished her signature with a flourish and smiled at him. The orderly left as quickly as he had come and shut the door behind him.

"Yes, I'm serious. Why wouldn't I be?" Christian was in

a daze at his newfound luck that he couldn't find the right words.

"Because... because... I thought the dream I had last night ruined my chances for getting out this week." Aceso looked at the door almost as if to make sure that they were completely alone before she continued.

"Christian," her voice was different this time. Lower. More personable. More imploring. "Do you see the books on my shelves? I read each one while a student at Parthenon many years ago. No, I didn't just read them. I lived each one. But I lost myself in them. I sacrificed healthy friendships, lucrative internships, and the general normal life in pursuit of..." Her voice trailed. With a slight nod of her head to the window behind her "... my own forests."

Christian gave her a puzzled look.

"What are you saying, doctor? That you understand what it's like to be misunderstood? That you understand what it feels like to have your entire world on hold. That you live in fear each day of..." Christian paused. "...of hearing voices that you don't ask to hear? I can hardly imagine that to have been your case. So, what are you saying?"

Aceso looked at Christian intently. Her jaw stiffened and her eyes dilated.

"Do you know the story of Jacob's ladder, Christian?"

"Vaguely," he responded.

"Jacob falls asleep and a ladder appears as he does. He wakes up and ascends it, only to find heaven. When I was a child, I was so inspired by that story that I used to wait till my mother was asleep and go sleep under the staircase in our house. Every night, I'd wish for heaven to reveal itself to me through my very own ladder. Ha, even now I still ponder why the ladder never showed, why my staircase remained mundane. But you... dear Christian, have your own ladder don't you? Where I failed, you can succeed. Climb it... after all you're a senior this year. It's about time for you to..." There was a slight pause.

"ASCEND."

Her last word went up Christian's back like an electric current and he almost fell out of his chair. Before he could reply, Aceso went on as if she hadn't seen the involuntary spasm of his arms and legs.

"With that, you are discharged." Just like that.

Christian teared up, attempting to conceal the sob of relief that was welling up within him. Aceso's compassion for and faith in him broke the dam of anxiety, isolation, and fear that Christian had been suppressing because of the voices. No one had ever been that honest with him before. No one had ever tailored their words to fit precisely what he needed to hear. No one—not even his parents—had ever dared let him get that close.

Parents. Christian had been so focused on getting out of Angelsfire that he hadn't thought of what would happen when he got out. Parents, that was what. A crippling fear gripped him.

"Do my parents know?"

"Yes. I spoke to your mother before our appointment this morning. They will actually be an hour late. They had a meeting this morning. You're welcome to wait here until they come."

But Christian didn't want his newfound freedom overshadowed by the unapproving stares of Stone and Mrs. Belvedere. Leaving now meant an hour of... life... liberty... and the pursuit of... the voices?

"That's ok. I'll go now. I can do with some fresh air."

"But where will you go?" Aceso looked startled. Christian vaguely remembered the surrounding geography of Angelsfire.

"Isn't there a cafe about fifteen minutes from here?" Aceso blinked her eyes.

"Yes. Delos' Meat and Three."

"Well, that's where I'll go." He slid to the edge of his seat, waiting for Aceso's permission to leave.

She pulled a smartphone out of her middle desk drawer and slid it across the table to Christian. It intermittently blinked green which meant it was on.

"If you need to check in with me before your next appointment, use this. It's an encrypted line and will alert me if you call."

Christian picked it up warily.

"Thank you," he said.

Dr. Aceso stood up, only 5 foot 3 to Christian's 6 foot 2. She put out her hand.

"Best of luck to you, Christian." She stepped over to the door and opened it. Christian grabbed his baggage, swiveled it around, and paused.

"Thank you again, Doctor."

"Nolite te bastardes carborundorum," she murmured in reply. It was Latin, but Christian understood the translation: Don't let the bastards drag you down.

And with that, Christian walked through the door.

***

As soon as Christian descended the twelve stone steps at the entrance of Angelsfire with his luggage banging behind him for each one, one of the wheels on his suitcase jarred loose. And by the time he had navigated the hospital's winding gravel drive to the main road, he was winded. But despite these minor inconveniences, he was free. Free of the voices. Free of his parents. Well, for at least another ten minutes.

As he took a left onto the busy University Boulevard, something caught his eye in the heavily wooded forest beyond the cyprus trees that lined the road, shielding Angelsfire from a street view. At the same time, he heard something crashing through the brush just ahead of him. Squinting, he caught the hindquarters of what looked like a giant dog.

A blue dog? Christian asked himself. But then it was gone. He shook his head, remembering that he had chosen to be free of the voices.

This is a new beginning, he assured himself as he picked up his pace, struggling along with his suitcase that would momentarily bounce off kilter at every crack in the pavement. He distracted himself by counting each crack, but lost track when Delos's flashing fluorescent sign came into view. Christian's confidence was suddenly replaced with a heavy depression when he made out the shape and color of his father's chrome-colored Bentley Bentayga.

So Mom drove with Dad. That means that Mom is under his thumb, Christian thought bitterly as he approached an intersection and pressed the WALK sign.

Christian's mother was a very forceful person in her own right. If Christian didn't believe things in the same manner that she did herself, she wouldn't try to persuade him in a reasonable manner. She would scream until he became unhinged and doubted himself. Throughout the ordeal with his psychosis, she had kept trying to convince him that he

21

was delusional despite how closely her own traditional religious beliefs mirrored his own departure from reality.

But all of her mother's bravado would melt away in the presence of Stone Belvedere. He was really the force in the house to be reckoned with. Behind the deception of his dark wavy hair slicked-back like a mob boss, tailored mustache, and his wide, winsome smile, it was the sinister way his honey-colored eyes would almost involuntarily darken as he peered into your own. It was a dark magic, and Christian was beginning to panic at the thought of being under his gaze. Maybe leaving Angelsfire was a mistake.

When the WALK light turned on, Christian stepped into the road with his head down and pulled his luggage behind him. Because his head was down and his thoughts were awry, he didn't see the oncoming pedestrian until he had walked into him. His luggage flipped and his duffel bag flew into the street.

Startled, Christian looked up to apologize, but then realized he had run into a homeless person. Not that Christian didn't apologize to homeless people he bumped into. But there was simply the notion that this homeless person might have actually been at fault because he immediately righted Christian's suitcase and retrieved his duffel bag. He was wearing a tattered black hoodie that concealed what appeared to be a massively built frame, and Christian didn't catch his face until the man retrieved his duffel bag.

The man glanced at Christian without losing his stride.

"No need to rush," The man nodded his head toward the diner. "Nothing's going to change in there."

Then the man was gone.

***

Christian peered through the smudged window of the door below the flashing fluorescent sign that screamed De-los's Meat & Three in an arc above a poor logo depiction of a lion that looked more like a grimacing seal. He was hoping to catch sight of his parents to gauge their mood, but no sooner had he scanned the diner than he caught his mother's frantic wave of excitement beckoning him in. Christian groaned. The fifteen-minute walk in the scorching sun had actually taken eighteen because of the dozen or so times that Christian lost control of his luggage. Along with the sweat pouring from every pore of his thick brown hair, matting his shirt to his back and giving him an uncomfortably haggard appearance, Christian didn't look presentable and couldn't handle a scene about his appearance right now.

On top of that, Christian would have preferred that his father had seen him first. That would have released the tension that had been creeping into his soul every damned step along the way. He wasn't bound to his father like he was to his mother. To his father he owed obeisance and fealty in exchange for the suspension of judgment and wrath. Their relationship was transactional and, therefore, simple. His mother was a different story altogether. It involved intricate levels of gaslighting, a panoply of psychological gymnastics, and the occasional slap. The emotional contortion of their relationship was, well, complicated.

But his mother was already standing up and gesticulating in a way that was already making a scene, so he reluctantly pulled on the sticky door handle, a cacophony of bells jangling his arrival, and entered the dark diner, bracing himself for the verbal jiujitsu that would undoubtedly ensue.

"You look well!" his mother all but threw himself into Christian's arms, beating him to the punch.

"Thank you," Chtristian said with strained consternation as he tried to ward off her tight squeeze. His mother stiffened and pulled back. Ah, the sweat did it for him. He waited for her to berate him, but she feigned a smile and motioned for him to follow her.

Here we go... He lugged his baggage to the booth where his father was sitting with his back to him.

"You know, I realize that I have put you and father through a lot, but please..." Christian blurted out the words soft enough for his mother to hear but also loud enough for his father to pick up on his contrite tone. If you weren't his equal, you had to be contrite before Stone Belvedere. There was no wiggle-room. Christian's mother responded loud enough for Christian to hear but also loud enough for Stone to figure out that she hadn't started the conversation.

"No, honey. You misunderstand me. I'm not trying to make this about me or your dad anymore." They both now stood in front of the booth where Stone Belvedere sat, nursing his coffee.

"Son," Stone stood up, flashed a winsome smile, and reached out his arms toward Christian. "Son," he picked up where his wife left off. "No, this is about you, and, despite appearances or hasty, insecurity-based investments, I am just sick thinking about how much you have had to suffer at just such a young age." Eager to fulfill her role, Mrs. Belvedere interrupted.

"I've even been talking to a therapist myself, who has been a godsend, and I have gained some perspective." She looked nervously at Stone. "So has your dad."

Christian began to shake.

Like I said, Here we go again.

Christian sat down across the booth from his father and scooted against the far side of the wall to make room for Mrs. Belvedere.

She slid in next to him until her shoulder touched his.

"Why are you wet?" She asked innocently as if she had just noticed.

Oh, my God, Christian grimaced as the tremors started in his hands.

His anxiety had gotten the best of him already, and he hadn't even ordered pancakes yet. Lately, he had been shaking all the time. But since Angelsfire had lowered his meds a week ago, he knew that he was shaking from emotion.

Christian's mother had never had perspective. She planted the fault and burden of his alleged bipolar disorder firmly in his lap: the shame and parental disapproval for something that he couldn't control.

Dr. Aceso had told Christian that since his imaginings were from religious systems and myths that his parents did not themselves believe in, it scared them on a variety of levels: spiritual, emotional, and mental. This trinity of effect had created a web of bigotry not aimed necessarily at him but at the gods who were "speaking" through his psychosis. Christian tried to shake these thoughts from his head in order to ward off any chance of a scene, but his thoughts tumbled forward effortlessly.

They're telling me that their suffering isn't greater than mine? They are telling me that they are sorry for me, for how they have behaved? Now she is telling me that she has gotten help.

Christian had been prepared to prove to himself that he could go toe-to-toe with them in an argument. He had waited for weeks, punching pallid pillows and shadow-boxing through empty colonial-style halls just to convince himself that he was now articulate enough, brave enough, and clear-headed enough to overcome his anxiety and deliver a verbal ass-kicking when argumentation would ensue once he was released.

Now, they had decided to be good parents so it wasn't necessary? He was beginning to experience the downer: crushing shame with a slight hint of relief.

Stone Belvedere beckoned a waitress who sauntered over with a pot of coffee, swaying her hips from side to side in an exaggerated fashion, her eyes for Stone only.

"What will it be, Boss," she drew out the word "Boss" suggestively. Stone had that effect on women.

"A stack of pancakes for the young man, honey." The waitress melted.

"Sure, sweetheart," she chortled back. Stone Belvedere didn't hide the fact that he enjoyed the view of the waitress as she walked away, a view she made clear was meant especially for him. Stone smiled to himself as he blew into his coffee mug, looking at Christian through the steam.

Christian sneaked a side glance at his mother to see her reaction to the back and forth between her husband and the floozy of a waitress. No reaction. Literally nothing. Christian couldn't tell if she was trying her best not to notice or if she had somehow internally resigned herself to the fact that Stone would always be a chick magnet, whether or not she liked it.

"It's good to see you, son." Stone slurped. Mrs. Belvedere turned to Christian who averted his eyes to the window that faced the parking lot just beyond his mother's face. She turned to follow his eyes.

"Do you want to drive it?"

"What?" Christian started.

"You can't stop looking at it." She nodded towards the parking lot, pulled the key of the Bentley out of her purse, and dangled it teasingly in front of Christian's face.

She set it down on the table and slid it over to him.

"Your father got it for me yesterday. I've only driven it once… here… but you can drive it back home."

Christian internally groaned again. In the last few months, Christian had noticed that nothing his mother ever offered or gave him was for free. She wanted something of equal or more value. What that, Christian could only surmise, was peace. That he agreed with everything Stone said before they got back to the house.

"Maybe on the way to school?" Christian tried not to show his disappointment.

When Mrs. Belvedere didn't meet his eyes, Christian slid her keys back to her.

"Is everything OK?" Christian could sense that something was wrong. It was probably something to do with the school and his senior year. Perhaps, the school had decided to expel him. But Stone ignored the cue.

"It was a fight to get the school to take you back after what happened last semester," Stone started. Mrs. Belvedere cleared her throat, an obvious warning sign to Stone to remember how much they both had "changed."

"What your father means to say is…" she began.

"What I mean to say is that it isn't your fault that the school is a fantastical place of prestige. It's the best school in the country, the stuff of legend, a collegiate Olympus.

27

It offers students a glimpse of perfection: a life 'free from realities' even." Stone took another sip of his coffee. "But perfection," he added, "can play with the mind." He took a deep breath and blew it out slowly into the coffee mug. "Son, your psychosis is perfectly understandable and not a big deal at all under the circumstances..."

"What your father means to say..." Mrs. Belvedere cut in. But she didn't find time to finish.

"What I mean to say is that there's just one problem. Your psychotic episode—your manic outburst at the Politics Department Building—just doesn't fit with the school's 'ambiance.'"

So there was a letter.

"What your father means to say..." Mrs. Belvedere offered again.

"But what about my privacy?" Christian cut in, irritated and surprised even at the boldness of his own voice. "How did a dean or student rep have any business knowing my diagnosis? And what qualifications do they have to judge me?"

Stone began fiddling with the handle of the coffee cup.

"Christian..." he started calmly.

"What your father means to say..." Mrs. Belvedere tried again. Stone had fiddled with the coffee cup so much that some of it spilled over the side and scorched his hand. With a curse he stood up in a fury partially overturning the table onto a surprised Christian and his mother.

"WHAT I MEAN TO SAY is that this is earth! This is the Iron Age of blood, sweat, toil, and ambition! Unless you display those qualities, you will NEVER realize your rightful place in the order of things. Even if you are my son!"

The entire diner had gone quiet at Stone's outburst. Patrons in the adjacent booths sat in shock, forks mid-air. The cashier stood frozen in place, and even the cooks in the back had stopped tending to the food and were staring out the breakfast window gawking at Stone with mouths open. Stone slowly opened the hand in which he had been holding the coffee cup. The cup, now pulverized, sprinkled down like sand in an hourglass on the partially overturned table and into Christian and his mother's lap.

"Waitress." Stone flashed a smile at Miss Hips. Pulling a $100 bill out of his wallet, Stone slipped it into the pocket of her apron. "Keep the change." He flashed a smile.

There would be no pancakes that morning for Christian.

***

Home for Christian was in the middle of a condominium complex surrounded by the highway and an amalgam of Chinese takeout places, dollar stores, banks, and a shwarma restaurant. An odd mix for a town in the suburbs of Long Island, but when one has a psychosis like Christian, it's the odd things that can keep one invested in reality.

After the commotion from the diner had died down and the Belvederes returned home, Christian went to his room to put his luggage away. As he entered the foyer with the staircase to the left, he saw a black cat dart up the stairs. Stone was allergic to cats and Mrs. Belvedere detested them, so Christian couldn't understand how this feline visitor had crossed the threshold. Was he hallucinating? Was it another messenger?

Christian followed the obsidian cat up the stairs to the guest room far down the hall where his grandmother resided. He approached the room cautiously, wondering if the cat was an unsuspecting companion of his grandmother.

Christian's grandmother was in bed with a breathing tube up her nose, sleeping. When he saw her, it took him by surprise. Over the last few months, he had been so focused on his own enfeebled situation that he had missed his grandmother falling this ill.

"Don't fret the tubing, Christian. It's just the umbilical cord of life keeping my spirit connected to this bag of bones." Grandma Sophie smiled in his direction without opening her eyes.

"Grandmother, I'm so... sorry..." Christian walked over to the right side of her hospital bed, leaned down, and kissed her.

"Don't be. You've had your own battle, keeping the umbilical cord of your mind tethered to your body, I've heard." Sophie erupted into a coughing spell that wracked her poor little frame. Christian passed her the cup of water that sat on her nightstand in the dimness of her small, undecorated room.

"You know... no matter what happens, you'll always be a Parthenon man. They can't take away what you've accomplished for three years."

How did she know about the fight between him and his parents already? They had barely been home for five minutes.

"Even if I don't graduate?" Christian asked after a pause. Sophie opened her eyes, blinking a few times at Christian.

"You got in. Your name is in their ledger. In ink. That's forever." She swallowed. "Not everybody finishes." she swallowed again, but harder this time. "But they'll come for your alumni donation anyway in a few years, so what's

30

the difference? You stay strong now. You're a Parthenon Man."

"I love you, Grandma," Christian smiled reassuringly.

"Meyn getin! And as fate would have it, we have a visitor."

"Who?" Christian turned to the door to see who had entered..

"You don't see the cat!" The ethereal feline perched on the end of the bed. Christian saw it for the first time, remembering why he had come up the stairs in the first place. But he was certain it was an illusion. His brain playing tricks on him.

"You can see it, too?"

"When I worked for the Department of Education, they had an exchange program. I was lucky enough to be selected. Imagine, someone like me getting to travel all over the United Kingdom, Europe, and the Middle East. But no place spoke to me like Egypt. I traveled the corridors of the pyramids and what I found… the secrets I unearthed… I wish I had the time to tell you." Christian was confused and it showed in his face.

"The cat is telling you that?" Sophie stared at Christian for a moment.

"Cats are servants of Osiris, the King of the Afterlife, a man who deserves his vengeance. When he was betrayed, all cats swore an oath that they and their ancestors would exact his will. They often appear at a time of great change, including death and awakening."

"What are you saying? Maybe the cat is here to give you strength." Christian thought better of it. "Or maybe it's just a stray."

"It's not here for me, honey." She winked and gestured to

the cat with her eyes that were fixed on Christian. Suddenly, Sophie's vocal register changed. A deep, tremulous alto.

"Even then, as fate would have it, it's my time."

"It's your time?"

Sophie pulled the white sheet up to her chin.

"Give your grandma some space. This will require all of my focus."

The cat jumped off the bed and ran through the doorway down the dark hall. Christian gave his grandmother one more kiss on the cheek and followed. No sooner had he gotten to the door that Sophie called out.

"Christian?" Christian turned.

"Yes, grandma?"

"No matter what happens when you go downstairs, ascend."

Sophie closed her eyes and was out.

Welcome Back, Mr. Belvedere

The next day, Christian was sitting in the dean's office to learn about the fate of his senior year. He hated wearing suits but gave in at the insistence of his father.

"No, not the damned seersucker one. Do you want them to think you're a pimp?" Stone had said in disdain. "The Navy pinstriped one. Now that's classic."

Not only did Christian feel claustrophobic in suits, but the button at the neck reminded him of a noose. Christian despised these institutional bougie trappings. But in the end, the Navy pin-striped suit with the scarlet tie won out. And while Christian's mother fussed over him by brushing imaginary dust from his jacket lapels, Chrisitan actually thought that he saw a tear in his father's eye as he beamed at him.

Christian's parents were required to sit in the waiting room of the dean's offices while he was interviewed privately. His mother looked the epitome of anxiety as she fidgeted, swallowed up by the gargantuan couch next to his equally gargantuan father who flashed him a smile with a hand gesture akin to something between "Go get 'em, Tiger" and "Or else."

Sitting before the dean reminded Christian of the previous day's meeting with Dr. Aceso, and he wondered if it would end with a surprise ending as well. Dean Maiden was an attractive dean who looked like she might double as a model for muscle cars. On the other hand, the authority she held made her equally intimidating.

What bothered Christian even more was the line of questioning she would take with him. Was it possible that she could trigger Christian's psychosis to take center stage? He had already been prepped by Stone to "admit nothing" that could make him look culpable in the eyes of the school leadership and should questions get too direct. To admit loss of memory.

Dean Maiden arranged a few stacks of paper on her desk, folded her hands, and looked Christian in the eyes.

"So, am I right that last semester during Reunions on June 1st you thought that you were being telepathically attacked by other students and driven to a state of madness by them because you are a 'chosen one' and all the other 'chosen ones' have all failed?

Christian froze for a moment. Damn, that was a loaded question.

"I… I don't remember… ma'am."

"You don't remember anything? You claim that by climbing the Politics Department Building, you were doing what 'chosen ones' had historically been afraid of doing: exposing 'evil' to society and risking your reputation to do so. Something that 'evil' never thought you'd do, you say."

Christian squirmed in his chair, and then corrected himself to make it look like he was adjusting his tie.

"I didn't… I mean… I'm not sure I used those exact words…"

"Those exact words?" Dean Maiden repeated. "Do you

34

remember this, Mr. Belvedere? Your fellow students—terrified—say that you called out the names of each student you sought to expose. And there were many—almost seventy-two. I'm sorry, it was seventy-two."

Yes, seventy-two in all... Christian thought.

Shh... Christian reprimanded his psychosis.

"Did you just shush me?" Dean Maiden said agitated.

"No, ma'am. I was... just... trying to... I'm breathing too fast."

She continued.

"Your girlfriend at the time—a Ms. Dité Laguidas—showed up to talk you down. And this is where things take a very interesting turn."

Is it not all an 'interesting turn' as you say, Dean Maiden? The voice almost erupted in Christian's left ear.

"You give up."

"I wouldn't call it 'giving up'..." Christian said aloud.

"Excuse me?" Dean Maiden questioned.

"What I meant to say was that I don't recall what you're talking about. Really, I don't."

"Why did you stop, come down, and give up this 'quest' when you saw her? The notes say you said nothing to her when the authorities took you. Please, elaborate if you can. I know this is hard and you were unwell—but if you could?"

Christian cleared his throat at the same time that Dean Maiden looked at her watch.

Because... Christian's psychosis prompted.

"Mr. Belvedere, could you answer the question."

At that exact moment, a shrill beep announced the five-minute change-of-class for the second period. Dean Maiden looked at her watch in surprise,

"Well, looks like I'm a little bit behind schedule. I need to speak to your parents. If you would wait in the lobby." She stood up and motioned to the door.

Christian didn't want to see his parents when he exited the office, so he walked to the cooler on the opposite side of the room and nervously got himself a drink. Clutching the paper cup, he walked to the window, resting his head on the cool glass, and looked out the foggy window at the campus from his second-floor vantage point. As he stared at everything and nothing, he couldn't help but notice the sob wanting to erupt. He was being expelled from Parthenon, and he knew it. The only question was, what in the world was he to do now? Where would he go? What would he do? What school would want a broken senior with psychological problems?

He stared enviously at the people walking by, a mix of students in their various cliques, the teachers walking doubletime as if they were afraid to be late to their next class, and even the Mighty Bread delivery man who was having a hard time balancing a stacked palette of whole wheat on his dolly. None of them seemed to have a care in the world. For them, Parthenon was a paradise.

Mighty Bread man lost control of the dolly while trying to navigate it down the ramp onto the curb. It looked like he had a conniption, holding his arms up in the air as if he were appealing to the god of delivery men, Why me?

Even you, Christian thought. Even if you have it better than me.

Now the delivery man was really working himself up by kicking at one of the palettes that caught onto a latch on the ramp and wouldn't easily dislodge when a muscled figure clad in a dark hoodie casually stepped up to the irate delivery man who was now sitting on the ramp smoking a cigarette with his head down in utter defeat. After what looked like a short exchange of words, the muscle man began picking up the bags of Mighty Bread, reorganizing them in their crates and stacking them back on the palettes. He looked up at Christian and gave him a thumbs-up.

Christian's paper cup went flying in the air when he jumped back in alarm.

Oh, my God, he thought. Maybe I am sick.

Dean Maiden's secretary peered over her desktop computer.

"May I help you with something?" She inquired.

Instinctively, Christian pointed to the window and "Out there" was all he could manage to say. Before the secretary could get up from behind her desk, Dean Maiden's office door opened.

"Mr. Christian Belvedere. You may come in."

No, I am definitely sick. Far too sick to be a student right now.

Christian froze momentarily. Up until now, his incredibly toxic line of thinking not only had been the product of shame and weeks of isolation. It had also been a rage that up until now had been simmering. Now, in the matter of a moment, it was a steady boil. On the one hand, he was embarrassed by his illness which had lain open exposed like a raw nerve. On the other hand, for all of the theories that his parents, Parthenon leadership, and Angelsfire had made about Christian's weird behaviors, he understood at that moment that there was one person who had the answers to Chrstians problems that they had not consulted. And that was Christian himself.

While he had been aware of how much his recent behavior had changed things, he finally heard the voices telling him that now was the time for anger.

Christian took one quick peek out the window. Sure enough, the blue muscleman and the delivery man were sharing a cigarette and laughing raucously.

Christian smiled grimly to himself.

Whether or not it was at Parthenon or elsewhere, he felt a tugging— a calling. He wasn't crazy, and he wasn't going to let anyone try to convince him of that again. And they say that's the compelling feature of mania: the doorways that depression closes, mania opens to nowhere and everywhere at once.

Well, here goes nothing, Christian muttered to himself as he stepped through Dean Maiden's office door to face his parents who were seated opposite Dean Maiden. Stone with a self-satisfying smirk on his face, and Mrs. Belvedere pantomiming her excitement.

"Have a seat, Mr. Belvedere. I'll be back in a moment," Dean Maiden ordered while she left the room.

Christian's mother moved to the chair on the left, making room for Christian to sit in between her and Stone, and he reluctantly sat down between both parents.

"You're back!" Mrs. Belvedere whispered as loudly as she dared.

"They said that they were so impressed with your defense." Stone leaned in and patted Christian's back comfortingly, making him flinch.

Instinctively, feeling that this praise was short-lived, he decided the route of self-sabotage.

"Well, it is all my fault, right?" He said to no parent in particular, his words aimed to miss any specific target like a bad archer.

Mrs. Belvedere shushed him.

"It's all in the past now. Dr. Aceso's testimony to your health and readiness was just what we needed. Although they did have their reservations, I made sure that I explained to them just how wonderful you are." That's what Christian meant by the praise being short-lived.

"You're a fighter." That was Stone. "You'll keep taking your meds and you'll fight this. You're back. Water under the bridge." Stone winked at Mrs. Belvedere.

"I'm back. Yeah, you're right," Christian sighed. "As long as I take my meds, it's just water under the bridge."

Dean Maiden walked into the room, shut the door quietly behind her, and sat down. Christian's parents sat up, anticipating the acquittal to come.

"Well, Mr. Belvedere..." Dean Maiden started.

"You asked me a question," Christian interrupted. Dean Maiden raised her eyebrows.

"Excuse me?" she questioned. Christian took a deep breath.

"You asked me a question this morning." Christian could feel both parents tense up on either side of him.

"You asked me why did I stop, come down, and give up this 'quest' when I saw Dité?" Mrs. Belvedere audibly groaned.

"Christian..." Stone interrupted.

"Because... Christian's psychosis prompted.

"Mr. Belvedere, why did you do that?" Dean Maiden prompted.

"Because when she showed up, I saw what no one else saw and heard what no one else heard. The sky turned black, the stars disappeared, and I couldn't differentiate students from these evil ones, the shadows. And when I saw Dité, she was the most evil one of them all. What's so hard to understand about that?"

On the car ride home when Christian's parents were berating him for his "Incident in the Deans' Offices," he couldn't remember whether or not he had overturned Dean Maiden's desk before his father became enraged or after his mother's breakdown. But when he came to, he had a sense that things were different now. He had gone too far this time which is exactly how far he had meant to go.

The papers that had been on Dean Maiden's desk were scattered all over the floor and her desk was on its side. Mrs. Belvedere was wailing in the corner, and Stone was seething expletives at Christian. And there was Dean Maiden and Christian standing in the middle of all the mess.

Dean Maiden reached out her hand to Christian and smiled.

"Welcome back to Parthenon, Christian Belvedere."

***

After the ordeal in Dean Maiden's office, everything would have fallen apart were it not for her authoritative tone with Stone who instinctively positioned himself to grab for Christian's jugular and her stern admonition of Mrs. Belvedere who almost had a nervous breakdown on her haunches in the middle of the office. Seeing their son flip Dean Maiden's desk had been the ultimate betrayal a child could have for parents who had sacrificed reputation, time, and money to have their only son succeed them at their alma mater... until it wasn't. Mrs. Belvedere almost fainted in shock when she heard, "Welcome back to Parthenon." Even Stone was tongue-tied for a second.

Being a parentified child who simply wanted everything to go back to normal, Christian didn't offer any explanation for the incident once they left the office. Instead, he shrugged in agreement when Stone suggested that it was the psychosis again but that the school knew they had a genius on their hands. It would have been foolish to let Belvedere get away. Mrs. Belvedere nodded in agreement. No sooner had they reached the car that Stone was congratulating Christian on his decision to "let those bastards know who runs this place."

That afternoon, they moved Christian back into his old dorm room, a single room in the center of campus.

"Close to the gym," Stone remarked. That was so that he could stay in shape in case he wanted to rejoin the rowing team.

"Close to the church," Mrs. Belvedere countered. That was in case he wanted to "Let go and let God" as it was Mrs. Belvedere's God who had given Christian a second chance despite his uncalled for behavior.

After the last carload of Christian's belongings were piled into his dorm room, Mrs. Belvedere commenced to decorating his room by setting up the bathroom in robin egg blues and chocolate browns, organizing the drawers in the kitchenette, and hanging pictures on the wall while Stone arranged books on their shelves in alphabetical order, pontificating on every other title and then setting up Christian's computer. With nothing to do himself, Christian sat on his bed in the corner for the next three hours while his parents fine-tuned the feng shui.

"Time for dinner," his mother announced after straightening the last picture on the wall, a portrait of the family

41

when Christian was about eight-years-old.

"Anastasia's," Stone powered down Christian's computer. "If that hospital couldn't do a good job with you, Anastasia's will help you forget your troubles." Stone winked at Christian and grabbed for his coat.

Anastasia's was an Italian restaurant with a menu that screamed Only for alums. It was where parents always took their kids when visiting the campus. Other food joints were college-cultured, but not Anastasia's. Not only did this place say Up yours to your normal diet of fat sandwiches and wings, but it also said that you'll deliriously crap yourself at their prices, too. Yet despite the promise of stomach cramps and hours precariously seated on the toilet, the wine still flowed and the conversation was as light as the Moscato. So, for two hours and forty-nine minutes, Christian was, per his father's word, happy.

Mrs. Belvedere was on her third glass of wine and Stone's cheeks were glowing when Christian caught sight of a group of students entering the restaurant along with several of his closest friends among them whom he hadn't seen since his incident. The maître de greeted them, grabbed menus, and led them down the aisle toward Christian's table. Christian saw the open table next to his own and realized their destination. He braced himself to smile as the party approached.

However, as the group moved closer, Christian recognized the lead student and instinctively flinched to hide his face. His name was Brock and at one point was the bane of Christian's existence. Brock made eye contact with Christian, whispered into the maître de's ear, and, like a flock of birds that suddenly changed direction mid-air, the maitre de led them to a table several aisles away. Relieved and de-jected, Christian dropped his eyes, but not before a girl he had known since his freshman year looked back at him. In pity? He couldn't tell. He heard her laugh at something she probably barely heard from someone else in the group, and he died just a little bit more.

"Another glass of wine," Christian gestured his wine glass toward his mother, feeling the need to distract himself from the angst that was creeping up his back and around his throat. She didn't hear him as she was busy relaying a story to Stone.

"Another glass of wine, please," Christian said "please" in a tiny whisper. Still no response. Christian reached for the second bottle himself and downed half of it. No glass needed. No permission required. No one noticed him. He was invisible once more. And just like that, things were back to normal in the Belvedere house.

CHAPTER 3
Now You Face a Power

Christian's first week of classes went with little incident.
It was almost a conspiracy that no one noticed him. He at-
tended classes in sunglasses and a hoodie despite the soar-
ing 80-degree weather. He would sit in the back of the class
and sneak out the back door just as the professor would
begin to wrap things up.

The courses he registered for that semester were im-
posed on him by the registrar in conjunction with his pro-
bationary re-admittance. All were easy, and unengaging.
All but one, that is. Econ.

Christian was captivated by that class, and no one in that
department knew or knew who he was. He had chosen Religion as his major because it was a sure steppingstone to
law school, or so he had convinced his parents. In truth,
religion had always been a burden and point of contention
with him. He had known many religious people and simply didn't feel their fervor. But Christian couldn't reconcile
a genuine belief in an afterlife that was all shits and giggles
in a world where people were born into extremes of poverty and disease and where psychosis could be a loose, rusty
nail on the pathway to freedom.

And he laughed at the ardent believer who claimed

that they had all evidence to the contrary, that there was a beautiful path destined for everyone to follow and that out of the trillions of compounds in the solar system, a far-off deity cared about which graduate school they got into (only to never finish there) or who they would eventually marry (only to divorce a few years later).

However, when Stone would tell the young Christian stories from ancient times about Zeus and his lightning, Shango and his thunder, and Amaterasu and her love for her people, he felt goosebumps. He felt something pure, something that couldn't be easily manipulated, because myth is a religion most recognized as too ridiculous to be real. So he had immersed himself into the study of mythical characters for the last three years of his university life.

But psychosis had destroyed all of the comfortable and translucent forces for which Christian had gained the respect: the anxiety, depression, disappointment in life and (he guessed) the disappointment in God for letting psychosis happen to him. During those first three years, he would bring a book to his merry mount, Liger, which had been established in the early 20th century as a social and eating hall for its members.

The book could be on a reading list from a course on Buddhism, Islam, or the Talmud. He would wait a few seconds until someone with a cold brew and a members-only pizza would query him on the majesty of the literature he was holding. One person would swell to five, even ten, and conversation would ensue deep into the night. As pretentious and bubbly as this sounded, he really needed that back in his life.

But each time during that first week of senior year classes, Christian would try but could not bring himself to go to Liger. He felt nothing but Apollo's poisonous arrows in his chest and the creep of doubtful Anansi up his spine. Both were warning him that his time in paradise was over because he had committed the worst of all sins: he had "weirded" people out. Among that group was his ex-girl-friend who was also a member and an ever-present pres-ence in the merry mount. And he hadn't heard one word from her since.

But Christian quickly fell back into the rhythm of college life with no incident. His symptoms seemed to have abated as his parents were no longer an ever-present factor and he had recommitted himself to his grades and sobriety.

One evening towards the end of the first month of col-lege, he decided that he was doing better and could walk down "The Street" and venture into Liger.

"The Street" was a nickname for Potential Street where all the merry mounts were situated. He was feeling so good that night that he considered the possibility that he had been making everything up in his mind about how forgot-ten he was and that, perhaps, people really missed him and were wondering where he had gone. So why not pregame a bit with his favorite champagne, play a drinking game by himself, and celebrate life? It's what Dionysus would do. In fact, he could almost feel the moral support from all the Pantheons cheering him on with words like, We made mortals for times like these. Go ahead. Live a little.

So that night, Christian closed his book on the Jaguar in Ancient Mayan cosmology, put on the ultimate Liger at-tire (a merry mount-themed tank top and patterned board shorts), and made sure that he had his student I.D. with his membership sticker on it so he could get in. Then he left his dorm.

He didn't know if it was the thrill of feeling like himself again or if he was still euphoric from his workout a few hours before, but Christian could swear that he was walking on air as he strolled to his destination. The trees were swaying in unison to the music playing in his head. The skyline was a rich rainbow of dusk so totemic and tall that he could feel his ancestors' adoration of the same skyline fill his heart and bestow an extra bounce to his curls.

As Christian turned the corner, passing the Summit Center where students watched Premier League soccer matches, ate at a buffet-style dinner, or listened to a small cafe concert, he danced a jig in front of it to honor the sense of restoration he felt inside. Onlookers cheered him on. A few old friends asked him where he had been.

"There and back again," was all he said. Christian didn't care how cryptic he sounded. He was entering the realm of the gods.

As he approached the large front door of Liger, he found himself face-to-face with three men dressed in black.

"Where's Leon?" Christian asked.

"New security company. Are you a member?" The shortest yet most intimidating one nodded his head in Christian's direction.

"I certainly am," Christian retorted, a little too defensively.

"Haven't seen you here. Why is that?"

"Indigestion. I've been working on my... on my microbiome."

"Your what?" The tallest one asked, squaring his shoulders.

"Yeah, beer is terrible for your healthy gut bacteria so I've just been working on that. Made good progress. Right, stomach?" Christian rubbed his stomach and laughed in good fun. The bouncers weren't amused, so Christian handed them his student I.D. The shortest one peered at it closely and then scowled.

"This is an old sticker. Unless you have a proper pass, you're not getting in."

"But..." Christian protested.

"No buts. Or asses," the shortest one added with a snigger.

"I'll vouch for him." Christian turned to see who had spoken."

"They mailed out the new stickers a while ago, and I know for a fact that Christian never checks his mail. He's a member, guys."

"You got it, Mr. Texas," the shortest one said as he glared at Christian.

"You guys do good work. And thanks for helping me with that freshman problem. You all are lifesavers."

They all laughed in unison, unclipped the barrier, and let them through. Once inside, Christian gestured his chin toward his advocate.

"Thanks, Aussie. I appreciate it," he said cautiously.

Aussie didn't turn around to acknowledge Christian.

"Just go upstairs and get a new sticker, OK. I don't want this happening every time or whatever," he said as he sauntered down the hall. Christian stood watching him disappear into the dark eating hall and get lost among the crowd.

All of a sudden, Christian was tackled from behind, immediately being slammed to the floor. He turned over quickly and saw Zaluski, his old friend and a mountain of a man. They called him "The Boa" because his hugs were constricting.

"You bicker with me and then don't show up until a month into school! Bastard!" he shouted.

"So you're happy to see me?" Christian wheezed as he sat up.

"Get up and come here!" Zaluski yanked Christian up with one arm and embraced him while a couple of juniors Christian knew flanked him, patting him on the back. He was back home.

***

"We all have bad days, Christian. I know you've been an enemy of the state around here with all the crazy things Dité has been saying about you, but we've always had a good time with you. Right, boys? We can't quit Belvedere. You're a legend!"

"Thanks, Zaluski! Eliot and Will, it's good to see you guys too!" Christian lifted his beer stein.

"Been waiting to keg stand with you all summer!" Will smirked.

"Christian, what's your thoughts on Apollo's role in the kidnapping of Persephone? Righteous, impartial witness, or bitter enabler? Got a paper to write in Classics and I'm asking the guru for some help," Eliot grinned pleadingly at Christian.

Will and Eliot were always eager sidekicks. Christian had met them soon after he met Zaluski, and this was the first year they were allowed to be full members of the merry mount after they bickered the semester before. Christian had a great time bickering these three. There was something old-fashioned about them. They respected institutions like friendship, they never rushed conversation, and

49

it didn't take much for them to warm to you.

As the four of them walked away from the bar downstairs that was serving beers from around the world that night, Christian saw a man with a gold eye patch staring at them. Zaluski called out to him.

"Christian you haven't met our new house manager, Mr. Grimly or Big Grim as we call him. Thanks to him losing a beer pong game to me, we had pizza all week. Thanks for keeping your word, All Father," Zaluski said affectionately.

Big Grim smiled

"Who's to say I didn't lose on purpose. Pizza is a rare treat where I'm from."

"Where's that?" Christian asked.

"You know where," Big Grim winked.

"Guys, Tash and Sysy are signaling us. It's our turn to play," Zaluski beckoned Will and Eliot. As Christian turned to follow them, Big Grim grabbed him by the arm.

"I finally see you. Took many deaths but this time I see you," he whispered.

"Excuse me?" Christian protested. Big Grim squeezed his arm harder.

"The last time you called for me you were a Moor fighting with Hadrada. You asked one last time. You screamed, 'See me!' Now I do!"

"The Norwegian King from like a thousand years ago?" Christian wondered. "I'm sorry. I know what you're going through with delusions. I have them, too,"

Christian walked to the beer pong table where his three friends were huddled around. Tash and Sysy stared at Christian, rudely he thought. While he didn't know exactly what Dité had been telling others about his incident, it was obvious to him that it was bad enough to make people think he'd never show his face in Liger again.

Without taking her eyes off Christian, Sysy whispered to Tash which made Christian so uncomfortable that he began to feel warm at his neck again. He had never before been able to infiltrate their elite social circle of water polo athletes but he supposed that, this close in proximity, both were going to treat him like a pariah unless he approached them.

"Ladies," Christian nodded to Sysy who still hadn't broken eye contact.

"Christian Belvedere," Sysy said matter-of-factly. "What a... surprise? Where've you been?"

"You know... here and there?" he tried out with a mysterious grin. Both girls gave each other sideways glances. Tash crossed her arms & squinted her eyes.

"It's not cool what Dité has been saying. You look normal. No, actually you look... better."

"What does that mean?" Christian retorted defensively. Tash took a step forward until she was inches from Christian's nose.

"Look," she whispered. "I've had people in my life who had mental breakdowns. It's nothing to be ashamed of."

Sysy chimed in.

"If you don't have at least one person in your life with all the craziness in this world then you're the crazy one." All three laughed, though Christian pensively. He was touched by their ardent defense of him but also troubled at what it was exactly that Dité had been saying about him.

Tash handed Christian a drink.

"If you need us to be your ears, we can be that." Christian took the glass.

"What I need is your advice in choosing a more moral

51

person to date." They all three laughed again, and Christian downed his. This was the love of Liger that Christian remembered. This was precious. This was worth protecting. This was worth losing his mind for a bit.

Then he blacked out.

***

When Christian awoke, he was in his rival's merry mount, Pithon, sitting in a leather recliner. He must have traveled with Sysy and Task to several other merry mounts first as he noticed wrist bands on his right wrist for at least five. As he sat up, his head pounded and he immediately came back to consciousness in the middle of a conversation with Woodrow. And Woodrow was drunk.

"I didn't know... I didn't know... I didn't know she would do that," he apologized on the verge of tears. Woodrow was apologizing for drunkenly letting slip out the details of Christian's meeting to Dité, the girl Woodrow was currently pursuing.

Christian was feeling like Humpty Dumpty with his head split open and all the contents dribbling out onto his chest.

"I'm sorry, who are you again?" Christian asked confusedly.

"Really, chap?" Woodrow started to tear up again. "We've been talking for shirty... shirty... thirty minutes and I've introduced you to several of my closest friends. You're the bloke who made that scene or whatever," Woodrow stood up too fast, wobbled, and sat back down, fighting the black out to come

"Oh," Woodrow's face came back to Christian in a flash.

52

He was the nosy student services officer he saw in the dean's offices a few weeks before.

"I'm sorry," he decided, not sure what else to say in front of a grown man whose feelings he evidently had damaged.

"No problem, love. You're a handsome guy. I should have guessed that's why she kept looking over here." Woodrow pointed behind Christian. Christian turned. It was Dité.

She was staring at him and not with an unfriendly look either. She was still so beautiful that Christian wondered if he was watching the birth of Venus. Snatches of the merry mount's shallow conversations about calorie intake and selfies and the almost Victorian attention to fashion and etiquette faded as their eyes locked. Her lure was strong, and Christian's curiosity even stronger, but he knew that Sysy and Tash wouldn't advise a do over with her.

"Not going to happen," Christian muttered to himself as he stood up, struggled to steady himself, and headed for the door.

As he walked to the door of the Grayson Center for a sandwich to cap off his night and suppress his pounding headache, he suddenly had the urge to puke. He burst through the double doors of Graysion and ran into the bathroom to dry-heave over a dirty toilet in the last bathroom stall. As he sat there staring into a floating cauldron of floating cigarettes and submerged chewing gum, he heard it.

The sound of the instrument was majestic, reminding him of another sound from another place in another time. When the dry heaves stopped, Christian recognized that the instrument was a saxophone playing so tragically beautiful that it caught him off guard. Music had been his first experience with the divine as a child, but tonight he was in the presence of the gods.

But what song was it that made him feel nostalgic? Rather, who was playing it? At that thought, the music ended and Christian bolted out of the bathroom and up to the stage in the dimly lit cafe. And there he saw him.

It was the same blue-headed wolf figure he had seen thrice in the last few weeks. Reality went backward and forward at once, and Christian was faced with a choice. A choice he had been training to avoid at all costs. The choice was psychosis or not?

Ignoring the way his brain framed the question, he slowly approached the figure, expecting it to disappear if indeed it was psychosis. The figure, about to start another set, paused. Christian started the conversation.

"Ok. You can stop this now."

"Are you talking to me?" The blue figure quizzed.

"So you talk? Look, you've been following me around for a month. If you want my attention, you don't have to play jazz to get it."

"But it worked, so you're wrong."

"Wrong?"

"About me being fake."

"Well, let's sit down for a drink. Maybe we can figure out getting you back to the Canyon of Unreal Imaginings in my subconscious."

"The Canyon of Unreal Imaginings in your subconscious? Damn! That sounds scary. So 'no' to that, but I will take a double mocha latte, light on the whip with extra cinnamon. And I'll get us a table. And since you think I'm not real, then obviously you know I don't carry cash."

Shit. I'm just going to give into it. Just like grandmother said, Christian thought.

"Sure..."

Christian doubled the order. Not only did a latte appeal to him but, believing the apparition before him to be an extension of some deep recess in his mind, he assumed that was what he really wanted. After ordering, Christian approached the table cautiously, balancing both lattes on saucers in his palms.

"Ok, kid, I'm not some figment of your imagination. If my suspicions are correct, you have The Sight. Or Vision."

"I see. So I must be some great hero, too... like a messianic figure? Does the world need me? That delusion is so first century." Christian took a sip and burned his tongue.

"Damn. Look what you made me do," he said to know one in particular.

"Your cynicism is a good quality. With parents like yours, you should be skeptical. But it's true what you said. That's exactly what's happening. Last semester, you had a wake-up call. You saw into the world that really is. The world of the supernatural. It revealed itself to you with no consideration for your mental health. For that, I understand your chariness. I've been following you around long enough to know that you still struggle. Sorry about the incident with Dité."

"How do you know about Dité? How do you know anything about me if you're real and you weren't there?" Christian emphasized the weren't.

"You're talking to an Egyptian god. I've got many ways of getting info and doing weird shit. Plus, I'm invisible to those who don't acknowledge me. And here you are talking to me. So you know what that means.

The apparition had Christian's attention now.

"There are things that have happened to you today that

you don't even remember. When you slipped and fell in Foam and Folly merry mount? Caused your blackout. I did that."

"That's why my head hurts like hell?"

"See? Could a figment do that?"

"Ok, so you can be invisible. So are people thinking right now that I'm just crazy for getting two fucking delicious lattes for myself and my imaginary friend? Is someone going to call the security on me because I'm having a heated conversation with myself?"

"Bro, I'm a friend. More of a friend than you know. And, no, I wouldn't have people thinking you're crazy. My name is Wepwawet, Wolf God of Opening Pathways among other things. Call me Wep. When they see me, they see a regular person. Here, give me your phone. Let's take a selfie."

Wep took Christian's phone, grabbed him by the shoulders and pulled him in.

"One, two, three..." He leaned his head against Christian's and duck-lipped.

"Now, what do you think about that?" Wep handed Christian the phone. Christian gave it a look while taking a sip. He set his latte down with a clatter. The photo looking back at Christian was him with Sophie. His grandmother. Christian grimaced.

"Why my grandmother?" He spat out through clenched teeth. "Why are you fucking with me like this?" Wep grinned and raised his eyebrows knowingly.

"Now, you're getting it. Sophie is an old friend. Surely, you know that your grandmother was different from most geriatrics her age." Wep took a dainty sip of the latte.

"Damn, they make a great latte here! I can even taste the cup, too." The charm was wasted on Christian.

56

"What I experienced last semester, what I knew was real yet have talked myself into expressing was not real and was just psychosis, was actually real?" Christian asked in disbelief.

"Really real!"

Christian stared at Wep for a long minute.

"No, I can't give into this again. I'll lose everything. I'll be right back in a mental ward. I'm sorry. Maybe you are real, maybe you aren't, but I can't join your quest or whatever you call it." Christian stood up to go, but Wep grabbed his arm.

"Look, take this. It's a sacred rope. You might even have called it a magic rope if I was having this conversation with you in grade school. Just take it." Wep produced a length of rope, sturdy but worn, bound and loosely tied, the length of about five feet. Christian sat back down and took the rope.

"What the hell is this for? Why would I take it? Why would I take anything from you?"

"It's your choice, but if you want to be sure…"

"Sure of what?" Christian interjected. "Sure that this conversation with you has ruined all of the time I've put into my therapy?"

"Christian, just do me this simple favor so that you don't waste any more of your time or mine thinking that you're The Chosen One that I… we… think you are OK?" Christian locked eyes with Wep for another thirty seconds.

"So, I just take the rope? That's it? Fine."

"Well, that's a start. What I want you to do with the rope is… well… it's gonna sound weird, but initiations are always challenging." Christian squinted his eyes.

"I'm not bickering for another merry mount. I've already

got one.

"And I certainly don't need you to be entirely nude," Wep continued, ignoring Christian, "but what I need to catch does."

"What are you talking about?"

"It's a long story, but… I need you to strip butt-naked, climb to the top of White Hall, tie yourself to the flagpole with the rope, and wait for it." Wep braced for Christian's reaction by noisily slurping the rest of his latte. Christian stood up.

"And I'm out. Nice meeting you, Wep. I'll take what you said to heart. And I'll take this rope because it's mine now, and I feel like being an asshole." Christian turned to go and did a 360. "And since you've thoroughly scared the latte I just downed out my rectum with the absurdity of your initiation offer, I'm going to pretend this never happened and get myself a sandwich. Somewhere else."

And with that, Christian turned towards the door of the cafe.

" It's real, Christian," Wep called out after him. "Just one more time. Take a leap of faith. Do it when no one is looking. There's no risk." He was shouting by the time Christian reached the door.

Christian went through the door and was gone.

CHAPTER 4

Now You Face a Power

A week later, Christian was sitting in his dorm room blaring jazz over the liquid gold he was drinking and the sideways rain that was pounding on his dorm window. Since his encounter with Wep, another side of his character had emerged. Every night, he routinely went out to his own merry mount and had even set an alarm on his watch to go off around 12:30 am just to wake himself out of a blackout as a precaution from ending up in another merry mount. Foam and Folly, Gatsby and even Musket were friendly to him, but he just couldn't risk going to Pithon again. He had begun eating his meals at Liger, too.

He also hadn't seen Dité who suddenly was of the mind to switch her merry mounts from Liger to Pithon. He saw his old clique though, the one he shared with her. They didn't have the clout to switch, nor were they brave enough to bicker again. Bravery... even those who torture others are capable of it.

So as Christian drank the IPA from his favorite liquor store on Withering Street and sunk into his futon and a nostalgic mood, he found himself thinking about his conversation with the apparition called Wep. And he found himself considering that it might be better to preemptively confront his psychosis once and for all because the fear of it coming back out of nowhere was ruining his streak of a "good time" of interrupted functionality that kept his parents at bay.

Yes, Christian thought to himself. Wep would come back, and I can't have that. He enjoyed going to class during the day, going out at night, and handling both lifestyles seamlessly as many Parthenonians did. Like his father before him.

Unconsciously, Christian put his hand deep into the futon, rooting around for something. When he withdrew his fist, he had the rope Wep had given him. Christian could have sworn that the rope was pulsating in his hand. Or maybe that was imagination? Either way, he was reminded that his father was coming to visit him the next day and he wanted to greet him without the baggage of this newly acquired mission.

That's it, Christian murmured to himself.

That's when Christian decided that in about an hour from then while it was still raining outside, he would be strung up naked on the tower at the right corner of White Hall.

***

Forty-three minutes later, Christian was drenched to the bone, shivering in the courtyard of White Hall, standing at the base of the flagpole. The rain was pouring sideways in sheets, and the wind was howling so fiercely that each snap of the Parthenon University flag filled Christian with dread.

"Fuck me!" Christian screamed up at the dark sky to

no one in particular. Even though, under normal circumstances, the flagpole at White Hall was visible from a hundred vantage points on campus, Christian had chosen to
take on Wep's challenge after hours under the blanket of
darkness and in the middle of hurricane-like weather in
order to minimize his exposure. In case, Christian had
said to himself, it's really my psychosis speaking.

Raindrops as fat and hard as marbles slapped Christian
in the face, causing him to wince as he stared up at the
flagpole, planning his ascension. Scaling that slippery pole
would be a feat in and of itself not to mention that the medication Christian had been taking the duration of the time
he was in hospital gave him enough weight gain he hadn't
yet been able to shed. At this thought, Christian realized
that part of the challenge required him to be "butt-naked."

"You motherfucker!" he roared through chattering teeth.
That was for Wep. If he were real. And if he were around.

But how much was butt-naked? Did that mean no pants
and just boxers or did he have to discard his boxers, too?
What if some student or faculty member decided to go for
a late night jog in this weather and found Christian inde-
cently exposed? What would the deans say? What would
his parents say?

Christian's sweatpants were already soaked and sagging.
He was sure that his butt crack was exposed to the elements
because his glutes involuntarily seized up against the frigid
rain. Was that good enough? No, that couldn't be what Wep
had meant. Wep meant to give him clear instructions that
this task was intended to challenge every claim to decen-
cy that Christian possessed. Literally, half-assing it might
ruin the magical part and Christian might get nothing out
of this ordeal but expulsion and double pneumonia.

"Fuck it." Christian yanked his pants and boxers down to his soaking shoes, kicking each shoe and pant leg off while trying to keep his balance. When Christian was done, he had on only his Liger sweatshirt, socks, and the rope Wep had given him tied around his waist. "This had better work," he muttered as he stepped up to the pole.

Damn it. How was he to shimmy the pole with nothing between himself and his balls?

"I'm losing my shit!" he screamed one more time to no one in particular. But he was also losing time. The longer he waited, the more likely he wouldn't follow through. He had to get up that pole as fast as possible and "wait for it."

The first pull up the pole felt like his man parts were being assaulted in what might not have been such an unpleasurable way if he were anywhere other than where he was. He grimaced, tightened his legs to brace himself, and shimmied up again. At about six pulls up, his balls encountered a metal peg and he almost lost his grip. But he maneuvered over it and, to his surprise, found himself about three feet below the flapping flag. Christian guessed that he was about 25 feet off the ground, and he felt every inch of it. Up there, it was pitch black, the rain hit harder, and the wind that filled his ears and swayed the flagpole sounded angry.

Bracing his legs against the pole, he unwound the sacred rope from his waist. He had previously tied it with an Italian hitch that was popular with belayers which he had learned at the rock climbing facility on campus during his sophomore year. Very carefully, he positioned it over each leg until it fit over his crotch like and hips securely. He secured the remaining length of rope around the pole into a single constrictor knot.

"Here goes nothing," Christian let go and tipped sideways, parallel to the Parthenon flag.

BOOM! went the first unexpected lightning strike of the night.

Christian yelled in fright. It hadn't been thundering all night. What was this?

"Wep, you have thirty seconds before I'm done! 29... 28... 27... Fuck that! I'm out!"

As Christian angled himself to undo the simple knot he had made, he noticed that it was double-knotted. A surge of panic shot up Christian's spine and he struggled with frozen fingers to undo it before the next lightning strike. The knot didn't budge.

"Psychosis? This isn't funny! It's tight! I didn't do this!" Christian protested, bracing for the next lightning strike.

But he saw no light and felt no sound roll over him. White Hall now had a large dark spot cast by the Parthenon flag that Christian hadn't previously seen. He peered at it through squinted eyes and perceived what looked like a human figure emerging from the dark shadow. At first, he couldn't tell if it was a man or woman, but then very clearly he could make out the voluptuous figure of a well-endowed woman. The figure moved the shadow obscuring it across the entire turret. Then it began to glow. Christian couldn't believe his eyes.

"Daphne?" Nothing. But he was sure it was her.

"Daphne? What are you doing? How did you get up here?"

The figure said nothing. Christian was suddenly aware that he was naked.

"It's an initiation," Christian offered, covering his manhood with one hand.

63

Daphne said nothing.

"We'll laugh about this together over a beer before graduation," Christian offered.

Before this incident, Daphne had been a beautiful and good-natured soul. Now, her attractive frame began to distort. From her face protruded a distended jaw with what appeared to be rows of teeth. Her eyes glowed red. Christian was shocked to say the least and paralyzed with fear. Is my psychosis going dark, he wondered, or was my original assumption from months ago true: that monsters are real and they were among us at Parthenon?

Daphne appeared to grow larger and come much closer to Christian.

"Daphne? Daphne! Are you OK? What's wrong?" But despite his questioning, Christian understood that this creature, Daphne or not, meant him harm. Gauging by the size of her jaws now, the harm she meant was to eat him.

BOOM! The second lightning strike struck Daphne's outstretched hands. She was illuminated and much closer to Christian than he wanted.. She was enraged and hungry.

The wind started to blow more fiercely, and Christian felt himself blown back and forth like a flag himself. Daphne was now on the flagpole directly beneath Christian. He was done for.

"Wep!" Christian screamed out as Daphne latched onto his right foot with her jaw and began swallowing.

BOOM! Without warning, the third bolt of lightning caught Daphne in the throat and she exploded, her flesh, blood, and sinew all over the flagpole. And Christian was covered in it.

"Well, it looks like you're in one piece. Instead of pieces." Wep chuckled to himself as he worked out the constrictor knot that affixed Christian to the flagpole.

Christian was in shock.

"O, my fucking god!" he screamed.

"O, my fucking god!" Wep screamed back.

"O, my fucking god," Christian tried to wipe what was left of Daphne off his sweatshirt.

"O, my fucking god.!" Wep screamed into Christian's face. At that moment the knot came out, and Wep, holding Christian slid down the pole.

"O, my god, the smell! Is that...?" Christian sat up and tried to wipe Daphne's remains out of his hair and off his face.

"Oh, yeah. Sometimes when I get them, they release their bowels." Christian looked at Wep's grinning face.

"O, my fucking..." Christian rolled over and threw up until his insides were empty.

"Congratulations, Christian. So you do have the Sight and they are drawn to you, willing to blow their covers and betray friendships. I'm afraid the worst is what is true."

"You used me as bait," Christian wailed. "Why did I have to be naked?"

"Maybe you don't know how to pick them, but you sure have a way with the ladies. That monster Daphne has a nose for human flesh. Your human flesh anyways. Your clothes would obstruct the smell."

Wep brandished a large ancient Egyptian styled curved sword that he flicked back and forth.

"So, what I saw last semester wasn't psychosis. It's real. There are monsters? The 72 called out... those are monsters?"

Wep swung his khopesh back and forth.

"Yes."

"I knew it!"

Wep grinned.

"What you're experiencing is 'The Awakening.' When a reborn god walks the path of self-discovery, it can look like psychosis to mortals..."

"Hold on, " Christian interrupted. "Reborn god?"

"Like I said, you might have psychosis, but you shouldn't have it forever. Just until you come into your powers. It's been a long while since Lord Osiris has made himself known to the world..."

"Wait. Are you saying I'm Osiris?"

Wep grinned conspiratorially.

"The transition will be bumpy. Earth's gotta adjust...

"Reborn?" Christian struggled to stand, losing his footing in a puddle of gore and then regaining his balance.

"Yes. Reborn. Welcome back.

Christian doubled over and wretched. Wep jumped back to avoid the splash and then looked at Christian pitifully.

"You ok, kid?"

"Excuse me as I faint," Christian began to keel over, but Wep caught him mid-fall."

"Let's get you cleaned up."

And with that, Wep and Christian disappeared leaving no trace of the initiation in the courtyard at White Hall.

***

An hour later, Christian awoke in his dorm bed, half awake and entirely disoriented.

"Reborn?" He murmured.

"Reborn it is," a voice answered in reply.

Christian jolted awake, wildly throwing the covers every

which way and jumping out of bed.

"Wep!" he shouted. "O, my God. You're in my bed now! That wasn't a dream?"

"I'm afraid not. I, you, last night, this is very much real. How about some smooth jazz to calm the nerves?" Wep snapped his large furry fingers, and the first of a hundred songs in a new playlist on Christian's computer began.

"Come on... I don't have space for all this fucking music."

"Calm down." Wep stood up and stretched. "You're still in shock. Even though Daphne got the jolt of a lifetime." Wep laughed at his own joke.

"Whatever you did to Daphne, just because you're Wep-wawet, Egyptian God of Ruining My Life, doesn't mean you can just come in here and add this shit to my laptop." Christian was pacing the room now like a caged tiger. "You called me 'The Reborn.' That's more like 'The Mental Case.' Worse than the last time I was in the hospital."

Wep yawned.

"Either that or you're bipolar and a god. Doesn't matter which it is. Your condition is our only hope to defeat them."

Christian stopped pacing and whipped around to face Wep.

"And by them does that include Daphne? Daphne and I were really close before all of this, you know."

"You're still close," Wep said matter-of-factly.

"What the hell do you mean by that?" Wep walked over to Christian's mini fridge and began rooting around.

"Christian, you didn't even thank me for cleaning you up and putting you in a new change of clothes before tucking you into bed like you were my own child. But for all those little kindnesses, I wasn't about to touch your balls.

So Daphne is still close until you wash her off you completely."

At this point, Christian lost it. If this were all a mind trip, there would be no escaping the pull of psychosis. He would be trapped in this house of mirrors until apprehended and committed to the hospital again. If, however, this were not a mind trip, then he was witness to the murder of Daphne. And the evidence was between his legs.

Neither was a good choice. But choice number two made the better sense. After all, Daphne was one of the 72 he whistleblew on. Wep noticed Christian's silence and perceived that he was weighing his options. Options in favor of Wep's claim that, indeed, he was Osiris.

Christian flopped onto his futon in resignation.

"Ok, Wep. So I'm Osiris? Go on."

Wep's ears perked up.

"Don't mind if I do."

"About 12,800 years ago during a period now called the Younger Dryas, the gods of ancient mythology came to this planet, Earth. From the Olmec, Shinto, Egyptian, Greek, and other gods, many orders of the gods seeded this planet in their designated areas. Each order had its own ambitions for its part of Earth and they spent their days in vastly different ways.

The Greeks, however, made up for lost time because while the Sumerian gods first began to dabble with genomes, it was the Greeks that sought to pleasure themselves with the new human creations.

It was innocent at first, no different than a child playing with stray puppies. But for the next twenty centuries, a highly advanced civilization of both god-and-man hybrids created a trans-oceanic society on this planet. This is where legends like the Buddhist Western Paradise, the Celtic Tir Na Nog or the Atlantis fabled by Plato all emanated from,"

Unlike today, people didn't know discrimination on the basis of visual attributes, so different peoples coexisted peacefully. There was also no poverty in this Golden Age, and death for mortals was like falling asleep into the sweetest dreams of the smoothest jazz.

But the Greek Gods, the Olympians to be specific, valued experimentation, and their philosophy classes were filled with debates extolling the virtue of things the other gods deplored like lust and envy. They got to a point in their thinking that because anything could potentially exist, everything that potentially could, should.'

The Olympians were so obsessed with logic and the notion of no absolutes that they lost their way on the wide road to immortality by trial and error. One of them, Dionysus, discovered that if he mixed his blood in the Greek wine, those who drank it would become, well, different.

It started as a joke at first, just a way for this often left out and frivolous deity to have some kind of influence. But it spiraled out of control as the gods became aware of Dionysus's trick and craved more of the bloodied drink. Addicted, they squeezed every last drop of his blood out of him on one fateful night and made an everlasting pool of it. They became vampires: fanged, hollow, and ravenous.

Those who refused to partake were forced until each Olympic god became tainted by the cannibalization of Dionysus. You see, wine is good in moderation, but blood wine from the death of a god created something unprecedented. We called it 'The First Perversion.' And we hoped it would be the only one."

By this time in Wep's monologue, Christian was so thoroughly intrigued that he got up from his futon and went to his desk where he logged onto his computer. Wep eyed him suspiciously.

"What are you doing?" Christian continued typing.

"There's nothing about 'The First Perversion' online. But when I search 'First Perversion' and 'Osiris ' together, all I get are dick pics."

"You won't find anything online, Belvedere," Wep scoffed. "You mortals have the story wrong. You've imagined it to be an elixir of life that grants mortals immortality. It's the 'First Perversion masked as the pursuit of eternal life. Your kind has killed for it. You see, the Greek gods treated their humans with a disgusting imagination to do all manner of evil to them in order to turn them against each other in every way imaginable. The horror-filled stories from Classical Greek myth happened during this time. Gone was order and morality. Now was a time of tyranny. True, it was an age of heroes who defied these wicked gods, but it was also a plague of locusts that never should have had a harvest to eat.

The other gods, fearful of the drink, abandoned the earth. Except for a few led by… you…"

Christian interrupted Wep's train of thought.

"Hold the fuck up. By me?

"If you let me finish," Wep reprimanded.

"Go on," Christian permitted.

"Except for a few led by Osiris who sought to protect humans from the wrath of the Olympians. Ever since then, we have been fighting on behalf of the humans. We've had some good and bad ideas along with losses and a few victories.

Oddly enough, the rise of Christianity which preached a

hatred of the gods actually helped us rebrand them for the average Medieval as demons. This new marketing strategy turned the entire world against them. In fact, the battles during the Middle Ages were largely battles against these fallen gods. These battles didn't stop when the Dark Ages became the Enlightened Age. No, these battles morphed from The Crusades and Inquisition to the Bubonic Plague, Colonialism, Slavery, the World Wars, the Holocaust, 9/11... These were all battles against the Greek gods.``

Wep paused. "And I wish that I could say it was over. This is where you come in."

"So how do I fit into this as Osiris," Christian asked impatiently.

Wep pulled his head back in surprise.

"You mean you don't know? The gods have come to Parthenon University to deploy their most devious plan ever."

Christian looked incredulous.

"The 72 I called out?" Christian mused.

"Devious bastards," Wep affirmed.

"So tell me, why am I human now?"

Wep crossed his massive arms and lowered his head.

"Because you were betrayed by your brother Set. He and his 72 co-conspirators caught you in a spell, a spell full of errors as they had no mastery of magic. All gods, even the Greeks, took on human bodies becoming mortal as the spell spread throughout the world."

"But why does Osiris have to be human?" Christian reiterated.

"Because... well, you know how the story goes?" Wep said nervously.

"Which story?"

"The story of Osiris. Set, his brother, you know... had

71

him killed. But then he came back to life." Christian sat up slowly and bored his eyes into Wep's.

"Are you saying..." Christian began dangerously. Wep opened a box of cornflakes.

"Yes. The spell requires your death to work. And you can't die unless you're mortal."

"Damn it. Isn't psychosis enough? I'm not sure how much more shit I can handle."

"But in death you'll become almighty," Wep comforted.

"You just ruined my senior year," Christian moaned, walking over to his futon again and falling face down into it. "I was doing so well without you! No parents. No psychosis. I've been going out at night. Some of the old friends have gotten back in touch with me. I was on top of everything. And now you're telling me that I'm going to die! I can't do that!" Christian's face was buried in the cushions so that all of this came out muffled.

"Take heart, Christian. Within you, are powers that are unprecedented. We just need to unlock them and undo the trauma that psychosis has done to obstruct your memory and your... libido."

"Libido?"

"You're a virgin, right?" Wep raised a hairy eyebrow.

"Well, that's just a choice I made."

"Choice," Wep chucked. "I'm here for you, bro. In fact, I've got someone for you to meet. She's been an ally of mine for a few years now. She'll be able to help you face death like a champ." He dumped the rest of the cornflakes into his mouth, getting a white coating of cornflake dust all over his snout.

"Who the fuck taught you to eat? One last thing before we go. A student is dead now... Daphne, my friend."

"One of the 72 co-conspirators," Wep corrected.

"Doesn't matter, Wep. We can't just kill students. Plus, won't the Olympians know what we're up to?"

Wep groomed his whiskers.

"Karma is a funny thing. When it's deserved, it takes a long time to right wrongs. But with the gods, it tends to behave like an obedient pet. When we need it, it's there. So, yes, Daphne will be missed by gods like you and those Greek bastards... but to reality at large... humans like students and administrators... it will be like she was never here in the first place. Karma will act like a rubber band returning to its unstretched self. We call it Karmic Elasticity."

"Oh, my god," Christian started.

"'Oh, me' is a more appropriate term," Wep smirked.

"But won't the same thing happen to me when I die?" Christian asked with concern.

"I thought you might ask that. You have the potential for resurrection on your side."

"And Daphne?"

"There's no resurrection for Daphne. The way we deal with these 72, well, 71 gods, will specifically sentence them to oblivion. So, we've got to do it right. We'll have to be selective in our skills, draw them to us, one by one."

"Potential for resurrection? But what if I die and that resurrection doesn't happen? It'll be like I was never here?"

"If you die... it will be like none of us were ever here. Look, the Olympians want to remake the world into a dark, cracked, volcanic series of islands. They want a New World Order. They want to break our connection to each other, make mothers' milk rotten, erase our histories, revise them as lies, turn the sky and seas red, and kill every one of any gods left to stand against them."

"The odds aren't really in our favor, are they?" Wep protested.

"It looks that way. But you've got to realize that your whole life has been a lie. You've never had psychosis. You're coming into godhood now and these demons began aligning themselves to play a role in your life the second they smelled your divinity when you were a teen and they're scared shitless. So the odds are in our favor."

Christian was chewing his lip nervously.

"It's hard to separate the psychosis from my alleged divinity," he explained. But Wep wouldn't have it.

"Get your shit together, Belvedere. Your powers need to start coming back or else we'll be shit out of luck now that they're ready to come for you. Stop all that negative thinking. In fact, I think it's time for you to level up. Follow me."

"It's after 3 a.m."

"Doesn't matter." By this time, Wep was holding the door open for Christian. Having no other choice, Christian got up, grabbed a windbreaker off the countertop of his kitchenette, and followed Wep.

Outside, Christian was paranoid. The events of the evening before were still deeply embedded in his nervous system and he felt invisible eyes on him. In under two minutes, they arrived at a nondescript alley that Christian had never before seen. Wep stopped.

"Ok. So, anywhere paths cross we can enter. This time I'll help you, but if you ever need to access the lair on your own, you'll have to recite a line from the Book of the Dead. It's my password."

"Where are we?"

"The masons built a sort of cosmic doorway underneath Parthenon to feed off the other side. But it's not really below. It's more like somewhere else, we're just going down to get there. Ready? Good! I am he who rises and shines, a wall which comes out of a wall!"

Out of thin air, a wall of fire appeared. At first there was a low hum, but then Christian recognized it as a sing-song chant of a deep bass voice. Then it turned into a high-pitched buzz. Christian felt the sensation of movement and could see, in real-time or his imagination he was not sure, images of hieroglyphs, sphinxes, and obelisks. At one point, he saw a girl, beautiful and winged, smiling bashfully at him. He thought she shed a tear.

Then they were there. Somewhere.

"Welcome to my side of the Duat." Wep was grinning.

The place where they were had a space-like quality. Statues of ancient gods aligned its walls in marble and limestone. The statues glowed fiery with life-like animation. The ceiling had a magnificent depiction of the Zodiac on it filled with stars and constellations. But the floor was the real show. One could see any location in the universe through the floor.

"Don't be shy. Walk around and make yourself at home. Technically, this is your home since this is where Osiris went when he died and where you will go when you…" Wep realized he was saying too much. "Anyway, I told you I wanted you to meet someone."

"Now?" Christian spat. "You brought me all the way here for a hookup? You could have warned me or given me a few pointers," he tittered.

"Pointers won't be necessary. You might be Osiris, but it's the 21st century. Leave that incest shit on the other side." Christian turned around abruptly at the sound of the voice, and there stood Sophie.

"Grandma?" He hadn't seen his grandmother stand for two years. And here she was, standing and beautiful. Christian instinctively reached out to touch her. His hand touched nothing but space. But there she stood as solidly as she looked. She smiled and gestured with her hand at their surroundings.

"We were just talking about all this Egyptian stuff about a month or so ago, and here you are!" She reached both hands out and laid them on Christian's shoulders. To his surprise, he felt their weight and their grip. His heart leapt at her impossible recovery.

"Grandma, you look so healthy. Are you all better?" Christian asked, confused. Sophie laughed dismissively.

"No. This is just my projected image. My body is still in the bed at your parents' house. Dying." Christian felt the air leave him like a balloon, and Sophie gripped him harder.

"Honey, don't be troubled. I've lived a long and adventurous life. Wep can tell you, I've cheated death many times. It's only fair that he gets what he's due. But enough of that. I'm on my way to see you, Osiris."

"Me?"

"You're the Lord of the Afterlife. You judge and allot the dead. A part of you is still in the Duat somewhere, carrying out your duties."

"Why wasn't I told about this when I was younger? Do my parents know?"

Wep and Sophie look at each other. Sophie let go of Christian and folded her hands behind her back.

"Your parents are what we call 'under the veil' as were you. They only see what they want to see. The veil prevents mortals from seeing the truth unless it's lifted."

"Then you knew I didn't have psychosis?"

"Yes, but you didn't know. Nor were you ready to see that you didn't. I could have told you and, because of the adoration you have for your grandmother, you would have played along. But you weren't ready." Sophie stole a glance at Wep and continued matter-of-factly.

"But now that the veil has been lifted for you, the hourglass has been turned and time is slipping away."

"Slipping away," Christian wondered.

"Even if the veil lifts for a person, it can drop as well. And without warning. Sophie's facial expression softened.

"When you were barely out of your toddler years, I would watch you? Remember? We used to play with cups." Christian's face brightened at the memory.

"That's one of my strongest memories of childhood," Christian mused. Sophie smiled.

"That wasn't just cups, Christian. I was teaching you Furie counter-magic. Old power before there were gods and goddesses. It takes mastery to control. That's why we spent hours playing." At this, Sophie stopped abruptly. "But your father put an end to that." Christian recoiled at the mention of his father.

"He did?"

"Yes. The intuitive power you already had as an Egyptian god grew stronger the closer you were to its history and culture. But Furie power works in all worlds. I tried to arm you in case your god powers failed you one day or never came to full strength at all. So, one day, we were playing hide-and-seek, and you, I couldn't find you. But your parents did."

The hair on the back of Christian's neck stood up.

"When they pulled up in my driveway, your parents

found you on the roof of my house. I had no idea how you had gotten up there. It was your mother's blood-curdling scream that brought me to the front porch. You had seen your parents pull up and got excited. One moment you were on the roof, and the next moment you were… on the ground running around the yard in circles, you were so excited. Stone was furious at me, accused me of meddling with your 'education,' and whisked you away. He suspected that I had been helping you hone your powers and, for some reason, he didn't want me… you knowing."

Christian was tingling with excitement.

"Didn't want me knowing what exactly?" he urged.

"He didn't want you knowing you were a god." The entire lair was quiet for a moment. The silence was broken by Sophie's sigh.

"Moved you across town into a ritzy suburb, put you in a private, high-dollar Kindergarten that specialized in enrichment classes. The next time I saw you, you knew the Greek alphabet as well as you did the English, and they had you reading out of Hellenic primers far more advanced than kids twice your age. Stone used to have you reenact scenes from The Iliad & The Odyssey at dinner parties that they threw several times a month. One Halloween, you dressed up as Archimedes. All of the other little boys chose superhero costumes, and here you were running from house to house, half naked with your little toga trailing behind you screaming, "Eureka, I found it!" You were an odd little boy."

Not sure that he should be upset or humored, Christian looked up at the ceiling.

"Grandma, are you trying to tell me that Stone… my father… hated his own… kind? I mean, it sounds like he tried to immerse me in Greek culture. Why would he do that if he knew I was Osiris?" Sophie pointed at Christian knowingly.

"Your parents didn't leave you alone with me for another three months."

"And why did they do that?"

"True, Stone was the reason I didn't see you, but your mother was feeling bad about my estrangement and convinced your father to let you stay with me for a night or two. What harm could there be in that?" Sophie laughed a deep belly laugh.

"You were so happy to be back with me though your powers waned to almost nothing. But you remembered those cups and insisted that we play with them. After a couple of hours of playing, I was surprised how much you remembered. Maybe it was curiosity or maybe I was trying to make up for lost time... I don't know. But I decided to teach you an Infernus charm which is the highest level of defensive wills. I didn't suspect that you would take to it so quickly, but your Infernus was so powerful that it shook the neighborhood. I knew that in a matter of time, the energy would attract the likes of dangerous beings, so I tried to counter the Infernus."

"A counter counter charm?" Christian said incredulously.

"I know. Maybe it was rash of me. But at the time that I called upon the counter, the power of the veil lowered at the same time. The veil missed me but hit you. You were never the same."

Christian was growing uncomfortable by this confession but perceived what his grandmother was getting at.

"Is that when 'it' started," he asked almost apologetically.

"If by 'it' you mean 'psychosis' then yes. Almost immediately, you began doing strange things. Like lucid sleepwalking where your parents would routinely find you wandering the streets at night... asleep. They couldn't figure out how you got out of the house because the doors would be locked. Stone had a customized security system put in, and that put an end to it. Oh, but then the nightmares started."

"This is incredible," was all that Christian could say. Sophie stepped up close to Christian and laid her hands on both of his arms. Her presence was airy and the pressure of her squeeze, though light, was the equivalent of a grasp.

"You would never know me like that again until the veil was removed. Well, it has been removed, and like I said, time is slipping away. No one knows when it will descend so you don't have a lot of time. The Olympians are closing in on Parthenon, and they are closer and further along in their plan to bind and abolish the ancient gods... the Furies... of which you are a descendent. You need to find and destroy them before the veil descends."

"That's virtually impossible," Christian argued. "I mean... literally... of all the tasks that gods have been given, this is the worst. There's no certainty in it. I can put a day or week or year into this mission and then in the next moment be oblivious to this world once again... like I was sniped in the head."

"Christian, while I don't have the power to move the veil, I do have something to give you that will help you in your journey."

"What is that?"

"Your parents... and my own negligence... has done a lot to suppress your confidence. Waffling back and forth

80

about 'deity or psychosis' poses a problem. You need to be able to function at a high level of god-awareness. So right now, I'm going to reinstate the Infernus charm that I suspended almost sixteen years ago. It will reinstate that vibrant energy that will allow you to think like a god without the doubt of psychosis. Pure energy."

"And it can help him with his other problem, too," Wep had been uncharacteristically quiet the entire time but now interrupted.

"Rhymes with divinity." Sophie laughed.

"He's got enough charm in there somewhere to find someone worth losing it to when he's ready. But Christian, I must also warn you that this charm comes with a liability. When unleashed, it will cause such a ripple throughout the worlds in which the Furies operate that it will attract a lot of dangerous beings, chief of which are the Olympians who are set on identifying and eliminating you. Now, my question for you is 'Are you ready?'"

Over the last few minutes while Sophie had been talking, a calm came over Christian. While he had no words to describe it, he would later use the word "indescribable."

"Grandma, I am." Sophie's eyes crinkled when she smiled.

"Now, this Infernus spell will require a little bit of me and a lot of you, Christian."

"Whatever it takes. I want to remember our lessons if it will give me more of you in my life," Christian said somberly.

"I locked the Infernus spell in with a riddle. If you can solve the riddle, the runes will appear on your seven chakras. By accepting this, you must carry out the mission in full, no matter what. Do you accept?" Christian took a deep breath.

"I accept."

"Here is the riddle: What rises but never fell, what sustains but never stains, and is more valuable than money, more variety than what is funny, goes good with everything perhaps even honey, and adored as a ceiling and a floor but never a ceiling without a floor, but sometimes a floor without a ceiling?"

Christian combed his fingers through his curls.

"Christian, you only have two minutes."

"Two minutes? Ok.... a ceiling with a floor, good with honey, rises but never falls? Can't be an empire unless it's an empire in some way that history is wrong. So maybe Rome? No? Ok, not Rome. More variety than what is funny, so maybe it's a thing? Ok, it's definitely a noun. Honey? So maybe it's a thing because it's food? Or a beehive, damn it! Ok, more valuable than money. For some reason I see an image of the French Revolution. 'Let them eat cake...'"

"Twenty seconds," Wep and Sophie said in unison.

"Ok, bees maybe? But they don't have floors without ceilings or whatever. Floors without ceilings? Ok, if it is a noun then what can have a bottom with no top sometimes, a top and a bottom most times and never a top without a bottom. Oh, my gods! I think I've got it! Bread! It's bread!" Christian shouted victoriously.

"That's my boy!" Sophie beamed and Wep howled.

All of a sudden, the three of them felt the concussive energy of a sonic boom release and the entire lair reverberated.

"Oh, look, he's glowing!" Wep chortled.

"I feel funny!" Christian said suddenly.

"This is going to be… challenging." Sophie said to Wep.

JUSTIN WILLIAMS

"He just followed the instructions of a talking wolf-man he believed to be a figment of his imagination. I think he can handle it," Wep approved.

"What do the runes say?" Christian shouted.

"You have to save one of the Greek gods," Sophie responded. The cave was silent for a split second.

"Save?" Wep and Christian reacted at the same time.

"They're hard enough to kill!" Wep complained.

"Wep, maybe this is the way we should be going about this. Daphne was messy business and I'm not sure I have it within me to dispatch the 71 others, even as Osiris. Maybe grandma is on to something. Maybe we can reverse their plan instead of just destroying them. Make them allies," Christian mused. Sophie nodded in response.

"But the whole point is to stop them once and for all. We can't risk having them show up even in another thousand years. Your own death…," Wep corrected himself. "I mean everything you're doing would be for nothing. You can't negotiate with terrorists. One of your presidents said that."

"Christian is right," Sophie spoke up, but this time her voice was fainter and her body more translucent. "And Wep is right. You can't simply murder them but you also can't negotiate with them. That's why it's up to both of you to come up with a third option. Christian, the blood of Osiris runs through your veins. Now that you've been reborn, you exude a power that has already made you a god-magnet before you've even left the halls of this sacred lair. As Yahweh said to our wily ancestor Cain, 'Everyone who sees you will want to murder you." You have been put on notice. Now, you can live looking over your shoulder for the rest of your life, or you can do what you need to do to end this now."

83

Wep was pacing the lair like a caged tiger.

"Ok, we know they are drawn to you," he addressed Christian. "So you need to do what you can to appear vulnerable. Get a bit drunk and so forth, flash some shoulder. Then once you notice someone giving you extra attention, lure them to where the two paths meet. We'll trap them here in the lair and then figure out the reverse spell to turn them back into gods from the Greek demons they are."

Sophie's image was waning even lighter when she spoke.

"Christian," she almost whispered, " Wep is right. You must experience the ultimate betrayal in order to reverse the spell, but that will require you to experience the ultimate vulnerability. When the time comes, your heart will be broken in a way that no spell or power can reverse. But you must remain still. That is the only way..." Her last words trailed like a wisp. Christian moved forward as if to hug Sophie, but as soon as he reached his arms out, she was gone.

"I love you," he whispered.

"She'll be back," Wep comforted. "But you heard what she said, right? We risk blowing our cover and alerting these Hellenic bastards to our plan if you can't control your... psychosis or whatever you call it. But it's worth it if we get you some power. Right now, you're like an intern without the right qualifications."

"I'm Osiris," Christian said quietly.

"Osiris or not, you've yet to be proven. Here, drink this. It's my own batch of heqet." Wep walked over to the corner of the lair and tapped on a glyph. Out came a brown clay bottle.

"Festival of Drunkenness 2361 B.C.," Wep murmured. "This is one of my newer batches of beer from the old days. Full-bodied. Hoppy. Smooth going down. You'll love it. Most importantly, it will give you the vulnerable edge Sophie was talking about. It will help make you vulnerable and subtle like flypaper so that we can start catching these gods."

Christian took the chalice Wep handed him.

"To… victory," Christian said somberly.

He took a sip.

"I think the stars on the ceiling are moving," Christian said after a moment.

"We're ready then!" Wep said gleefully. Christian felt himself slowly rotating until the momentum caused him to black out for a few seconds. When he came to, they had risen back to street level. Wep steadied him and pointed him in the direction of his dorm.

"You need to go get yourself a proper shower. I can't come with you now but I'll be close by."

Christian started to walk away unsure of his footing.

"And Christian," Wep added. "Beware. They're onto you. Once you go through that door…" Christian waved Wep off.

"I've got it," he said inebriated while irritated at the sound of his own voice. "Don't worry about me," and he stumbled down the street like a cocky jock with a hangover.

When Christian reached his dorm door and touched the door handle, a thought startled him back to reality. I have to save one of the Greek Gods.

"I wonder which one it will be," Christian slurred as he fumbled with the deadbolt, "Cause I will fuck him up."

The deadbolt unlocked, Christian went in and closed the door behind him.

"By my Furie powers," he giggled, and flopped face down

on his futon.

"Your Furie powers?" a deep bass voice echoed. Christian turned over quickly, falling off the futon onto the floor, startled at the voice of the intruder.

And there he saw him. Stone Belvedere sitting in his chair at his desk with Christian's laptop opened. And he didn't look happy.

***

"Furie powers?" Stone repeated.

For a second, Christian was paralyed by a specter of darkness that pulled him back to a moment in a dark living room with Mrs. Belvedere cowering with fear in a corner while a younger Stone towered over a much younger Christian, yelling with so much vehemence that Christian could see the bulging vein in his neck, pulsating angrily.

The scene of the gigantic Stone gesticulating threateningly with his meaty fists over the smaller Christian froze for a second, and then something strange happened. Stone began to shrink smaller and smaller. And Christian began to grow larger and larger. For a split second they were the same size but then Stone kept shrinking and Christian kept growing larger and larger until his head hit the living room chandelier.

The scene was so absurd for the short period of time that it lasted and Christian was so taken off guard by it that he laughed. Stone, still sitting in the chair at Christian's desk, was not amused.

"Son, have you... been drinking?

Damn it, Christian thought. Grandma's spell... I must be acting like an irresponsible addict right now. Get it together! he chastised himself. But as Christian began to explain how not only was he not drunk, but he also wasn't spiraling for lack of taking his medication, it didn't come out as he planned.

"Drunk? More like I got pissed at every fucking merry mount on Potential Street!" Stone's right eyebrow arched visibly.

"Out drinking at every merry mount? I called you." Stone's consternation was palpable. "I told you I would be over tonight. I've left you a dozen voicemails today."

Despite Christian's attempt to respond in an agreeable manner, Wep's hequet had a different course in mind.

"Calm the fuck down. I just forgot what time you were coming." Christian regretted every word as it left his mouth.

This time, both of Stone's eyebrows arched and he sat up in his chair.

"Son, have you been taking drugs? Because I know that you sure as hell didn't just tell me to calm the fuck down."

Careful, Christian chided himself. Act normal...

"I am a little drunk," Christian offered, pleased at first with his contrite tone. But then he had to continue. "But you shouldn't be surprised. I've heard the legendary stories at Liger. Like father, like son."

By this time, Stone was staring daggers at Christian through bushy eyebrows. Slowly, he turned his attention to Christian's computer and clicked a key to refresh it.

"Looks like the similarity between father and son ends here," Stone said dangerously, nodding his head at the computer screen. "'Thick & Juicy', 'Nibbles & Bits', 'Erectionmania: Men at Work'?" he read. "What are all these dick pics doing on your computer? Is there something I should know?"

At the mention of "dick pics," Christian's hangover disappeared and he was a little child again being interrogated and reamed out by his father.

Damn it, Christian said to himself. He had forgotten about leaving his search history open. Almost instantaneously, Christian felt the effects of the hequet disappear and suddenly knew what it meant. His signal had grown strong and he was on the Olympians' radar. In fact, they could even be closing in on him now. He had to scramble fast.

"Oh, that... well... I..."

"Is there something you need to tell me, son?" There was a smirk playing on the corner of Stone's mouth. "Are you a Greek poof?"

"No, sir," Christian stammered. Then a diversion came to him. "I've been, uhhh, 'kicking it' with some chicks, you know... 'doing' them." Christian couldn't look at his father while he said it because the fact of the matter was that he had never "done" it and didn't know the first thing about "doing" it.

Stone stared at him unconvinced.

"These are dicks. Not vaginas," he retorted.

Christian mustered everything he could remember about sex.

"Dad, I was really 'giving it' to them... you know.. 'hammering their nails' and 'banging' them like a... uh... like an Uzi. It was crazy... they... they kept wanting it. They were making such a big deal of me that I wanted to see if ... uh... how I measured up to ... you know... other guys." Christian averted his eyes from Stone who sat quietly for what seemed like a long time. Then Stone guffawed. He threw his head back and laughed until he cackled like Sophie used to do. Stone laughed uncontrollably until he cried as Christian winced in embarrassment. Stone was finally done.

"O, my God!" Stone said, wiping his eyes with his sleeve. "And here I thought you were some Greek poof! Son, we Belvedere men have no competition in that field, believe me.

Christian almost breathed a sigh of relief.

"But what's Dité going to think of all this when she finds out? I know you two aren't speaking but I didn't realize you would go all Casanova behind her back."

"How do you know Dité and I aren't speaking?" Christian's voice was tight.

"I just know," Stone said coolly. "You seem very agitated. Have you been taking your meds?"

My meds? Christian thought. He hadn't taken any in the last 24 hours, but he wasn't about to admit that to his father. Stone tapped a ziplock bag of pills sitting on Christian's desk.

Did he really even need them? He wasn't psychotic. Or was he still? Maybe all of this wasn't real. Maybe he was still psychotic like Wep said could be the case.

Just as Christian was about to lie about how he takes his meds in the late morning, he felt the sound of distant thunder.

But it came from below.

There it was again. This time, it reverberated through him. It had to be the Olympians. They couldn't be more than a block away.

Because the hequet had worn off, he had to get to a drink of the strongest sort really fast to mask his location or he was going to be cornered and torn limb from limb.

"Dad, ... I actually have to meet Dité for brunch." Christian jumped up to leave.

"Dité? After, what did you call it, "hammering the nails" of all those broads? I don't think she's going to like that one bit when she finds out," Stone clucked his tongue.

"I'm going to be late," Christian mumbled. Another vibration crescendoed up his spine. The Olympians were in front of the residence hall now.

"Don't forget your meds," Stone said as he flung the plastic back of meds at Christian, hitting him in the back of the head. The next vibration was violent, and Christian thought that his vertebrae would come apart. The Olympians were now on his hall, just steps from his door, and there was no time to escape when an idea came to his mind.

He wondered if he could double on his pills and scramble the signal. It was worth a try. So, Christian picked up the bag his father had thrown at him, took the largest bottle out, opened the lid and poured a few capsules into his mouth.

"Whoa!" Stone warned, "what the h..." But by the time Stone got up from his chair, the effect of the pills kicked in and Christian felt the reverberation of the Olympians roil right past his dorm door.

By this time, Stone had reached Christian, grabbed him from the back and attempted to do the Heimlich on him just as the warm relaxed sensation hit Christian's bloodstream. But to Stone's surprise, he couldn't lift him.

"Calm the fuck down," Christian said casually. "I've got shit to do."

***

Amid Stone's protests, Christian peeked his head out his dorm door, looking up and down the hall. Mid-morning was usually when the majority of the students on his hall would stir, their music devices blaring a wide variety of morning music. But the hall was silent. Christian smelled the hint of sulfur in the air and smiled grimly to himself. Without a doubt, the Olypians had just been here, but Christian's quick thinking had outwitted them.

They're probably pissed, he thought to himself. And he did it. He allowed himself to be vulnerable just as his grandmother had instructed him. Would it be this easy every time? With this newfound confidence in the sanity of his mind and in the power of Osiris inside him, Christian stepped into the hall, closing the door behind him. If he could stay in this state of mind, his Furie powers might be restored to him quicker than he anticipated.

Wep. Christian needed to find Wep and report to him his first success, how he foiled the Olympians. He decided to opt for the stairwell instead of the elevator. Small spaces were too much a hazard. And when Christian opened the stairwell door, not only was it abandoned of late students scrambling for their mid-morning classes, but he caught a faint whiff of the Olympians who evidently opted for the stairs as well.

Cautiously, he made his way down to the ground floor and pushed on the breaker bar of the door that opened to the back of the dorm. Still no one. And from his vantage point, there was no one behind the building either. But there was a mountain bike leaning outside against the air conditioner to the left of the door. Christian grinned at his luck. He would take the mountain bike, climb on the dumpsters behind the dorm and toss the bike over the

91

fence. From there he would ride the bike down the old, windy but muddy aqueduct that was an effortless downhill ride. At the end of his ride he would end up in an alley on the south side of Potential Street. From there, it was a short pedal to the intersection where Wep and Christian had entered the lair last night. And he could do all of this without having to expose himself to the rest of the campus where the Olypians could be lying in wait.

The first part of Christian's plan went smoothly. He had no problem getting up on the dumpster and getting the bike over the fence though he was breathing like a freight train once he jumped the fence. Even his descent into the aqueduct went easy and was exhilarating because it was almost entirely downhill with curves that were easily negotiable if you were moderate in your speed, especially with the aqueduct being muddy.

But on the last curve that led into the alley of Potential Street, Christian thought he was home-free and so allowed the mountainbike to accelerate, his feet off the pedals, his windbreaker flapping behind him, and the wind in his face.

Later on when Christian recalled the incident, he wasn't sure if she magically appeared before him or if he was just so tunnel-visioned and euphoric about completing his escape plan that he didn't see her. But he didn't have time to brake or to warn her. When he made impact, Christian thought he had hit a low wall or maybe a tree lying in his path, but when he tumbled through the air, he was tumbling with someone else.

Christian landed against an alley wall with a thump while his mountain bike somersaulted two or three times until it skidded to the end of the alleyway. The person he hit landed halfway on him and halfway on a bag of trash.

"Are you ok?" he groaned, not yet knowing who he had hit but trying to be respectful all the same. "I didn't see you..."

"I think I took on more of that than you somehow." a familiar voice responded. It was a female voice and she got up as quickly as she dared, brushing her knees and backside off from mud. When she was done, she reached her hand out to help Christian. It was then that he got a good look at her.

"Dean Maiden?" he squeaked in horror. Despite the growing knot on his forehead, Christian got up as quickly as possible, embarrassed.

"I am sooooo sorry. Oh, my God, are you ok? What were you doing?"

Dean Maiden smiled wryly.

"I should be asking you since you were speeding towards me like you were fleeing for your life. Are you ok?"

Christian tried to control his level of energy, because Dean Maiden was known among the faculty and students for her ability to cipher even the most obscure of details when it came to making decisions about a person.

"I'm just doing a little calorie burn before I hit the books," Christian said nervously. Dean Maiden looked around the alleyway.

"Did you lose your books?" she asked knowingly? "Or are you on your way to Liger for a beer this early? Which is it? Beer or books?"

There was an awkward lull in the conversation interrupted by a low rumble that Christian could feel in the soles of his feet. Dean Maiden was studying Christian's face as she waited for an answer. Then there was another rumble. This time, it made Christian unsteady on his feet. He lurched to balance himself.

"Are you ok, Mr. Belvedere?" Dean Maiden asked. It was then that Christian realized that hitting his head must have woken him up from his inebriated state. That rumble was the Olympians. They had zeroed in on him again. They had to get out of the alley fast.

"Beer!" he shouted a little too loudly. She looked at him quizzically. Christian tried his best not to look too panicked, but he needed to scramble the signal as fast as possible before the Olympians found them. In the alley, they were in a kill zone.

"The merry mounts are on the north side of Potential Street. You're kind of in the sketchy part of town." But Christian was panicked when the third wave hit. They were closer.

"Let me take you for a drink," he grabbed her hand, almost yanking her toward the sidewalk.

"Is this a date, Mr. Belvedere," she teased, somewhat pulling back from him as he squeezed more tightly on her arm.

"Or is this another episode?"

Another rumble rolled through the alleyway from the direction Christian had been riding his mountain bike. He looked frantically around and tugged Dean Maiden toward the street end of the alley.

"An episode? Come with me if you don't want to see an episode."

***

By the time Christian burst through the doors of the nearest bar, in his anxiety he was unaware that he had been

94

dragging the delicate Dean Maiden behind him the entire time.

"Mr. Belvedere!" she whispered sharply as the bells announcing their entrance jangled loudly. But Christian was preoccupied with adjusting his eyes to the dark and dank interior, his eyes flitting back and forth until they spied a booth with an amber growler on the table top. He beelined for it. No sooner had he slid into the sticky cushion bench that he had the growler to his lips, sucking deep pulls at such an alarming rate that Dean Maiden felt compelled to follow him, the concern growing in her voice. She sat opposite him, glaring at him as he finished, set the growler back down with a thud, and tried to catch his breath.

"Mr. Belvedere," she whispered sharply. "Are you going to explain yourself? Do you know…" she looked around the bench carefully at the bar where three characters, nursing various drinks, were turned around looking at the couple, distracted by their whirlwind of an appearance. "Do you know where you brought us?" She turned back around. Christian, more docile than when they entered the establishment, half grinned at her.

"All I know," he began. "All I know is that Fate has brought us together." Despite being sufficiently inebriated once more and avoiding capture by the Olympians, Christian's metaphorical speech evoked double entendres. Dean Maiden was a young 23, no more than two years older than Chritsian, but she was also a dean, and a celebrated one at that. The bike accident was forgivable, but Christian had definitely crossed the line when he brought her… by force even… into a dark pub on the southside of town and played the drunk. From her perspective, the latter act was a breach of the student-faculty relationship. But from

Christian's vantage point, he didn't see her as someone far above him

There was a commotion at the bar. The three regulars were speaking to the bar attendant who had just emerged from the back. By Dean Maiden's estimation, they were letting her know that she had two visitors. She grabbed a couple of coasters and made her way over to the table.

"Mr. Belvedere, I insist that we get out of here. You don't know where we are, and my premonition radar is on high alert. We are not in good company..." As Dean Maiden finished her conspicuous warning, the bar attendant was at their table. She was a beautiful lady with large, sultry eyes that betrayed her Middle-Eastern background, her high cheekbones accentuating them. Her unique noseline gave her an overall modelesque look. But, perhaps, her most stunning feature was her hair which was a platinum champagne against the background of brown skin.

"Hello, I will be your server. But it looks like you've helped yourself already." Christian was captivated by both her beauty and her accent.

"Asara? Beautiful name." She was fairly tall, with a long, sleek neck and a tongue piercing which might have lent to her accent. Asara ignored Christian's compliment and reached for the growler.

"What will you both be having? Or have you had enough already." She held the growler up to the little light inside the bar and saw that it was empty.

"Well, aren't you a comedian?" Christian asked playfully.

"And aren't you the irresponsible frat boy, drinking before noon. With a teacher, nonetheless." She shot a piercing look at Dean Maiden for a split second. Dean Maiden looked alarmed and even Christian sat up a little at this response.

"Hold on, hold on. Give me a stein of your best house beer... on draft."

"And for you?" she asked Dean Maiden who looked out of her element.

"A tea. No sugar," she said nervously.

Without a word, Asara turned and headed back to the bar. Once she was out of ear shot, Dean Maiden leaned in to speak with Christian who looked a little more sober than he did a few minutes before.

"Mr. Belvedere, do you think you're living in a simulation where your actions have no consequences? " she began.

"That's Descartes," Christian said abruptly. "And call me Christian."

"Excuse me," Dean Maiden said aghast.

"Stop the act," Christian sat up. "You've got as much explaining as I do." Christian's tone was aggressive but petulant.

"And how do you mean?"

"I mean that why in the world would a dean allow a student who in a mental health crisis made accusations of students and faculty members in the most public and vulgar way... why would that dean let him back in the university as if it didn't happen?" Dean Maiden breathed in sharply through her nose and let the air out slowly.

"Why do you think that is, Mr. Belvedere?"

"There's only three reasons I could come up with? One, you really think I have a mental health issue beyond my ability to control. Second, someone put you up to it. Third, you put yourself up to it." Dean Maiden paused before she spoke,

"And which do you prefer to believe?"

"You mean which do I prefer?" Christian fired back. "I don't think it's number one because I know the school's protocol for mental health outbursts that were less than mine. I don't think it's number two because you made the decision almost spontaneously. I saw it in your eyes."

"So, it's number three." Dean Maiden said matter-of-factly.

"Yes. I choose number three. So let's talk mano a mano. I'm not who people believe me to be, but you're also not who you say you are. So cut the crap. What's going on?"

Dean Maiden's eyes bored into Christian's so that he squirmed uncomfortably. Before she could respond, the waitress was at the table. She seemed in a better mood, setting each beverage down in front of each person with care.

"Anything else I can do for you?" She smiled sweetly at Christian.

"How about a name?" Christian raised an eyebrow expectantly.

"I don't give out my name to customers." She glanced at Dean Maiden who lowered her head. Christian offered Dean Maiden a puzzled look.

"Am I missing something here?" The waitress abruptly turned, snapping her ponytail.

"Let me know if you need anything."

Christian shook his head confusedly and reached for his beer. Dean Maiden quickly reached out and covered it with her palm.

"Don't drink it," she whispered between gritted teeth.

"Oh, no, I need this. More than you can think."

"It's not what you think it is. Look, I'm not even going to drink my tea." She pulled Christian's beer to her side of the table.

"What is going on?" Christian demanded. Dean Maiden glanced quickly at the bar. The waitress was nowhere to be seen.

"Quick, let's get out of here." Dean Maiden began scooting out of her booth. By the time she stood up to head towards the door, she noticed that Christian was still sitting in the booth, pulling his beer back to his side of the table. In one quick move, faster than Christian's could register, Dean Maiden grabbed his hand.

"Christian, let's go." Almost as if under a spell, Christian obediently got up, grumbling and began to follow her out.

"What about paying for it..."

"We didn't drink, so we don't pay." This time she was dragging Christian out beneath the jangling bells above the door. Once they were out, Christian looked up and down the street.

"Where are we going?" he asked bewildered. "I still haven't gotten my drink. And why were you acting strange in there?" With her hand still firmly gripping his, Dean Maiden took a right into the alley from which they had come.

"Mr. Belvedere, it might surprise you, but I happen to know that those drinks were tainted. They were drugged. With what, I don't know."

Christian pulled away from Dean Maiden's grip briefly.

"You've been here before?" he said, the revelation lighting up his face. "She's seen you before."

"Maybe," Dean Maiden admitted.

"But why would you patronize a bar that drugs its customers?"

"Christian, there's a lot that you don't know about me,

and there's a lot you don't need to know. Let's just say that you and I are on the same team." At that moment, someone turned the corner into the alleyway.

"Christian? Christian Belvedere." Both Christian and Dean Maiden turned towards the voice. It was the waitress, approaching them carefully.

"I believe this is yours?" She reached out and presented Christian with a prescription bottle with his name and address on the label. Awkwardly, he took it from her.

"Thank you…"

"Asara," the waitress said with a grin.

"Thank you, Asara," he corrected.

"Asara Stern."

***

"Hop from bar to bar much?"

Christian had been hunched over a beer up at the bar of Liger, lost in thought. But the familiar voice startled him back to the present.

"Remember me, Christian?" When he turned, he found himself face-to-face with Asara Stern. He froze. First, because he hadn't expected her. Second, because so much beauty so close found him tongue-tied.

"It's Christian, right?" Asara cocked her head at him and squinted her eyes teasingly.

"I… hello… I… didn't expect…" Christian did a 360, "How did you get in?"

"So, you do remember me." Asara enunciated each word insultingly as if Christian were hearing-impaired.

"Do you not have places to be your senior year at this prestigious university or are you a trust fund baby who daydrinks for sport?" She reached over and grabbed Christian's beer.

"Yes, I remember you. Yes, my name is Christian. And, no, I'm not a drunk." In response, Asara swished the beer around, sniffed it, and took a gulp." She made a repulsive face.

"You're not a discriminating drunk. This is piss water." She scanned the merry mount.

"The lady you were with yesterday. Is she here?" Still captivated by the beauty who was giving him her attention, Christian was quick to deny the presence of Dean Maiden even though she wasn't there.

"No. She's a dean. I accidentally ran into her on my bike yesterday and your place was the closest place to… recover." After one more scan, Asara grabbed Christian's arm and got off her chair.

"Let's take a walk to remember," she ordered while Christian downed the rest of his beer and obediently followed her out past the front door.

"Where are we going," Christian asked carefully, aware that he was being led by a stranger as well as a stranger to his campus. Once they went through the door, they were greeted by a blast of wind that made Asara lean into Christian tightly, her right breast pressed against his chest in a kind of side hug. A rush of warmth spread through his own chest and added to the buzz from the alcohol. He didn't protest.

"You must have been drunk earlier today when you told me that you wanted to see me," Asara breathed into his ear and gave him a peck on the cheek.

"Did I?" Christian asked, not knowing what else to say.

"You did when you left your bottle of pills in the booth.

An empty bottle," she added, playfully bumping her hip against his.

"I did?" Christian repeated.

"Yes, you did. This is why you shouldn't drink during the day. It would improve your memory. I would know, I remember everything. And I don't drink. So why were you carrying around a bottle of empty pills, and why were you with a dean from your college in my part of town? You don't belong there, prep. And why is it that the second time that I see you, you're still drunk? Now all of this can make for an excellent conversation should you want another kiss, so indulge me and perhaps we'll both get a reward out of the next fifteen minutes or so. The time it'll take for the good knight to move on, drink, and black out far away from me. Christian? What irony. It's a Christian to save me from a crusader."

"What are we waiting for?" Christian perked up at the likelihood of a makeout session. Even though he was on a mission to figure out the runes, fulfill his duty, live, and receive his long hidden and much needed power, that mission couldn't compete against the chub that was quickly working its way north.

By this time, they had walked into the center of campus, right by the famous cathedral simply called The Chapel. A small cathedral, it was scaled in such a way that it preserved the sense of magnitude and awe that evoked for many the hope of Christ but for Christian the imposing Gothic belief evoked in him both fear and dread. However, if this cathedral provided both of them temporary shelter from the cold and some privacy in order to get closer to each other, then praise God.

Asara picked up on Christian's reluctant energy once

they reached the threshold of the large door.

"Are you intimidated, heathen?" Asara teased.

"Heathen?"

"Many times throughout history, kissing a girl like me would make you a heathen, especially in front of places with stained glass windows and flying buttresses." She kissed Christian again.

"What do you mean by that?"

Asara ignored his question.

"Whoever is writing our short story had better keep on with their best material, because this is too good to be true," Asara breathed in his ear. While they were commencing to kiss, Christian thought he heard a sound deep into the recesses of the cathedral. As faint as it was, it reminded him of the moving of stone and the groaning of metal. The sound got louder. Concentrating on the sound caused him to lose momentum with Asara.

"Have you never done this before?" Asara whispered. Christian, keeping one ear out for the sound, protested.

"Loads of times," he attempted to come off convincingly.

Asara stared into his eyes for a few seconds and then pushed him in the chest with both hands.

"You've never done this before," she laughed wickedly. "You're Christian the Virgin."

"I'm not new to this!" In his attempt to be convincing, he pulled Asara to him and proceeded to kiss her passionately. Asara pushed him away.

"You bit my damn lip!" She shrieked. "You're a virgin! Admit it!" Christian was out of his element and wasn't sure how to respond.

"Say it!" Asara ordered. "Say, I am Christian the Virgin!"

"Look, I'm sorry about your lip…" Christian started. But

Asara wouldn't let him finish.

"Say it and I might forgive you." There was a twinkle in her eye. With a deflated ego, Christian decided to give in. But as he opened his mouth, another sound came out. Someone else's voice. Ancient and in Beowulf's Anglo-Saxon.

"I am William Marshal!" The voice came from behind the doors of the chapel.

"Ha. So you're William Marshal now, too?" Asara joked.

"It came from the church," Christian tried to say, but what Asara heard was something that sounded like, "Leaveth mine own chapel!"

"What the hell are you doing, Christian," Asara yelled.

"It's not me!" Christian pleaded. "It's coming from inside the church!"

But all Asara could hear this time was, "Leaveth mine own chapel, Jew!"

BOOM! The doors flew open. As if on cue, the sound of an organ playing in an ominous Gothic key filled the room so instantly and loudly that it made both Asara and Christian duck behind a low stone wall. In a flash, the form of a Medieval knight emerged in sleek, metallic armor, overlaid chainmail, and adorned with a large scarlet cross in the middle of his chest: scarlet that matched his soulless, pupiless eyes.

Though Asara and Christian were concealed, they could see that he carried two red swords and was advancing down the corridor in a lurking manner.

"I am William Marshal!" he screeched several times in succession. Christian glanced at Asara as if to say, "I told you it wasn't me." Asara whispered, "Frat boys. They take shit way too far."

104

Each time the knight screamed, the wind would stop briefly, then pick up again in a howl.

"What the hell," Asara's mouth hung open. "Are you hearing this? Tell me this isn't a joke. Tell me you don't have anything to do with this." By this time she had lost all of her former confidence and was frightened. Without waiting for a reply from Christian, she peeked over the wall as much as she dared and saw the character who addressed himself as William Marshal slouching closer to them, searching every anteroom he came across." She knelt back down.

"Shit. I think that's the William Marshal. The 12th-century Anglo-Saxon knight and notorious bigot."

As if in response, the knight screamed again.

"I am William Marshal! Where art thou, Jew!"

"Asara," Christian interrupted. "I haven't had time to tell you that... since we've only known each other for a little bit. But I might be responsible for this. I mean, I'm not behind it but he might be here for me." Asara scrunched up her face.

"I knew it. I knew there was something going on with you and that dean. She's been frequenting the pub for the past month. I've only been working there for three months, but there's something going on in those meetings. But, look, if you're right and that's really some form of William Marshal, then we need to run. He won't like the fact that I'm here."

"What do you mean?" Christian took a peek over the wall and saw William Marshall lurking about fifteen feet away."

"I'm Jewish." All of a sudden, a horse appeared on the chapel steps behind where Asara and Christian were huddled down. It reared up on its hind legs and neighed hauntingly. The knight Marshal ran past them and mounted it.

"Let's go!" Asara grabbed Christian, they both leapt over the wall, and took off down the opposite way that William Marshall left the chapel. But not before William Marshall noticed them.

"Maketh thine self known, Jew!" he howled, kicked the ghost horse in the guts with his stirrups, and took off back into the church, down the corridor after Asara and Christian.

"You would think it wouldn't take a horse appearing out of nowhere for me to believe we're in actual danger here." She yelled at Christian as they ran down the corridor to the opening of the school museum with the sounds of a malevolent windstorm and the echoey hoofbeats of William Marshall and his horse behind them.

When they reached the museum, it was open on the outside but the inner door to the gallery could only be opened by an employee with keys.

"Shit, we've pinned ourselves in here!" Christian cursed. But Asara had picked up a stone from a discarded pile along the wall and hurled it through the glass door which shattered a head-sized hole on impact. She thrust her hand through, opening the door from the inside.

"Get in!" she urged Christian, withdrawing her bloodied hand and pushing him through.

Asara pulled the door behind both of them. William Marshall and his steed were on their heels.

"I am William Marshal," he screamed and charged the horse first into the glass with such force that the doors flew off their hinges. Asara and Christian scurried deep into the museum foyer, waiting for the alarm to sound. There

106

was none other than the sound of Marshall's horse flopping around concussed and William Marshal swearing up a storm and retrieving his swords.

Looking for a place to hide, Asara dragged Christian into a side room and shut the door quietly behind them. Chrisian flipped on the light. To his surprise, they were in the museum's archive where they processed, packaged, and stored artifacts. Laid out on a table before them were a Morningstar sword and khopesh. Christian couldn't believe his eyes and lunged for the sword as William Marshall approached the door knocking on it with one of his swords.

"Out, filthy Jew…" He paused.

When Christian grabbed the hilt of the Morningstar, he could hardly lift it. He tried again to no avail. Asara directed him.

"The khopesh!" she whispered.

The khopesh was obsidian black with green streaks and a golden handle that fit Christian's grip like a pair of gloves. Marshall spoke again, but this time his tone was more subdued.

"Treacherous," he murmured. "A Jew but then, an infidel?" It was a question.

Asara put her finger up to her lips to warn Christian to keep quiet. William Marshall continued.

" A Jew and an infidel? Impossible?" He knocked on the door again. This time with the hilt of his sword.

"Infidel, doeth thou the work of God. Out with the Jew!"

Asara pursed her lips, looking at Christian desperately. Christian pulled her behind him and cleared his throat.

"William Marshall," he began. "Fuck off." Asara groaned audibly. When William Marshall responded, there was a playfulness in his tone, as if he were teasing Christian.

"Lord of the Underworld. Infidel of infidels. Precursor to Christ. Friend of Christendom. Wilt thou turn over the Jew and be called brother?"

"Fuck off. I mean it," was all that Christian could say, holding the khopesh in front of him with both hands like a sword. William Marshal laughed.

"Wouldst thou be in league with a Jew, the plague of thy people? Pharoah-hater. First-born destroyer. Plunderer of thy country, and murderer of thy people? Usurper of thy birthright? Wouldst thou be in league with a Jew?"

"Why are you here?" Christian asked strongly. "Why are you here... now... at Parthenon University. My beef isn't with you. But if you want to go there..." he let the threat hang in the air.

William Marshall's response was to beat on the door.

"I have been summoned to this place to do your bidding for thou art in danger. And I shall avenge thee if the Jew harmeth even a hair of thy khopesh."

In a moment it all made sense to Christian. William Marshall must have been summoned by someone or something to come to his aid to stop the Greek gods from taking over Parthenon and, therefore, the world. But critical information had been lost in translation and William Marshall thought Asara's presence to be the target of annihilation.

"Sayeth the word," William Marshall offered, "and the Jew is as good as dead."

Christian's next move was a mistake. Instead of explaining that Asara wasn't the enemy, he opened the door to William Marshall who was on him in a flash.

"I am William Marshall!" he screamed as he lunged at

Christian, presumably to get Asara behind him. He sprung through the door with superhuman ability and lunged at Christian, launching both of them into the air and across the room, breaking through a wall into the Greek exhibit. William Marshall punched Christian several times until his nose and lips were a bloody mess. The armored punches were like rocks breaking through the clear surface of a pond. His blows were strong and lingered. He kneed Christian in the neck and threw him through another wall into the Egyptian exhibit where Christian lost his grip and the khopesh in the process.

Marshall summoned his swords, cornering Christian in front of a statue of Wepwawet. He raised both of them.

"I am William Marshal!" he bellowed. Another voice echoed him.

"And I'm Asara Stern!"

William turned around. As he looked her up and down, he became confused. He muddled his words and started to stiffen his neck and froth at the mouth. William suddenly lost his red eyes like two flames going out and fell to his knees. He keeled over onto his face. And in one final show of the supernatural nature of this encounter, William Marshal and his blades erupted in flames and disappeared, leaving no trace of his appearance that night.

"Tell me I'm drunk," Christian asked Asara.

"You're drunk," she obliged as she watched the last of the smoke from what was William's body dissipate.

"How is this happening? I'm not drunk anymore," Christian surmised. "This is Karmic Elasticity. When someone supernatural dies, the world snaps back as if that person were never alive in the first place. It's like the "undo" edit option in a computer program."

"It will fade," Christian responded somberly. "In time."

"Well, I want to remember this. I want to remember you," Asara whispered. And before Christian could register how it happened, they were both in each other's arms.

***

"Morning," Asara said timidly, searching Christian's face. She was leaning over him, covering her front with a blanket. Christian opened his eyes slowly, blinked a few times confusedly. He was in his dorm, in his bed with…

All of a sudden, he jumped up instinctively, pulling the blanket from Asara to cover his own naked self, leaving Asara gloriously exposed.

"Mmm… so… good morning," he stuttered, tripping over the bedspread to the chair where the majority of his clothes were piled up. There was a slight look of amusement on Asara's face.

"So, we must have met last night and got a little too drunk."

"Drunk?" Christian stammered as his heart began to sink.

"What's your name? You know what, never mind. Let me get my clothes and head out. I've got work in an hour."

"No, don't go!" Christian pleaded." You don't remember last night? You came to my merry mount to find me and…"

"And what?" Asara asked as she bent at her perfect waist to grab a blouse off the floor. "Where's my bra?"

Christian was crushed. Clearly, he had lost his virginity to this goddess of a woman but couldn't remember a minute of it. Tears of regret filled up in his eyes as he helped her look for her bra which, she recalled a few minutes later, didn't exist because she hadn't been wearing one. Damn karmic elasticity!

She found her panties and put them on slowly as if she had done this sort of thing a million times.

By this time, Christian had donned enough of his clothing to feel comfortable going underneath his bed to retrieve her shoes. He wished that she knew he was different. He didn't want to be a number. He had never before treated women like numbers. Didn't she know they had just defeated William Marshal together?

When Christian stood up with both her shoes, she was in front of his mirror combing her fingers through her hair. "Say, what's your name though? You seem upset. Least I can do is catch your name. Maybe I'll brag about you. Increase your rep on the south side." She smirked at his reflection in the mirror.

"Christian," he said as a last-ditch hope to jog her memory as she headed for the door to leave. "My name is Christian.

"Is that so," she stopped and turned around briefly, having opened the door already. "Well,...." she paused. I 'm William Marshal, the Jew-hating knight of Parthenon Chapel."

Christian felt a surge of relief like resurrection climb up his chest like he had just caught the Holy Ghost, and his knees felt so weak that they almost buckled.

"You really thought I didn't remember?" Asara laughed and shut the door. " I was fucking with you. Wanted to do the whole gender role reversal, you know. Act like a guy who just had a one-night stand with a girl and was going to...." Christian interrupted her

"Leave her? Like a jerk." Asar stepped right to him a nose-length away.

"But then you started crying while rummaging under the bed." She kissed him. He kissed back.

Suddenly, Christian began to glow. Asara stepped back, startled. She put her hands on Christian's bare chest. His runes were shifting and changing. She marveled at them and let out a sound that can only be described as unbelief.

"Christian, what the hell is going on?" She looked down at his bare feet that were glowing, too. "Is this happening…"she paused, "all over you?"

"Pretty much," Christian struggled to say before she was on him.

He wasn't sure how long they were under the covers, but he thanked the gods that this time he was conscious of it.

"Crazy how just the realization that I am Jewish snapped him out of the spell he was under," Asara wondered out loud as she snuggled up to Christian post-coitus.

Christian didn't know what to say, so he smiled and wrapped his arms around her, pulling her close.

"With Killing William Marshall and two sessions with you, I need pancakes and waffles. How about you? What are you still hungry for?" Asara winked at Christian."

"I could do that as well. Hey, you said two sessions with me. What happened with the first one? I don't remember all that well?" he said sheepishly. Though Christian was now a full-fledged man now, he still had some boyish kinks to work out. Flirting and being flirted with was one of them.

"Do you remember anything?" Asara sat up.

"I don't really. It's like that part of my memory is erased. Asara pointed out the bottles on the kitchenette island."

"Maybe that has something to do with it?" Before we left the museum, you were complaining that the building was shaking and you thought there were more of them.

More William Marshall's I supposed. You said you needed a drink fast, and all of the merry mounts were closed, so I followed you here, and you got sloshed."

Christian smacked his hand on his forehead.

"So we didn't "do" it." he asked. Asara laughed.

"I was game. But for all of the things you said you'd do to me, you passed out before I could get your socks off." She playfully poked Christian in the side then jumped out of bed to get dressed again.

Before Christian could reply, he felt a faint rumble. He groaned internally.

"Shit, not this again," he jumped up off the bed and began hurriedly dressing.

Asara whirled around.

"Are you thinking about waffles like I am?" She joked.

"Asara, I need to tell you something," Christian said nervously as he hopped on one leg trying to keep his balance as he tried to don his boxers.

"I already know. You were a virgin before tonight, and now you're in love with me.. Not a problem. But right now I'm hungry for waffles. You coming?" She pulled her blouse over her head without unbuttoning it.

"The windows began to rattle.

"But seriously," Christian started, "we've got to get out of here."

"Asara whirled back around," Don't tell me that after saving me from that knight, he's actually a relative. That's low."

"No, it's not that…" The air in the room shifted, and an ominous feeling caused Christian to speed up the niceties.

"Will we see our friend again?" Asara asked as she began to put her jacket on.

Christian suddenly grabbed Asara by the shoulders and

113

looked at her alarmingly in the face.

"Don't you hear… don't feel that?" As if in answer, the building shuddered. Asara looked quizzically at him.

"Hear or feel what?" The building shuddered.

"They're getting close…" he whispered, a look of panic spreading over his face.

"It's like… it's like like like William Marshall. I've got a feeling we're not safe here…" Christian left the room briefly and emerged with a bottle of vodka.

"What the hell are you going to do with that?" Christian uncorked the bottle with his teeth and grabbed Asara by the hand.

"Trust me," he instructed her. "After I drink this, give me two or three minutes and I need you to take me as quickly as possible to a specific place on Potential Street. I don't want to make a scene, so just let me lean on you. Don't stop to talk to anyone. When we get there, I'm going to disappear but I'll be back before you know it." He gave her directions to the location and then downed five draughts of the burning liquid.

Suddenly, there was a thudding and the breaking of glass above him. And before he lost consciousness, he could have sworn he felt Asara, who's hand he had a grip on, flinch.

***

The walk to the portal of the Duat was the most awkward couple's walk that Christian or Asara for that matter ever remembered taking, though Christian hardly remembered it. The first problem was that Christian in his inebriated state became paranoid, babbling about monsters coming through the ceiling. He was also convinced that they shouldn't open the door to his dorm and so opted to jump out the window were it not for Asara's athletic reflexes that stopped him from doing so. She convinced Christian to leave with her the more civilized way, by taking the elevator downstairs. They left arm-in-arm, Asara having to direct him with all the strength she possessed to walk the right way. When they emerged from the Christian's dorm, Christian was delirious and chatting up a storm, so, though it was beneath her dignity, Asara put on a loud, Valley Girl persona to drown out Christian's descriptions of the minions who were following them. There were two in the lobby of his dorm. And a faculty member responded in irritation when Christian described him as a "an academic sot who, though a trained professor in classic studies, was a traitor to his profession." It was a chore to get him off the campus proper but they eventually ended up at the intersection Chrsitian described to Asara.

"Here we are. You owe me an explanation, Belvedere. And it better be a good one. I'm not even fucking student."

But before she could give him a thorough tongue lashing, he disappeared in what Asara could only describe later as a conflagration of fire.

***

When Christian entered the Duat and opened the giant emerald-colored door to the lair, he was greeted by a cascade of multicolored balloons raining down on him and a bear-hug from Wep before he even crossed the threshold.

"You did it!" Wep yelled as he twirled Christian in several circles around the room. "Missions accomplished!" He set Christian down who was dizzy and grinning.

"What?" he asked. "I came back here because I've gotten so mixed up that I lost track of the first mission."

"Nah, nah, naw! You're the man! You did it!" Wep was beaming and wiped invisible tears from his hairy face. Suddenly, Sophie appeared, more solid and lifelike than she appeared the last time Christian saw her."

"And my little mocha mensch has become a man in the process." Christian was elated to see her, but she also read the worry on his face.

"Don't worry," she said with a twinkle in her eye. "We stopped watching once it was clear you two required privacy."

"As private as you could get," Wep interjected. "We could hear you two in the Afterlife... But, go Furie power! Osiris is back!"

"Wep," Christian changed the subject. "I'm not sure what you saw or didn't see, but I didn't complete the first mission yet. And I'm back because I think that the Olympians are a step ahead of me. Third time's the charm, they say, and I've had exactly three encounters with them. I've spent my time avoiding them, and really… it's because of them that I've come back here. I need some help."

"What are you saying, Christian?" Sophie protested. "You completed the first mission with flying colors. You saved a Greek god." Christian was incredulous.

"But I didn't come across a Greek god."

"The dean chick," Wep said eagerly. " You ran her down in the alleyway on the southside. Instead of killing her, you disabled her and then, cloaking her in your Furie power, got her out of the alley to safety before the Olympians appeared. You both would have been dead, fraternizing like that." Christian was incredulous again.

"What? Dean Maiden, a Greek god?" He began pacing the room. "I knew there was something strange about her showing up at the exact same time I showed up in the alley. But even then, you said missions, Wep. You only gave me one mission. Was there another?"

Sophie motioned for Christian to sit on a piece of furniture that resembled a loveseat. It was surprisingly comfortable.

"That encounter you had with William Marshall?" She asked softly. "You weren't due to complete that mission until after eliminating several members of the Olympians."

"But that other chick," Wep said, handing Christian a chalice of mead, "that chick you ended up banging. She led you to him."

"But she didn't," Christian started. "It was entirely accidental."

"But was it?" Sophie whispered. "Do you think that you could have escaped such powerful magic with little warning? She didn't take you to the museum to make out. She could have taken you to your dorm first and avoided the possibility of death for you both."

"You're still Osiris, but that museum is filled with real power. The figurines, artifacts, and guardian spirits don't choose just anyone to protect. You have to be very special. Keep it in mind and visit again should you require that sort of help when shit hits the fan with the Olympians. Go spend time with them. They're probably dying for a good conversation."

The shock on Christian's face amused Wep.

"But that khopesh... it was the only fake artifact in that museum because it's not made from the Benben stone. Each Egyptian God was given a real khopesh. Currently I'm in custody of three. Mine, yours, and another one. Now that you're ready, I'll give it to you."

"It's strange how old Christian warriors have returned," Sophie wondered out loud. "I had this problem in the 40's. So, tell me, Christian, will you be seeing this girl again?"

Christian jumped up.

"Shit! I left her at the intersection!"

"Slow down," Wep soothed. "There's no time lapse between here and there."

"She flinched?" Christian said with panic in his voice.

"She what?" Sophie asked. Christian repeated.

"She said she couldn't hear the Olympians when they were about to show up this last time. When I grabbed her hand, I felt her flinch." All three paused for three seconds and then said in unison.

"Whose side is she on?"

***

Asara stood, frozen in disbelief, as Christian disappeared. At first, she thought that her mind was tricking her. Maybe it was the alcohol. She had, after all, pretty much half-carried Christian from his dorm to the intersection and he had been breathing in her face the entire time, talking nonsense.

While she stood there, contemplating her next move, a slim figure stepped out of the shadow of an alleyway.

"Asara is it?" the voice asked. Asara turned around quickly. Asara didn't immediately recognize the person because she was dressed in a black trench coat and matching hat with a wide brim, strategically angled on her head so as to conceal her image.

"Surely, you remember me," continued the voice. Then Asara did remember.

"Yeah, I remember you. You came into the pub with the college student the other morning. He was soused before he even sat down." Asara said this dismissively but she also mentioned it as a jab. She didn't like Dean Maiden. Dean Maiden laughed light-heartedly.

"Well, it seems that you're more acquainted with 'the college student' as you say."

"What do you mean?" Asara asked irritably.

"You were just with Mr. Belvedere," Dean Maiden rebutted. "Before he disappeared. In a burst of fire." Asara held her gaze for a few seconds.

"I don't know what you mean." They both stared at each other coolly. Dean Maiden tipped her hat back so that Asara could see her full face.

"I'm not sure what game you're playing, but you're up to no good. I know you stayed on campus last night. And you're not a student. I can have campus security ban you. Hell, I can have security stop you from coming to this side of Potential Street."

Asara didn't bat an eye.

"Is that so? Well, I'm sure I know what game you're playing, and you're up to no good. You think I haven't seen you come and go from Lair… little Miss Prissy you… at all hours of the day? I'm sure your bougie colleagues would find it interesting that you patronize the south side. And for what? Is Parthenon dick not thick enough for you?" Dean Maiden, though trying to present herself as even-keeled, flared her nostrils slightly.

"Listen, bitch," she said through gritted teeth, "you've got no business this side of Potential or on Parthenon at all. If you won't stay out, I'll keep you out. I think a quick call to ICE is in order, Asara Stern." SOME OTHER REVEAL.

***

"Asara. You need to watch out for that ho," Wep scowled ferociously. "Spitting image of Isis. She did a number on him, Sophie, you remember?"

"Grandma? What did Isis do?" Christian started. Sophie sighed.

"It is all rumor and hearsay about her actions leading up to and after your death. Whatever anyone tells you, it's not a simple story. You'll find out for sure when Fate deems you ready. Just remember that even when a goddess, a woman is not given easy choices." Christian looked incredulous.

"What the hell does that mean, 'a woman isn't given easy choices? I need to know. I'm the one who has to go back down there. If I'm in danger, I need to know."

"Anyway, Christian," Wep interjected dismissively. "You leveled up once. Now you need to level up again. You have to unleash your Furie powers, and the only way to do that is to put you in difficult situations. If you do that enough times, your god powers should awaken. I'm talking super strength, invisibility, telekinesis, control over elements, awesome laser shit out of your appendages. And sex. The sex will be fantastic beyond belief." Christian grimaced.

"We must go way back for you to talk like this in front of my grandmother."

"I'm not a prude nor is this the 1930's" Sophie challenged. "Besides, I'm a grown-ass Furie. There's nothing Wep has said or done these last few thousand years that have made me blush."

"That's enough information," Christian headed off the conversation. "I need to get my head straight because it looks like in addition to picking these Greek gods off one by one, I've got woman problems on top of that."

Wep laughed.

"Alright, you need to head back to your dorm, get some studying done, and give off all the appearances of Parthenon normality because we must capture a god tonight and interrogate them to find out their plan. But that Asara chick? Careful. Hold your cards close to your chest, and hide your balls. She's up to no good."

And with that, Christian disappeared in a green flame.

"He has to kill her." Wep said affirmatively once Christian was gone.

"Wep, whoever you plan to capture tonight, Dité cannot die yet. First, we do not know enough about Asara. Their meeting cannot be mere coincidence. The way she insinuated herself into his night tells me there's a story there. I know my grandson. He's a sweet boy who isn't lucky with the women he meets. Dité is the key to solving this mystery, and your plan to just kill her and all the Greek gods will not solve anything."

"Sophie Craft, the bleeding heart. I never thought I'd see the day. What do you want us to do? Love thy enemy hasn't historically worked out so well, has it? It didn't work out for Jesus or his followers like Martin? They're both dead. Boom! Blown away by the enemies they loved so much. They can't be saved. They must pay."

"So this is about vengeance," Sophie questioned. "All of this. All of these thousands of years are simply about getting even?"

Wep sipped heqet from a jeweled chalice in response.

"I feel for you, Wep. I know what you've been through. What the people you represent have gone through. But my grandson will not risk the precious little life he has experienced so far for some revenge tour. He has vision. Let's let the night play its course and trust that reborn Osiris has a plan buried deep in his subconscious but there all the same. Like lava deep within a volcano about to erupt, let's hope it springs at the time predicted."

"How many days have you left, Sophie?" Wep mused.

"Anubis is giving me until late December. He won't say the day specifically. But it's around Christian's birthday. Apparently, this birthday has been foreseen as a day especially heavy with death. Anubis wants me to bear witness, a penance for my folly. Asshole. I know what I did to him was wrong all those years ago but can't he see that my grandson will need me beyond that date? I can still be of use. The end of the world is a cyclical thing but it doesn't have to be."

"Well, the end of the world may yet be averted," Wep said cryptically.

"And what does that mean, Wep?" Wep downed the rest of his hequet.

"We can all - all the gods who deserve it - ascend and with our full powers. We can have one last war against these foreigners, these demons that came from far, far away. These Greek Gods who have plagued dimension after dimension since first arrived on the scene. We can end this."

"That's just a rumor."

"But it isn't. You weren't there. I was and I'm not crazy even though that's what they always called me: 'Infidel Wep', 'Two-Brained Wep'. The origins of the Greek gods are more lies than mystery. You say it's the blood they drank that made them evil. I say Ragnarök will not come until we are committed to sending them back to where they came from."

"Like I said," Sophie turned her back on Wep as she spoke, "Dité and Asara are to be unharmed."

***

Dité stood outside Pithon merry mount, wearing a beige trench coat, high black boots, and a simple, brown hat over her hair that she had tied up in a bun. She wanted to come across as understated and unmemorable because she didn't want to get noticed yet for switching to Pithon. Also, she liked the effect she had on people when she had more to take off. Men and women watched her every move upon command. She was fierce, desirable, and lived up to her namesake.

As his fans regretted him leaving their conversations a galavanting student strode out of the merry mount, slowly approaching Dité while fiddling with his acoustic guitar. Sporting a cream-colored, cashmere turtleneck and thousand-dollar, black jacket that offset his golden, Rastafarian locks and caramel skin, his cadence was like the power of an army. He told people that he did his own shopping for the accolades, but he actually hired a team for that. His fans lingered at the doorway pining for him like Sirens for the shipwrecked.

"Excuse me, nonmember. Who do you know here?" He asked sarcastically. Dité gave him a smoldering look.

"If I take one step into your establishment, I'll have every member wanting to know me, begging me to bicker. Hell, they'll bicker for me." She kept her distance.

"Dité, of course. How could I have forgotten you? Especially after last night." He shivered excitedly at the memory.

"I do my best after dark, Far Shooter."

"Well, come in. Everyone is waiting for you, my dear. The brisket Bolognese tonight is like a touch of the Rome we once knew with all the remorse for why it had to fall and unfortunately give us Texas. To die for, really."

"Last night's catch?" She asked sternly.

"On ice downstairs with the others. I've been playing music for them all day, but they haven't been the best audience. A bit… stiff… I'd say." He chuckled at his own joke.

"Apollo, you've become so devious. If only the Trojans had really known you, would they have been so devoted?"

"Ah, you wound me, sister. How I long for the old days when a fresh plague had no cure but more prayer. But wait till your old boy Christian joins us. Then you'll see devious." He put his arm around her waist and his eyes twinkled. Almost instantaneously, sacks of horse manure erupted all over the Liger lawn.

"Fuck em," shouted a member. Apollo smiled at him and kissed Dité full on the lips.

"Fuck them all," Dité repeated.

***

A few hours later, Christian was sitting at the desk in his dorm listening to music and doing his best to study Econ. He hadn't paid attention to the volume at which his music was playing until a couple of students who had been walking down the hall banged on his door, complaining of it. In Christian's world of psychosis, that was how he formerly dealt with the voices: loud sounds, multiple distractions, tension, and pressure all made him rise to the occasion to give his best output. Given ease and relaxation, he would drift into indiscretion and arrogance.

And right now, Christian had to do everything he could to stay focused because his next task, with the aid of Wep, would happen that evening. Who they would capture or how they would go about doing the capturing was a mystery to him, and that made him nervous. Especially with Wep in the mix. Who knew how things would go? He thought about Daphne's abrupt ending and a shiver went up his spine.

A message popped up in a chatbox on his computer. It was Asara. She had something for him but he had to find her with the aid of clues. Flirtatiously, she gave him the first clue, and the prospect of meeting her soon gave Christian a buzz of serotonin.

But then the door to his dorm opened, and in walked Wep with a box of hot pockets.

"Hey, hey! Got you a box of these." Christian closed his laptop as conspicuously as possible.

"Thanks, Wep."

"Is that your medication?" Wep pointed out three bottles lined up along the edge of Christian's desk. "Just out like that for anyone to see or abuse?"

"O, yeah. You're right, I should be more discreet. With all the friends I have and all the time I have for parties, these could end up missing..." Christian joked.

"But you never know what someone may do with these. Can I see it?"

"Sure, catch." Christian tossed one of the bottles.

"Hmmm. All three the same?"

"Yep."

Wep examined the ingredients.

"Really sucks you can't just take an injection. Much more efficient uptake, better results. Here you go." He tossed it back to Christian.

"You're pretty suspicious about my meds. I may really need these."

"You're a god, Christian. I understand that you have to play the role with your parents and all, but you don't need em."

"Well, they've proven pretty useful to scramble my signal when the Olympians are on the prowl. Saves me from having to down a fifth each time I hear them approach. Why don't they just come to my room to find me. I mean, where else would I be?"

"Don't know. Maybe Summoner has the answer. I brought it here for you as well as your khopesh. You used to call it "All brighter." All brighter my rage, for thee I soothe the anger of the oppressed with the judgment of the righteous."

"What are those words from?"

"A poem you wrote. It's in Summoner so I haven't read it in eons but that part I remember."

"Wait... you've read my diary... er, journal?" Wep laughed and tossed a box of hot pockets into Christian's microwave.

"Let's talk about happy stuff... like killing demons. Tonight, we hunt a demon and get them to talk. We'll need your vision skills so don't take your medicine tonight."

"Already took it."

"And now you haven't." Wep waved his hand

"What? You can remove the meds from my body?"

"From your entire system," Wep affirmed.

126

"So why don't you just remove the blood of Dionysus from the demon Olympians. Turn them into good people again?"

"Those motherfuckers? And take away the pleasure of ending them? Well, Christian, some things stick too well. It's been in them for so long and honestly, well, like I said, I prefer to just bash them rather than help them. I've been on my own in this fight for a while, been to some dark places inside. Perhaps if you and I put our collective effort toward reforming the Olympians, it could work but we'd need you to get really powerful. That means a lot of power practice and lots of sex with a lot of women."

"I like Asara." Christian said matter-of-factly. "I'll stick with her."

"Christian, don't get too attached. We may need to kill her. We don't know whose side she's on."

"Maybe she never drank the blood, you think of that?" Christian protested. "I wasn't even on my meds the night I met her and I saw no signs of her being in alliance with the Greeks."

"She flinched," Wep reminded him. "You said that she flinched, so she could be with the Greeks."

"But," Christian started to rebut.

"Seriously, I may just be a seven-foot wolfman telling you this, but you need to be careful of falling for her too quickly with this new lease on life you have. And remember the danger this campus is in. If she isn't one of them, then we might need to protect her. But even by doing that, you're distracting your efforts which means putting both your lives at risk."

"Noted," Christian grumbled. "So, it's Sunday. The only merry mounts open today are Future, Foam which I think is having a members only night, and Pithon which is having something but I don't know what or why."

"Good enough for me. Ok, so take the khopesh and shake it downward. Wala, it fits on your hand like a ring. To open it back up again you just whisper your intention into it. That way only you can open it and use it. It's an extension of your desire. You ready? Good. Let's go save the world." Wep smiled grimly.

***

The sun was just about to go down as Christian and Wep emerged from the dorm building. Christian mumbled at Wep as they merged onto the sidewalk heading for Potential Street.

"Are you going to be invisible or just freak people out?" Christian asked nervously. Wep manifested a giant mirror.

"How about Plop. I love being Plop" As Wep spoke, he morphed into a character with a very large, dirty belly, tank top, basketball shorts, and a ponytail down to his butt.

"You look like a fat me with a ponytail."

"Yeah, no good. Let me try something else."

"While you do, answer me this." Christian cleared his throat. "Are you currently the only good god on this planet that isn't mortal?" Wep had refined his character into a classic, preppie-looking mook, complete with seerseker shorts and boat shoes.

"Hard to say. I should be. While I can't die like you can, I can be manipulated, trapped, and used against my will. It would take a very strong spell wielded by another divine being though."

"But why didn't Set's spell turn you mortal?" Wep shook

his Preppie-tousled head of hair out of his eyes.

"Let's just say that the author of the spell and I were close." Christian gave Wep a sideways glance.

"I can tell I would have liked you a lot back then. You're earnest and have rage. Both qualify you for some form of psychosis. I've raged ever since becoming a mental case. But I can also tell that this work doesn't have to be work if we can figure out how to remove the blood."

"To remove blood in the classic sense, young Christian, you must spill it. And it would be a lot of blood with these fiendish Olympians outnumbering the remaining gods by at least 10 to 1 if not more. So what do you think of my look?" Christian studied Wep at an angle.

"Believable." He complimented.

"Yeah, I am Bjorn Bjornson. Icelandic exchange student. My hair says, "Blondes have more fun" while my fashion sense screams "Parthenon fun, that is." I'm the brisk of an Icelandic Fall day with all the chest pumps of a true son of Big Grim."

"Big Grim? The Liger house manager and amateur chef?"

"No, Big Grim as in Grimnir, one of the names of Odin, King of the Norse Pantheon. Big spear, more wives than Zeus, only needs one eye to see the world. Hasn't been seen in ages."

"So... he hasn't been seen in ages," Christian mused, studying his khopesh ring.

"So why can these kill them?" He pointed at the ring on his finger as they passed High merry mount.

"At the beginning of our time on earth, the great creator we call Atum gave us the material to make what we would need should we ever have to defend ourselves. Atum foresaw conflict, so the same stone from which Atum arose, the BenBen stone, came the material or Heka that we used to make our khopeshes from. Each Egyptian god had their own. Yours is Allbrighter, mine is Road Warrior. They are irreplaceable."

"What about Set's?"

"Bitch, don't kill my vibe. We don't mention him when hunting. He's the reason we're in this fucking predicament in the first place. If I could destroy all memory of him I would, including his khopesh."

"Where's he now?" Christian asked curiously.

"Hopefully dead. As long as he's alive, he's a threat to our mission. That's for certain. Maybe he got stuck in a Catholic dungeon and forgot about it in the 12th century, overdosed in the 80's, or maybe he's sorry and wants to give us a big ole hug. He was the first person to ever be called an asshole. Look his name up in a dictionary in ancient Egypt, and you will see "asshole." If you ever run into him you kill him."

At this precise moment, Christian could have sworn that he had just seen a female woman stop at the intersection ahead of them about a block off and enter the Duat in a burst of light. However, because he was in a deep and intriguing conversation with Wep and because neither Wep nor Sophie had revealed they had allies aside from each other, Christian didn't mention it. Besides, he supposed it might have been the side effect of Wep removing the meds from his body.

"Listen," Wep admonished, "You need to grow up and fast. You like Party? You want to graduate and have Parthenon trust fund-fried-chicken-and-knish babies with Asara and spend weekends in Bermuda laughing at the flying fish while drinking Dark and Stormies while your NGO saves Togo and Benin from cyclical recessions? Then discover your inner hakuna matata and leave off asking too many questions about the past. The past is a place of great pain and it'll only be a distraction. Once this is over, and we've stopped these Greek motherfuckers, then I'll fill you in. Maybe it's all the hequet I've been guzzling in the Duat, but I think we're in for one wild night."

"Got it," Christian affirmed. "Where to first?"

"Foam and Folly," Wep decided.

Foam and Folly looked humble enough with its monotone and understated facade. While it lacked the girth and magnanimous spaciousness of Gatsby, it didn't have the frill and pomp of Pithon or even a real color scheme like Liger. What it didn't have in material overwhelm, however, it made up with its close-knit members who came from all walks of life. Some were Division 1 athletes, others were merry mount sports stars, a few were acapella millionaires, and the smallest category were those who simply liked the proximity of the merry mount to the science building. To get into Foam and Folly, in short, you had to be well connected. They didn't fraternize with those they didn't trust, and they didn't come from circles that couldn't be validated.

All of the merry mounts at Parthenon had their affiliations: groups you had to be associated with in order to have a good chance of getting in. But while Liger always loved the one random kid who, released from his or her high school identity, would bicker like a crazed wallflower ready to make a splash, merry mounts like Foam and Folly preferred a more subdued approach. The vibe at Foam and Folly was conformity which equaled clout which in turn equaled packed nights on Thursdays and Saturdays.

131

Today was Sunday, however, and that meant it would be a members-only night. And Parthenon students took their members' nights seriously. It was tribal, pure and simple.

As Christian and Wep approached the door, the sun had gone down. Of the two, Christian was the only one with a membership sticker. He didn't know how Wep would manage to get into the merry mount, but Wep had told him not to worry."

"It's like jazz," Wep had assured Christian. "We improvise. Ba boom boom bah."

"Members only tonight boys," Brick, the bouncer, lifted his hand up, palm forward. Christian recognized the petit junior standing next to him and nodded at her.

"Christian?" the girl asked quizzically. Christian smiled at her confidently.

"So it says on my membership ID." The girl eyed Wep from his boat Chad-styled messy hair but then nodded at Christian.

"Neme. We were in Antiquities last year. You always interrupted the professor with questions. Lots of them." Taking this as a compliment, Christian nudged Wep that he would handle getting into the merry mount for the both of them..

"Hey, Brick, funny thing…" Then Wep interrupted, snatching Christian's ID before he could hand it to Brick.

"Christian, please just shut the fuck up. Liger must always humble itself before the doors of the great Foam and Folly and the panini makers within, right Gabriel? This place is Constantinople before Mehmet the Conqueror, and Istanbul after. This is 8th-century Baghdad, This is Los Angeles, creator of Smooth Jazz! We must prostrate ourselves before its holy and horny doors!" Wep spoke pretentiously in a flawless Icelandic accent.

"You damn right, Bjorn Bjornson! You update that sticker like I told you to?" Brick chided with a sideways grin.

"Word to your mother," Wep teased back, raising his hand, "Up top." Brick gave him a high-five and both engaged in a brief bro hug.

"As you know, Christian has sadly been a victim of weeks of hotdog dinners and scurvy-ridden women. I'm allowing him to tag along with me as a sort of anthropological study in what experts call 'a good time.'"

"Bitchin.' Yo, go easy on him, Bjorn. You're too much. See you at band practice tomorrow?" Wep winked.

"You bring that trumpet of yours and we'll charge admission."

"Word to your mother," Brick gushed, pleased with the compliment.

"Be careful with... Christian. He seems timid but I know there is a savage in there somewhere!" Brick made as if he was going to hit Christian in the balls to which Christian doubled over in mock defense. Wep and Brick laughed while Brick let them both pass.

Once they entered the merry mount, Christian chastised Wep.

"You've really doubled down on this secret identity." Wep shook his hair out of his face.

"I've been using that one since 1985. Once you get bouncers laughing, they never wonder why it's taken you thirty years to graduate."

"That's some dope god power," Christian admitted.

Right as Christian finished speaking, a beer caught Wep in the face. All activity immediately surrounding Christian and Wep came to a standstill. The flinger of the beer can stepped into the circle that surrounded the duo. He pointed at Wep.

"This bitch right here has the nerve to come on a member's night? I thought we revoked your membership after you came here last time dressed up as a bigass blue wolf," he leered. The curious crowd moved in tighter.

"Hey, Michael, chicks dig wolves. Sue me. And," he added, "I think you're drunk but you owe me an apology."

"Like hell I do," Michael spat, moving into Wep's personal space. No one could say exactly who was the cause of it, but the one called Michael fell to the floor with all the apparent signs of having been knocked out cold before he could advance close enough to get chest to chest with Wep. Christian, who was already uncomfortable at the attention they were receiving, whimpered.

"Oh, my God. You just killed him!" The crowd recoiled in disarray, not understanding what happened to the aggressor. Someone knelt down and pulled back Michael's eyelid.

"He'll live," Wep laughed. He turned to Christian. "He's just sleeping," Wep assured him quietly. "Now, go get us both a beer. I smell something funny. Above us. Keep your head on a swivel."

Christian made his way over to the bar among the massive crowd, buzzing with friendly conversation. Ordering two beers on tap, he stood at the bar waiting for his order when a stairway caught his eye. As crowded as Foam and Folly was, with students not only filling up the downstairs hall but also milling in and out of all of the antecedent room, he noticed that no one was going up or down the stairs. It struck him as strange as he surveyed the crowd of people by the staircase, packed like sardines, and not one

of them went up the stairs or even appeared to acknowledge it.

Strange, Christian said to himself.

Once he got his beers, he bumped his way back over to
where Wep was, engaging with several females.

"Excuse me, ladies." He handed Wep a beer. "I'll be
back. I'm going to check on something," he nodded at Wep
knowingly.

"Well, if she doesn't meet the standard of these beau-
ties, you can do her anyway. Just don't bring her back here!
"Wep guffawed as he put his arms around two of the wom-
en in his new entourage while skillfully keeping his beer
from spilling. Christian rolled his eyes internally and non-
chalantly sauntered off in the direction of the mysterious
staircase.

Once he reached it, he peered up as far as his eyes would
allow. The staircase was a deep red and polished mahogany, spiraling to the right so that he couldn't see the landing.
He took a quick look around him, then stood on the first
stair.

He remembered a Furie trick his grandmother Sophie
had taught him when a child. If you enter a corridor or
room and want to know whether or not what is beyond it
has something that you want, knock twice on the wall. If
you hear a knock back, you're right where Fate wants you.
So Christian knocked on the wall. After what seemed like
a minute, Christian heard a firm but faint knock in return.
Needing no more than this invitation, he made himself up
the winding stairs.

As he slowly approached the landing and peeked into
the room ahead of him, he realized that this must be the
officers' lounge, where the elected student officials typi-

cally spent their time organizing events, gossipping, and smoking bongs.

A calendar pinned over a desk against the far wall caught his eye. He moved over to it and set his beer down on a coaster that he almost felt anticipated his arrival. On the desk was a bong belonging to a student, Christian figured out by the decor, whose name was Iceman. Where had he heard that name before? Christian scanned the calendar and noticed that the current day, which was November 19th, had been adorned with an elementary drawing of two dicks in the square for that day, bracketing the word "birfday." Clearly, someone had a birthday. Maybe even one of the officials who had been blending in the crowd downstairs.

As Christian surveyed the room further, he noticed that the wall to his left was covered by drapes. He went over and poked his head behind the velvety partition and noticed a door with steps leading downwards. Curiosity got the better of him, and he descended another staircase with the same polished mahogany finish that spiraled down twice putting Christian below ground.

We've got to be in the basement, he wondered to himself.

As Christian stepped out of the staircase into the room, he was startled at what met his eyes.In the center of the room was a large obelisk-shaped structure with a hulking figure tied to it. Moving forward carefully so as not to make a sound, Christian got close enough until he sucked in air.

Tied to the obelisk and slumped over was none other than Babby Drake, or "Iceman" as they called her on campus. Babby Drake and Christian had been on the same rowing team his sophomore year. She was six foot three, broad like a bodybuilder, and an accomplished athlete who could hold her own. For someone to overpower her and bind her against her will could only happen if she had been incapacitated in advance which looked like what might have happened with her hulking frame pitifully slumped over.

As Christian moved towards her to examine her restraints, he felt the pulsation of a strong, dark magic as if warning him to keep his distance. Ignoring it, he jiggled at her chains and jumped back when two things happened at once. First, he felt the frigid presence of an entity enter the basement. Second, he saw Babby's body transform from human flesh into what he could only describe as stone: the same stone as the obelisk. This was magic to which Christian had yet to be introduced, so he headed for the stairway only to find someone blocking his way.

It was Neme. The girl who was with Brick when we tried to get into the merry mount no less than a half hour ago.

"Leaving so soon?" Neme asked coldly. "But you just got here, Christian Belvedere." Her voice was dripping with hatred. Escape had been Christian's plan A. Now he had to pivot.

"What's going on down here? Do you know anything about this?" Christian gestured towards Babby on the obelisk behind him. A look came over Neme's face that could be construed as a half smile as if she were amused at Christian's question.

"You down here to save your girlfriend?" Neme stepped down into the basement floor from the last step in the stairway.

"She's not my girlfriend. But that's beside the point. It looks like she's been drugged or worse. And she's tied to that... that thing," he couldn't find the words. Neme interrupted him.

"It must be some magic you have, coming in here like that. A spell was put on that stairway, the room upstairs, and even this stairway, but even then, the alarm bells were set off when you touched that obelisk. So I need to know how the hell you got in here, what the hell you're doing down here, and why you touched that stone. You don't belong to Foam and Folly, and you don't belong here."

"It's not really magic," Christian confessed. "It's more like counter magic, I suppose. Accidentally." When Neme bristled at Christian's explanation, it was all he needed to level up to his god powers. Before he even consciously anticipated an encounter, he was braced for what came next. Her nondescript pale-as-paper face turned dark and lightning shot from her eyes. Christian leapt into the air higher than he needed, smacking his head on the 17-foot cathedral ceiling. Falling back down to the floor, he rebounded with a sprained ankle. Taking a deep breath, he attempted to do the lightning-out-of-the-eyes thing but all that happened was a beer burp. Neme leapt to intercept Christian.

"I put a spell on Babby's room. You said you use counter magic. I've only heard of one kind. That means you're a Furie! Osiris! It's been so long since the original three stood against us, creating their rules of engagement. But where are they now? Where are any of the other gods now? It's just you." She sent three ocular lightning strikes at Christian who, learning the new rules of flight, evaded all three.

"Perhaps I shouldn't even kill you for the clout," Neme taunted. "Maybe I should corrupt you. Turn you against yourself! You've been a hero for so long that maybe it's time that you'll become the villain." It was only at this moment that Chrisitan noticed Neme's dark wings spread across the length of the cavernous basement and a sword in her

138

right hand.

"You must think you're inescapable! But I'd rather roll my ankle a thousand times than join the likes of the Olympians. So fuck you and your Greek posse."

Why Christian would antagonize her with conversation was a part of pivoting that he hoped would buy him some time. As Neme swung back her sword, she paused, confused.

"Wepwawet!" She shrieked. Christian turned to look behind him and saw Wep hunched over, ready to spring.

"Bitch, you guessed it!" Wep shouted.

While Neme's attention was distracted with the presence of Wep, Christian summoned Allbrighter and stabbed her. It was really more of a poke and did so little that Neme didn't even turn around fully to address him. She began a careful, compelling dance around Wep, accessing a scorching and dangerous energy which was the opposite of her frigid presence when she first appeared in the staircase.

Wep stood resolute, as if he had seen this trick before. He stomped on the stone tile, sending out a wave of granite that attacked Neme. Wep lunged at her, but she freed herself quickly and kicked him in the gut. A punch and a slice from her sword followed and strikes from her wings ensued.

Christian's cardio was lacking, even as Osiris, and he fought on with Wep, tag-teaming when one or the other was tired. As his lungs got the best of him and he began seeing double, Christian heard a voice deep inside him.

Call upon it. That inner power! Speak to it. Coax it out of hibernation and rise! He heard.

Then he saw it: the memory of his own death centuries ago. There he was being put in a box by his brother Set.

139

Christian felt a rage rise. Memory was the key.

Allbrighter felt warm for the first time on his finger… in his hand… as if he had unlocked a terribly profound secret. Suddenly, he heard it… the cry of a frightful nature, the cry of an angry king advancing to exact judgment. Christian's sprained ankle suddenly felt better. He grew seven inches, his eyes beamed brightly with a supernatural energy, and his grip on confidence was secure. He found himself back to back with a surprised Wep.

"Welcome back, Osiris!" Web grinned with tears in his eyes. "Let's do some damage."

Neme, aware that the balance had shifted, panicked, showering the basement with multiple bolts of lightning. Noticing the underwhelming effect of the lightning show, she flew at Christian, closing the gap faster than he could lift his arm, and struck him in the face.

Ironically, it didn't anger Christian. It woke him up. Maybe it was because this was the first fight he had ever been in without anyone else's intervention. Maybe it was the newfound realization that leveling up on his divinity brought a calm he had never before experienced except when irresponsibly drunk. And as painful as Neme's blows were, her assault on Christian's face was the most cathartic and authentic moment of his life up to that point. Psychosis could never have offered him self-realization like this.

"Wep," Christian called out, his eyes on Neme who was hovering a few yards away angling herself into position for another onslaught. "Know what I'm thinking right now?"

Wep transferred his khopesh from his left to his right hand without taking his eyes off Neme as well.

"Tell me, brother." Out of Christian came a foreign language chant-like, that sounded Aramaic at first but then took on the dimensions of a more primordial language.

"Ahh…" Wep quipped satisfactorily. The words, ancient and echoey, took on a staccatoed cadence. And seemed to anger Neme.

"Blasphemy! That Faerie magic is not allowed here!" Neme became unhinged.

But it wasn't Faerie magic. It was Psalm 23.

"You know that prayer. Christian. It's got Egyptian symbolism. The rod, the staff, the valley, and the amen. These bind our worlds, principles, our mythology. And it came before… them… the filthy Olympian,s"

"You wretched Egyptian fuck!" Neme screamed at Wep. "And you little half-breed Hebrew prick. You dare think you can interfere with us Olympians? Your rod? Your staff? Against our thunder? Our lightning?" You think you can take our sacrifice? Circumvent our destiny to rule this world and rid it of all mongrel deities that have dirtied the pantheon. This will be your last time. You can be sure of that." As Neme narrated this interlude, she rose until she reached the ceiling, seeming to expand to fill the width of the basement. Christian sensed that she was winding herself up to deliver an incapacitating blow that, though Wep and he might survive, Babby, the mortal, certainly wouldn't.

With newfound catlike reflexes, Christian was at one point standing on the basement floor in front of the obelisk and on the next he was face to face with Neme. Grabbing her by the throat she flew around the room screaming, taking Christian with her.

"Wep!" Christian called out, "Take her. I'll get Babby." Wep paused for a millisecond before he realized the implications of what Christian was offering him.

141

"Happily," Wep said grimly, intercepting Neme's trajectory toward the obelisk. Wep reached out his gigantic hands and snagged Neme by the hair. The momentum carried Christian forward and he crashed into the obelisk, waking Babby who was moaning. Once he got his footing, he began attacking the restraints around Babby's waist and on her hands.

Full of rage at being yanked by the hair, Neme turned on Wep but didn't have a chance. Wep was at her throat. The expression on her face hadn't even registered her plight by the time her body hit the floor. She gargled something indecipherable as she expired, writhing in death throes.

By the time Wep was done, Christian was finishing up the ropes around Babby's legs.

"Christian," Wep warned, "we need to get out of here. Neme said some dark magic before I snuffed her out. And I'm feeling the presence of some dark power descending on us. Hell, it might even be the veil. You got her?" Wep turned to assist Christian but Christian already had Babby over his shoulders in a fireman's carry.

"Wep!" Christian said in alarm. "The staircase!" The staircase which was the only entrance and exit to the basement was darkening. Disappearing.

Without a word, Wep grabbed Christian who had Babby.

"Hold on," was all he said. Then Christian blacked out.

***

What Christian remembered next was sitting against the wall next to the secret stairwell on the main floor of Foam and Folly. The crowd had thinned out, but those who were

142

left were in several large groups clearly on their fifth or sixth pint for the night. Babby sat next to him, her head against the wall, groaning.

"Shit. Got wasted and can't even remember it." She turned to Christian.

"Christian? You didn't come with me tonight, did you?" She looked around frantically. Christian's world was slowly spinning, making him wonder what exactly had happened. When he saw Babby, it all came back to him.

"Where's Wep?" he murmured to himself, trying to move from a slumped position to a sitting one. He turned to Babby who was glowering at him.

"It was you, you motherfucker."

Christian squinted his eyes until she came into focus.

"What are you talking about? Where's Wep?" as if she would know.

"You lured me upstairs. Told me you had a surprise. And I followed you like some kid getting into a van of candy with a pedo. What the hell did you do that for?" She was irate, not to mention intimidating when triggered.

"No. It's not what you think. I went upstairs and happened to go down into the basement where I found you. Unconscious." Not knowing how much he should say, he eliminated all of the unbelievable bits.

"Hold on. Did you say that I took you upstairs?" Babby calmed down somewhat.

"Yeah. I know you, Christian, and I'm not drunk. You told me there was a secret upstairs. I thought you had a few of my friends throwing me a surprise birthday party even though we're not in the same friend group. It was all believable, you know, for a surprise party. Once I got upstairs, I saw a couple of the Foam and Folly officers just chilling or

143

so I thought. The next thing I knew, I felt a cold that came out of nowhere all of a sudden and then I started blacking out. I've not had a drink tonight yet, so I wasn't drunk or roofied. But the merry mount President was looking at me all weird like before walking out of the room. Someone must have hit me. My head hurts like hell."

Christian surveyed the room and then whispered to Babby.

"Do you see them? The two officers who were upstairs? Are they in this room?" But before Babby could answer, Wep showed up as Bjorn but Christian could tell he was rattled.

"Babs, you doing OK? You must have had some night… not that I'm judging… it's your birthday after all, so live it up and all of that. Christian, can I talk to you?" But giving Christian no choice, he yanked him up by his arm and pulled him into the stairwell.

"We've got to go. Some weird shit's happening up there (he pointed up the stairwell) and I received a strange pulse from the Duat. It's not normal. Something's wrong. Not sure if it's Sophie or something else. We've got to split." He peeked out of the stairwell. Christian bristled.

"You annihilated Neme, so we're good to go with that." But Wep protested.

"No. This feels familiar. I don't think I killed her. Entirely."

"Wep, what are you talking about? We saw her." Wep looked alarmed in a way that Christian had never seen before.

"No. If I had to guess, I think there's some reanimation shit going on. Either way, it's not safe to split up, and I don't think any harm will come to Foam and Folly too soon…

with a name like that at least." Christian peeked out of the stairwell momentarily.

"You think it's a good idea to leave Babby here? She thinks I had something to do with her… loss of memory. She says that I was the one who led her upstairs."

"Interesting," Wep rubbed his chin in thought. "Did she mention anyone else upstairs?"

"That's the strange thing. She said that there were two Foam and Folly officers in the meeting room upstairs and that the merry mount president gave her some look and started to leave as she passed out. What's that all about?"

"I say we haul ass to the Duat ASAP. There's too much commotion going on here for the Olympians to wreak havoc tonight. Check on Babs and meet me outside real quick." With that, Wep was gone.

Christian walked up to Babby who was still in a sitting position with her knees pulled up to her chest. Her head was down.

"Babby, like I was saying. That wasn't me you saw but it might have been my doppelganger."

Babby kept her head down, picking at the denim knee of her pants with a jagged fingernail.

"I'm not an idiot, Christian," Babby said quietly. "I know what you look like. I know who you are." Exasperated, Christian stopped trying.

"Well, look, I can see you had a hard night, and all I'm doing is trying to help." He turned to leave but then turned back around.

"Did you ever learn what the birthday surprise was?" Babby looked up, furtively at first. And then her pupils disappeared until all Christian was looking at was the whites of her eyes. Then her face twisted into what Christian could

145

only describe as a distorted smile.

You will find the child lying in a manger. He thought he heard her say.

"What? Christian was taken aback. Babby continued.

And Herod killed all of the children in order to get to the Christ child… she gurgled.

"What? Christian asked again, alarmed. And then Babby smiled.

You're next, birthday boy.

***

Christian, chased out of Foam and Folly by the haunting words of Babby, had double-timed back to the intersection and entered the Duat. When he entered the lair, he didn't see Sophie but he saw Wep, and, to his surprise, a visitor. From what he could tell when he entered the lair, Wep had recently responded in kind because the visitor, a young woman, looked like she was getting over an intense fright.

"Who the hell is she? What is she doing here? Where's my Grandma?" Christian demanded of Wep. Wep motioned for Christian to calm down.

"Christian," Wep started, "you remember when we met. Officially, that is?" Christian was irritated.

"What does that have to do with anything?"

"No, remember." Wep demanded. Christian thought for a second and then recalled.

"It was the Grayson. You were playing sax and I ended up hurling in the bathroom." Wep chuckled at the memory and then regained his serious composure.

"This. This person here was the server that night. Look familiar." The woman stepped into the light so that Chris-

146

tian could get a better look at her. Christian glanced at her but his eye went to the khopesh she was carrying.

"Wep, you know whose sword that is, don't you?" Wep smiled grimly. As if in response, the female put the sword behind her back as a sign of respect or so as not to agitate Christian more than he already was.

"I do," he responded with no further explanation.

"Can you tell me what this… this person who sells sandwiches at Parthenon is doing here? And where's my grandmother."

"This person who sells sandwiches happens to be family. Sophie summoned her here and will be back soon. She thought you both needed to… talk." Christian looked at their visitor again.

"Ok. Then talk." The visitor took this as an invitation to introduce herself.

"So I guess you know whose khopesh this is?" she asked as she pulled it from behind her back.

"That… that's Set's khopesh. How can she carry that…"

"I am not Isis. I'm not Set either. I'm their daughter. My name is Tess." Christian's eyes got as large as quarters.

"Wait a second," Wep growled. "Let's hear her out. If Set is as evil as you say he was then why would he save us. Please, Tess, explain."

"I was born twice. Once to Isis in the Valley of the Kings and then again in England to a virgin. My father was always rubbish with spells. When he realized that Isis was going to have me kill him, he fucked up a spell that found me incubating in the womb of a 40-year-old psychoanalyst named Melanie Klein. Trust me, I needed all the therapy I could get as I grew up.

The servants of Set eventually tracked me down and

convinced me of my heritage. They also told me that Set wanted to use my powers to aid Osiris. I know, strange, isn't it? But Set was dying. And because he was dying ten years ago, that means he's dead now."

Wep arched his eyebrows at Christian as if to say, Sounds legit. Christian turned his attention back to the one called Tess.

"What killed him... your father... and why would he send you to help me?" It was at that point that Tess teared up which wouldn't be the last time in the conversation.

"A broken heart, I suppose. He really regretted ever betraying you. He said that you two were close and he let others get in the way of that. Isis herself bore a similar regret and wanted to use me to kill Set. It caught up to him... knowing he had ruined the world. He just didn't want to live anymore." For a moment there was reverent silence. Then it was broken with a snort. Then a guffaw. Then Wep couldn't contain himself.

"Hahahahaha!" Wep shook with laughter and the cave reverberated in response. Christian glowered.

"Wep! So my wife ended up with Set. Big deal." Wep wiped tears from his eyes.

"I'm sorry, but gods don't die and if Set did, he'd just go to Osiris for judgment which would be the last place he'd want to be. I hope he is dead, don't get me wrong, but you being his daughter is ridiculous? C'mon." Tess squirmed uncomfortably.

"But she can wield his khopesh. Almost owned my ass," Christian said, nodding his head slightly to Tess. "Wep, you said that the khopesh can only be wielded by its owner. Well, she's the closest thing to the owner of this khopesh that we could have. They have the same... I dunno...god-

DNA. Plus, she looks like me. We have to be related." Christian's explanation encouraged Tess to speak up.

"Wepwawet, my father was many horrible things. But I do believe he wanted to change. That's why I exist: to be that change, I guess. All I'm asking for is a chance. For you to trust me. I know of your mission here. It's my mission, too. Please..." Wep crossed his arms and frowned at Tess.

"You work at Pj's?"

"Yes."

"Can you get us a table?"

"Probably."

"Do that and pay for my pancakes and we can discuss whether or not we'll be working together."

"Deal. I have an idea for him." Tess was referring to Christian.

"Wait. Before I do anything Wep, did you know that my wife ended up with my killer?" Wep raised up his hands defensively, showing both palms in confession and protest and shaking his head..

"Don't call her your wife like you know what that means. While you are Osiris and while, technically, Isis is your wife, there's much you wouldn't understand. She framed you for sleeping with Set's wife then flipped a switch when Set took his revenge too far. It was then that she realized how much she loved you. She was with Set long enough to connive a way to kill him to win you back. But I never knew that a daughter was involved. That's a spell so forbidden that not even the Set I knew would use it." Wep, Christian, and Tess stood there awkwardly until Tess broke the silence.

"I'm sorry, uncle. I know this must be... upsetting."

"First, don't call me uncle," Christian quipped. "We're

practically the same age. Second, this is actually liberating. Evidently, I've already moved on so it would just complicate things if I had a wife. Especially one who framed me." Tess lowered her voice.

"This whole situation is one problem but I know about your other problem as well. The Olympians. I know about that."

"And what's your opinion about them," Christian folded his arms.

"Well, working in the food service industry on campus, I do a lot of hosting for different events like coffee shop nights, awards banquets, galas, things like that. And I oversee events at other merry mounts. So I'm familiar with the people on wait staff as well as in the kitchen. And I can tell you that we've got cloakers on Parthenon." Christian squinted his eyes.

"What's a cloaker?" he asked.

"A cloaker is when a god poses as a mortal. Olympians are posing as mortals on this campus.

"We're well aware of that," Wep interjected. "They're at the top, running the school." Tess nodded.

"But they're also in other places. "We had one at Grayson, a dishwasher, but I fired him. Because he was a cloaker, yes, but also because his hands were so large and awkward that he broke too many dishes."

"The mortals would sue you for that, Tess," Wepp guffawed. "That's like divinative discrimination." Tess went on.

"However, there are three who are working the kitchen at Pithon which has a wine & dine event tomorrow night. It's a big deal. The problem is that the main sous chef is a cloaker as well as one of the cooks. So is the head of security for tomorrow night's event." Christian nodded his head at the direction the conversation was taking.

"So what's this idea of yours, Tess?" There was a twinkle in her eye.

"Anyone who's anyone in Pithon will be showing up. That means Dité will be there." Christian's heart almost jumped out of his chest at the mention of her name.

"And?"

"Well, you know the one reality show where a private investigator helps one party prove that the other is cheating? Then during the big reveal, the party doing the cheating has their face on camera and either confesses or makes a scene trying to get away? Either way, they're forced to respond like a cheater so that now everyone knows they're guilty."

Wep rubbed his chin and looked at Christian.

"That could work. If we could catch Dité by herself. Like in the woman's bathroom or when she's going out to her car." Tess shook her head vigorously.

"No. You need to expose her. In front of everyone. She's the lynchpin for what the Olypians are trying to do in Parthenon and to Pithon. You need to put her on blast before the other Pithonians who aren't shitbags. You know, 'I can slap my sister but I'll kill you if you do?' We've got to turn the good Pithonians against the bad ones. Let them take out their own kind of vengeance on them. But, Uncle, you need to be the one to confront her. She's walking this campus uncontested while the Greek vermin infiltrate every level of campus. You know that overweight woman who oversees the salad & fondue bar at the large campus cafeteria? That bitch an Olympian, too."

Christian took a deep breath. It was true that he had

151

been avoiding Dité but that was before he realized his new identity and latent Osiris powers. When he called Dité and the other 71 Olympians out, he was ignorant, non-strategic, and overcome by psychosis. He thought he might be able to elicit a confession this time.

"So, how does this work?" Tess beamed.

"Glad you asked. Pithon hired a band, bartenders, waitresses, and workers for their evening event. I'm on that list. I can get you in, Uncle, as waitstaff. Wepwawet, you can play your sax like you did back at Grayson. Uncle, you would walk the room taking drink orders and serving hoity toity hors d'oeuvres. We'll have to get you a tuxedo. Don't worry about people recognizing you because we can cover you in a Furie spell so that only Dité recognizes you. You serve until you see her. When she sees you, she'll notice that you haven't been identified yet and will assume it to be the doings of the Olympians and not you because she's not aware that you're aware of who you are. That will get her to begin talking. Once she starts talking, I'll terminate the Furie spell, and those good Pithonians around her will hear her. That's all that it will take."

"Nice," Wep and Christian said in unison.

"But there's one thing," Tess said almost apologetically.

"What's that?" Christian braced himself.

"When I terminate the Furie spell, that terminates your cover. People will know who you are. So once you get her going, you'll have to figure out an exit. They hate you in Pithon." Christian nodded grimly.

"That sucks balls. But sounds like a plan."

***

Getting Christian in was pretty easy. Tess had a suit for him that was nicer than any he had ever had. Something that Stone Belvedere would wear. But Wep took the hard route.

"Dude, have you seen my sax?" Wep had said, peeking into Pithon's green room. Thomas, the saxophonist, turned to see who was speaking to him.

"Oh, my god!" he yelped, then immediately fainted. Wep put Thomas in the closet and assumed his form.

Meanwhile, Christian was getting a pep talk from his niece.

"To be a good server you need to remember a few things. While a few customers might appreciate your service, most won't even notice you. When they do pay attention, however, ignore the blanket stares they give you that say, What sucks so badly in your life that you're a fucking server and simply stick to the mission under your nose: keep delivering the hors d'oeuvres oh, and make sure you offer them breadsticks… Python breadsticks are a hit here. Oh, and if they call you sugar tits, ignore them. That's a Pithon favorite, too. And keep bringing in the extravagant drinks that they'll eventually spill on their even more extravagant clothing." Tess went on and Christian's head swam. Tess, sensing his overwhelm, stopped talking for a few seconds.

"Got it?"

"Got it." Christian echoed

"Good. Come here. Ok, your bowtie looks good and here's a tray! Go kick some ass, Uncle."

***

It was just as Tess had described. Christian even got

called sugar tits to which he responded, through clenched jaws, as humbly as he could muster, by offering to bring out more breadsticks. A tipsy junior from the men's water polo team at this particularly obnoxious table of Pithons asked Christian, "Are you threatening to whip out your dick, waiter? Date rape!" he fake screamed. The others at the table howled in laughter. Christian had walked back to the kitchen seething but kept his temper despite it all.

Aside from the occasional blistering insult hurled at his expense, Christian's Furie magic was working. As he went from table to table, pouring drinks and taking orders, he was pleasantly surprised that nobody recognized him as Christian Belvedere though they most were familiar with who he was, especially from his reputation last year as the guy who placed third in the keg toss and second in beer chugging during the annual Liger vs. Pithon merry mount Olympics. Or the incident that landed him in the psych ward.

While Christian was playing his part, keeping an eye out for Dité, Wep was playing a beautiful saxophone rendition of "Onward Christian Soldiers'" which Christian took as code for "get the fuckwith it before the damn song ends because it's like one of the only songs I know this well." Christian circulated around the three main rooms of the first floor of the merry mount several times until the house manager, an alumnus named Argo, told him to see if anyone upstairs wanted champagne.

The walls leading up to the second floor were decorated with images of cornucopias near the bottom steps and constellations like Draco and Ophiuchus the higher he ascended. While the overall effect was to feel as if one were ascending Mount Olympus, it didn't feel like heaven to

Christian. A heavy miasma hung in the air, and Christian felt the uncontrollable sensation of a pending jump scare the closer he got to the landing. Higher and higher until he could barely hear Wep's sax. Instead, it was silent.

Once at the top of the landing, Christian followed the curvature of the narrow hallway until it opened into a room gaudily decorated in thirteen shades of white and dripping with crippling privilege. The room was filled with beautiful people at various decibels of conversation. Christian scanned the room once, rebalancing his tray of three, ready-to-pour bottles of champagne. Several couples were intertwined here and there in such steamy PDA that Christian thought he might have happened upon a swingers' merry mount. But then his eyes lighted on a couple in the far left corner who were engaged in such an intense makeout session that Christian blushed red. He already knew who the female was before he fully identified her. It was Dité.

Although Christian couldn't hear Wep's saxophone, he could almost feel Wep telepathically urging him to continue before his elaborate, one-song set ended. He braced himself, reminding himself why he was at this event in the first place, and began to weave in and out of the tables to see whether or not Dité and her partner were thirsty enough to take a break from sucking each others' faces off.

"Champagne… er… for the couple?" Christian had no idea how a server at a Pithon event would interject himself into a live porn flick at an elite establishment the likes of this one, but both parties unlocked lips long enough to glance at Christian and eye his tray. Dité, giving no hint that she recognized Christian, grabbed a bottle and slowly poured it all over the matted dreads of loverboy. Christian, taken back, managed to chuckle nervously until Dité began slowly licking the champagne off the face of her partner who sat, blinking in surprise. Dité paused and glanced at Christian.

"It's been 173 days," her eyes were smoldering but Christian couldn't tell if she was teasing him or angry. Whatever the case, he needed to get on with what he came to do.

"Since you last saw me or disappeared yourself? If it's the latter, then that was 174 days ago." He tried to be firm but nonchalant. After all, he was a waiter.

In answer, Dité smirked at Christian, and then promptly emptied the rest of the bottle onto Bob Marley's crotch. Marley yelped and jumped up, his pants soaked in a 1995 Dom Perignon White Gold 3-liter Jeroboam with a retail value of $21,459.99 (Tess had briefed Christian on the cost). Marley's flailing caught Christian in the chest, knocking the tray out of his hands and sending the other two bottles flying through the air toward the next table where one bottle hit a dapper dressed sophomore between his left eye socket and the top ridge of his generously-sized nose. Almost immediately, blood sprayed in several directions and the sophomore jumped up, not registering what happened for two seconds until he looked down at his shirt.

"You fucking oaf," he bellowed. "This is a Stuart Hugs Diamond Edition suit, you fucking retard! It cost me $778,290!" Why all the exactness with numbers this evening, Christian wasn't sure and he cringed at the attention he inadvertently brought on himself. No, that Dité brought on him. Lucky for Christian, the bougie sophomore was addressing Bob Marley, the likely culprit (he wasn't even from Pithon) who himself was taking the heat off Christian by cussing Dité out about his own ruined suit.

Attention drawn, the surrounding tables took up the side of the insulted sophomore and began booing Marley with interjections like "Wah Gwaan!", "Ya Mon" and "Bomba-clod" until the agreed upon abusive "Come Gwope!" ("Get out!") was the decided upon chant that half the room was taking up. Marley, pissed, but no match for a room full of Pithons, beelined for the nearest exit with two middle fingers in the air. The room let out a raucous cheer, then a table of mooks started up the Pithon merry mount song. Christian, surprised that he emerged from the event unscathed, realized that this distraction must have been the work of Furie magic.

"Took you long enough to get here." Dité chortled, crossing her long legs. Christian stared at Dité briefly, and a wave of grief swept over him. Her presence still had an affect on him.

"Seriously, Dité? You did that shit to spite me?" Dité offered a pouty smile.

"Why does it seem like you don't want to be seen with me?" Remember why you're here, Christian told himself.

"Can we talk about this in private?" Dité smiled again.

"No one's paying attention to you, Christian. You're forgettable." Christian held back an insult.

"You're right. I've been gone for almost six months and no word from you." Dité stiffened.

"Do you not remember what you did to me with your public display of disrespect? To my reputation? To my parents?"

"That was my... my psychosis," Christian decided to play that angle. It was best to get a reaction from Dité without revealing the new things he had learned about himself. "And I was put in the hospital for three lonely months.

That's punishment enough."

"Your psychosis?" Dité said, disbelievingly. "Your psychosis? Christian, you specified 72 people by name, and many of them whose names you didn't even know. You think that's a coincidence?" Christian struggled not to look uncomfortable at his next question.

"What do you think happened?" He left it open-ended. Dité drummed her long nails on the table and then looked Christian in the eyes.

"I think you're pretending to know less than you know?"

"About what?" Dité stood up and stepped up close to Christian, her breasts almost touching his tuxedo.

"Christian Belvedere, you've never had psychosis," she whispered into his ear. "Munchhausen syndrome, probably. God knows you come from a fucked up family."

"What do my parents have to do with this?" Dité detected his nervousness and laughed.

"You're still playing that obedient son role, Christian?" Christian couldn't think of anything to say. Being face to face with Dité like this after long months of absence, a girlfriend who he was madly in love with but a relationship he never could consummate, and all of the references to his dysfunctional family found Christian at a low point.

"Do you remember each of the names you publicly called out? What we all had in common?" Dité asked innocently? Christian thought for a moment. Honestly thought for a moment.

"No. I can't remember. A few of them I can." Dité nodded her head knowingly and feigned to straighten Christian's bowtie.

"Christian. You have a gift. The question is whether or not you're going to be honest about it or have the truth forced out of you." She lightly brushed his collar with her fingertips, turned to pick up her purse and began walking towards the door. Christian called after her.

"The names I called out... what do you think you all had in common?" Dité swayed her hips until she got to the door and turned around to address Christian who was standing in the middle of the room bustling with conversation again.

She opened her arms widely, gesturing with one arm across the room and slightly bowed.

"You don't see it? We're all Pithons."

And that was the last thing Christian remembered.

CHAPTER 6

Now You Face a Power

"Yes, Christian Belvedere. Lose yourself where the ivy grows thickest," the voice said. Christian stirred.

"He's back," someone said.

"Yeah, but he doesn't know where he is." That was another voice. Female and dismissive. The first voice spoke again. "He's coming round. Gosh, what a night you've had." Christian opened up his eyes, taking in the disorienting scene like a newborn. The person who belonged to the first voice was waving a pamphlet in Christian's face, presumably to administer some version of CPR without actually putting his hands on him.

"He's awake!" the voice victoriously announced. Scanning the room slowly, Christian saw that he was in what appeared to be a library. The cavernous room was lined with mahogany bookshelves and gaudy, 17th-century French furniture of rich red and purple tapestries. Christian realized that he was reclining on a couch among a circle of lounge chairs and couches in the center of the room underneath a chandelier of dazzling light. Several people were in the room, but three... the original voices he learned later... were standing over him in some manner of concern.

160

The first voice, ticked with himself at this resurrection, addressed Christian.

"You evidently had quite a scare in there," he pointed to the double doors inset in a wall, indicating to Christian that the gala room where he had been was next door. "When you collapsed, few paid attention. They thought you were in league with that Rasta troublemaker, but then Dité told us who you were and left you in our charge. And now here we are." Christian sat up a little too fast and was instantly greeted with vertigo. A dozen or so people were sitting on the furniture around him, looking at him curiously.

"Is this some kind of book club?" he asked, noticing that each had a booklet of the exact same dimensions as the one that the first voice had been waving in Christian's face when he awoke. The first voice paused for a second and then realized that Christian was referring to the book in his hand.

"Oh, this! Well, I suppose you can say we are some kind of book club." He handed the book to Christian who didn't touch it but eyed it with curiosity. When the World Was Black: The Untold History of the World's First Civilizations. Christian looked up at the three people closest to him, each of them with eager eyes.

"Ok," he started. "Thanks for the help. I've got to go. I'm a server here, you know."

The one with the first voice laughed and the others followed suit.

"Oh, but Christian, indulge us, your hosts. Take the evening off from your waitress fantasy and come play a bit of Risk!" Christian surveyed the room again but could find no Risk board. The first voice saw his confusion and then laughed again.

161

"Oh, Christian, Dité told us who you are. Join our discussion… book club as you say… I'm sure we will find your… perspective enlightening. I'm Guerro by the way." He reached out his hand to shake Christian's. Wary, Christian declined.

"I'm not sure what Dité told you. I hardly know her." He added with a tinge of bitterness, "And she hardly knows me." Guerro shook his head.

"Let's start over. I'm Guerro. That's Paulie," he pointed to an Italian pretty boy who Christian decided was gorgeous… not pretty… had gone to retrieve champagne and glasses and was sauntering back.

"Nice to have you here," Paulie nodded his head and grinned, showing pearly teeth that sparkled almost absurdly white. Guerro continued.

"And that's Tess. But you must know her because she's running the show here tonight." Tess walked up from behind him with a blank look on her face that said, Keep it professional, Belvedere.

"Take it easy the rest of the night. It looks like you got lightheaded and passed out. It is warm upstairs." There her face said it again. She wanted Christian to read into her choice of the word warm. She addressed the one named Guerro.

"I'll make sure to adjust the thermostat on the way out of the room because it's pretty hot in here." With those words, Christian internally groaned, realizing that he was where he was meant to be because Tess had planned all of this. But why hadn't she told him? He could have at least had an idea of what he was meant to do. But one thing that Christian knew about Pithon: if you were willing to lose yourself a bit and indulge, you wouldn't be lost alone. And it was

162

necessary for Christian to get lost. After all, the mission was for him to fit in too well, to seem too lax, and eventually attract evidence of a god or goddess lurking in Pithon so that he or she could be captured, interrogated, hell, even tortured if that's what it took to uncover what subversion was happening at Parthenon. So he changed his tune.

CHAPTER 4
As Thieves

"So what's the topic of discussion," he asked no one in particular. By this time, it had been about twenty minutes since he awoke, and here he was about to get into the middle of a conversation with Guerro and the others about something that promised to give him more information on the 72.

Someone lit up a blunt and began passing it around, counter-clockwise which made Christian the third person to take a hit. Smoke layered the room like humid pillows in the air.

"Ok, enough of the introductions, good sport. Obviously, we're metaphorically playing at a game of war, not an actual board game." He grinned at Christian. "You know, you have a keen mood-setting way about yourself, a true Capricorn? You seem like a practical leader, perhaps one who spends too long alone in his own world? Step outside yourself. Evolve beyond the Neanderthals and misanthropes of your… your merry mount. Live a little! What say you?" Guerro's elaborate language underscored the slithery nature for which the Pithons were best known. But Christian went along with it.

"But are we ever going to play the game?" Christian said

with a raised eyebrow. Guerro paused ever so slightly, indicating that he wasn't sure whether or not Christian was insulting him. He smiled from ear to ear.

"Haha. To the point. I like it. You're very different from the timid person you were when you woke up. So, Other Christian, do my bidding, dear! See now he is other Christian now." Guerro gestured to the others around the room who murmured in compliance.

"They all agree. That's how excited we are to have you! Other Christian, Paulie, and Chastity, and the rest of you, we're playing Risk." It was at this moment that the blunt hit Christian. Paulie, who up to this point had been silent, began the questioning.

"Tell me, Christian Prime, do you have a father? To have a father is to have trouble. Some males (need I say all males?) would do better without a belligerent, covetous, and haughty male telling them what to do," he sat his ginormous frame back in a wing-backed chair. Though a little dizzy, Christian was still in his right mind enough to take the question as strange.

"The Black community. They're pretty consistent. No fathers needed," Christian heard someone say. There was tittering among the group. A combination of weed brain and the admission of the petty racism of the ruling class.

"Wallace, please! Offensive much? You're not in Alabama anymore! You can't just say shit like that to our guest. Sorry, Christian Prime. Not everyone is like that. I love Blacks. I had a Black Nanny who lived with my family until she passed once I hit my teen years. See?" That was the one named Paulie again.

"I disagree with the comment about not needing fathers," Chastity interrupted. "It's the pressure the father provides that makes men so sumptuous and tender. Men tend to be the opposite of their fathers, so if you want a good man, give him a bad father. For example, your father works at the World Health Organization, my father works at the Council on Foreign Relations, and Guerro's father was friends with Castro and the Kennedys. They are insiders, men who climb ladders and begrudge the more impressive cock sizes of their sons. I want an outsider, a rogue. A real man is the struggling musician my daddy will hate, the poet with interesting friends, the one with a habit that makes my daddy scream, and the guy who is unlucky in relationships but so blessed by Tyche in the sack!" A few of the women in the group cheered Chastity's speech.

"So what about you, Christian Prime? Got a father? Got a bad father? You seem tender?" Guerro half-mocked.

"Um... my father can be difficult at times when things are going well and a good ally when things are at their worst."

"Well said!" Guerro applauded. "Evasive enough." The room went silent. Christian decided to change his approach.

"Do you not think I have a dad because I'm..." but Guerro wouldn't let him finish.

"No... I'm not saying that...," Guerro waved his hands as if to push away Christian's bad energy.

"But the author of this work," Guerro held the book up, "Seems to think that the family tree of the earliest known Black civilization seems to... how shall I say... have gaps in its family tree." Guerro sipped from his glass of champagne while Christian flushed red with anger but then just as quickly dissipated it at will.

"Well, there are gaps in the family trees of later mythologies. Take the Greeks for example." You could have heard a pin drop. Christian continued. "Patricide, matricide, fratricide, sororicide. Hell, on every side the Greeks have huge gaps missing from their family tree like a set of bad English teeth. So the question isn't one of fatherlessness on the African side only but of fatherlessness and the violence that ensues on the Greek side as well. Either way you look at it, we're all fatherless." It got so quiet that you could have heard the angel on the head of a pin drop. And then Paulie broke the silence.

"Yes! Very! And I thought I was the poet of Pithon merry mount. You sure you don't want to bicker here?" Paulie said with awe etched in the dimples in his cheeks and the crows feet of his eyes.

"A toast then!" Chastity stood up and raised her glass, beaming. "To our fathers! May we be content knowing that even the gods have daddy issues." Christian didn't have a glass, nor did anyone offer him one. As everyone downed theirs, he added wistfully.

"But it's true. Some of the first human stories were about paternal conflicts."

"And bold Cronus castrated his father Ouranos with his mighty sickle, liberating the world from tyranny!" Pualie chortled, pouring himself another glass.

"And hot-for-Hera Zeus conquered his father Cronus, liberating the world from tyranny!" Chastity retorted.

"What about Apollo, son of Zeus?" Christian asked carefully.

The room fell silent again until Paulie broke it.

"What about him?" It sounded more like a challenge, and Paulie mad-dogged Christian a couch away with a combination of bitterness and amusement. Everyone looked down to their drinks or up at the ceiling. Only Christian dared to look Paulie back in the eyes.

"To be determined?" It sounded like a question because Christian meant it as one. After all, he had no former knowledge of these Pithons or of this secret book club, but Tess had told him he was hot on the trail and that took some improvisation. Guerro broke the silence.

"Perhaps an actual game of Risk is in order. He walked across the room, rummaging in a chest and came back to the group with an actual game of Risk in his hands.

"Christian, would you do us the honor?" He handed the game to Christian who opened it and set it up on the coffee table in the center of their lounge. Taking this as their cue, the others (minus Guerro, Paulie, Chastity, and Christian) dismissed themselves and left the room.

Over the next two hours, they played Risk during which these four discussed world politics, the companies they planned to build (or seize from their parents), and their dreams of a better world. Other than Christian, the other three seemed in earnest and he learned a lot about them indirectly. They shared a similar dislike of their own fathers as Christian did his. They talked about the virtues of everything Pithon in a way that, at first, Christian took as a subtext that maybe he should rebicker but then rethought his opinion about them an hour into the game when they didn't follow-up with evangelistic fervor. They were simply confiding their most cherished beliefs as Christian used to confide in his own.

But Risk is a game of war, fascism, colonialism, and the worst parts of the 20th century, and Christian had been so taken by the brotherhood of their intimate little group that he didn't realize until too late the subtext of the board.

While Geurro and Chastity engaged Christian in conversation, Paulie had been making bold moves against Chrsitian which Christian thought he had properly countered until it was too late.

At first, it looked like Paulie was about to challenge Guerro's small army in the Middle East with his own formidable battalions from Southern Europe but then he changed tactics, eyeing Christian's five game pieces in the country of Egypt and then boring his hazel eyes into Christian's. "Egypt," Paulie said coolly. Christian picked up two dice and rolled a total of 5. Paulie rolled a 7 with his two and Christian had to forfeit two pieces. It was only then that Christian noticed something... something that sent a chill up his spine. Chastity owned the continents in the Western Hemisphere including the South, Central, and North America. Paulie's dominion began with Greenland, included all the blue of Europe and several Eastern countries beginning with Ukraine as far East as Siberia. And Guerro had the southern part of the Eastern Hemisphere, Asia, and the island of Australia. But Christian. Ironically, Christian was relegated to the continent of Africa, meagerly spread out along its southern border countries and amassed on its Northern border.

The other three noticed the mild look of shock on his face. Paulie's cool look gave way to a severe smirk, and Christian could have sworn there was a hint of a smile at the corners of Chastity's lips. But Guerro, Guerro, was the only one who tried to look neutral.

"It looks like art imitates life," he said softly, surveying the board. He then looked Chrsitian in the eyes. "And it looks like you've got quite the gamble here, Cyrus." Christian flinched.

"What did you call me?" Guerro ignored him and lightly tapped the country of Egypt.

"Or maybe it's destiny? Either way, it looks like Egypt is going to fall into the hands of..." he looked around the room at each of them. "What would you call...us?" The three Pithons had, in their gameplay, formed an Axis power against Christian, pinioning him on the continent of Africa in a defensive position he couldn't win. Paulie picked up his two dice to roll again. Christian prepared to roll again, but then the irony hit him. Here on this microcosm of a Risk board game, he was imitating the last three thousand years of history. He should have paid more attention to the moves he was making and the moves they were making against him instead of being sucked into how impressive they were and how they made him feel a part of the group. Now he felt betrayed. And embarrassed. But also clear-headed, and resolved. If he had any chance of beating the Olympians, he needed to get out of this room, get out of this gala, and get out of Pithon fast. He would have to take the game off the board.

***

Getting out of Pithon ended up being more difficult than Christian had imagined. Guerro had picked up on Christian's shift in energy, and just as quickly, Christian shifted it back to his friendly, happy-go-lucky self, trying his hardest to purge his thoughts of what was actually going on in the game. He pretended not to see the way the game was stacked against him, focusing the scant resources he had in Egypt to target the two dozen or so game pieces Paulie had in Southern Europe. He made casual conversation as he rolled against Paulie time and again while making light conversation with Guerro who applauded his war of attrition. Paulie had gotten pissed when he sustained a loss of fourteen pieces in a row. Chastity had actually laughed at Paulie's consternation when he examined the dice to see if they were loaded.

Right when Christian thought it opportune to bow out of the game gracefully and leave Paulie his dignity, Guerro left to retrieve four more bottles of champagne, returning quickly, teasing Paulie and applauding Christian for his "will to power that could get a chub out of dead Nietsche."

So the drinks kept coming and Christian couldn't just up and leave. He thought he remembered trying to leave twice after leaving a wake of destruction through Europe to Greenland and then descending down into North America which, when he crossed the Canadian border into the United States proper, he noticed that Chastity wasn't as supportive. Again, there was so much drinking.

But when it was all said and done, he had awakened in a thicket of shrubs between a bike store and the post office on Potential Street, with barely enough time to make it to Econ class which he couldn't miss because he had already used up his limit of absences in that class for the semester.

Christian couldn't concentrate in Econ. All he could think about was the game he played at Pithon the night before. The new world he had encountered. The sinister subtext of it all. The revelation that Pithon wasn't only housing a few Olympians but was infiltrated at every level with them. In that light, why the hell was he in some stupid-ass college classroom instead of reporting back to Wep, Tess, and Sophie? He had sacrificed the normal college version of himself over the last week or two that he was likely on the dean's watch list. Again. Christian was slowly spinning out of control. He was scared, but unlike last summer he wasn't fighting this alone. He had a reputation. He had real friends. He had to make it look normal, so he got some lunch, something healthy for a change, and then went to the Duat.

***

By the time Christian reached the Duat, Wep and Tess were already there. Neither had changed out of their outfits from the night before and both were barely talking to each other. In fact, they were on opposite ends of the lair just staring off into the distance.

"These Olympians have this sort of effect on you two, too?" Christian asked. Tess broke her gaze from the nothingness she was looking at.

"There are just so many of them. I did what I could to watch for the mortals that were there but…"

"Thanks for looking after me. With Dité and the others." Christian said softly.

"Anything for you, Uncle. For Parthenon. For us."

"We've got to check on Babby. We've got to make sure she's safe." Wep interrupted.

"Virtues constellation," Tess responded.

"Virtues what?" Christian asked.

"It's what Neme said when we were fighting her. I've never heard of it before but it has something to do with Babby and the obelisk," Wep interjected.

"What's weird is it isn't like Babby just disappeared a day or two ago. Now that I think about it, I haven't seen her since… last year?" He said it as a question. "But I'm only noticing that now."

"Karmic Elasticity," Tess said.

"So maybe there were two people taken. You saw the room snapback to normal, which is a spell to cover one's tracks. Let's say we thought that would have been Babby but she may have been down there since last November? That means whoever lived in that room was taken last night. Two people missing." Wep said.

"Yes, on their birthday, too." Christian added.

"Think about it," Tess said excitedly. "I mean this type of arrogant boldness and partying must mean that whatever the Olympians are planning in Pithon must be happening soon and it's time sensitive. Babby was born in November, she disappears in November, this other guy disappears on his birthday. It's like right at the tip of my mind," Christian mused.

"Yeah, I have no clue, maybe something from the museum can help," Wep wondered.

"Or my grandmother! Can you summon her, Wep!" Wep and Tess nervously looked at each other.

"Wep?" Christian said. "What's going on?"

"Kiddo, look, we tried to summon Sophie, but she's too sick to make the astral journey."

"It's time to tell him the entire story," Tess prompted Wep.

"Your grandmother made a deal a long time ago: a set number of more years to live if they were in ultimate service to a god. Any attempt to get more time beyond that or break her agreement and she would risk illness and then death followed by angry judgment. Your grandmother is a firebrand and she is stubborn. She just had to do what she felt was right, against the demands of Anubis. Now he has come to collect her and has given her until the end of the year." Wep stole a quick glance to gauge Christian's reaction.

"I can't do this without her!" Christian almost wailed.

"Your grandmother isn't entirely an innocent, Christian. It's all about reciprocity. Your oaths are your bond and following rules… that's very important to Egyptian religion. It's time for her to face judgment. She's had a long and full life."

"But I'm the Judge? Right?"

"Well… that's yet to be seen." Wep corrected.

"What does that mean?" Christian shouted. "Is she in danger of Ammit the Devourer? Is she in danger of being sent into the void never to return?" There was panic in Christian's voice. "Will she be alright?" He was panting now. Tess put her arm around Christian while Wep continued.

"It's 50/50. Osiris will judge her like he does every mortal that comes to him: no special treatment. It will be as if she isn't your grandmother."

"I can't handle this right now. The way you're talking to me now… and breaking this news to me now. Does this even sadden you, Wep? You seem so matter of fact. It's as if you've judged her yourself! Shit. I need to clear my head."

And with that, Christian was gone.

***

Soon after Christian disappeared, Tess left the Duat to walk the campus of Parthenon, looking for him. It was raining but she didn't mind and proceeded without an umbrella. Tess had always found walking in the rain an enjoyable experience. No creature to loneliness, rain was welcome company.

When she reached the halfway mark across the campus at a north to south trajectory, she reached the center of campus where ginormous menacing lion statues sat on guard, one on it's haunches and the other on the prowl. Though the rain was a steady drizzle by now and Tess was thoroughly drenched, she mounted the statue that was on all fours and sat there, pondering Sophie's situation and the precarious situation it was putting Christian in. It was throwing Christian off his game which meant that he was distracted. That wasn't good for anyone, including Parthenon.

Tess made a mental calculation of all the incantations she knew. Nothing powerful enough came to mind that would shelter Sophie from punishment. Who do gods pray to when they're screwed? she wondered.

While deep in thought, Sophie hadn't recognized that a figure had approached her and was standing just feet away from where she was sitting. Umbrellaed, in a black suit, and carrying a leather satchel stood Professor Khufu, looking stoic like the relief of an Egyptian pharaoh. He wore his hair long and curly like the style of his people, the Beja of North East Africa.

"Hello, Ms. Deshret." His words broke Tess's concentration. She blinked.

"Professor Khufu, hello," she struggled to say. He tilted his head and umbrella, looking up at the rain.

"I see you're enjoying this beautiful Jersey weather." He said lightheartedly, an immigrant's attempt at a joke.

"Oh, yes. It is rather comforting," Tess said nervously. Professor Khufu looked at her kindly.

"And I suspect you are in need of comfort. I noticed something very strange today. You weren't in my Econ class. Are you OK?"

"No, I'm fine. I just…" Tess started to well up but didn't try to hide it as her face was already wet from the rain. Professor Khufu looked down at his shoes for a moment as a sign of respect until Tess composed herself.

"I see. You seem to have a great burden. I am not your usual confidant but as we say in Sudan, A child is a child of everyone. You may share if you wish." Tess thought for a moment, composing herself.

"My… someone I really care about is losing someone they love. She is dying and my friend is worried about how she'll be judged. You know. In the afterlife. For some reason he thinks she may be in some trouble for… for breaking some rules." Professor Khofu made a sympathetic clucking noise with his tongue.

"Ah, yes. Anubis and his rules. Very serious. He sits in a big chair in the underworld, doesn't he? But a big chair does not make a king." There was a twinkle in Professor Khufu's eye. "Even he is subject to rules, which come from the highest law. It's like economics, Ms. Deshret. There are some things that will always be, but then there are times for deviation. And deviation can be…"

"Bad?" Tess finished his sentence for him

"Bad," Professor Khofu pondered. "Sometimes, yes, I suppose. But when they are bad, they are very noticeable. Remember Anubis does not judge. He simply weighs the heart against the feather of truth. This is a modern world. Most young people may not even believe in the great jackal god. But rules must be followed, and if your friend's dear one is worth saving from obliteration, that will be measured by the heroes she inspires. One moment of inspiring another can lighten the most ponderous of hearts. Perhaps you should try to meet this person yourself?" The last sentence was a question. Tess nodded.

"Now that I have shared my wisdom with you, will you now please attend my class next time?" Professor smiled, showing pearly white teeth. Tess grinned in response.

"I'll be there. Thank you."

"Good." he nodded his head, approvingly. "And tell your friend, Mr. Belvedere, to please not drink on the day of class. He smells worse than a hippo and answers problems like a drunk one."

"Oh… I will, sir," Tess stuttered.

"Many blessings to you. Enjoy the lion and wherever it takes you!" Professor Khufu nodded. He turned and Tess watched him walk away with his large umbrella until he vanished in the fog.

Tess sat there for a few moments contemplating their conversation, especially his remark about Christian which seemed to be random at best and suspect at the worst. Thoroughly drenched, she decided to dismount the lion statue to continue her quest to find Christian when she heard heavy breathing. She looked around her, expecting to see an asthmatic student huffing their way across campus but no one was there. There the heavy breathing went again. For a moment, she almost believed that it was the lion she was sitting on. No, the breathing was coming from beneath the lion. Tess dismounted the statue and looked under it. To her surprise, she found a student huddled in the fetal position. She couldn't believe that she hadn't recognized her presence before.

"Are you ok?" Tess asked puzzled. The girl was clearly

frightened. She was a young student, probably a freshman, and slight of build. Her windbreaker hadn't done the best job keeping her dry, but neither did sitting under a lion statue with rainwater that ran along its sides and underneath its belly only to drench her. And for how long?

"What's your name? What are you doing down here?" Tess tried again. The girl's eyes darted between Tess and the direction that Professor Khufu left in.

"Who are you?" The girl quizzed Tess. "How'd you get here?" The girl's voice was hoarse.

"Can you see them, too?" Tess reached out to touch the girl's shoulder.

"See who?" Tess replied gently. "Is someone after you?" The girl pulled a few strands of soaked hair from her face to get a better look at Tess.

"I don't know. I was in the common room when my roommate came out of her room with... with this guy. And... she's not my roommate anymore." The girl looked at Tess pleadingly.

"She looked... I don't know... evil. So did he. I was the only one in the common room until they came in. I'm not sure why... I knew I had to get out of there. But I couldn't move. And I'm not sure, but I felt that no one could come into the common room either. Like a force field or something. But a negative one. I must have panicked because both of them came over and stood over me. I was sitting at a table studying for Chemistry, not that that matters, but it was horrible. They both started taunting me. He said that I would do wonderfully. What's a girl to think when a guy says that? I thought he was going to... I don't know... assault me or something and there she is standing there grinning like she knew what I was thinking." The girl had found her tongue and the floodgates weren't closing any-time soon.

"Maybe it was a few minutes or a few seconds, but it seemed like forever. I couldn't move my arms and legs. I was sure I was going to die, and all I could think about was how my parents and sisters would miss me. I was supposed to be going home this weekend for my birthday."

Tess froze.

"Your birthday? Your birthday is this month?"

"November 31st. I was almost a December baby, but two of my sisters were born in December, three years apart from each other. My Mom wanted to make sure she had me in November. I mean, two birthdays during the month of Christmas makes for an expensive Christmas." It was her attempt at a joke, but Tess was distracted by the men-tion of her birthday.

"Your roommate... do you both get along?"

"We did. Until she started seeing that jerk. He's a jock and all, but looks more like a full-grown man. Like an MMA fighter-type."

"How long has she been seeing him? Tess asked.

"That's just it. No more than a week or maybe two. Pretty quickly, I felt like I was intruding on them when he was over, so I spent a lot of time in the common room, library, or at the local coffee shops doing my homework. You know, I thought they needed the privacy because they were... be-ing intimate. But then that's the strange thing. I don't think they were being intimate. It felt more like he was recruiting her. Like he was some sort of cult leader. And then she said some shit yesterday." Tess's ears perked up.

"What did she say?" The girl broke eye contact with Tess for a second and swallowed nervously.

"My father's from Jamaica, the nicest father in the world. My mom's White. Beautiful. Brilliant. I've had a photo of them on my desk all semester." The girl took a deep breath.

"Yesterday, she… she asked…no she told me to take it down. That it made her sick to look at it." The fine hairs on the back of Tess's neck bristled.

"And?" The girl continued.

"Well, I thought she was joking at first… a sick joke but a joke all the same. When I laughed. She reprimanded me. She said I should be ashamed and then went off on me about how I needed a dose of the red pill. That I'd been a spoiled suburban half-breed for nineteen years, living with a false notion of diversity that's been nothing but a bad experiment. She said I needed to wake up. I swear it was like listening to one of those television cult leaders. But that's when I realized they weren't having sex in our dorm room. He was turning her. Against me. And that's the other thing he said in the common room."

Tess had been squatting the entire time, and finally squeezed under the statue next to the girl.

"Said what." The girl took a deep breath and dropped her head.

"It was sick. He said he had a big black dick that would fit me perfectly."

"Yikes," Tess said quietly. "I think that would pass as attempted assault." The girl looked at Tess out of the corner of her eye.

"Maybe. But that's just it. He was a White guy."

Babby came to Tess's mind instantly. She had been chained to a black obelisk. The entire environment of the upstairs office and basement had the feel of a rape.

"They were sure they had me but at the last minute I

made it to the common room bathroom and locked the door. I don't know how I can go back… back into my room. Tell me I must be crazy."

"You're not crazy. How did you escape?"

"Escape? I locked myself in the bathroom." Tess was confused.

"You're not in a bathroom."

"Yes, we are."

"Then how did I get in?"

"You were in here when I came in. You were in the next stall. They're probably still out there. They're going to break in at any minute."

"No one's going to hurt you…"

"They're coming!" the girl shouted.

"I promise," Tess said desperately as she hugged her hard assuringly. But then the girl went limp and her eyes rolled up in the back of her head so that Tess was looking into two white veiny orbs. Tess shook her.

"Hey! Wake up! Stay with me!" No response.

It was at this moment that Tess felt what she could only describe as a pressure pressing in on her and the girl in her arms, a kind of suffocation. Tess swiveled her head to the right and then to the left, peering out from underneath the lion statue. The air pressure intensified so much that her ears were popping. Her heart was beating so fast that she was having a hard time catching her breath. Now her head was pounding with a migraine of epic proportions, and her vision was fading in and out until she imagined she was in a bathroom stall. No, she was leaning against the toilet with the girl in her arms. She could feel the cold of the porcelain through her wet shirt.

Stay with it, she chided herself.

And almost as if the girl in her arms heard Tess's thoughts, she reanimated, sitting up, and looking into Tess's eyes with fear. Or was it hope?

"Happy birthday, Rioghain, we're coming in!" Who the hell was Rioghain, Tess thought, but then the girl began convulsing and Tess did all she could to keep her from going into shock. But then she realized two things at once. The first was that the girl wasn't having a seizure at all. She was channeling… or attempting to channel… her assailants. Her former roommate and boyfriend were no longer unpleasant, college-aged mortals but had fully manifested into the Greek gods they were with every intention to capture and use her in similar fashion to the way Babby had been used before Wep and Christian rescued her. The second thing she learned was the girl's name. It was she who was named Rioghain.

Tess realized that the only way to save Rioghain and herself was to take the fight out of the bathroom to the gods on the other side of the door. When she stood up, the world started to spin around her.

"Damn it," she said as she opened the bathroom door and stepped into the common room. No one was there. Perhaps, the duo were in Rioghain's dorm room. So Tess entered the hallway where she surmised Rioghain's room to be, using her keen sense of hearing to zero in on Rioghain's door. She was able to quickly find it and kicked the dorm door in. In the process, she dropped her khopesh but didn't have time to retrieve it because there they were: Thanatos and Athena, the demons they had become.

There was an awkward pause as the three of them sized each other up. Tess called to her khopesh but Thanatos lunged and tossed Tess's khopesh out of the window and in one quick motion, grabbed Tess by her leg.

"Look, Caroline, it's the waitress." Thanatos's face was twisted in derision. "Should we take her? Perhaps, her birthday is next month," he sneered.

Athena attempted a grin but it came out a grimace. "She does have a strong kick. There's much we could do with a woman with strong thighs and a fighting spirit."

"She's hard to hold down. But I think she'd be perfect for dinner all the same." His fangs came out.

Tess squirmed herself into an advantageous position and kneed Thanatos in the groin and tossed him down the hallway in a single throw where he landed against the elevator, leaving a body-sized dent in the door. She then turned her attention to Athena.

"Fuck the pretense, Athena. There's no way I'm going to be another one of your conquests. What a shame, you were once so different, a pillar of virtue. Now, you're exactly what the Christians fear at night and you're not as attractive as Hera or Aphrodite." The women faced off with each other.

"Who are you, cunt?" Athena's eyes were red. Then Tess heard a scream. It was coming from the common room.

"Help me!" screamed Rioghain!

"I heard you the first time! I'm… trying… to.." Tess grabbed Athena by her breastplate, dragging her into the hallway and beautifully maneuvering her from the hallway into the common room with a hip toss strong enough to pulverize steel.

Being a clash of goddesses in a college common room, bursts of lightning and fire razed down posters and framed artwork on the walls. Tess struck in the Egyptian style of combat, heavy with elbows and grappling while Athena scratched and clawed with her sharp nails, kicked, and used her spear against Tess's improvised movements. Rioghain, overhearing the commotion, peeked out to see this supernatural phenomenon in action.

A combination of strikes between Tess and Athena knocked out the wall on the window side of the common room and both continued the fight into the parking lot. Thanatos, who had regained being thrown into the elevator emerged into the common room and through the broken wall. A dark storm gathered over him as he yanked Athena away from Tess, ready to kill Tess and take Rioghain.

"Why is this your fight, waitress? Do you even know who you are up against?' Thanatos's eyes were glowing red."

"You've proven yourself worthy." Athena added. "Join us! Leave the mortals to their fate," Tess, breathing heavily, stared daggers at Thanatos but answered Athena.

"No, thank you…. I've met Fate. They'd tell me to keep kicking your ass!"Athena and Thanatos both guffawed.

"Once you have a drink, you'll change your tune. You'll have a hymn of your own as Apollo does. As Aphrodite does. You'll be worshiped and feared, and you'll have the might of the most powerful force in this universe: Chaos. This I foresee, waitress!" Athena declared triumphantly. As Tess prepared to answer, Rioghan half-praised the two and half-begged Tess to bring this to an end.

"They are the Greek Gods, aren't they? The ruiners of Troy, the bane of Hercules, a religion with no final account of the end! Please, don't let them take me," Rioghain begged. Tess looked sharply at her.

"You seem to know them pretty well!" She retorted.

"The veil is too far removed! We've done too much here. We still have time in the day. We'll get her later. Come,

Darko," Athena spat.

And within seconds Thanatos and Athena had fled out of sight. Tess heard her ring call to her and summoned it. Rioghain was still on the rubble of the wall. Tess knelt in front of her and grabbed her hands.

"Tell me what's going on. You're not telling me everything."

Rioghain gestured to the hole in the common room wall. "I'm not sure I understand myself, but this is certainly a start."

***

Museum idea as protection from the veil

On Potential Street, Christian walked into Pithon to keep his dinner with Guerro. After peeking around with no Guerro in sight, he checked his phone which revealed a text from Guerro asking Christian to come to the back. So Christian exited and walked around the left side of the building. He had to remind himself that he was ultimately here for information: not for revelry, especially after the nightmarish events from the evening before. Just being in the vicinity of the great Pithon merry mount gave Christian the feeling of being Perseus in Medusa's lair.

As Christian approached the back lawn, he ran into Chastity who looked the part of a Greek goddess. Her hair was piled high on her head with a few rebellious, curly strands lying on her neck. What was more noticeable were two coy deer horns protruding from either side of her forehead. Her lips were red, and at first Christian thought her lipstick had smeared until he noticed the pomegranate in her hand. She gave him a suggestive smile and teasingly spun one rotation. Tongue-tied, Christian struggled to respond to this gesture.

"Very fashion forward person. I'm sure that…er…antlers will be the new black this season." Inwardly, he cringed at his inability to respond appropriately to this beauty.

"And pomegranates make a great accessory. The Persians believed it gave men superior strength in battle. It's a robust and vigorous fruit which completes my ensemble." She meant this in a light-hearted way. Or did she? Again, Christian, tongue-tied couldn't manage to say the right things.

"To be honest …and don't let this get back to Dité… I think you are the most alluring woman I've ever met. Probably. There's a … a Homeric quality to you. I feel like Odysseus…." Chastity winked at him.

"You're flattering me. A man who knows beauty and the classics. But, alas, I don't look this way all the time. I'm actually in costume. I'm a nymph. For Guerro's directorial debut of The Bacchae by Euripides."

"I've heard of it. Congrats on the lead," was all Christian could say.

"Anyway, enjoy your little man date with Guerro. He's waiting. I'll see you later tonight?" It was a question.

"Tonight?"

"Yeah, we're having a little initiation for Dité. She just bickered Pithon and got in, so we have something special for her." Christian winced at the sound of Dité's name.

"Ok, see you then."

Christian could feel his heart drop down to his stomach. If Tess were right and the Pithons were able to see through his ruse of pretentious friendship, then Dité's initiation

185

might turn on him and ferret out his intentions.

Keep to the plan, Christian told himself. Get them one on one, discover their weaknesses, and annihilate them quietly and quickly before the veil descends. Up until recently, Christian thought that the number of Greek infiltrators might have been a pantheon's worth. But the last twenty-four hours had him thinking that there could be a hundred or hundreds. Clearly, Guerro, Chastity, and Dité were a part of the devious plot. Cut off the head and you kill the body. Unless you're a Hydra a voice said to him.

When Christian finally came round to the back lawn, what he both saw and heard made him reconsider his plan. Guerro was facing the raised stage, addressing a caste of beautiful women. Clearly his actresses.

"Ladies, my wonderful, ebullient nymphs, this is the fun part. When you gorge on King Pentheus's flesh, I want this to make the audience squeal like its 405 B.C all over again. I want you to tear into this poor unfortunate soul. Start slow, tease your prey, show a certain sensual curiosity as nymphs do. Then commandeer him. Make him know he is yours, not his mother's who birthed him, not his wife's who loved him, and not his father's who taught him. Yours. Then, let him think you mean love and kindness, that this is all one flirtatious game. And once he has your trust, taste spinal fluid! Got it?"

"Hi, Guerro," Christian interrupted more from the desire by the nymph characters staring down at him from the stage not to be perceived as a Peeping Tom

"Ah, Christian! My muse! My raison d'être, come, come. I want you to judge if you think this performance…it's only practice, of course…is authentic. I want even the ghost of Euripides to say, 'That is my vision!' And Scene!"

The ten girls surrounded the male actor playing the unfortunate Pentheus and did exactly as Guerro directed. They hissed and hummed which was the theatrical part. Christian wasn't sure if his eyes were tricking him, but while the actresses played their role, Christian had the sense that they were devouring the male actor. He didn't scream because you don't really scream when your bowels are let loose. But Christian's confusion turned into fear. But it was just acting, right?

"What do you think?" Guerro asked Christian with a twisted smile. Again, tongue-tied.

"It's remarkable. Really. It's as if they really are eating him." Guerro called the scene and smiled approvingly at Christian.

"Acting, good Christian, is reality. We're just made to believe it is imagination. These are the best. You see, I held auditions over the summer and it took me a very long time to cast the perfect King Pentheus. Someone who would elicit sympathy at maximum. It's university, so finding women who are hungry to devour men is not hard. But finding a sympathetic male lead who is both brawny and appetizing yet so tragic... well, ha, it's like how I guessed you are: a Capricorn... it takes a gift that is rare. You must be hungry. Let's go inside and eat, yes?"

"Sure."

At Pithon, it was customary to sit wherever there was an empty seat, regardless of where that seat was. This was intended to stimulate conversation and camaraderie among members who may not have known each other very well. A strategy to cross-pollinate talent. Guerro found an empty table for two, and they both took seats across from each other.

187

At first, Guerro quizzed Christian about his background: family, travel, and then eventually why someone like Christian would bicker Liger given his lineage.

"Pithon is your true birthright, Christian. If you and Dité had joined as sophomores, you both would have been king and queen of this establishment. Your reign would have been called the 'Golden Age.'" Christian thought carefully about how he would answer.

"You know, we met at Liger. She was on the fence about Pithon and I bickered Liger without having any affiliation to the merry mount. I did it because I was feeling brave. She did it because, well, because she decided to follow me."

Guerro found this story riveting.

"Let me tell you a deathly serious version of your story. You see the other Christian and you run parallel to each other, like Athens and Sparta. I'm sure you know the Greeks. You are Athens: compromising, didactic, temperate, perhaps unsure of your own power so you make sure no one around you takes advantage of their own. There's a democracy of voices telling you what to do and who to be, heroic but known more for your wisdom than warrior ferocity. You aren't desired. You are loved softly. But other Christian, he is a true Spartan, he will abstain from all pleasures in pursuit of his goal, he is ripped and muscled as if ability and power themselves live in his fibers. He has rage, and he is desired. Unlike your pensive calm, when he is calm he is at his most terrifying because it is the edge of his sword called rage. He pierces through the history of others as a legend we falsify and idol worship. So it stands to reason that Dité was quite passionately smitten with him before meeting you, his alter ego. Other Christian found Dité to be too conventional, too predictable, not death-defying. Kind of the opposite of how she makes you feel: star-crossed and out of your depth. So when she saw you go into Liger, he saw you enter as well. We all knew of your father. Some of us knew him well. You were a wanted man. Everyone thought that the great son would follow the father. We were feverish with excitement, drunk off of the possibilities. But Dité never joined in such revelry. She wanted you to lick her wounds and lean on someone else, or to see if Athens would become its southern rival. And the other Christian? He wanted you to." Chiistian perked up in interest.

"Why?"

"You don't remember meeting Chastity all those years ago do you? Secret kisses, a memory spell. Ha, joking about the spell. Well, let's just say wars must have a winner and only one Christian can be vindicated by history."

"Still cryptic, but OK. I feel as though there is a threat coming."

"Oh, no I don't provoke. I equivocate that you are the better man of course. You have Dité on your side, like he did, and Chastity, well, she tucks the poor Spartan away for when the clouds turn dark blue so she can appear available when the sun's out for a reason. Both Christians have the same things, just not at the same time. All I'm saying is forsake Liger. Live your life here, and have both or more. Don't be a savage, it's beneath you. Be memorable, have a story, embrace your heritage. You know I know ten girls that would love to have a bite of what you're cooking. Historically speaking, Athens was known to have much better food than Sparta. Pig blood."

"So," I began sheepishly, "if you're all his friends, why do you all torture Paulie so?"

"Please, you must take Greek history with me next semester, then you'll learn... nothing and no one tortures Spartans like Spartans. What we do is just... risk. And if the gods will that, so be it. They are the Pithon of the sky."

They spoke for another forty minutes over filets and wine. Guerro wanted Christian to stay with him, going over his script over champagne and finger-food until Dité's party. He even tried to cast Christian in his play as the understudy for one of his leads. Christian declined as politely as possible, citing homework as the reason. With that, Christian left Pithon. But when he walked out the back and turned the corner to go along Pithon to the front lawn, he got a Spartan greeting.

"Christian, hello." It was Paulie from the night before.

"Hello," Christian said back.

"What brings you back here? Wild times last night, right?" Christian whistled, trying to come across casual.

"No doubt. I was just having..."

"Dinner with Guerro. Yes, I overheard you two arrange that. It's good that a drunk plan becomes a sober action. Although are any of us ever really sober?" Paulie winked at him. Christian noticed that they had the same color eyes.

"That's very meta." Paulie laughed.

"I'm a philosophy major. Meta is the only carbohydrate I'm allowed. Been on this keto thing to get in shape for a marathon." Paulie flexed his traps, lats, and abs, respectively.

"I'm actually a carbatarian...well... carbovore as they say. You might need some more carbs running those distances." Paulie stopped flexing.

"You were a rower, yes?"

"I am. Well, was, last semester."

"Well, then you probably have some cardio left in you. I'm about to go for a run in an hour. Why don't you join me? I'd really appreciate the company. Everyone else is too busy pretending to be busy."

"Sure. Where?"

"Where do you live? We'll meet there."

"1901 Hall."

"Fantastic. See you in an hour." Paulie said eagerly at the prospect of having a new workout partner. "Hydrate, it's a long one."

As soon as Paulie left, Christian wondered what he had gotten himself into. Buddying up to Paulie wasn't exactly his mission. He walked about twenty-five feet towards The High merry mount with the intention to skip out altogether and then decided to call Tess. He pulled out his phone only to realize it was dead. He needed to charge it anyway, so he continued to The High, found a table near a wall and outlet, plugged in, and then drummed his fingers nervously until he heard the familiar beep of his phone turning on.

Almost immediately, Christian's phone pinged repeatedly. 17 missed voicemails and 23 text messages. Nervously scrolling through the texts, most of them were from a very frustrated and heated Tess, beginning with urgent imploring for Christian to call back, to text if he wasn't in a place where he could talk, to Where are you? With one question mark graduating to a dozen question marks, and then stand-alone expletives with a lot of "Motherfuckers" and the crown jewel of expletives "pussy-ass deity." Looking at his voicemails, nine of them were also from Tess, but he dare not listen to them.

What could be the problem, he thought, as he dialed her.

Tess picked up almost immediately.

191

"Where the hell have you been? You disappeared on me and almost cost me my life… no two lives!" Tess was irate.

"Wait, wait, wait. Hold on there. My phone was dead…"

"Christian, it's been the better part of a day! You were supposed to report back to me after your game with the Pithons, but nothing. Absolutely nothing. And the Olympians attacked. Almost killed a student and me. And, yes, they're recruiting. Pithon might be the head…" Tess began, but Christian finished her sentence, "But the rest of Parthenon is the tail."

"Exactly. Where the fuck are you right now." Christian explained that he was trying to get out of a running date with Paulie who he met when he met Guerro.

"No, Christian. You keep your appointment with Paulie and you work him over until he gives you something solid. You make him like you. You give him what he wants, but you don't leave that run until he's your best friend. Exploit his ego. He's a pretty boy and vain. You get him to invite you into the inner circle. Tonight. You owe me that much." She added.

Genuinely contrite, Christian agreed.

"Have you heard from Wep?" That question agitated Tess.

"I just told you that I was looking for you and almost lost my life. I haven't, but you don't have time to talk to him. Get to your dorm, get ready for this run, and you get into the right headspace."

"Damn," Christian said quietly into the phone.

"What is it?" Tess asked sharply.

Christian took a deep breath, "Now Paulie knows where I live. What if it's a trap? This could be a trap. Maybe the entire gang shows up at my dorm?" Tess scoffed.

"This isn't the time for you to have a crisis moment. I thought you dealt with that shit already. If it's a trap, then it's a trap. Deal with it then." Then Tess hung up.

Christian made his way to his dorm, looking over his shoulder the entire way to see if he was being followed. Once inside, he changed into his running attire complete with spandex pants and a fluorescent orange headband to shield his ears from the frigid air. It would be an understatement to say that he was nervous. Though a rower of notable repute, Christian hadn't done cardio for going on six months now, and he was nervous about his performance: gassing and falling out before they even hit the five mile-mark. He looked at his watch and saw that he had another twenty minutes before Paulie would show up. He did some light stretching and then found himself pacing, still worried at the possibility that this could be a trap when he heard a pounding on his door, intermittent with curses.

"Chris, open up. It's dad!" Christian jumped. What the hell was his father doing here?

"Hold on," Christian scrambled to get to the door.

"Open this fucking door right now or I'll break it down!" Christian fumbled with the latch and opened the door to an angry Stone.

"Chris, what the fuck is going on?"

"I was getting ready for a run..."

"No, I don't care about that, I mean you serving people at Pithon? As a waiter?" Stone towered over Christian and nudged him with his forefinger in the sternum. It hurt, and the surprise showed on Christian's face. He took a step back in an attempt to de-escalate.

"Oh, that? It was a favor."

Stone stepped forward and nudged Christian again, pinning him against his desk, and knocking over his laptop.

"How much have I paid for this school each year? More than most faculty salaries. What's the purpose of a Parthenon education? To be on top. Why did your grandfather do whatever he could for his descendants to come here? So that Belvederes don't ever have to serve people. Belvederes. Don't. Serve." Stone punctuated these last three words with three hard pokes to Christian's chest.

"It's not like that..." Christian started.

"Oh, it is like that. You demeaned yourself in front of people who should be your equal or lessers, and at my merry mount no less. I overheard board members laughing about it. You keep pulling shit like this and you can forget being respected, forget a job, forget a future with Dité!"

"I was helping out a friend." Christian protested.

That's when Stone grabbed Christian by the front of his tracksuit jacket.

"Leaders don't make friends. Leaders have followers, employees, servants. You get that? You mental case!"

"Please, stop putting your hands on me." As calmly as Christian made this request, Stone's anger ratcheted up.

"Excuse me?" He pushed Christian again. This time Christian was half sitting, half lying on his desk with Stone pressing him down to the prone position.

Something snapped. In Christian.

"I said STOP IT!" No sooner had Christian given this command that, to both Stone and Christian's surprise, Stone was launched up and backwards, knocking his head against the ceiling and falling against the door. Christian sat up. Then stood up. Then, realizing that the confusion on Stone's face abated to embarrassment, sauntered over to him, standing over him.

194

"You don't get to touch me anymore. Mom allowed it. Grandma couldn't stop it. But now I'm telling you that this shit stops here. Now get your ass out of here. I've got company."

***

Stone hadn't been gone ten minutes before Paulie knocked on his dorm door. Christian swung the door open almost immediately. To ensure that Paulie or any other Python who might have shown up didn't have a chance to corner him in his dormitory, Christian wanted to make sure he was ready to go.

"What's up," Christian said, quickly shutting his door behind him, trying to look as eager as possible for this run.

Paulie, decked out in light blue spandex pants with a matching pink top that exaggerated his muscular frame, looked at Christian quizzically.

"You alright?" he asked with one eyebrow up.

"Yeah, yeah, yeah. Never better!" Christian cupped his hands to his mouth and blew into them as if already anticipated the cold." Paulie smiled. While on the elevator to the first floor, Paulie briefly explained the route which was the better part of a marathon. Christian inwardly cringed but had no choice but to feign confidence like it was nothing. However, he was giving off more nervous energy than he was aware of, and Paulie saw it.

"You sure you're good to go?" Paulie asked again.

"Hell, yeah," Christian insisted.

"Well, then let's get with it."

Once they exited the dormitory, Christian was off. Paulie laughed and caught up with him.

"Dude, we're supposed to be doing this together. You actually want to race?" And then he was off.

Paulie's pace was ridiculous. He lured Christian in at first with a brisk speed that was manageable without Christian's having to breathe hard. Once they got to Route 1, however, Paulie exploded with Christian bounding in short bursts to keep up with him.

As they kept up this pace, Christian wondered if Paulie was trying to prove a point. Maybe he lured Christian into this run to embarrass him. By mile three, Christian signaled for Paulie to stop. They stopped in the middle of a sidewalk while Christian lay on his back, trying to catch his breath.

"Christian, you've got to slow it down. Slow your brain down. You're overthinking the run." Christian, still on the ground, tried to play it off.

"It's not my brain that's trying to catch its breath." Paulie laughed heartily.

"Tap into your energy source," Paulie offered.

"And what might that be?" Christian offered his hand to Paulie who pulled him up.

"Does anything make you angry?" Christian considered the encounter with his father that morning. His inability to think straight before his father's wrath, the helplessness he felt when pinned against his desk, and the paralyzing fear he felt when his father put his hands on him. It had never been an equal fight between him and his father. Ever. He was the four-year-old Chris Belvedere who, after a day of playing with friends in the creek behind the house, absentmindedly tracked in mud all over the Turkish rug in his father's office. Stone, in a fit of rage, had grabbed little Chris and proceeded to rub his nose in a muddy footprint.

A warm feeling crept up Christian's back, wrapping itself around his neck and proceeding down his chest. The beginning of a boiling rage. Paulie sensed it.

"That. That right there. That's where your mind lives throughout this run. You got this." Then Paulie was off. Christian followed him, slow at first, his mind playing over and over his surprise and humiliation, his instinctive calling out to his mother, his mother showing up and screaming at Stone, jumping on his back. Stone's flinging his mother against the wall, and his mother crumpling like a rag doll. But then Christian shook his head. He didn't need the memories. He just needed to tap into the energy right now. For the next eleven miles, Christian kept pace with Paulie. By mile sixteen, the anxiety in Christian's mind had disappeared altogether and both were settled into a nice conversation pace.

"I work on my sprint speed for the first part of the run, then I relax and pick up miles," he confided to Christian. Whatever Paulie's method was, it was working for Christian.

At mile nineteen on the way back to campus, they stopped by a small wood next to a convenience store to rest before the last leg. As they sipped water from their water bottles, Paulie addressed Christian.

"I want you to join us."

"Join what?" Christian asked for clarification though he knew exactly what Paulie was talking about.

"Us. It's in your blood," Paulie said nebulously.

"Blood?"

"Your father was a Pithon." Christian was halfway through his water bottle when he coughed at the mention of his father.

197

"And what do you know about my father?" Paulie gave Christian a grin.

"A lot more than you know. Stone Belvedere was a legend." Christian pursed his lips.

"We might have different perspectives on his legendary status. Look, I'm happy at Liger. Besides, it's too late for me to bicker."

"I'm not talking about the merry mount. As your father, I'm sure, has told you... life is about connections and connections are about alliances. The world is an ugly, piss-and-shit-ridden place. Not enough people collude to make it better. Our parents failed, so we need to succeed whatever the cost. So for the rest of the year and after graduation, I want...no... I need someone like you with us. You're one of the strong, you're a good person, and you know what toes not to step on."

Christian couldn't believe his luck. Was he being asked to join... the Olympians? But he couldn't give up that he knew this.

"Does this group have a name?"

"Ha, no. We aren't that pretentious. But we will overcome our fathers. They were all about titles and pomp, empty gestures and etiquette. We're all about results. I'm not the only one who feels this way nor am I the only one who has noticed how perfect you'd be with us."

"You mean Guerro?" Paulie nodded.

"Well, if you feel as strongly about your father as I do, we do have a resentment of our fathers in common."

"My father was a tyrant. Yours?"

"A Grade A asshole. But we're their sons, you know. How sure are you that we can really escape them?" Paulie downed the rest of his water, crumpled the bottle in his hand, and threw it in the general direction of a nearby trash can.

"You mean the sons complain then as fathers they reign? The notion that we will make our fathers mistakes? I don't believe that. Not for a minute They got lazy and fat off their success. Being fat and lazy, they made sure we were trim and industrious. They forgot about what pain and struggle teaches. Being pain and struggle themselves for us, they became our teachers. They forgot how to grind, and so they ground us down to the nubs we are. But we will act before they grind us out of existence. No mountain tops for me. Give me the underworld where the real work is done." Christian considered this a pep talk falling on deaf ears.

"But you seem so… shackled by all this. Is this pursuit really what you want? No intention to offend but your friends, from what I notice, don't seem to have your best interest at heart just as your father didn't. Guerro, Chastity, Dité. They all toxify."

"You only assume they have power over me because you don't know me well enough. I'm like music. They can choose when to play me, but they can't get me out of their heads when I'm at my best." He grinned almost wickedly. "And I'm always at my best."

Paulie stood up, turned his back to Christian and towards the road.

"Just a few more miles, Christian. What do you say?"

But Christian wasn't listening. No cars or other traffic were coming by this stretch of road. Other than the convenience store owner, they were completely alone. Paulie's back was to Christian. And then it hit Christian. He was supposed to kill him. This is what Tess set him up to do.

This is what Tess expected of him. And here was the opportunity he had to make up for his absence of more than half a day that almost cost Tess her life.

Christian's body tensed and he slowly stood up from where he had been sitting. Paulie's thickly muscled neck lay above the collar of his ridiculously fluorescent pink shirt, but it lay bare. Too good to be true, Christian thought as he stretched his legs, eyes still on Paulie's neck.

But was it a premature move? Paulie had just offered him an invitation to join the pantheon of Olympians who were planning to take over Parthenon and then infect the world of politics and economics in a centralized way through their undergraduate and graduate programs, placing their alumni into positions of authority in policy development, government affairs, and federal advisors until the entire system was infected with the Greeks once more and all other competing mythologies were choked out. Why would he want to kill one when he could kill them all?

Cut the head off the snake and the body dies, Christian said to himself as he took three steps towards Paulie. But then an ancient line came out of nowhere, wafting like a refrain into Christian's ear, Smite the shepherd and the sheep will scatter, it said as Christian reached his left hand out towards the back of Paulie's neck.

But was Paulie the shepherd here? Christian asked himself, his hand six inches away from the nape of Paulie's neck. Would Paulie's annihilation stop the undermining of Parthenon or would it escalate the timeline like a catalyst?

"I can't," Christian said aloud as he stepped up next to Paulie and draped his left arm around Paulie's shoulder.

Paulie turned. "Can't what?" Christian looked toward the road for a half minute before turning his head to look at Paulie, his arm still around Paulie's wide shoulders.

"I can't let an opportunity like this pass me up. I accept." Tess was going to kill him. Paulie blinked in surprise.

"Am I hearing you say that you'll join us, Christian?" Christian nodded his head, simultaneously squeezing Paulie.

"That I am," he grinned. Paulie grinned back.

"Well, we'd better haul ass back to campus so we can be ready for tonight."

"For what?" Christian asked.

"You're joining us at the right time. Tonight is Dité's initiation."

CHAPTER 7
Things You Miss

An hour after Christian returned from his run with Paulie, he was finishing up his shower when the phone rang. He checked the number only to see the words UNKNOWN blinking back at him. He picked it up anyway.

"Hello?" It was a question. There was a pause and then a familiar voice responded.

"So I hear you've got a date tonight?" It was Asara. Christian was almost caught off guard because he hadn't heard from her since the last time he saw Wep in the Duat.

"Where've you been? I've been looking for you."

"Have you come by the pub?" Christian set his phone on speaker mode and began drying his hair.

"Well, no. I've been busy on this side of town."

"Then you haven't looked hard enough." Christian couldn't tell if she was teasing or not.

"Hold on. What do you mean that you heard I have a date tonight?" Asara was silent for a few seconds.

"Word travels fast. In the right circles. Just make sure they don't hypnotize you." That caught Christian's attention.

"Is that a warning?"

"Christian, consider it a tip from a concerned citizen."

Christian switched the phone from speaker to private.

"Should I be concerned?"

"Christian, consider the luck you've had with women lately. Now throw in an ancient ritual of which you know nothing about and vows of secrecy to which you will be compelled to make and I think being concerned is an understatement." Christian looked at his reflection through the fog on the bathroom mirror.

"We haven't had that much time to talk, but, well, things have gotten more difficult than I expected. I was hoping to have a normal semester, but things have..."

"Gotten out of hand?" Asara interjected.

"They're manageable," Christian protested. He could hear Asara sigh on the other end of the line.

"Christian, your dean has been here in the pub at least three times since I last saw you. Not to drink, of course, but to attend what I can only guess to be meetings. But I'd bet an entire four years of tuition that the kind of company she's spending time with isn't the kind your university would approve of. She's corruptible. And I can't help but think that the event you're attending tonight is connected." Needless to say, this information stunned Christian.

"Dean Maiden? Are you sure? She's one of the good ones."

"No. Your dean is corruptible."

"But why? She let me back in school when it wasn't looking good for me." Asara sighed again, but this time Christian detected agitation.

"I can think of a few reasons."

"Humor me." Christian clicked the phone over from private to speaker again and began dressing.

"She's using you. Don't you still have a couple of lawsuits

pending from the defamation of character charge from last semester? And by students in that Pithon merry mount afterall? Why would the dean let you back in the university when there's still legal action against you?" Christian fumbled with the buttons on his shirt. He had forgotten about the lawsuits.

"I was hospitalized that summer. Maybe there's some loophole for students with mental health issues. Maybe she was being kind."

Asara scoffed. "Maybe you should talk to Wep. I'm sure that he doesn't share your opinion about Dean Maiden or any of them." By now Christian was tucking his Oxford blue shirt into his black pants. That comment stung because he knew that Wep was quietly frustrated with his pivoting... always in favor of sparing the reputation or life of the god in question. At some point he knew the killing had to start. But when?

"Haven't thought about that. You've given me a lot to consider. But do you think I'm safe tonight?" Asara got quieter.

"You must not let them hypnotize you." Christian's frustration was compounded by the fact that his pants, a relic from better days, were highwaisted on him. He picked up the phone again and switched from speaker mode.

"Asara, you've said that once already. It sounds like you don't trust me. I have the power to stop them. I stopped my father today. I fought a god in a basement. I've fought a knight. I've evaded the Olympians. I mean, don't you think this is my cosmic role?"

Christian could tell that whatever expression Asara formerly had had dropped like a stone.

"That's the issue right there! Most sound-minded people

would be fearful, reluctant even. And heroes? Heroes always see too much evil as well as the evil they seek to stop. And when something prevents them from stopping it, they become the villains or go insane. Heroes always suffer."

By now, Christian put the phone on speaker again in order to have both hands free to lace up his shoes.

"You're not describing anything other than a calling. This is my calling." Asara was silent for the better part of a minute.

"Asara? You still there?" He heard her take a deep breath.

"You know, Christian. I worry that you're not thinking clearly. I worry that your real enemy has a clinical name." That got Christian's attention.

"Are you saying I'm a basket case?" He felt the anger boiling up within him.

"Christian, self-defense against a ghost is one thing, but a secret society of psychopaths is masochism. I know how you're feeling, I've heard the call before, too. But you don't have to answer it. Not like that. It's preferable that you do what Wep has said and pick them off one by one. But infiltrating the group? That could backfire on you."

"I asked you if you think I'm a basket case?" Christian was surprised at his anger.

"What I think is that you should live in the real world with the occasional phantom, not espionage into a secret society of beasts and devils. The real world is where you belong. It's where you're safest."

Christian interjected.

"You just said that it was preferable that I remain in the real world and kill them one by one. So do you prefer for me to be a murderer? To choose mortal restriction over a quest?"

"Look, it's my right to do some thinking. One of us has to. When a better idea comes, you must concede territory. If they are evil, then they are a slow-moving evil and that means they are confident. And if they are confident, then they have reason to be. After all, these aren't college kids. They've been around for centuries, feeding off good people like you. They know how to draw in their prey. They get them hyped off their own heroism. You aren't the first to challenge them. They have faced down your predecessors and won. If you're going to be different, then you need a better plan. And if you have one, I'll hear you out..." But then Christian, finishing up the V-is-for-Victory knot in his tie, cut her off.

"We'll talk about this later."

***

Showered and well dressed, Christian reached the front of a loud Pithon, both visually and raucously. As Christian was about to walk up to the doors, he caught a glimpse of Liger across the street and realized he hadn't been to his own merry mount since he began his mission in earnest. His distractions had been almost pathological to not knowing what day of the week it was to treating the Olympians better than his own friends. But he shook it off. This is where it was all meant to lead him, Wep had said. So do what you have to do.

The bouncers checked Christian's student ID and his name against a list. The one with the bull neck nodded at him and opened the door.

Here goes nothing, Christian said to himself as he stepped into what irony told him was a dark cave. As usual, it was like magic... black magic... stepping into the world of Pithon. The most beautiful women wore the finest dresses from the season, all authentic versions of the scarlet red colors unique to the Middle Ages. The men with their suits cut perfectly, trim and debonair (well, most of them) set Christian a little on edge with his cheaper, more simplified version of Uptown Casual. The dress, the chatter, the energy was electrifying.

Christian glanced to his left. On the staircase stood the cabal: Christian, Chastity, Guerro, and Dité. They were taking selfies together, displaying their sleek plumage and subtle, sensuous power like they were royalty. Guerro noticed Christian and gestured to him to join the photoshoot. As awkward as it was to be in Dité's presence after their previous encounter at Pithon, she put her arm around Christian's shoulder while Guerro flanked the other side of Christian and the photographer commenced to shoot more photos. Evidently, all had been forgiven and forgotten or simply set aside for the event tonight.

Over the next two hours, Christian actually felt in good company as the conversation, intermixed with champagne and hoer d' erves spanned geopolitics, World Cup soccer, and literary pet peeves. Even though the evening was to celebrate Dité, she personally introduced Christian to a few dozen people who sauntered by to pay their respects.

After maybe his third or fourth glass of wine, Christian noticed that the mood in the room had shifted. Towards him. Chastity, glowing with a solid two couple of hours of throwing back glass after glass squeezed herself in between Dité and Christian.

"I love you like a sister," she said earnestly, hugging Dité. Then Chastity turned to Christian.

"It's time for initiation." Dité stood up and took one of Christian's hands while Chastity took the other. Christian immediately felt on guard.

"What are we doing? Isn't this Dité's night?" Christian tried to cover up his perplexity, but he was asking too many questions. Both ladies led Christian to the bottom of a staircase. One Christian hadn't noticed before.

"My night, your night... all that matters is that we're friends again and together. Right, Chastity?"

"True. That's the thing about you, Christian. You know you love the attention but you play off your showing up here at Pithon like it's accidental You're good at that." Christian felt himself blushing.

"I'm just here to support her."

"I'm sure you are," Chastity smirked as they ascended the steps. Christian felt himself in danger but could think of no way to separate himself from the group in a dignified manner. Especially as they were at the top of the steps now. Dité stopped outside a door.

"Christian, this ritual requires the inclusion of a guest or two. You're my guest. When you enter the room, follow my lead. And just let go. Don't overthink it. Understood?" Squeezed between the two women at the top of the landing, Christian had no option but to consent. Dité put her hand on the door knob.

Once they crossed the threshold, Christian immediately sensed the presence of magic. It was dry and old, like chalk on a well-worn chalkboard, but it spoke to him. As he made his way across the room, he listened and heard it speak about stories of sacrifice, blood oaths, and owls.

In the center of the room was a five-pointed star with the symbol of the Greek aegis in the middle, drawn on the floor. Christian glanced up and noticed that Paulie and Guerro stood in front of mirrors that were aligned with each point of the star below. Chastity took her place. Then Dité, standing in the center of the star with Christian, pulled Christian towards him and kissed him while she put her hands in his pockets. Christian wasn't expecting this turn of events but couldn't avoid reciprocating. Then he heard a bolt lock in the direction of the door they entered.

Instinctively, Christian felt for the ring on his hand. But it wasn't there. Also, in his frenzied rush to make it to Python on time, he had forgotten his khopesh in his dorm room. By the time he considered his third option, to conjure All-Brighter, his efforts were repelled by a countering force. He was screwed. Perceiving that the initiation was already in progress, he was somehow able to momentarily disentangle himself from Dité, retreating to the edge of the star.

Paulie picked up a lyre and began strumming it. Quietly at first. Complex arpeggios progressing from the middle octave to higher and then lower registers. Then a melody. A single note that hung in the air. A Mediterranean call-to-prayer kind of tune with a vibrato that found Christian tearing up. Then Paulie began to sing. And what a voice he had. It was a beautiful tremulous tenor. He sang a ballad of a restless wanderer who accepted an offer he should have refused.

Christian was so thoroughly transfixed by the music and storyline that he was unaware that Dité had completely disrobed. Christian only noticed her during Paulie's interlude at the end of the third verse. There she lay down on the star. Naked.

The members within the room began to chant in an ancient Greek dialect. It rose to a chorus of what sounded like a hundred voices though Christian was only aware of five people in the room which began to spin. Dité spinning along as well, around and around.

At once, the room transformed into the Greek Parthenon. Columns, doorways forty feet tall, marbled statues, and large windows of light appeared. Christian couldn't tell if he was caught in a time traveling warp or entering another dimension.

As Dité spun, she picked up where Paulie left off, the others spinning as well and chanting in accompaniment until the transformation was complete. Paulie shone golden like the sun. Guerro was red like blood. Chastity was white as the driven snow.

Dité, however, began to transform differently. Her beautiful image began to disappear, still spinning, and slowly replaced by a swirling whirlpool of a rose liquid contained in the center of the now marbled floor. The chanting stopped. Then Paulie spoke.

"This is all that we can conjure. This is all the veil will allow us to bring. But we share it with you, more sacred and potent than ambrosia, so that you may join us!" Christian's blood ran cold.

He knew at once then that this was the Blood of Dionysus before him and that one sip of it would make him like them: an Olympian. He was now trapped, had no weapon, and the powers of Osiris with which he had become acquainted over the last week, were waning. His power to resist was almost absent, and he felt the lust-driven lure to drink. Somewhere in the back of his frantic mind, he hoped that Wep and Tess could bring him back. Asara had been right. He had gone too far with a bad plan. He had gambled on his assumption that they couldn't conjure an ample defense at will. He had underestimated them. Maybe Stone was right, too. Maybe his enemy was clinical, and its name was Mania.

***

Fight them, the words bubbled up from deep within Christian. But the music, beauty, and euphoria of it all was so overwhelming that there was no way. If he fought, he would lose and be thrown in the pool anyway. At least this way, giving in to the lure with full knowledge of what he was doing, he convinced himself that he could be brought back. Somehow. Some day.

As soon as he thought that, Dité had entirely dissolved into the rose-red liquid that now was a rich burgundy color, slowly her form rose out of the whirlpool, her once dissolved body reconnecting, resurrecting more beautiful, more enchanting than before. Empowered by the blood, the flush of her skin pulsated with a delirious force of energy, her piercing eyes and irresistible voice inviting Christian like a siren. She had eyes for no one but than Christian.

Once more, the voice surfaced within Christian to back away from the symbol on the floor, that this was his last chance. But he kept his heels planted firmly on the outer ring like a rebellious child, tempting a fate too large, too all-encompassing for him to understand. Then it happened.

In an instant, Dité grabbed Christian firmly by the neck or torso, it happened too fast for him to comprehend. The voice he had heard playing the siren tune in his head was the voice of the Furies: silent like a screaming mute. Then she pulled him below the churning waves of Dionysian blood, too fast for Christian to take in a mouthful of air with the last scene he recalled of the others who had further transformed, their fangs and red eyes assuring him that he had no one else to blame but himself. This was it.

***

"Where the hell is Christian," Tess growled, checking her phone for the tenth time. Tess, Wep, and the little girl Rioghain had convened at a local deli waiting for news… any news… from Christian on the outcome of the event at Pithon. Rioghain pushed her plate away from her.

"I can't eat," she said morosely. Tess fussed over her as if over a child.

"Rioghain, you need to eat. You're recovering. Eating will give you normalcy." But then Wep grabbed Rioghain's plate, greedily dumping the contents onto his own.

"I don't blame her. She woke up this morning a 'normal' red-head and now she's really a normal red-head with a crazy story to tell. Don't worry about your pancakes."

"Stop undermining everything I'm doing for her," Tess chided Wep. Wep's fork hung in mid-air and he glowered at Tess for a few seconds."

"Look, I've known you for maybe a day and already I notice you cling to people too fast. Leave her alone and focus on your own inadequacies. And Christian? You said he would be here. Isn't this the second time you've lost track of him in twenty-four hours? How can you lose Christian? Nigga, please." They resumed eating while Tess fumed, then redirected her conversation to Rioghain.

"Listen, Rio, I've been fighting those that have been chasing you for a long time, and the only way you get out of this is if you listen to me. So, eat or don't eat, it doesn't matter to me. What I know is that this is probably your last good meal for a while because we're hitting the road."

"I'm leaving?" Rioghain's mouth dropped open in surprise. Tess looked at Wep and crossed her arms.

"This is your department now." She was agitated.

"I called in a favor with my cousins," Wep kept chewing and talking with his mouth open. "They've agreed to protect you, but they don't have opposable thumbs so Tess is right about this being your last pancake dinner for a while."

"Are they… like you?" Rioghain barely whispered.

"Bite the hand that feeds you. What does that matter? They are the Raiju. And, yes, they're weird. That's what you wanted to say, right? They love taunting samurai and sushi restaurant customers, but it's the best I can do. You want to live, don't you?"

"Yes." Rioghain said in a small voice

"Maybe Christian's plan will work tonight and you won't have to," Tess interjected. But Rioghain, knowing that she had changed handlers from Tess to Wep, sided with Wep on his growing animosity towards Tess.

"Your friend's plan seems a bit hasty. But I'll say a prayer for him, just in case God is real." Rioghain snarkily responded. Wep coughed.

"God? You mean gods are real, you little monotheistic smartass. My friend is on the Little Caligula path right now. Who knows who he'll be when we see him next?" Wep scowled at Tess.

"What's that mean? Caligula and Christian have nothing in common," Tess huffed.

"Christian was raised by Stone Belvedere, a man who is not his 'real' father. Christian's real father is the father of Osiris who is Geb, the Earth, who was the opposite of the intemperate Stone. Caligula lost his real father, who, like Geb, was honorable and good and was adopted by the hedonist Tiberius. Christian is sane and kind like Caligula was at first, but there lies in both of them the seed of madness. And since Christian left his khopesh in his room, now in my possession, he is defenseless to the will of the Greek Gods, as were the Romans who adopted them."

"That's a stupid analogy! Christian doesn't need his khopesh. It only focuses his power. His real power is within. Maybe if you spent more time helping him with better plans instead of playing some fucking smooth jazz set in front of college students that's not only basic but sounds like an 8-track, he would have fulfilled his potential by now!" Tess was livid.

"Shut your hip-hop-spewing-whatever mouth. You don't get it. Smooth jazz is the music of his childhood when his mother was aware of the world and his grandmother was teaching him. It unlocks all the doorways into his Furie and latent-god power. I know what I am doing. And I don't regret anything I did. They don't call me the Opener of Pathways for nothing! Respect that!" Rioghan, nervous at this escalation, tried to excuse herself.

"I have to go to the bathroom. May I? They can't get me in the bathroom, can they?" She stood up. Both Wep and Tess ignored her.

"And another thing, Tess, who is this Asara girl?"

"Hello?" Rioghain sighed unpleasantly.

"She's hard to figure out."

"Hello? OK, I'm just gonna go." Rioghain pushed her

chair in and left.

"She is...."

"What? She is what?" growled Wep.

"She's in love with him. From what I can tell, she is just another person who loves him."

"Love? How long has it been, a week? Is she a goddess, too? Who isn't these days?"

"If you can't tell, I can't either." Tess and Wep locked eyes at the same time.

"Hold on," Tess said, with a look of fright on her face. "Why can't we tell?"

"New-to-godhood people, meaning they just awoke. They're like baby snakes. They express their venom too much too soon, so it's easy to spot. But someone who has been posing as a mortal for centuries is good at it and can hide or show as much as they want. Makes them excellent shapeshifters. Like your waitress friend."

"Wait, waitress friend? As in the only other person here with us?"

"You said the waitress was fine. So I'm sure she's fine," Wep said dismissively.

"Yeah, but...what if you're wrong? What if I'm wrong? Zoie? Zoie!" Tess stood up fast, screaming out for her co-worker.

No response.

She looked at Wep frantically. Wep looked back, and they both read in each other's eyes what the silence could only mean. They both rushed to the women's bathroom, barging in, and checking the stalls like a SWAT team.

Rioghain was gone. And there were only twelve places she could be.

***

The world of the blood-drawing Olympians had over-taken Christian and not without his consent. Having been drawn under the whirlpool by a frightening, transformed Dité, everything reversed beneath the surface, the former-ly distasteful indulgences of the completely free and mis-erable now at the forefront. Unburdened by sobriety, com-mon sense, and good nature, the right to life, liberty, and the pursuit of happiness divulged into an orgiastic feeding frenzy where all persons present frolicked, fell on top of each other, and fucked.

In this underworld overrun by demons, Christian felt an insatiable pull toward the undercurrent of this new moral-ity. He wanted to experience the initiatory rites of baptism into this world. He wanted what he got when he first saw her: Asara But this night, he gave into the behaviors that society afforded bad boy tropes and noir women. He saw Dité with Guerro, Guerro with Chastity, at one point he was with Chastity: permutations of denial, trial, and sex that he had only ever feared rather than embraced. He had never before approved of this kind of animalistic behav-ior, but here he was in the middle of a round robin of be-ings. He was now a hypocrite, and a well-worn, sweaty, and spent one.

Christian wasn't sure how long it lasted, but he remem-bered slowly coming back to his senses, sitting in a wing-back chair in the corner of the room he entered at the be-ginning of the evening. Dité climbed out of the circle of pleasure seekers, beelined toward him, and sat on his chair.

"That's what it's about, Christian. To embrace sex on everyone's terms but still be a consort to who wins you."

She kissed Christian on the cheek. Ashamed, Christian instinctively pulled back.

"But you won't win. Not in the end."

"You're still talking like a priest, like a moralist, like a hero. But you're not, Christian. I made sure of that." There was smirk at the corner of Dités mouth.

Christian, utterly defeated now that he was in full possession of his mind and realizing what he had just done, attempted the high road.

"I'll never be like you. We're not the same. I don't belong here." Dité nodded towards the pool.

"Well, that just proved that you are and you do."

"No," Christian protested. "I was drugged or something. You and the others..." Dité rolled her eyes.

"And when exactly were you drugged? Was that just now under the pool? Was that during your afternoon run with Paulie? Or was that last night when you showed up at Python pretending to be a server? I'd really like to know when that was because it looks to me like you've been the one inserting yourself where, as you say 'You don't belong.' No one tied you up and brought you here. It's all your own doing." Christian was nearly inconsolable but tried not to show it. Had he blown his one opportunity to infiltrate Python?

"You're playing the hero, Christian," Dité cut him off. "I once wanted to be remembered as a hero, but the Greeks only allowed men to play that game. Heroism is a code. It's a prison. It isn't free to choose. She stood up and began to walk slowly back and forth, as if she were reminiscing about some long lost thought.

"That's why I feel such an intimacy with blood. With war. War allows women like me to be free. I can be fatal like the women of Sparta while their men spent over a decade away training for battle. I can be what the mid-century patriarchy feared about women after World War II when we had too much independence and too much experience outside of the home away from motherhood and housekeeping. I've been either before, but I can also be the or. Tonight I was the or. And you were the either." Dité grinned at her own play of words and pouted when Christian didn't seem to appreciate it.

"My God, I'm talking to a bi-polar manic depressive here." And suddenly, as if in a fit of rage, she lit on fire with dancing red and blue flames.

"I am a woman's true work upon this earth. I am the Goddess reborn. And you're mine. What a prize you have won, Christian! Men envy you. Women envy you. Your father envies you. And there's nothing I love more than a boy with daddy issues. You will never be rid of me and you'll never know why I picked you. But I'm the chase you'll always cut to, and the camera loves me at every possible angle."

She mounted Christian and kissed him. He felt himself once again powerless to resist her. Her legs squeezed him like the grip of a python. And as much as he feigned resistance, every attempt that he had to stop her failed. She was stronger than him at that moment.

In his previous life, just a few weeks before, Christian had played the victim card one too many times so as to become instinctive. Being controlled by an over-possessive father and paralyzed by an aloof and indecisive mother, it was second nature for him to give up in situations where he felt immobilized. To go limp like a possum before a deadly predator.

That's it, Christian thought to himself. Go limp.

And he did.

It took a moment for Dité to realize that her charms weren't working on Christian and it took less than another moment for her to realize that it was a protest.

"How dare you!" She grimaced in his ear.

By this point, the Olympians had stopped their cavorting, pulled themselves out of the pool, and stood staring like statues at Christian. Dité seethed, screaming ancient curses and with thunderous steps left the room.

No sooner had Dité exited the room than one of the Olympians began to laugh.

Belly laughs. The laughter spread until each was doubled over and the room resounded in echoey guffaws. But whether that laughter was directed at Dité or Christian, that was yet to be seen.

***

Despite his strong inclination to leave, Christian ended up staying in the upper room where the rites were performed. Paulie, who never jumped into the pool, continued playing music, an indication that the ritual wasn't yet over though Christian was over it. Though the music continued to stir within Christian nuanced feelings formerly foreign to his ability to experience, he sat in his corner, still relishing the humiliation of Dité.

I probably never knew the real Dité, he rationalized to himself. I only knew that she drank.

He glowered at each of them from his corner of the room. All of them had fallen, reversed like maggots who were once butterflies. And yet for all these negative thoughts, for pity's sake, Christian couldn't bring himself to end each of them. For all his good intentions, Christian understood that Wep would see his actions differently. And he wouldn't be as kind.

The music was intoxicating, so intoxicating that Christian thought he might be hallucinating. Paulie played a tune sensual and sinister. Christian was the dark knight of a kingdom abandoned and destroyed. The music was an enchantment that gave stamina to the sinner. Both Christian and the melody moved in unison. Each note shook the merry mount like the strides of prehistoric giants. It emboldened Christian, and saw him, like the infamous Gilgamesh, chase down these Nephilim to challenge them to do battle.

Luckily for him, Guerro and another Hermes got into a fight which escalated to both of them throwing lightning bolts at each other. One of them hit the chair in which Christian was sitting, blasting him out the back window across the patio over the bannister onto an embankment and down it into a deep wood where he awoke to find himself alone.

When he came to, Christian had no clothes on and his tongue was bleeding. He looked at his hands only to see that they were pale as alabaster. Each move he made was difficult and felt like the blood had congealed in his veins.

Suddenly, it was as if everything flipped. Christian found himself floating up, rather falling down, into the sky which was now below him.

I've got to still be hallucinating, Christian thought to himself. All of a sudden, his vision blurred and he had to shake his head to clear it. Looking up at the ground above his head, Christian had a birds eye view of Parthenon, and things were uncharacteristically out of line for the Ivy League school. He saw students all over the campus experiencing, as it were, some form of psychosis. Some were running in circles, some were climbing buildings, and he saw several bellowing at imaginary creatures. A group of students in front of the school's post office were, as best he could tell, cornering some imaginary monster, beating the air with their belts and shoes. Three female students had completely undressed and were dunking themselves in the school fountain so as not to be seen, only coming up for air when their lungs were about to burst.

And then it happened. With no sudden warning, the ground rained blood. It shot past Christian from the ground below him and up to the earth above. He could hear, in waves, the frightened cries of students who were being pummeled. Christian himself was not immune from the stink and decay of the blood that covered him from head to toe. To his surprise, he found his footing in the air and ran for an hour, choking, mad, and directionless. He was desperate to get out of his supernatural disaster. Did I cause this? he wondered. Am I being punished for not, once again, killing the Olympians when it was in my power to do so? But the regret didn't stop the monsoon of body fluids from assaulting every orifice in his body, and he ran on.

Until he saw a revelation.

Suddenly, everything got quiet. For a moment, Christian thought he might be dead, but when he looked down at his feet he saw that they were still running. But the noise in his head had quieted and something strange happened. As if several cogs of an intricate watch had fallen into place, he felt a oneness with the minds of the Olympians. He saw

221

their plan. He saw through them.

Constellations lit up below him. He saw in the animated fashion of a few seconds the entire interplay of the gods in the forms of stars over the last two thousands years. Taurus, Aquarius, Scorpio, and the rest of them danced among each other, challenging each other for supremacy. Coming close to snuffing the other out yet at the same time keeping their distance.

These Zodiacs each called to Christian, thousands of voices shouting down the others, and warned him of their personal ends and aspirations. He heard snatches of complaints, grievances of broken contracts, vignettes of suductions, and details of murders. And yet, he saw the strange, standoffish balance among those worlds when they brought the gods to earth. They all appealed to him. To Osiris. To the Lord of Life. Of the Dead. Of the Afterlife. As if in a universal court, they were all bringing their aspirations for resolution, reparations, and redemption to Osiris's feet. They had raised him from the soil of the immortal benben to be the The Fire Next Time, the last defense against those who would abuse their power.

Christian felt a surge of power and evil ambition to mock them as they as Greek gods mocked each other. But they showed him the beginning. They showed him some of who he used to be.

He had been a great king: noble, didactic, kind, slow to anger, and, most importantly, happy. But then he had become too comfortable, he became unvigilant. His sign in this life, the Capricorn, stepped forward among the other constellations and sang a song which was a long lament that unveiled Christian's past as Osiris.

Then Pisces, the zodiac of the ending age, shoved Capricorn aside and showed Christian a warning of a great spell. The Virtues Constellation in which Osiris had become his own enemy and ironically privy to the solution would be a part of the problem.

Taurus and Aries took center stage now and verbally attacked and shamed Christian as an older brother would.

To his left, Christian could see Libra pantomiming the drowning in its scales of Christian like an uncle.

Leo, to his right, wouldn't look at Christian like a disappointed aunt. Cancer screamed out at Christian "Backbiter!" like a worried sister.

Virgo questioned Christian's logic.

Sagittarius called him the death of love.

Scorpio admired how he tried to play the game of gods.

Aquarius told Christian he could still arrive.

Gemini finally left Christian's double-poled mind alone. And he got it. He finally understood that for all of the abuse of the father, abandonment of the mother, and torture of the psychosis, each was a signpost to a greater truth. And that was that all gods and all places were in danger because Osiris hadn't stood up to evil and Christian, following within the same train, wouldn't either. And if Christian wouldn't take his rightful place as Osiris and do what was right, the Olympians, an imbalance of all deities and virtues, would recreate reality themselves. The Virtues Constellation.

***

Capricorn, Christian's natural sign, had yet to speak but stepped forward. Christian raised his head to meet and Capricorn noticed the pained expression. A glimmer of hope flickered in Christian's eyes as Capricorn laid a hand on Christian's shoulder. Here is the benediction, Christian thought. Here is where this horrible mess is made right. Capricorn studied Christian's pupils. The left one first. Then the right. And, discovering Christian's thoughts, sighed as only constellations can do.

"But at least there was hope in this world. Such hope for even the gods to change." He paused as Christian hung on his every word.

"Now, no more." And with that, Capricorn turned on his heels, as it were, and found his position in the sky once more. So did the rest of the gods, one by one, their combination of menacing grumbles and bitter complaints fading off into the distance until Christian was alone.

Once the last god was gone, Christian's emotions overcame him, and, though suspended in the air, he fell to his knees, and, kneeling on all fours, heaved and vomited all the blood of Dionysus. Every drop of it. It kept coming in waves until, asphyxiated for lack of air, Christian lost consciousness.

***

When he awoke, he found himself in Dean Maiden's arms.

Keep crying, he heard her say.

Remembering the court of the gods and their indictment of him, Christian began hyperventilating at the thought of losing himself forever. He was ashamed. He blamed himself for his lack of evolution in his learning curve since realizing that he was Osiris. He had reveled in his new identity, using his powers for scant little things like getting chummy with the Olympians, getting close to Asara, sparring with Tess, and putting his father in his place.

I've learned my lesson. I should have kept my resolve. I should have been true to myself. Damn the hero complex! I should have done what was needed, not what was asked. Help me! He cried out to no one in particular.

Just cry. It's ok, just cry. Let the circle be broken. This voice was different.

"Grandma? Is that you?"

I am.

"Yahweh?"

I am. All is not lost. Say this verse with me.

At once, the voice's presence filled the entirety of the sky so that the constellations glaring at him accusingly from light years away were momentarily shrouded by its glory.

Say 'No weapon formed against me shall prosper.'

No weapon formed against me shall prosper. Christian repeated.

Good. You never sing anymore. When you were a boy and your grandmother was teaching you lessons, I used to visit you. You would see me on the wall and you would sing to me because you knew I was sad.

Who are you? Christian asked confusedly.

Apollo used to sing like that. Such beautiful, holy music to the sorrowful. Just like his son Orpheus, to save a damned girl's soul. Will you sing this song with me?

Yes. I will sing.

It goes like this: 'When home is a far it's where I think there is love that is for knowing.'

When I think of home, I think of a place where there's love overflowing… Christian repeated.

Remember we pursue for justice, not for what makes

others happy,but what makes us whole. We pursue home !

And then he felt it. That feeling Christian had been chasing while improperly diagnosed bipolar, while being lonely since his prepubescent years, while needing approval in high school, and while disappointing his parents. Now he felt a surge of true freedom in this song. This being who he had never before met, decided to save him. He had never felt that salvation was possible, that salvation was like... home.

***

"Christian, wake up!"

"What?"

"Wake up!"

He opened his eyes warily and found himself sitting at a table in a brightly sunlit room. Someone had draped a warm blanket over his shoulders, and a steaming cup of hot tea was sitting in front of him.

"Dean Maiden?" He sucked in his breath and looked around him, disoriented. Dean Maiden sat across the table from Christian, her eyes twinkling mischievously on the other side of the bright red flowers in the vase that adorned the center of her table.

"Are you sure you're awake?"

"I could have sworn I was..."

"Where? You could have sworn you were where?" Dean Maiden's voice was light-hearted. Almost teasing. Uncomfortable, Christian took another look around and realized that he was in an apartment. Her apartment?

"Some night you must have had. On a Tuesday." She wrinkled her nose. "On a Tuesday two weeks ago." She emphasized the "two weeks ago." That caught Christian's attention.

"Two weeks ago? What do you mean? I don't know what you're talking about." Dean Maiden lifted her tea cup as if to drink.

"You don't, don't you?"

"No, ma'am. I don't." She set her tea cup down and gave Christian another flirtatious look.

"Ma'am? Seriously? After all we've been through?" There she was. Teasing again.

"Well, then I know something you don't know," Dean Maiden whispered in a sing-song voice. Christian shrugged the blanket off. That look she gave him made him a little too warm.

"What happened two weeks ago?" he offered, honestly miffed at his surroundings and the nature of his interrogation. He had only ever been alone in the same room as Dean Maiden in an academic setting on the second floor of the university administration building. This setting, however, was uncomfortable.

"You went missing the last week of November." There, she did that seductive thing again, but this time she was stirring her tea with her forefinger. Slowly.

"What? What day is it?"

"December 12th." Christian's heart almost stopped. Dean Maiden stopped stirring in response and looked him straight in the eyes. "Last time anyone saw you was entering the Pithon merry mount. A friend of yours. She said she saw you walk in." Christian's heart was beating a mile a minute. Could this be true?

"Gone? For that long? This isn't good. Where do people think I've been?" He looked around the room as if expecting his parents to appear in the doorway.

"But that's not what's odd." Dean Maiden's voice changed. Just a little bit.

"How can anything be odder than that?" Christian squinted from the sunlight bouncing off the fresh snow outside her glass sliding door and reflecting through the window over Dean Maiden's left shoulder into his eyes.

"Oh, after that, it looks like you disappeared. And you did. But then you didn't." She said "but then you didn't" almost accusingly.

"What?"

"Someone has been fooling your teachers and parents into thinking that he is you. Attending your classes. Having dinners with your parents. Though your dorm room shows no evidence of your living there, we have located your phone signal at times. No where around here."

"What? That's strange" He saw the flinch in her lower lip before he heard her words.

"It's neither. It's fraud." Christian saw now that her demeanor had changed. As if she had taken his disappearance personally. It lay in Dean Maiden's power to kick him out of school. He needed to play this safe. But then how do you play "it" safe when you don't know what "it" is?

"Now I'm going to assume that you weren't murdered because you're... well, here. I'm also going to assume that you weren't kidnapped because you seem to be in OK shape. But I am going to assume that you planned this." She paused, but Christian didn't say anything because he didn't think she was finished.

"But I could be wrong. You do have a history of uncanny

behavior given your illness. But you've suffered too much to stoop to planning deceptive plots. So unless you want the school to assume you defrauded them, let's work on an alibi for you."

"Why are you helping me?" Christian asked suspiciously.

"You really want to know?" he could tell it was a rhetorical question because she continued without waiting for his answer.

"You've been off your meds. Didn't think you needed them. Got to holing yourself in your room studying like a madman for quizzes, tests, hell, even for finals coming up next week. Got to feeding on Doritos and Doseqi's in your dorm fridge, no sleep, godlike ambition. Then you snapped. Snapped and took a walk. God knows where you were all that time. Patronizing the sketchier sides of Potential Street or shacking up with that whore from the bar. But then you wandered, getting lost in the woods near Parthenon. Maybe you were no farther away than the small woods nearby. Your father didn't know about your absence or appear to have any opinion of it when he found out, but I'm sure your mother noticed. Mothers always know when their babies are gone." Her last words agitated Christian and he interrupted her.

"People keep thinking it's me, but it's really my mother who hasn't been herself for a long time. Maybe once my mother would have shaken the foundations of heaven to find me." Dean Maiden almost looked regretful for a moment.

"I'm sorry to hear that, Christian. It's hard to be a woman. My father was like yours."

"My father's will is her command," Christian continued.

" So believe me when I say they weren't looking for me half as hard as parents would if they were looking for me at all." Dean Maiden absorbed Christian's words quietly.

"Like yours, my father was the kind who would disown his child because of perceived disappointment."

"Or who would make his child build a wall only to find the wall trapped the very thing the child loved most," Christian said bitterly. Dean Maiden arched her eyebrows.

"That last thing you said, Christian. That's exactly what another student told me his dad did."

"Seriously?" Christian was interested.

"Yes. He's in Pithon. He's been through some rough times. He's a bit psychopathic because of it." Then Dean Maiden caught herself. "I shouldn't have said that. Student confidentiality and all." She perked up as if she was now entering Dean Maiden mode again.

"Ok, so, I've spoken to you for a few minutes. You seem of sound mind even though you've been off your meds now for two weeks. If I were you, I'd rush to your room, take them, and tell the 'friend' who has been covering for you that he can stop now. You can only cheat the rules for so long before you've gone too far. And you're skirting the edge."

"Thank you, Dean Maiden."

"Of course." It was then that Christian felt the urge to use the restroom.

I haven't pissed in two weeks or since the last time I remember? He thought to himself.

"Just shy of two weeks by three days," Dean Maiden responded then she caught herself and stiffened. "Yes, you may use the bathroom," then she caught herself again, averting his eyes.

230

"Down the hall to the right."

***

Christian got up from the table and all but rushed to the bathroom, mulling over Dean Maiden's comment, Just shy of two weeks by three days. That was just 11 days. Why didn't she just say eleven days?

Not only was Christian's bladder as tight as a new pigskin on game day, but his legs, which he hadn't recalled using in the last two weeks shy of three days… he had a difficult time moving on command. So he hobbled as best he could down the hallway toward the direction of the bathroom.

When Christian reached the end of the hall, he saw only an open door leading downstairs, provocatively ajar. Puzzled, but panicked by the possibility of wetting himself in Dean Maiden's house which meant in front of Dean Maiden, he entered the door. As he closed it behind him, he felt pulled down the dark pathway of the stairs almost magnetically towards a lit area. Shit. It was fire. Hold on. And lava.

That bitch… he muttered.

Suddenly, he heard the combined sound of grunting and the metallic hum of some machine down the corridor. Probably a central heating unit, he thought. By this time, he wasn't sure if his urge to piss himself left or if I had already wet himself, but curiosity drew him down the corridor. As he moved toward the loud sounds, Christian felt a strong nostalgia. He had been here before.

You have, said a voice behind him. Christian jumped and swiveled on his right heel. He couldn't see anything.

"Where is this?"

You breathing? You feet not on fire? You no worry?

"Who are you? What's your name?"

You say name first.

"You work for Dean Maiden?" Christian was panicked. Was he talking to a ghost?

Pretty lady.

"You know her? This is her basement, isn't it?"

You breathing. Tell me name. Though Christian found it unnerving, speaking to a disembodied being, maybe bargaining would work. This being, after all, didn't want to be seen.

"First, step from the shadows. Into the light where I can see you."

It did. Well, they did.

A gigantic, looming figure shifted into the light so large that Christian's eyes couldn't take it in completely. All at once, he noticed three pairs of gray eyes staring at him across a twelve-foot spectrum. Six eyes meant three heads. That's when he realized that he was standing face to face with Cerberus, Guardian of the Underworld. Christian's urge to piss himself came back.

"I know your name though I don't want to say it…"

Say it, they said in unison.

"Cerberus. Guardian of Hades."

At the mention of his name, a loud howling from what seemed like a thousand voices rose in such a tenor that it made the hair stand up on the back of his neck. And he peed a little. Cerberus seemed satisfied. And as if in exchange, Cerberus's former clipped speech became both eloquent and conversational.

I am Cerberus. But Hades is here no longer. He is about

to be disposed of and decided not to put up a fight. We call this place Tartarus now. And we are under new management.

"Persephone?" Christian asked.

You know your stories.

"I know more than I used to."

Then you know where you are then.

"I mean, I wasn't shown everything. All at once."

Tartarus seems pleased with you. Unless you are an Orpheus giving it a second try, you must be a Furie. The first male Furie in a long time.

"I am. I am Osiris."

That name has no power here. This is a place the children of Atum don't believe in until they witness it. An Egyptian God reborn to a Furie heritage? Fascinating. I can smell from your piss that you are a great Warrior with useful power sets.

"Useful?"

You reek of many of the gods. They always saw in the potential of a novice a great opportunity for manipulation. You've been asked several times to choose a side. Haven't you?

"What? You mean psychosis or deity? I chose both."

Both? How is that possible? That would cost you your sanity. Christian lowered his voice.

"Sanity? Maybe. But it has certainly almost cost me my soul."

At the mention of the word "soul" the quiet storm of the monstrous, three-headed dog began to grow excited..

Furies, when young, are often indecisive. Nature gives them years to normalize like other children. But Nature also makes them a powder keg as they mature. Furies are obsessed with justice and its pursuit. They will hunt evil with all they have. If I make you piss yourself, then try getting between a Furie and its prey. Wait just a while, my new friend, and you will know what I mean. For a few seconds, Christian forgot the terror of being in the presence of a frightening entity and almost felt a respectful devotion as to a mentor.

"You're unlike the stories that have described you."

Perceptive, aren't we? I have been alive since the beginning and have witnessed the punishments of the slain.

"Are all punishments alike?"

Oblivion is the fate of those whose hearts are heavier than the feather. The fate of one Furie alone, for now.

"You're talking about my grandmother. Sophie."

She was taught by the Queen Three themselves: Megara, Tisiphone, and Alecto. Their best student. They raised her right. Too right. Furies always defy the gods. They don't mix. Gods never take justice as seriously as Furies do.

"So I've heard."

Sophie had a rebellious streak and didn't know her place before Anubis. She chose pursuit over obedience. The pursuit of a man who sinned yet was fated to save many lives. Sophie couldn't let him go. And, thus, our situation. You look like her. I smell that you've met Voida. Haven't you?

"She came to me."

The mother of all Furies. If she came to you, then perhaps all is not lost for Sophie. But I'm afraid your time has run out.

"Excuse me?"

I let you in. I thought you were a dead soul. Either way, once you enter here I cannot let you leave. My base programming is all-consuming and obeys divine orders. You

234

must stay. It paused. Or be flushed.

"I didn't ask to come down here. I wasn't looking for this place, and I am not dead," Christian argued. Shouldn't I get a pass?"

With the Queen gone for now and unable to vouch for you, my hands are tied. Rules are rules. I love one thing more than conversation, and that's new prisoner intake.

"I see that the odds are against me. Only Hercules has ever defeated you."

That is not true. You may run. I'm sure you will want...

And before Cerberus could finish his sentence, Christian ran. He ran for what seemed like hours but might only have been less than ten seconds. As he ran, he saw vignettes of the Underworld. Sisyphus carrying his boulder of infinite failure. Tantalus stuck between thirst and hunger. Ixion rotated like rotisserie chicken on a wheel of damnation. The Daughters of Danaus, who carried fifty jugs of water to wash away their sins, in a bath that cracked at the pouring of the last drop. A gray forest in which was a beautiful garden with a Reaper calling out to him with a crown on which was emblazoned "Crown Us."

He heard the sounds of those who were getting their just desserts in the Underworld. But then he heard those who had been enduring long past what was fair. The enslaved, the captives, those who simply weren't famous enough to break their chains. Those who did not deserve to be.

My allies against the Olympians.

Christian became consumed by this thought and grew wings of green and a surge of such strength that he reversed his trajectory and flew back towards Cerberus who wasn't certain how to respond and froze while Christian like a green phoenix maneuvered high above him and then dove down behind him until he came to a spike. Christian could see that the spike held a chain that ran into a deep darkness.

A light went off inside Christian, and it was then that he remembered them... their stories he heard as a child but that were real all the same: Helios, Thetis, Perses, Leto, Zealous, Styx, Pallas, and others. How their freedom would thwart the plans of the Olympians, he did not yet know. But just as his grandmother Sophie, his Furie pursuit of justice over obedience would initiate a series of monumental consequences that would make him that much more a target in the eyes of the vengeful Greeks.

So he removed the spike.

That little motion, that little twist of the wrist, that little rebellion immediately created a violent upsurge as if all the water in the world were draining in reverse. Christian was surrounded by thousands of swiftly moving bodies, heads upturned as it were, swimming to the surface for that lifegiving gulp of air. It was all Christian could do to keep himself from being carried away with them. Christian held on to the spike with all his Furie strength as it fought to burrow itself back in its hole. So he held on.

The Rapture of souls lasted a good eight minutes and then Christian's deed was done. His mission was complete. His pursuit was ended. In what felt like a melting, he returned to mortal form once more and found himself in Dean Maiden's basement, the howling Cerberus looming over him.

What did you do? Cerberus howled.

But then a woman appeared.

"Dean Maiden?" Christian asked embarrassed. But it wasn't her. The figure stepped into the light and up to

Christian, eye to eye.

"I had given up hope for them. For doing this, I will help you against Cerberus." It was Eurydice.

Noooo, Cerberus howled behind her.

"You can make me as strong as Hercules?" Christian half joked.

"No, as strong as Orpheus. Stronger. Take this. It is the lyre that Orpheus dropped."

Christian took the lyre from Euridice.

"Remember the pain of those you just freed. Listen to the regret above and below. They are all sorry. Remind them they deserve a fair trial, a jury of their peers, the dignity of humanity."

One of Christian's fingers struck a string. Cerberus stopped howling. The lyre wasn't just an instrument. It was a weapon.

"Christian, think of a song so beautiful…"

So Christian searched his mind. He searched his heart. And then a melody filled his soul. He strummed an F: F for Furies. No, they deserved more than that for saving his ass. F sharp.

And so Christian sang.

"Hail to the Popular

Hail to the popular
Hail to the glean
Hail to the royalty
This one's for everything

Hail to the popular
Hail to what's before

237

Hail to the ones that aren't thought of anymore

I was so popular
Beloved like a Queen
Ripe for the taking
Coming apart at chosen seams

Hail to the popular
To songs they used to sing
In palaces, in halls, and acropolis springs

Because you won't let me die
Because you won't let the past lie
Because you must pursue where no one prys
Because you deny we all deserve just one more try

Because you won't let me die
Because you won't let the past lie
Because you just eat our cries
Because you deny we all deserve just one more try

So if you are unpopular
Remember this one thing
Shadows once were fed and trampled
now light as the songs we sing

So Hail to the Popular
Hail to effort even more
The damnation is the end of voice, we deplore

Hail to the popular
Hail to our place in lore

We are sorry to ever doubt that someone else was keeping score

Christian, singing the song lustily at first, got quieter with each quatrain. On the last stanza, he tiptoed past Cerberus, which, one of his heads wept, lost in some ancient grief, the other two lay silent in a deep daze.

I have to come back, Christian thought as he reached the basement steps. Enough is enough. Look to your fellow man and ask yourself, 'Should someone be in hell forever simply for believing in the wrong thing? Jails reform, nations forgive. Why can't the gods?'

Just as Christian reached the top of the steps, he heard Cerberus say one last thing.

Whispers of hidden agenda in covert plan. Waiters change world balance if not stopped. You, friend god, who changed Hades for one time must stop them for good. Christian turned.

"I'll be vigilant," he said as he opened the basement door.

Just as he was about to shut it, he felt a hand on his shoulder.

"You get lost?" Dean Maiden was standing there with concern (or maybe curiosity) in her voice.

"I got turned around. Was I gone long?"

"Long enough. Where were you? The bathroom's right here."

And there it was. To the left as plain as day. But for some reason, Christian didn't need to use the bathroom anymore and dismissed himself from Dean Maiden's.

As he started down the street, Dean Maiden ran up behind him.

"Are you ok, Christian?"

"What do you mean?"
"Campus is the other way."

***

Chapter 1

Gamerinn or Gods

Meanwhile Tess was on the opposite side of Parthenon where, attempting to enter the Duat, she was refused and diverted to Sophie's bedroom. Already pissed at Christian's absence in two critical scenarios, she wasn't in the best of moods when she suddenly appeared at Sophie's bedside.

"I was expecting many things today, but not such a sight as you." Sophie was sitting up in her bed. Tess whirled around. And stared.

"Sophie?" she asked. "You look like him. Well, I should say that he looks like you," Tess said matter-of-factly with an edge to her voice.

"I would hope so. I'm his… oh, nevermind." Sophie closed her diary with a mischievous grin.

"What's wrong? You don't look so… friendly," Sophie finally decided. Tess relaxed but her voice took on a cautious tone.

"Christian… I don't know. Something's not right with him. He's not focused, and he doesn't seem to take this, this onslaught seriously. He stood me up, and I almost lost my life on account of him. And he stood me up again. And, he, he's… Osiris or not, I don't think he's up to it." Tess plopped herself on the edge of Sophie's bed in frustration.

"I'm sorry. I shouldn't be saying this to you in light of… of what may come next for you."

"You're a bright one. So you know?" Sophie smiled.

"I do. Death☒given that there are gods☒is rarely restful. And just so that you know, I think it is unfair."

"Ah," Sophie mused. "So many gods just won't let shit go… even after all my time on the proverbial treadmill like I'm stuck in the Book of Psalms." Sophie raised a small book for Tess to see. "At least I have my kiddush to read☒ my mother and father taught me. At least I'm not alone."

"You're not alone. Now that I'm here, I'll stay until…" Tess started.

"But you didn't mean to come. Not here anyway. You had other plans," Sophie winked an eye at Tess knowingly.

"Thank you. But if I'm the one dying today, why do I sense that you're the one afraid of Fate? Do you plan to die any time soon?"

"Well, with your grandson at the helm, I just might beat you to the Underworld." Tess's frustration bubbled up. "And I'm the one who feels guilty about it? Why?" Sophie rubbed Tess's shoulder.

"There now, I sense that. And while it's admirable that you feel so responsible, it isn't your job to defeat the Olympians."

"Actually, that is my job," Tess shot back.

"I see," Sophie said decidedly. "Well, I'm just an old wanderer, but I believe that if one bad person does one good thing as a final act, then that person deserves to be remembered. Redemption."

"What does that have to do with my situation?" Sophie sat back against her pillow.

"Do you know the story of Set?" Tess perked up.

"Of course, I do. He's my father. He murdered his brother, took his brother's wife, and basically ruined the world."

"Yes, he's got a long dark corridor to walk through when it's his time to be judged, that's for sure. But this same god was once a noble warrior, a caretaker of the great god Ra, who battles the Chaos monster Apophis day and night, stopping him from devouring the world. Set was unlike his brother Osiris who appreciated the attention of many women. Set wasn't handsome, yet he was ever loyal to his bride Nephthys."

"What's the catch here?" Tess asked suspiciously.

"Well, where some get it wrong is that Set didn't just live in the desert as if he were banished to it. He was all that kept the evil there at bay. If you ask me, he overcame a lot to be trusted with the highest of duties to fight evil⊠ without gratitude, I may add⊠while Osiris received all the adoration and credit. So you see, even he⊠wherever he is now⊠has a redemption song to sing."

A light turned on in Tess's head, and she stared at Sophie incredulously.

"Are you saying…" she began. Sophie cut in.

"No matter what Set did, Osiris himself would tell you that Set is the god you want on your side when there's a battle like the one you're up against. To remove blood from the equation, you need to spill it. No one knows that better than Set."

"Spoken like a true Furie," Tess affirmed. "But are you saying…" she started again.

"And while we Furies talk of blood until we are bloated with it, we still pursue Set for his fratricide. You need to redeem him. You need to find a way to stop us from haunting him and by helping the brother he hurt. That's your

243

duty. And that's my dying wish."

Tess tried again.

"Are you saying that I've been going about this all wrong? You want me to kill those sons of bitches, don't you, because Christian doesn't have the stomach to do it himself?"

"Help him is all I'm asking," Sophie said quietly. Tess sat with her mouth open.

"If you don't, I'm more afraid for the world I will leave behind than for whatever world I will be sentenced to."

"Isn't that a gamble? A shot in the dark?" Tess asked. Sophie lifted her hand and motioned for her to relax.

"Not if you play your part. I'm a person of faith. Redeem Set." Sophie coughed.

"But what if you are being deceived? Osiris had faith, too. Then my father put him in a box." Sophie lifted her hand to motion that she was slowing down.

"Not blind faith. Experience." Tess squinted at Sophie.

"You won't say goodbye to Christian, will you?"

"If he sees me go into Ammit, he'll lose what we Furies call agape, the love from beyond. If he sees me go into oblivion, he would give up and it would be two of us who die. As you said, he's already distracted."

"But if you could inspire someone else☒someone other than Christian☒to do a great good, then maybe that would tip the scales enough in your favor?" Tess suggested.

"Who said that?"

"It's just a hunch," Tess said innocently.

Sophie's voice dropped a decibel.

"You're a child of darkness, of blood-red rage, and fear. It's this same energy that inspires usurpation, fascism, and domination. Yet, still, you believe in using those qualities for good. So you see, there is a chance for this world. So

244

go ahead and do a good deed. Prove that the apple can fall far from the tree, but not so far that it cannot redeem its parent. You have everything to gain and only me to lose, young Tess. Do it."

Suddenly, an avalanche of emotion poured out of Tess at Sophie's words as if her heart would irrevocably break. She howled like an inconsolable two-year-old. Sophie, weaker, held her and rocked her until her sobs subsided into sniffles. Sophie murmured little comforts to her until early evening when Sophie's transfiguration began to take full effect.

"It's happening," Sophie whispered from the bed. Sophie's body took on a warm glow.

"Sophie," Tess cried out. Then there was a flash of light. Sophie's body faded into wisps of shadow. Sophie was gone.

Tess took a moment of silence in the room, sitting on Sophie's bed. Strangely, a calm came over her… for Sophie had given her permission. Permission to be the daughter of Set.

***

In order not to further arouse the suspicion of Dean Maiden, Christian rerouted himself campusward. But once out of sight, he double backed, maneuvering three alleyways until he ended up at the intersection of Potential Street where the portal to the Duat was. It had been a while days since Christian was last in contact with Wep, actually two weeks shy of one day if Dean Maiden was right about his absence for Christian had yet to consult a calendar or watch. All he knew was that Tess had been angry with him the night of Dité's initiation. What was she to think now?

Wep, his assigned Guardian, must be beside himself.

Christian looked both ways before crossing the street and entered the Duat as casually as if he were taking a stroll. Once inside, he headed for Wep's lair but stopped shy of entering it. He heard several voices in conversation. Peeking into the room, he noticed Wep at a round table with several different beings standing around it. All had some unique quality that made each human. One looked like a wolf, another was composed of flames, and yet another was made of frost. The last was a giant bird that reminded Christian of happier times when he was younger. Wep was clearly in charge.

"So again, no sign of him?" Wep addressed the great bird who shifted from one foot to the other and flapped its wings.

"I've seen him," it said in a raspy voice like a smoker's lung.

"Where?" Wep implored.

"He's behind you," chirped the great bird. Wep turned around so fast that Christian wasn't able to retreat from the doorway fast enough. As good-natured and unperturbed as Wep, Christian could see that he took great pains to keep his emotions composed. But by doing so, he showed Christian his hand. He was disappointed.

"So Osiris is back from the dead once again." It was more of an insult than a statement.

"So you're back," Wep repeated. "But back from where is what I'd like to know." By this time, the various creatures had formed a semi-circle around Christian, studying him curiously.

"Osiris you say?" Flame asked Wep. "But he's merely a boy."

"Irresponsible, too," observed the wolf creature with the languid eyes that circled Christian slowly, sniffing him. "And he's pissed himself."

"Did you say he's been gone for a fortnight?" Cackled the bird. "Doing what I'd like to know." Wep's game face had taken on a combination of worried eyebrows and receding lips so that he bared his fangs.

"They think you owe us an explanation," Wep scoffed. "So why don't you humor us and give us an account of your activities. You had one thing to do, but pray tell what feats The Young Lord Osiris, nay, the naive Lord Osiris has accomplished this last half a moon."

Christian fidgeted.

"Look, I can account for two of those days. I don't remember the others…" At this, Wep reared back his arm and smashed the table into splinters, scattering the creatures in his company.

"Oh, I can guess why you can't remember. You were probably using your newly-discovered powers bedding the women of Pithon, our sworn enemy or, at the least drinking their poisonous elixirs. More like Odysseus than Osiris." While Wep had both the size and strength advantages, Christian's green eyes turned into serpentine slits and almost involuntarily he began to swell in size, taking on a scaly, green skin.

"Take. That. Back." Wep's eyes widened.

"Take what back? The time you stole from us?" he challenged. But that didn't help. Somewhere deep inside him, Wep hit a nerve.

"That comment. About me being Odysseus." Christian was visibly shaking large wings out of his back, and his hands grew into talons three times their normal size.

247

"Do I look like Odysseus now?" Christian shouted. But Wep wouldn't back down.

"So now the Furie in you is awakened? And you would dare threaten me? A friend? The one sworn to protect you since the foundations of earth were formed? You can cavort and party with those wicked Olympians who have sworn to erase you, your family line, your future seed, and every memory from the face of the earth, and that doesn't trigger the ire you've reserved for me? What kind of a fucking god are you?" Wep was breathing hard, glaring at Osiris.

And just as quickly as Christian had transformed, he deflated to his former self, clearly frightened at his unintended transfiguration.

"Well, no thanks to you. You basically sacrificed me. Left me to the Olympians while you played that shitty jazz set. I've had to improvise and figure things out on my own. I nearly lost my soul."

This time Wep fidgeted.

"Did you even put up a fight?" he growled. "Or did you pander to their bougie facade of being snotty-nosed trust fund babies?"

"Perhaps, you would have put up a fight. You're a god. But I'm just a college kid who suffers from psychosis, remember? I don't have your resume. I haven't been doing this for centuries."

"Centuries my ass," Wep retorted.

"Should we go?" the great bird interrupted. Wep refocused on the group of beings.

"Yes. I mean thank you. I won't be requiring your services anymore." And within seconds, all were gone. Only Wep and Christian remained. The awkwardness between them filled the air.

"So you were looking for me?" It was half question and half statement. Christian was fishing for any amount of sympathy Wep was willing to conjure.

"Yes. And Tess was worried," Wep said, agitation still in his voice. "We figured you just walked away."

"Is that so?" Christian tried to suppress a surge of anger. "You know, these past two months have flown by like a few hours. I've experienced a number of strange things⊠mind-fucks. But nothing is stranger than what was obviously your plan for little me. You brought me into this conflict, and then sent me off to do what you⊠a fucking Egyptian god⊠couldn't even do in six thousand years. And if I die, then great, I suppose. At least that would prove that you weren't being a coward in exercising all of your options. Mission accomplished." Christian was shaking like he did when he went a day or two without his medication. But he wasn't done yet.

"But you've got to believe that I didn't just disappear on you. Something happened to me, and I'm not even sure what." There was discouragement and forgiveness in Christian's tone.

"Tess," Wep started. "We've been tracking the Olympians' movements, protecting anyone who has a birthday. It's only two of us⊠which is somewhat a reliable team⊠and we've been effective so far. We could use you. We think that this Virtues Constellation is a spell that requires a person from each astrological sign. Each obelisk represents a sign and..." All of a sudden, Christian perked up.

"I've read somewhere that the Olympians can use mortals, usually those descended from a deity, or actual gods. Perhaps, under the guise of "good, clean fun" these merry mounts have been hiding their true purpose as quarters

249

for these powerful obelisks for decades, each representing a Zodiac sign's highest power in the solar system. And if they tie someone to an obelisk this month, on their birthday, the day in which they are most empowered by their Zodiac sign, the Olympians can conjure a megaspell to bring fabled and much feared Olympus back and its nightmare of a new world order. Permanently."

Wep paused, incredulity etched in his eyes.

"I think you're right. Will you help us?" Now Chrisitian had the leverage of negotiation.

"I will, but with a plan of my own. I think it's better that way. I can't pay attention to the person I'm supposed to become with you or anyone else in my ears all day."

"What about Tess?" Wep asked.

"What about her?" Christian retorted. "I'm sure that if she wants to find me, she will. But she can't be ordering me around like she has. So let her know that if you see her before I do."

Wep nodded his head in agreement and Christian turned to leave. But before he reached the door, he paused and turned around to say one last thing to Wep.

"Thanks for attending my classes and being 'me' these last two weeks. I know it was you. You're a really good friend." Then Christian turned and headed out the door without further explanation of what his plans were. And this time he wasn't sorry. He had to hurt Wep to establish his own boundaries. Otherwise, Wep would walk all over him in his signature carefree way. This was the only way that Wep would see beyond his own ambitions, whatever they were. And Christian wasn't going to feel bad about that. After all, Wep had almost pushed him to a point of no return.

And even though Christian knew that it was his fault for taking the drink at Dité's initiation, such an admission was better left for total reconciliation, not the first hit. Because there were many more hits to come.

***

When Christian left the Duat, he didn't know what his next move would be until he appeared on Potential Street. It was early afternoon, and Christian's belly growled, reminding him that he hadn't eaten since he didn't know when. Having been absent from his own merry mount for the last month, he decided to go to Liger, make an appearance, and during lunch mull over what his options were.

When Christian arrived at Liger, he was surprised to see that the cafeteria was empty, minus Will, Duel, Sysy, Brisin, and Zalewski who were sitting at a booth in the corner having beers and sharing a birthday cake. It was Thursday.

"Well, look at that... it's Christian... back in his natural habitat." Duel, who was puffing on a cigar, greeted Christian with a grin and nervously adjusted his glasses. CHANGE NAMES (WILL, ELLIOT IS DUEL, TOSH IS BRISIN, ETC. FROM THE FIRST TIME THEY ARE MENTIONED)

"How was the Pithon initiation? Still recovering?" Brisin teased. "Haven't seen you around here in a bit. Or maybe it was you? Who knows?"

"If we didn't miss you so much, we'd call you a traitor, traitor," Sysy quipped.

"Ha, that outfit you were wearing early this week assured me that you didn't join Pithon. You looked like a tourist from one of those 1980Ss brochures for a small European

251

country. And not in an endearing vintage way." Will guffawed and they all laughed.

"Ok, we're done," Zalewski said affectionately. "Come
drink with us like old times. You passed our cold shoulder
test. Enjoy some beautiful cake." Zalewski cut a slice for
Christian and Brisin rolled her eyes.

"That's all he's been talking about: cake and where the
hell the real Christian Belvedere is." Christian, who hadn't
a moment to get a word in edgewise, took the comments
in jest and grabbed a free chair from a table nearby. Liger
was eerily quiet.

"So where have you been, Christian?" Sysy quipped.
"You haven't been yourself lately." Christian could see by
looking at the others that there was ample eye diversion
happening.

"What do you mean?" He asked, playing the question
off as if he were confused. "I've been hitting the books and
going to classes." Duel started to change the subject but
Sysy jumped back in.

"About that," she started, sneaking a glimpse at Zalewski
who was concentrating on the beer in front of him and
waving away Duel's cigar smoke that he was furiously
pumping out.

"Since when do you play saxophone?" Christian inwardly groaned wishing that the question was a rhetorical one
but realizing that it wasn't. What the hell did Wep do while
he was me? Christian wondered. It must have been bad.

"Oh, that? That's a new thing I've picked up." He smiled
at Sysy self-consciously.

"Oh, I'm sure it's a new thing you've picked up. Sounds
like it. You know, you could do with more practice before
you start giving impromptu concerts during Econ." Brisin

252

snickered. Christian wasn't sure how to proceed. Zalewski, sensing the mounting tension, cut in.

"Christian, you know, you can tell us anything, right?" Christian shrugged off Zalewski's question, sensing that he was being funneled into an intervention.

"Did I do something to offend you or anybody here?" Christian offered.

"We're just concerned that you've been exhibiting some... well, strange behavior lately... and we wanted to know if everything was OK. In light of what happened last summer and all."

Oh, so that was what this is about. Well, it's better to play the part then, Christian internally agreed.

"Well, now that you mention it, I haven't been well. I've been stressed over things. Things at home." The others at the table nodded in unison which encouraged Christian to confess more. "I'm also concerned about some friends. I think they might be in trouble. But I can't say for sure. And then there's graduation. I've got a lot of work to make up..." he trailed off, hoping that one or all of these excuses might stick. Sysy began to answer, but then Zalewski raised his hand to stop her.

"Christian, you're our friend, and your troubles... or secrets... will stay with us. Just know you can trust us. Now," Zalewski stood up, raising his beer, "We've got much to be grateful for. We've got Christian back, it's almost the weekend, and we've got all this cake to eat."

At the mention of all this gratefulness, Christian was relieved at first but then felt ill at ease when he turned his attention to his piece of cake. He glanced around the cafeteria which was still empty minus his posse of friends and a server behind the counter.

253

"Whose birthday is it?" He looked around at the group as each began eating.

Brisin smiled conspiratorially.

"Well, if you bring in a cake on a Thursday but don't put a 'Happy Birthday' on it, people get suspicious." Christian stared blankly at her.

"Everyday is someone's birthday," Brisin teased. The hair crept up Christian's neck and he dropped his fork.

"Where is everyone?" Duel stole a glance at Zalewski as if to say, Here he goes again. Our friend isn't well. Zalewski, aware of Christian's total change, tried to allay his concern.

"Before you came here, there was a full lunch room. You just missed the lunch traffic."

Christian fidgeted with his fork and nodded his head in the direction of the lunch counter.

"Who's that?" The group looked over at the counter.

"What do you mean," Sysy scorned. "That's Chef Udunn." Christian squinted.

"Are you sure?" Duel was unnerved at Christian's behavior.

"You haven't touched your slice, Christian." Duel finished his piece. "Did you know that there's quite a bit of salt in cake? Helps the flavor, but also seals the bond between those who eat it. It's why Berserkers went to battle first. They thrived on cake."

"And mead!" Zalewski raised his glass.

"Isn't that beer?" Christian countered, confused.

"Beer, mead, what's the difference. It's a Warrior tradition."

Christian, unsure of whether or not the table talk was an attempt at wordplay to distract him from the awkwardness his friends felt toward him, picked up his fork again. But then it dawned on him, the conversation he had with Wep in the Duat about the Olympian tactic of Virtues Constellation which required the sacrifice of twelve Parthenon students on their birthdays. Was it possible that since he had liberated himself from the agendas of well-meaning Wep and Tess that his Osiris intuition had guided him to Liger because Olympians were close by, planning mischief?

"You should have some of the cake, Christian." Sysy interrupted Christian's thoughts. "You're going to offend Brisin. Have a piece."

Christian stared at the uneaten slice before him. He was sure that it was much more than cake he was being offered, despite the ruse of Brisin's birthday, so he decided to change tactics. He decided to tell the truth.

"Look, guys. When I say that I haven't been well... that's, well, that's code for a lot of things have happened this last month and I've not had time or maybe even the courage to share with you." They were listening.

"I think something wrong is happening at Pithon. I've seen visions, if you will, that Parthenon is in danger. The school, yes, but then the... the world." Christian looked at the group to see how they were taking this.

Then Duel cleared his throat.

"Well, just so that we're being honest here, where have you been these past two weeks? Were you just keeping it low-key or have you been trying to bicker Pithon because of your new friends?" Christian could tell they weren't buying it.

"Look, no one in Pithon is my friend. Well, yes, I know Dité but that's over. And, yeah, there are a few people I've met, but they aren't students... I mean, they're much more than students. They're dangerous." Christian paused a few seconds before he let it all out. "They're gods." No response. This was a hard crowd. Sysy put her arm around Christian's neck, but her touch was cold.

"Well, you've grown bolder in your tongue these last two weeks," Zalewski said seriously. "In the Old Country, that sort of talk would be dangerous. You could lose a limb or be labeled a warlock."

Silence.

Then laughter.

"Ok, now you've earned our keg and our loyalty. That's a good one," Zalewski swapped Christian's beer for his pitcher of ale.

Christian wasn't sure if it meant that they believed him or didn't care, but for once in the last several weeks he felt relieved. He felt he had nothing to hide.

Christian stood up and raised Zalewski's pitcher. It sloshed over the side and everyone laughed. So did Christian.

"To great friends," he began. "And to Brisin. Happy Birthday." And he chugged the entire pitcher to the cheers of all at the table.

"Then it's settled. Eat your cake." Sysy ordered. And Christian, forgetting how famished he had been, ate not only the piece of cake before him. He ate two other pieces. He was so focused on the third slice that he didn't realize the table had fallen silent.

"And all this time, I thought something was stirring in Pithon." Sysy looked Christian in the eye with a suspicious glare. But Christian protested.

"No. No. No. All of that's true. Something is happening in Pithon and it's not good. I am in need of a stronger, bolder strategy, but that means food first."

"Then you've come to the right place, the right people, and the right time." Brisin approved. Everyone but Sysy seconded Brisin's motion.

"Well, enough chatter," Zalewski ordered. "Let's hammer this afternoon home with some beer pong! A toast to..." but he didn't have time to finish.

***

A commotion outside the room began as a scuffle then crescendoed into mayhem when someone barged through the cafeteria door, headed straight for the table where the birthday party was happening, skidding on his knees, knocking over tables and chairs in the process, and half landing in Christian's lap. It was Aussie. Christian jumped up, but Aussie held onto his legs, preventing him from getting out of the booth.

"Help me, please!" Aussie grabbed both of Christians hands, now that Christian sat back down, and he held on for dear life. The friends were each looking at Christian, dumbfounded.

"Aussie, chill out. What's wrong?" Now Aussie was crying. Like a toddler.

"I'm an asshole is what's wrong, I know," he bellowed. Then he lowered his voice to a hoarse whisper. "But that doesn't mean I should die, does it?" But then he got loud again.

"Especially not on my birthday!" He wailed so loudly that Christian tried to hush him.

"Come on. You're not making sense." Christian pleaded with him, helping him up to his feet.

"Now tell me what's wrong."

257

"I'm petty," Aussie confessed. "Maybe even vain. But I'm not bad."

"Ok," Christian said, trying to follow his logic.

"The sun shines on the just and the unjust alike, right?"

"I suppose," Christian responded.

"And Osiris is the Sun god, right?" Christian froze. His table was looking at him curiously as he responded.

"I suppose you're right," he nodded.

"So, please, Sun god, help me!" Duel jumped out of the booth, looking at the door where Aussie had burst through.

"Is this one of those Pithon freaks you were talking about? Because if so, there's more. Quick... look!" he warned.

But no sooner had Christian turned his head than Aussie was suddenly ripped from his grasp, sucked out of the cafeteria door, and, by the sound of the emergency alarms going off, completely out of the building through a forbidden exit door.

Instinctively, Christian sprang up and shot out the door in close pursuit with his birthday party friends close behind in succession. But it wasn't until Christian reached the exterior door that he understood Aussie's terror.

***

When Christian reached the exterior door, he didn't have to open it. It was twisted metal, blown from the outside inward and barely hanging on by the middle hinge. It was probably Aussie's poor body that did that when he was pulled in and out of the corridor of Liger.

But what Christian and the others hadn't anticipated was what they would see outside the door. For where a parking lot had once been, there now was a scene that Christian could only describe as a scene straight out of Dante's Inferno.

Just on the other side of the door threshold, the ground dropped into a bottomless cavern that made Christian's stomach lurch. Where there was once a parking lot, Christian now witnessed what he could only describe as a scene right out of a war movie. For as far as the eye could see, Christian saw only darkness backlit by fires that traversed the landscape, sometimes erupting with earth-shuddering pulsations. A hot, dry wind howled across this scene, sending flickering ash and smoke every which way so that it was difficult to see clearly for more than a few yards. But once the air cleared for a few seconds, Christian saw them.

Nine hysterical Greek gods had arranged themselves in a semi-circle around a central god.

"That's Thanatos," Christian said to no one in particular. He had Aussie: held high up in the air by the neck, kicking his feet like he was on the end of a noose.

"Shit," said Sysy. It was only then that Christian realized that the party had followed him to the door and were seeing what he was seeing. He turned to warn them to stay back but was stunned to see that his friends had transformed into a posse of dynamic super-heroic personalities. Duel was wearing the skull of a wolf on his head and swinging a mace. He nodded at Christian. Sysy answered for all of them.

"We're here for you is enough that needs to be said for now. Explanations can come later. Now, let's to it."

Christian nodded and viewed the scene before him again with Aussie wailing. Though beyond the threshold looked like a chasm, Christian observed that the Greek

259

gods appeared to be standing on solid ground.

The rules are different here as they are on the other side of any threshold, Christian mused to himself. It's best not to overthink the process. So he stepped over the threshold.

Once he did and the others followed, all eyes of the gods went from Aussie to Christian. Thanatos, anticipating an encounter, lowered Aussie with his hand still around Aussie's neck.

"We've been long-awaiting your reintroduction, Osiris." Thanatos sounded like a pretentious thespian affecting an English accent. A thunderous murmuring of the gods in response started a quaking and several volcanic fires burst in response. Thanatos took a few steps forward.

"When I had my first drink, I, too, went on sabbatical. But two weeks? You must really have had quite the transformation. We've had to be very patient with you, and, according to leadership, you're worth it. Besides, what takes its time more than death? Isn't that right, Good Judge?"

The excited murmuring increased.

"Would you like to do the honors?" Christian knew by the tone that Athena was referring to chaining Aussie to the obelisk that was slowly emerging from the ground where the front lawn should have been. It rumbled the ground so thoroughly that several car alarms in their dimension erupted into a cacophony all could hear in this hell of a place. It was the last obelisk that needed to be filled.

A change came over Christian. His eyes turned a deep purple and fangs grew from his mouth, distorting his face into a grimace.

"Sounds good to me!"

Christian walked up to Thanatos with outstretched arms. Understanding his gesture, Thanatos handed the struggling Aussie to him. And with one quick thrust of his arm, Christian threw Aussie against the obelisk.

Thanatos, energized by Christian's swift execution, turned to the Pantheon behind him, who now, their excitement galvanized, were loud and joyous. Not only had Christian been waiting for his arrival as Osiris in full regalia, but they had also been awaiting it. The final piece of Virtues Constellation was complete for the Olympians.

It was then that Christian realized that Pithon's leaders weren't there. No Dité, no Apollo, no Chastity, no Guerro. Not one of them. Only the B-team was there. And they were so confident in Christian's transformation that they did not anticipate what was to come next.

More than the others, Thanatos, drunk off the victory, was laughing heartily and so violently as to be entirely consumed with himself, lurching his head back until it almost touched the ground. What happened next was unexpected by all, even Christian. Swifter than the thought could bubble up in his mind, Christian took advantage of Thanatos' victory laugh, and was on him in a confusing blur of activity. When it was over, Thanatos lay decapitated, his mouth still twisted in a grin. Energized by this first kill, Christian turned at the remaining Pantheon who were blown back away in the direction of the Pithon lawn.

And just as quickly as Christian had transformed into Osiris, he assumed his normal size, his wings receded into his back, and hands diminished in size with talons disappearing into fingernails, and his face was back to normal. Christian looked about him in surprise and then down near his feet where Thanatos's body writhed in a death squirm until finally he lay still and joined the Underworld. The extra-dimension in which Christian confronted the

Pantheon shivered away, and they were in the parking lot once more: just Christian and his party of four.

Zalewski laid a hand on Christian's shoulder which caused Christian to redirect his gaze to the party, each pulsating with the afterglow of their own transformations until each was back to his and her normal self. While the others looked on with pride, Sysy was the only one staring at him with consternation on her face.

"Christian," she said carefully. "Did you just pick up on what happened just now?" Christian, in a daze, looked at Sysy at first not comprehending that she spoke. But then he did.

"These obelisks. They're all connected to me... when I was Osiris." He corrected himself. "When I am Osiris." Sysy nodded.

"Yes, they're vessels of your power," she explained. Christian interrupted.

"However, I can be used against my will to empower the obelisk or, while unattached by a spell, be used to command the obelisk." Christian looked each of his friends in the eyes and then the light dawned on him.

"Shit," he said quietly. "Now that I've killed Thanatos, the Olympians will be coming for me to put me on the obelisk on my birthday. That's a few days away." Despite the outcome of his victorious ordeal, he couldn't help feeling objectified. That the only reason they sought to make him one of them was to command a spell so powerful that it could never be broken. But with Thanatos raging now in the Underworld, they would have to go with plan B. The Blood of Dionysus simply didn't take as they thought it would because the Blood of a Furie is immune to it.

"Christian. Hey, Christian.," Brisin started to say. Christian had been trying to make sense of these details that he was momentarily distracted from his surroundings and didn't notice the glitching happening between the dimension of Parthenon and the scene in which they had confronted the Olympians.

But when his eyes adjusted, he saw what looked like fifty Pithon students through the veil, who had emerged from the direction of Pithon, and they each were looking right at him.

"How is that possible?" Brisin wondered. "They're students."

"Doesn't matter. Oh, they're pissed," Duel murmured, and the friends resumed their Viking forms.

"Maybe this time we'll get some action," Sysy said grimly. "Christian, was a ball hog last time."

Athena began screaming. At first it was indiscernible. But then Christian realized it was the obligatory speech that villains often make about how offended they are and why vengeance would be pursued to the point of bloodshed. If it weren't for fifty of them, Christian would have been amused, but his involuntary transformation to Osiris underscored the severity of the situation they were in.

He took a deep breath. Almost on cue, the Pithonians transformed into looks more befitting Greek gods than league students. They spread across the lawn like a horde of maniacs with Cretan tortures on their minds.

Suddenly, Christian felt a drop of rain and saw that a quick and loud storm was gathering above in the alternate dimension they were staging the battle in. He heard a thunderous cry and lightning struck behind Christian, revealing what he evidently had been led to Liger for. He turned around and saw a fist with a hammer in the air. The cry of a Valkyrie, Jötun's Flame of Fire, the Binds of Fenrir. Pure power of gamesmanship.

Zalewski, Brisin, Sysy, and Duel who had each transformed into their god forms, weren't from the Mediterranean like the Olympians. They were from the cold and bitter North. They were made of fire and ice, of Hamr and Hugr. They were made of Ragnarök. Christian, realizing that he needed these allies, was warmed by this act of their friendship.

The Olympians manifested spears and swords to match them. Aussie, freshly freed from the obelisk, though emotionally traumatized, had crept inside Liger and watched from a window. Despite his fear and buckling knees, however, he couldn't look away. The fight of the gods called to him.

Christian was immediately attacked by Nike and Phobos while each of the friends were beset by two or three Olympians at a time. Meanwhile, students and faculty casually walked in and out of the glitchy bedlam, unaware of the battle they were walking among. The veil was being held strong by the obelisk.

The friends,nVikings gods, knew the power of harmony in battle, so they chanted in unison as beautifully as they fought ferociously.

While Christian, who had never before fought with his Viking party, observed their heroic feats from the corner of his eyes, it was impossible for him to intervene. Phobos and Nike were proving to be hard competitors for him alone. Both Olympians attacked Christian with no reservation that they feared injury. Nike met Christian's chest with her foot, and Phobos struck, approaching from behind, grappling Christian around the neck. Christian could sense an ebb of energy from his group as if victory were slipping away.

While Nike angled to level Christian at the knees, he decided to employ an old trick. He sprung into the air about forty feet or so, paused at the top, suspended momentarily as if he were able to fly. Catching him by surprise, Christian appeared in front of Phobos, to his side, behind him, as well as above him in an illusory way as if he were all places at once.

Confused, Phobus struck out indiscriminately, missing Christian every which way which gave Christian enough time and power to crush Phobus with a collisional force that took the disoriented Greek out of the fight once and for all.

Out of the corner of his eye, Christian saw Nike head inside Liger, presumably to retrieve Aussie who was observing from his self-appointed post at a second-floor window. Sysy perceived Nike's intention as well and screamed at such a crescendo that the ground where the parking lot was opened. Lightning and thunder suddenly filled the sky in a fearsome way, and the Olympians, though more in number, scattered at the fear of what was to come.

Along with the lightning came a strong wind with a sting that reminded Christian of the Northern Gods from days long gone by when Jotunns, dragons, and monsters of earth, ice, and flame dominated the world. These were hard gods created steel-like by the riddle of struggle and pressure. The lavish Olympians relied too much on parlor tricks and showmanship and knew nothing of blunt force trauma. Christian himself was of the harsh sands, the pounding heat of the Egyptian jungle, the betrayal of 72 people whom he had loved, a brother, and the negligence of those who stood by. Christian knew struggle. Christian knew perseverance. Together, these were the gods of grit.

But something puzzled Christian as the strength of the Olympians began to wane. Apollo, Artemis, Ares, Aphrodite, and Zeus, the legendary pantheon, could offer a challenge these minor gods could not. But they were not here. Why? Christian wondered.

These lesser Olympians lay sprawled out on the ground either dead or otherwise incapacitated. Phobos lay gassed in a heap, partly on a sidewalk and partly on the lawn. Athena, for all the bloodthirst that legend attributed to her, was sitting on her ass and leaning against the fire hydrant trying to catch whatever breath she had left.

And though Christian looked around at the panoramic scene of defeated Olympians and at his friends, the Norse gods that helped him wreak this havoc, a worry buzzed in the back of his brain like a panicked mosquito. For Nike was on the loose.

***

Once Christian entered Liger, followed by the Vikings, he ran upstairs to where he last saw Aussie. The room told a story of struggle with drywall smashed and floor joist broken so that one could see through the floor to the downstairs. No Aussie.

"Find him," Christian ordered and then took off for the basement where the taproom was.

When Christian reached it, he was surprised to see that it was filled with students who were casually having drinks and talking. Having still the appearance of Christian the college student, he walked through the crowd until he reached the old kitchen area. Scanning the room, he saw random perishables on a table in front of him that butted up against a wall. Christian quieted his breathing and then put his ear up against the wall. Then he knocked on it. Faintly but as sure as he was standing there, he heard a knock.

Aussie, Christian thought. He moved the table and in one powerful punch knocked a hole through the wall. He didn't even have to peer in to see him. There was Aussie. Stiff as stone but breathing.

Christian pulled Aussie out of his tomb, knocked the food off the portable table and laid him on it to determine if Aussie needed medical help when all at once he felt a crushing blow to his back, knocking Christian against the table and Aussie off the table onto the floor. Before Chrsitian could turn around to see who had done this, Nike grabbed him by the nape of his neck and lifted him up. She was stronger than the others, and hungrier, too. She turned Christian around so that they made eye contact momentarily. Then without any warning, she bit into Christian's ribs.

Christian screamed in pain but couldn't remove her grip as much as he struggled. She had latched on tightly and Christian resolved to stick both of his thumbs into her eyes when a thought occurred to him.

Let it be, were the words that he heard, so he lay limp as a rag while Nike dropped Christian and fell back in surprise. She began to cough and then vomit. Christian yanked Aussie and retreated to the back of the kitchen where Nike's vomit hadn't yet reached. But he could still see her.

The blood of Dionysus, Christian mused grimly from

his place in the corner.

Nike's eyes turned brown and rolled back into her head. Her fangs, which had been protruding, fell out of her mouth. In fewer than twenty seconds, Nike reverted back into her ancient self. Before she ever had drunk the Blood of Dionysus. As she sat in a stupefied silence, taking in her surroundings and recovering her ancient self, someone drove a spear through her chest so suddenly that Christian spun around.

There stood Big Grim, or more specifically, Odin, in all his glory. Surrounded by two giant ravens, Hugin and Munin, and two wolves, Geri and Freki, he lifted his spear on which Nike was kabobbed, turned abruptly around, and disposed of her in the trash chute. When he was done, he came back, wiping the end of his spear on a pant leg.

"Good thing I saw you come in," he grinned at Christian. "Lucky for you—for us—my spear never misses." He offered Christian a hand and pulled him up. Christian looked at Grim in wonderment.

"So the gods of Liger finally reveal themselves to each other." Christian offered. Big Grim put his right hand on Christian's shoulder.

"Like I said, I finally see you. Now let's do a body count. Hugin tells me we've won the afternoon."

The bodies were stacked together by the time they emerged outside, the sole deed of Sysy, evidenced by her sitting atop the pile, drinking a horn full of mead. Christian surveyed the others and saw that each had produced a horn and were reviewing the battle.

"I could do with one of those," Christian gestured to Sysy's horn. She grinned.

"We've been waiting for a long time to give this back to you. Sysy produced a horn and handed it to Christian.

"What do you mean 'back to me'?" Christian said incredulously.

"Don't be coy," Brisin teased. "We know you must remember" Christian closed his eyes and concentrated. He finally opened them.

"I only see snow, an arrow, and people standing over me."

"One of your many deaths, no doubt," Big Grim affirmed.

"That was when we gave you a sacred name," Duel added.

"And made you our brother," said Sysy.

"Baldur!" said Zalewski.

"That's a strong name," Christian smiled.

"It means bold," Will said.

"You said 'many deaths.' Wep told me I only died once," Christian took a sip from his horn.

"Wep? He doesn't see all there is to see. Before Set killed you, you spent time with us. You learned our ways. It was important for you to walk among more than one pantheon, given what was to come," Big Grim explained.

"Psychosis must be the doorway from one pantheon to the other, I suppose. At least for me." Christian replied, a weak attempt at a joke.

"As initiations go, it's your thorn in the flesh," Zalewski rationalized. "Those who survive initiation are most awake, waiting for the imminent arrival of that which they hope for as Jormangandr waits for me."

"As Fenrir awaits me!" Big Grim nodded.

"As Heimdallr waits for me," Sysy agreed.

"As Garmr waits for me," Will followed.

269

"As mead and another cigar waits for me." That was Duel.

"And I await them all," finished Brisin. All eyes were on Christian.

"Who waits for me?" he asked.

"This time," Big Grim started, "This time is different from the others. Haven't you felt it, Christian, that in this life you have been paying for actions done in another one?"

"Yes. For sure. There's no other explanation for all of this."

"All our lives and individual incarnations are woven by the three sisters into a thin string which leads to a final knot where all destinies will meet," Will explained.

"And Wep knows what is to come. The stories in the Norse Eddas are but a child's account of what awaits us all. A time when the sun no longer shines, and the moon runs for its life."

"That's pretty apocalyptic. But again, who waits for me?"

"Who waits for you?" Sysy almost spat. "Don't you know?"

"Speaking of apocalypse," Will attempted to change the conversation, noting the agitation in Christian's demeanor. "If Norse gods see the folly in fighting and will only engage the Olympians as a matter of defense and not offense, then what might that tell you?" Christian mused.

"That the end of all of this is still far away? That there are many more battles between now and the end? That we still haven't faced their strongest deities? That Apollo, Artemis, and Zeus are probably really upset now and are going to give us more trouble, now that their cover is blown?"

Will nodded,

"So we need a plan," Christian decided.

"No," Will said curtly. "We need a trick?"

"A trick? What's a trick going to do?"

Sysy laughed.

"Sometimes, the absence of your multicultural sensitivities baffle me. Different mythologies have different strengths when it comes to battle. For us Norse, our martial code is No tricks, no justice. So if we're going to help you defeat these Olympians at all, we need a trick."

Christian nodded his head in understanding.

"Well, as the saying goes, it's hard to teach an old dog new tricks. Working with me, you've got your work cut out for you."

***

After more talking and a little more drinking, the former dimension was restored, Christian said bye to his friends, and he headed across campus to his dorm. Unaware, he began to sink into his feelings for Asara. Should he try to see her or should he leave her alone? She hadn't tried to contact him. It was clear that she was angry with him.

Someone called out his name.

"Christian Belvedere." When Christian looked up, he was surprised that he had ventured a route which passed the building where he encountered William Marshal. And there William Marshal was, barely visible in the large doorway of the entrance. He was beckoning Christian.

Confident that his powers were much more superior than the last time Christian encountered him, Christian walked boldly to the entrance.

"I am William Marshal!" Marshal bowed low.

I know who the fuck you are," Christian said snidely as he scanned his periphery in case other knights were flanking him. Marshal finished his bow and beckoned Christian deeper into the doorway. Noticing Christian's hesitance, he beckoned all the more.

"I've come to ask for your help. Please, following our battle I was able to shake off a long spell."

"You mean that getting your ass kicked brought you to your senses?"

"Yes, perhaps, because of your Jew. She's blessed with great power."

"Not my Jew! She's a Jew... her own Jew." As this comment sunk in, Marshal looked puzzled.

"You mean to say that you did not lay claim to her after defeating me?"

Christian rolled his eyes.

"Again, why are you here?" That question brought Marshal back to the present.

"I've been judged. I had been appropriated by the Olympians who found me and used me for their evil purposes. But I have since been enlightened and find rest in knowing that, besides the extremes of my former cruel beliefs, I have no reason to fear them. I'm free." He finished and bowed lower this time. When he stood back up, Christian looked bored.

"So how can I help? You seem fine," Christian commented.

"For a warrior like myself, facing a Black and a Jew. Well, oh my, that was much more than I could bear and thus it broke the spell."

"So?"

"I tried to conjure that power again to release my brethren who are in bondage as I was. But the spell has adjusted or perhaps was only useful once? Osiris, I need you to help me free my brethren." Christian was moved to compassion at this confession.

"I have an idea," Christian said.

When Christian shared his plan, Marshal was noticeably uncomfortable at the mention of the Norse gods. But in the end he agreed that this course of action was best.

"Thank you, kind Osiris. May Christ bless you," he added, bowing his lowest at this point so that Christian could see a patch of balding hair on the crown of his head.

As Christian continued on to his dorm, his phone vibrated in his pocket. It was Tess.

"So you're alive?" He couldn't tell if she was being sarcastic or sincere.

"It's me." He thought brief was better when it came to Tess.

"Wep has an idea he thinks will work," she started.

"But what?" Christian asked, anticipating there was a problem.

"Well, uh, he's not... he's not himself." It wasn't like Tess to be tongue tied. "He's despondent. I mean his plan is solid. I'm just not sure he should be involved in it." Christian let Tess's explanation hang in the air. Christian knew that he hurt him the last time he saw him in the Duat. But that couldn't be helped. Christian was a different person now. He now knew enough about this strange underworld to understand that he had rights. As the hero, he had the right to veto any ideas that didn't give him a chance at survival. So he wasn't being petty. If you didn't stand up to Wep, he would just assume you were along for the ride. His ride. And there was ample historical evidence that this was Wep's modus operandi that made him quite unpopular in ancient times.

"So do you want to hear it?" Tess asked cautiously.

"Well, let me hear what it is," Christian offered and heard her out.

"I see its merits," Christian relented once Tess briefed him on the details. Tess perceived this admission by Christian as humility and some of her iciness melted.

"We missed you. That's all," she began. "Forgive Wep. That's all that was. Concern. Two weeks is a long time, especially when you're... new at this." Christian felt the slightest rise of irritation at Tess's last sentence.

"I'm not a novice anymore. That's what you both need to understand. Also, I don't understand how I was gone that long. Makes me think I could be taken at any time like the Evangelical Rapture."

"Well, two weeks for me... that's an entire paycheck from work."

"Fair enough," Christian admitted. "On another note, I'm guessing that things with Rioghain didn't end well?" Tess sighed.

"Well, we found her but we couldn't remove her from the obelisk. These Olympians are so assured of their plan that they barely guard those things or else the student forms they have taken on are handicaps and their inexperience is shining through. Either that or they want us to know we can't stop them." Christian countered.

"Yes and no. Remember, they aren't sober which makes them dangerous because it's hard to trick the incredibly blank. They have no preconceived notions. This kid, Aussie, was almost captured by them. I'm surprised you missed him."

"He must not be on our radar then. I mean, our system wasn't flawless. Here's the thing: we need them all in one place to stop them once and for all. Because when they scatter, they just regroup and rise again. But when they're in one place, their numbers are overwhelming."

"We need help." Christian agreed.

"The Raiju are fifty-fifty and all other beings that could help us haven't taken a side yet."

"We need my grandmother then. She's worth at least a hundred."

"I visited your Sophie." At the mention of his grandmother's name, Christian felt a jolt. Whether it was concern or love, he could not tell.

"My mom didn't mind?"

"She didn't see me. I came through the Duat. Which is what I want to talk to you about."

"About what?" Christian asked suspiciously.

"It's her time. She's on her way to your throne. That is, if she makes it there at all." Christian felt suckerpunched.

"She died?" Tess paused out of reverence before she spoke again.

"I'm so sorry, Uncle. I consoled her. She wasn't alone. She was strong, friendly even, and loving. She was worthy of a good death and that's what she got." Christian was silent.

"But she might need our help down there. It's troubled waters, even for a Furie. Especially for this Furie."

"The Guardians?" Christian suspected. "Yeah, I remember enough to know I don't like mentioning their names without a weapon near me. As much as I'm becoming familiar with my Osiris identity, I'm still Christian, too. That is to say, there are still things that cause me to involuntarily tighten my buttcheeks." Christian heard Tess catch her breath sharply.

"What if there were a way to attend her ceremony?" When Christian didn't immediately respond, Tess continued conspiratorially. "And if it goes awry, challenge the Judge himself?" Christian considered this idea.

"So you think that's possible?"

"Yes. of course. The Guardians have never faced me… or you for that matter. We're basically brand new." Christian was developing a newfound respect for Tess. She was the consummate strategist.

"Ok. Then let's do this. Let's leave now. By the time we get to the throne, she'll be there. And we'll bring Chaos!"

"Careful," Tess warned. "You sound just like your father. Let's just say that whether or not Chaos shows up is up to him. For our part, however, let's show them what team spirit looks like when aligned with all that is good, right, and beautiful!"

"Sounds like a plan," Christian agreed. "By the way, what are the names of the Guardians again? They can't possibly be too much trouble, can they?"

Chapter 1
Been Spending Most of Our Lives

Tess and Christian arrived at the Gates of the Guardians which was in the Duat but a long way from Wep's lair. That was one of Christian's non-negotiables with Tess: leave Wep out of it. When they reached the gates, Christian thought that he might be in Michelangelo's Sistine Chapel. Above the gates was a vision of earth. Just beyond it, as if they had been waiting for them, stood the Three Guardians: The Guardian of What Was, The Guardian of What Is, and The Guardian of What Could Be.

From what Christian recalled, The Guardians were once spells that had been brought to life long before Osiris died the first time. Over millennia, they had transformed. Originally, they were created to terrify voyagers and to guard doorways throughout the Duat. But they had evolved to much higher levels of sophistication, thanks to the guidance of Anubis who adopted them as he had also been adopted. In addition to threatening and imposing their wills if provoked, the Guardians had become sentient with a unified mind of their own, allowing them to both challenge and inform travelers on their journeys to the throne of Osiris.

As they walked up to the gates, they opened automatically like one of those large warehouse stores on Earth that carried everything from bubblegum to lawnmowers. Tess reached for Christian's hand. As she did, another hand reached out and pulled both of them inside. The gates closed. It was the Guardian of What Is.

Standing sentinel, The Guardian of What Was and The Guardian of What Could Be watched as The Guardian of What Is motioned for Tess and Christian to follow until they came to an open, leveled area several yards from the front gates. The Guardian of What Is motioned for both to stand on two squares: one on each. Tess looked at Christian warily as she stepped onto hers. Christian shrugged his shoulders slightly back at her and consented. No sooner had he taken his position than The Guardian of What Is nodded its head. Before Christian or Tess could nod back, their two squares expanded into four and then eight and then sixteen until it became obvious that they were on an expansive board. A game board.

It wasn't like any board either had ever seen. Tess and Christian were in a back row. For seven spaces on either side of them and two rows in front were beings from all across the Mythoverse. There was Raiju to Tess's left and Jotuns to Christian's right. Flanking both of them were nymphs and gollums. In front of them were windagos, coyotes, and feathered serpents. Christan noticed a couple of students from Parthenon whom he had seen around campus but hadn't spoken to. Two rows ahead of him to the far right, he saw the shaggy blue head of Wep. Christian turned to Tess and muttered.

Tell me that's not Wep. But no words came out of his mouth. He tried again. This is chess, right? No words. But that didn't seem to affect Tess's understanding of what he was saying.

Like chess, but not chess, she countered. Look where we're standing. Christian looked around for a moment, and a grin broke across his face.

You're queen and I'm king!

Tess bit her lip.

No. I'm a queen, but you're a hunter. Christian detected worry in her eyebrows.

Doesn't matter. We're going to kick ass!

It's not just us, Christian. Look. Tess pointed to her left and then gestured beyond that with a throwing motion.

At first, Christian thought he was seeing double. But when he blinked, he was sure that his eyes were playing tricks on him. He looked to his left and his mouth dropped. The same pattern was duplicated. They weren't just on a board. They were on a megaboard.

What does this mean? Christian was on the borderline of fear.

Tess put both hands over her mouth as if she didn't want any of the beings around them to read her lips.

You're not just a hunter, she said almost apologetically.

What do you mean? Tess took a deep breath.

You're not just a hunter. You're being hunted. Look at the board.

The board was twelve-sided with each side converging into the center where stood an obelisk. Each of the other eleven sides was an exact duplicate of Tess and Christian's. If that were the case, then that meant there were eleven other versions of Tess and Christian.

When Christian looked directly to his left, he caught the eye of his exact counterpart for a second. "Other Christian" evaded his gaze intentionally and looked to make conversation with the Tess who stood next to him. Christian swiveled his head to his right and met the glare of the Christian on that board in a game of "Who Blinks First Loses." Uncomfortable with these two very different versions of himself, he said in a panicky voice to Tess.

What does this mean? Tess flinched as if that were the question that she was expecting.

It means that only one of you is the true Christian.

And the others? He glanced at the Tess on the board to their left. She was mad-dogging Christian with a vindictive stare. Tess next to Christian interrupted.

Eleven of you will not make it. Eleven of me will not make it. There can be only one Christian. Only one Tess.

Christian surveyed the rest of the board and noticed something peculiar. Among his ranks were beings of myth that were not altogether good beings. On the row ahead of him were two dark and powerful dragons next to a sphinx and a ginormous leviathan so behemoth that he wondered how he fit on his square.

That was when Christian realized that each side was governed by a Zodiac that represented a possible outcome on that board. However, because there were twelve boards, one Zodiac sign would prove to be true. The Zodiacs were not so much determining the result but playing out the consequences of certain alignments of traditional gods, heroes, and villains. All twelve of them chose a side and engaged whoever was nearest. Who would make it in the end? Would it be Libra Tess, Taurus Wep, Scorpio Christian? It was in this game that the great board would reveal who could kill who, who could betray who, and who could be left standing.

Tess looked at Christian somberly.

280

Get to the obelisk, Christian. As fast as you can. I'll see you there. Well, one of me will.

Christian looked at Tess affectionately.

You'll make it. Just stay behind Wep.

Which one, Tess shot back.

When Christian attempted to point out the Wep on the board to her immediate left, he noticed that Wep had taken a pawn position. Other than that space that that Wep had taken, all other beings mirrored their board. When Christian looked to his right, Wep had usurped the space of the leviathan. The rest of the board mirrored his.

What the hell...

But even more shocking was the fateful revelations found on the board. Each side had its own version of Tess and Christian. There were too many variations for Christian to remember all of them but the few that stood out were the following as outcomes became moving scenes: Asara, wearing a crown of bayol leaves, was kissing Christian with her fingers crossed behind her back. Sysy in a wedding gown feeding him cake while he was wearing a hospital gown with wax versions of both on the cake, depicting Sysy with a bow and arrow firing at Christian and landing a golden arrow. Stone Belvedere was in a lotus pose with his hands crushing a crown while the earth swallowed him whole, Tess, many times, was trapped in a pillory holding the heads of a jackal and falcon in her arms.

Wolves surrounded them. One of the most terrifying things Christian had ever seen was a monster with dilated eyes, shivering spine, and reticulating jaw. It was the stuff of nightmares. The Wep directly across from them raised his khopesh and howled as to the moon. That further unnerved Christian. Did Wep know? Did these clones of Wep know that Christian had offended the real Wep?

The objective of the game was for a pair of Tess and Christian within a Zodiac to reach the obelisk in the center "alive." So all of the other characters, besides Tess and Christian, functioned as support and assault at the same time. An earth-shattering scream that almost burst Christian's eardrums officially started the game, and the Tess-Christian pairs were off.

What followed could best be described as chaotic with harrowing moments of gut-wrenching terrors for the real Tess-Christian pair. At first, Christian and Tess couldn't decide which route to take to get to the obelisk. Math said "the shortest route" but there were too many creatures surrounding them, heading their direction, or otherwise blocking the easiest routes. Out of the corner of his eye, Christian saw the Scorpio Tess give him the finger and then was immediately grabbed by the throat by the Arie's Wep who snapped her neck and pulled her arms clean off her body.

Christian grabbed Tess by the arm. She was running to the back of their side of the board to wait out the carnage or try to escape.

Don't, Christian ordered as he ducked the stinger of a scorpion as large as an SUV. You'll get cornered. You won't have a chance. Stay behind Wep. He's kicking ass. Tess for once followed Christian toward the fray. And it worked. Their Wep was enjoying the unbridled pleasure of dispatching creatures in dozens of gory but ingenious ways. Deep within Wep's thick and hairy paws were the sharpened curved claws befitting a velociraptor that slashed at the air so quickly that it was raining blood. Tess and Christian wiped the constant downpour out of their eyes and huddled behind Wep who was doublequicking it to the center.

Eventually there were two Zodiacs left: Christian's sign Capricorn versus, oddly enough, and Dité's which was Gemini. The real Tess and Christian's Wep suffered a fatal blow with a spear through the eye by one of the Parthenon students. Where he got the spear, no one knew, but it embedded deep in his brain, causing him to fall, and exposing Tess and Christian. But they were less than ten paces from the obelisk when their Wep fell. Without a moment to think, Christian grabbed Tess by the shirt and dragged her that distance, touching the obelisk a second before another Scorpion brought his tail down to finish Tess. The great obelisk in the middle shook, announcing the end of the game. Channeling the voice of the Guardian of What Is, it spoke.

The winner gets the riddle. It glowed in shimmering hieroglyphs. Christian was so exhausted that he could barely respond.

The winner gets the riddle. Ok, what is it? Christian channeled back.

Anyone can be blue underneath. Tess lay at the base of the obelisk, covered in gore from the game.

Anyone can be blue underneath, Christian repeated dizzily. Tess painfully lifted her head and tried to speak.

"It means..." but before Tess could finish, everything for Christian went dark.

***

Christian Belvedere. Former student, psych patient, and the de facto therapy group leader, woke up in his bed in

Nirvana Meadows Hospital. Blinking, he looked over at the bed of his roommate who wasn't there. His sheets were gone. His belongings in the open faced cabinet were gone. That meant that he was gone as well.

Christian lay still, taking a moment to lament the loss but then cried a tear of joy at his roommate's successful recovery and discharge if, indeed, that's what happened. Then Dr. German walked in.

"The staff must not have seen you sleeping there, Christian. They must have thought you were discharged and didn't wake you up for group. Not like you'd ever miss it. You never do anymore."

Christian opened his eyes sheepishly.

"Dr. German, I wouldn't miss it for the world or my college degree. It's the peace I have long been searching for. Having said that, I must have missed my alarm." Dr. German, looking very German, nodded sharply at Christian.

"You have come a long way. Your mother will be proud to hear of your progress." He smiled, which was so rare, that Christian wondered if he was in pain. "And it's pizza day, so there's an added incentive."

"For sure. Well, let the incentive do its work," he joked as he sat up.

A few minutes later, Christian was sighing with contentment. Freshly showered, and wearing his favorite sweatpants and T-shirt (well, they were only allowed one set of clothes in the hospital to be worn on special occasions like pizza day). Leaving his room which opened into a common hallway, he greeted the custodian who was mopping the floor and cordially nodded at the desk staff.

Turning right after the desk, he walked down a hallway beset by a rec room corner and framed picture of an exotic island in the shape of a sleeping human. Stopping for a few seconds to run his fingers through his hair, he turned the doorknob and entered a room of other patients in mid-discussion. All eyes turned on him. The group was small. Only six of them, including Dr. German.

"I'm sorry for being late," he said remorsefully. There were a few seconds of uncomfortable silence until someone broke it.

"The doctor promised us that all of our diagnoses would go away if everyone showed up on time today. Thanks for fucking that up."

Someone snort-laughed and another began to wail. But the number of laughs won out until the entire circle burst out in laughter. Someone scooted over and made room for him in the circle.

"So, please, Nikola, continue," Dr. German crossed his legs. A beautiful brunette with Slavic cheekbones closed her eyes as she began to talk.

"I guess what I was trying to say before is that it's been a blessing and a curse to have what's in my head. All the memories, all the conversations, and all the characters."

"You should really write that play," encouraged a plump man in the corner whose name was King. While clearly King had chosen not to be a part of the group, that didn't prevent him from participating. Nikola perked up.

"I know! I just... let me ask the group. Does anyone feel, after all that's happened before coming here, a feeling of equilibrium between what is outside and inside you? Yes? Yes! See, it makes it hard to really accomplish any task because I feel so ready to...," her voice trailed.

"Move on?" Christian suggested. Nikola turned and looked him in the eye.

"Yes. Exactly." Dr. German answered for her.

"You deserve that feeling, Nikola. It's your victory. Actually, all of you deserve to feel that way. I've known you all as a group for about a month now, and I know that what you left behind is something you survived. There was the breaking of teeth, the fascism of fate, so much mental anguish among you all as you tried to be normal. Now you feel like it's hard to accomplish anything without tribulation. That's normal. But how can we get past that? Should we even try to? Maybe this is what Nirvana is?" All eyes were on Dr. German. Christian interrupted.

"I've always thought Nirvana was this erasure. Like a... That a cosmic cop out. The path a coward takes."

"Uh, oh! Shots fired! Good thing Buddha isn't here right now." That was a teenager named Prince. A woman named Queen interrupted.

"That's a fight I'd pay to see. Not that violence is what we need anymore." Dr. German inserted himself once more.

"Christian, I'd like to pursue this. Are you saying that Nirvana strips us of our humanity? You've all been here for a month. Do you feel stripped? Like something is missing?" Dr. German looked around the room.

"I feel glad to have this company of people. And I would like to keep having them. That's my Nirvana," Christian initiated.

"I see. So connection. So having good people to be around is Nirvana, OK? Anyone else?" Queen motioned for Dr. German to look at her.

"Being listened to. Y'all know I wasn't singing much before I came here. But ever since Prince started playing his guitar and you all started to open up during music group, I can't stop singing. That joy, that soulfulness, well, you never get tired of that. That's Nirvana for me."

"Amen, sister," Prince agreed. Dr. German went around the room so that each person in the group had a turn until he got back to Christian. At first, Christian's eyes were glistening with tears as each member of their group testified. Now, it was full of waterworks so that the front of Christian's T-shirt was soaked.

"Christian, would you like to share?" Dr. German said quietly, sensing that Christian had struck upon a revelation. Christian turned to look at Dr. German. Then he looked down at his shirt, feeling how wet it was. Then he touched his face and looked at the wet hands. He looked around the room until he made eye contact with Dr. German who gently prodded him again.

"Do you have something you would like to share? Dr. German said. Christian, looking confused and nodded his head.

"Yeah, where am I and how the fuck did I get here?"

***

"I think we won," Tess's whisper was barely audible, but Christian registered it. He had slumped to the ground next to Tess, who had recovered from her former position of lying sprawled at the base of the obelisk and was nursing a sprained wrist.

"We're the only two left," Christian said cautiously as he surveyed the game board. "What's the reward? They never told us what the reward was for winning." Christian's head began to pound.

"Do you feel that?" Tess pressed her palms against her temples.

287

"My head's about to burst." She looked over at Christian who was pressing his palms to his temples as well.

"My head's about to split," he affirmed. Within seconds, both knew that this was no ordinary headache.

"I'm fading," Tess eked out in a panicked voice. "I'm about to pass out."

"Here, grab my hand," Christian ordered. Dropping his left palm from his temple intensified the sharp pain that he was feeling, causing his eyes to shut tightly so that he had to grope around for Tess's hand.

Then the vertigo started and Christian felt as if he were being involuntarily spun counterclockwise with Tess right along with him.

"I'm going to puke!" was the last thing he heard her say before both woke up side by side in a graveyard. The sky was overcast with a cloud barrier so low to the ground that Christian could see, as it were, the individual molecules of mist, giving the sky a pixelated look. A thunderstorm that sounded like muted artillery rang out in the distance, but there was no rain.

The trees and grass themselves had long been dead, giving the graveyard an eerie aesthetic unlike cemeteries back home. Tess stood up and approached a gigantic head stone that stood a good six feet tall.

"Christian," Tess said his name slowly, drawing out the syllables in a sing-song. "Look at this." Christian was at her side.

"Can you read it?" Tess asked. Christian rubbed his hand over the hieroglyphs etched into the marble. Suddenly, the hieroglyphs lit up and rearranged themselves in English. It took a minute for both to read the inscription from beginning to end.

"Uncle..." Tess started. "We all die."

"This can't be," Christian whispered to himself. But as clear as day, their names were inscribed on the tombstone along with several other names like Sysy and Big Grim.

"Tess, let's spread out. I want us to check every name on every gravestone." It took some time, but the conclusion was unmistakable. The names of gods from time immemorial, from every ethnic mythology possible were written on the tombstones with one obvious omission. The Olympians. Christian walked up another row, peering at names.

"But how, Christian," Tess demanded. Christian's face was set in a grim line as he studied each headstone he passed.

"Tess, these are mass graves. There was a battle. No, a war. Had to have been. Gods the world over are buried here.

Suddenly, they showed up to Wep's gravestone.

"Wepwawet," Christian read. "Opener of Paths. No more." The emotion caught Christian in the back of his throat unexpectedly, and he wretched until his guts were queasy with the emptiness.

"How did this happen?" Tess demanded again. Christian wiped his mouth on his sleeve.

"They made us drink," Christian said hoarsely.

"Made us drink?" Tess mused. "Christian, in what dimension would we ever be in the company of The Olympians and drink? That's suicide." Christian nodded.

"There are only two ways. We attend some sort of event where the Olympians are, and they poison the drink they serve us."

"Like hell," Tess retorted.

"Or," Christian continued. "We drink it willingly."

"What? How could that be?" That old edge was coming back in Tess's voice. Christian shrugged his shoulders, but his face was set.

"This is how we fight. We believe in the unthinkable. We trust in our reincarnation. We hope in the resurrection of the dead. We are crazy enough to be certain that death will bring us to the Judge who will sort shit out in the end. Come on," Christian beckoned. "Look at the lightning over there. It seems to be attracted to that acropolis-shaped building. I think that's where we need to go."

When they got to the city, they were greeted by an eerie silence. No one was out and about in the streets, getting along with the day. Of the several houses they did pass, Christian and Tess noticed through the generous-sized windows that its inhabitants were bowing before statues on mantles. After passing a dozen or so, Tess nudged Christian.

"Are you seeing what I'm seeing?"

"You mean the strange synchronized devotion of the people here?"

"Yes, but the statues. They look like they're bleeding."

"Yes. I think we're at the right place." Christian's jawline was set in a fierce determination.

"The people are under a spell of some sort. Keep your head on a swivel. Who knows what they're like when they snap out of it."

As they crossed an intersection, coming upon another row of houses, a voice called out from the shadows in an alleyway.

"Christian? Is that you?" More inquisitive than startled at hearing his name in such a foreign place, Christian took a step forward, peering as he did.

"Aussie?" He asked with surprise. Aussie stepped out into the street, cautiously looking to his right and left as if for danger. He looked Christian up and down, entirely ignoring Tess.

"No," he said with disappointment. "This is some ruse. You don't have the marks. You look far too healthy. Who are you anyway? Are you from elsewhere?" Christian and Tess glanced at each other knowingly. They were in a parallel dimension at the hands of the Guardians in which Aussie was unfamiliar with this version of Christian.

"I thought you were someone I knew. Clearly, you're not from here because you're out here instead of inside." Aussie turned to go back into the alley.

"Hold on. I'm Christian. This is Tess. We aren't from here but do I look like someone you know?" Aussie turned around.

"You did but now you don't."

"You. Why aren't you inside like the others? Are you even from here," Tess interjected. Aussie looked as if noticing her for the first time.

"You're correct. I'm not from here either but have no idea when I arrived. I awoke in this alley a few hours ago. It must be a punishment." Aussie muttered the last sentence almost to himself, but Tess heard it and wouldn't let it go.

"Punished? By whom? For what?" Aussie leaned forward as if about to share a secret.

"There was a prophecy spoken. Once a prophecy is spoken, it must be followed. I didn't follow it and thus…" Aussie's voice trailed.

"What was the prophecy?" Christian asked.

"Once let loose, it will take a son of Zeus. Make no stand. Make no truce. Why else does the sun rise but to cease yesterday's abuse?"

"I don't understand," Tess complained. Aussie now looked like he had disappointed Tess and Christian.

"I know. The rhyme part sounds contrived. Maybe I'm not remembering it word for word. What I know it means is that someone fucked up. In my world. Maybe it was me. I think I was banished here."

"Once what is let loose?" Tess persisted.

Crestfallen, Aussie gestured at the destruction around them.

"How do you survive this?" Christian asked no one in particular. Aussie shrugged.

"Do you believe in ghosts?" Tess and Christian looked at each other.

"What are you saying?" Tess cut right to the point.

"We all become ghosts. Some holy, some not. I'm sure your ghosts in this time sequence are haunting some miller who cheated locals or some weaver with a voracious appetite for young women. But only the living can stop these gods, these demon Olympians."

Thunder from a distance rolled through the scant village, feeling dangerously close to a miniature earthquake. Aussie waved them away.

"You must go now. But remember my last hope."

"What's that?" Tess asked.

"That you have one hell of a trick up your sleeves in whatever world you have that still has hope in it." Before Christian and Tess could respond, they found themselves back at the gate.

They were less confused this time as they understood the elastic nature of the world to which they were subject that increased the odds of their visiting odd places at the drop of the hat. They were also aware that the Guardians were behind it all. That there was a lesson to be learned or a clue to be extracted.

In the distance Christian noticed a figure. Tess noticed, too.

"That's Sophie!" Tess said excitedly. "If she's here and we're here, too, then we're making good time! I think we might beat her."

"You might be right," Christian tried to contain his excitement. "Let's find out." He called out to her.

"Grandma!" Sophie, who had been trudging along a road parallel to them, stopped at the sound of his voice. She appeared to be listening. He called out again.

"Grandma!" Sophie did a 360, looking confused.

"She can hear you but can't see you," Tess said.

"Let's try to get closer." Christian began to take a step forward, but then the gate closed. He grabbed the iron bars and rocked it. It wouldn't budge.

"There has to be another way," he said suddenly.

"I agree," Tess affirmed. With all they had been through, there was an unspoken decision among them that forcible strength was not the currency of these worlds they were in.

"Yield and overcome," Christian quoted one of the ancient Chinese masters. "Yield, overcome, and there will be a way." A voice belonging to someone they had never met, interrupted this newfound wisdom.

"Excuse me. Stranger. If you want to get into Olympus, this is not the way." Christian and Tess both jumped at the same time.

"No. We're not trying to get to Olympus. Hey, who are you?" The figure who spoke to them was backlit by a bright light that obscured his identity. When Chrsitian looked at the gate, he suddenly realized that it was no longer golden. It emanated a white hot light that occasionally sizzled like lightning. Had they shown up in a new place within the last minute without knowing it?

The person who addressed them had gotten closer and was less phantom as the light behind him faded. Christian squinted his eyes and then they widened in stark recognition.

"Paulie? Pithon Paulie?" Tess asked incredulously.

"Apollo, actually," Paulie-Apollo grinned. "Now that my pretense has dropped, Apollo will do." Christian was dumbfounded, uncertain what to make of this new revelation.

"Christian it is. Actually, Osiris. I didn't recognize you bathed in all that glory. Here, let me open the gates for you." And at the mere mention of it, the gates began to open. Apollo, showing his pearly whites, chuckled at Christian and Tess's response.

"It opens to Olympian hands only. But surely you knew that." As the gates stopped, wide-armed as it were, heart-filled music hit Christian and Tess so hard that they found themselves weeping before either comprehended what was happening. The agape had an intoxicating beat and both had to fight not to lose themselves.

"Happens every time," Apollo mused. "Visitors always love when the doors open. So what brings you, Osiris? Come to join in the celebration?" Christian found his tongue again.

"It's a wedding, right?"

"Ha, a wedding! No, for the Bacchanal! It's the first of its kind! Apparently, my brother, Dionysus, is revealing an aged wine that everyone 'must' try!" Tess grabbed Chris-

294

tian by the arm, yanking him close.

"Christian," she murmured. "The cemetery we just were at? The mass graves? This is it. This is the day Olympus fell. You were right. We drink it."

Almost immediately, Christian felt the urge to run. But where? Thanks to the Guardian of Things That Once Were, there was nowhere to run or hide. Despite revulsion of the knowledge of what would happen on this day, he had to remain calm. That was the only way he would be able to save his grandmother. That was the real Guardian's test. Not this.

"Are you well, Osiris?"

"Apollo, can you take me to Dionysus? He's actually who I'm here to see." Tess made an involuntary noise that sounded like a yelp.

"Dionysus is it? He's on the way to where I am going. You can accompany me." Apollo looked at Tess apologetically. "Both of you can accompany me." Tess started to protest, but Christian cut her off.

"Woman, you will do as I say," he grabbed her by the arm and shook her two or three times. Apollo looked on approvingly.

"Follow me," he gestured graciously. Christian followed with Tess in tow.

"Sorry," he whispered. "I have to warn Dionysus. This might be the trick we need."

***

In an instant the party of three teleported to where Dionysus was in Olympus. They stood before a massive Greek temple that almost blinded them upon first look because its alabaster exterior reflected the burning sun. When their eyes adjusted, they could see that it was accented with blues and reds and that its gigantic columns were decorated with wreathed leaves along its plinths and capitals. The steps rose up a story high to the entrance from which emanated a sweet smell they later learned was nectar.

"Smell that?" Apollo gestured for them to inhale deeply. "He's here." And with that Apollo bounded up the steps three at a time. Tess looked at Christian nervously,

"To the trick," she said somberly.

"To the trick," Christian said back. And with this reinforced agreement, they took off after Apollo.

They made it to the top ten seconds behind Apollo who, not having even broken a sweat, was eagerly waiting for them.

"I should probably let him know you are here, though he probably already knows because he is keen on what happens in his domain. Wait here." Apollo walked through the wide and dark entrance, disappearing about twenty paces inside.

"We can do this," Tess said encouragingly, as if she were comforting herself.

"Stop it. You're freaking yourself out and you don't have to do that. We're in the past which means there's a future. That's all we need to know right now."

"I just can't get that graveyard out of my mind. I don't want to screw this up." Christian looked at her comfortingly.

"Tess, you're the bravest person I know. Honestly." He held up his hand and they bumped fists as Apollo appeared back at the entrance.

"He's ready to see you," he flashed a pearly smile. "Come

296

on. Let's go."

Apollo led them through a labyrinth of vault-sized hall-ways with plenty of twists and turns until they arrived at yet another entrance to the throne room of the temple. Dionysus's throne was empty. Tess and Christian, having the same idea that this could be an ambush, surveyed the room until their eyes fell upon a pool that lay between them and the temple. In it lay a huge figure whose head was submerged just below the surface as if he were float-ing. Upon closer inspection, the pool was filled with a rich burgundy-colored liquid. Was it blood?

Dionysus hadn't budged and there was no sound, but Apollo didn't seem alarmed.

"Is he..." Christian began.

"Dead?" Tess finished.

Apollo looked at each of them with a combination of agitation and amusement.

"No. He's drunk! I just spoke with him a few minutes ago, and now he's pissed. Brother, awake. It's your superior. And your guests are here!"

Dionysus didn't move. Apollo walked to him and nudged him with his sandaled foot. Dionysus bobbed. Frustrated, Apollo grabbed him by a lock of his long, wavy, black hair. Suddenly, Dionysus thrashed around like he was being at-tacked, splashing all over Apollo and even getting the red liquid on Tess and Christian who backed away.

"No, I do not have a drinking problem, Radegast. You have a drinking problem since you have a problem with my drinking!" Dionysus laughed at his own joke as he strug-gled to get out of the pool, finally standing, and then wob-bling. Apollo helped to navigate him back to his throne.

"Ok, let's try this," Apollo said almost apologetically to

Tess and Christian. "He hates it when I do this, but time is of the essence. One snap of the finger and he's sober again. What a pity. I only do it sparingly. Ok, and snap!" Apollo snapped his finger and Dionysus's personality transformed immediately.

"Damn it! I was somewhere! Somewhere far away, fanciful and free from pain. The pain of boredom! I warn you, you boring, slurvish, burdensome sophist that I will have a drink so caustic and permanent that not even you will be able to snap anyone out of its effects," Dionysus complained.

"You have a visitor, jackass! You remember Osiris!" Apollo pointed Tess and Christian out as if Dionysus might need help identifying the only other two people in the room. Dionysus peered at Christian.

"Prince of the Nile. Warder of Evil. The Lean, Green Dean! Yes, I remember. How you were able to transform that wild and ferociously independent Isis into a dutiful bride, I will never know." He looked at Tess with a leer so thorough that it made her blush.

"We Olympians must take note: the key to subduing a woman is to be so shy and sweet of demeanor that they think they can walk all over you. But that was your trick, wasn't it? Because no one tramples over the King of Kemet under holy Amen Ra and the elusive creator Atum!"

"Dionysus," Christian said with imperative authority.

"Cousin," Dionysus shouted back. Christian walked forward within spitting distance of Dionysus.

"I must warn you and Apollo as well. I am not just Osiris, but a traveler from a faraway time. I have come to warn you. Someone will use your blood to defy Apollo's power and turn all of the Olympians into fiends. I don't know who betrays you. It must be someone you trust, someone you trust more than a brother. But I adjure you on your father and your father's father to cancel the party tonight. Cancel them forever. Be brave and take a pilgrimage to a world where you will not be in danger. It will be hard, but the price the world will pay because of your blood is too great for you to be here.

Dionysus scrunched his eyebrows and addressed Apollo.

"What is this? Tasted my blood?" He looked back at Christian. "How do you know about that?" You could hear a pin drop and couldn't mistake the shift of energy in the room when Apollo jerked his head in surprise.

"You are saying there's truth to this, brother?" Apollo bristled A smirk played on the corner of Dionysus's lips that he feigned to control. Then he burst out laughing, the intentional theatrics falling flat.

"You know that I bleed myself sometimes. I have to. Too much of my sanguine has, well, it has caused me problems in the past." He laughed again as if the reference to his diabolical behavior was something to be admired. "I have made concoctions with it. I did not want to see it go to waste, you know. I was curious to see if nectar lingers in the blood and why. A harmless pursuit," he waved his hand dismissively.

"Have you told anyone else about this?" Apollo asked.

"No. I go to the bed of others and no one comes into mine," he winked at Tess. Apollo shook his head in disbelief.

"I have no doubt of your sincerity, Osiris. It is I who have the power of foresight. Why I did not see this coming, I have no explanation," Apollo said almost apologetically.

"Have you been looking? Maybe you've been distracted by your damned music?" Tess had come to stand by Christian and was almost shaking with rage. Apollo and Dionysus were both surprised by Tess's reaction.

"She speaks," Dionysus said sarcastically.

"Last time I looked," Apollo started, "I just saw more of the same. Look, how about you look after my brother here until the celebration. Who better to protect him than you? I have to be on my way."

"Excellent! Now I'll have drinking partners in the interim. I'll only make it easy for you to protect me if you drink with me. I promise, no blood," said Dionysus.

"Did you not hear me, Apollo and Dionysus? There can be no party."

"But the preparations have already been made. It will be impossible to stop it from happening. I'm afraid that we will have to do the best we can to monitor Dionysus in this Bacchanal tonight. That is, I'm afraid, the best I can do. I'll be back as soon as I can."

And with that, Apollo left. An awkward silence among the three filled the air, generated by Dionysus who sat with a half smile playing on his lips, staring back and forth at Tess and Christian. Christian had enough.

"Do you understand the implications for yourself, your family, your people, your offspring, the world?"

Dionysus might as well have been named Narcissus. Not only could he not see beyond his own interest but he also seemed to enjoy the attention, negative though it might be. He was, as Christian was thinking while Dionysus smirked at him, emotionally underdeveloped and incapable of taking the threat seriously. But then why would he? He lived in a world without any threats. The gods there were vulnerable to evil simply because there never had been evil like that in the world that Tess and Christian lived.

But evil breeds evil. Surely, someone must have an evil intent in this world. Intentional evil. Perhaps it was an unknown puppet master who came up with the sinister plan to taint Dionysus with blood that converts the divine to devils. Perhaps their quarrel was with them. Either way, there was nothing for Christian and Tess to do but wait in the company of Dionysus who, once he saw both relent, made himself better company.

Dionysus, as he proved to be, was such a storyteller. He related tales of romance, love won, love lost, brotherhood, and even a few erotic vignettes that made Christian squirm and Tess blush. He had such an imagination.

He confided in them that he and Apollo had decided to bring back some long-lost traditions.

"Apollo has been sneaking around with Persephone. You know, daughter of Demeter. She belongs to Hades." Dionysus said this in a half-whisper, leaning forward as if he feared that someone might be listening in on them.

"Things are changing in Olympus, my friends. We're entering an age of clashes," he leaned back on his throne with an affirmative nod of his head. As if this secret were a burden for which a confession alleviated some pressure within him, Dionysus found his tongue. He was excited for how many great drinking stories this era would create but was melancholy somehow because he no longer felt that he fit in a world that was moving in the direction of conflict over merriment.

He, too, had fallen in love, but with nymphs who shared him, not goddesses. Nymphs loved as a collective and Dionysus had his eye on marrying the Nymphs of Aphrodite, chief among them a nymph named... Dionysus looked alarmed.

"What's her name," Tess asked curiously. Dionysus sat up in his throne befuddled.

"I don't think I should reveal it," he said matter-of-factly.

"Will Aphrodite seek revenge on you for such affection?" Christian half-joked. Dionysus laughed in response.

"The Olympian Gods never seek vengeance." Now it was Christian's time to laugh at the irony of that statement. For being a Greek, Dionysus seemed to be lacking the finer powers of logic. But Christian felt obligated one last time to give him some reality.

"You live in a gilded cage, Dionysus. Literally and figuratively. The way the world ends up, the ugly stuff that reveals itself that's right now just hiding and mocking you, it's heartbreaking. You become the excuse for every demon in this dimension." Dionysus considered this and then sighed.

"But you don't understand me, cousin. We believe, in Olympus, that our ancients imbued each of us with basic traits... that we Olympians are merely symbols of sacred absolutes. I am ecstasy incarnate: dangerous yes, able to unearth the repressed and unspeakable, yes, but also impermanent. My power, my being, is only for a short time, even when it's not for a good time. If my family partakes of me and my blood and eats of my flesh it will not sustain them forever. Whatever they become they will have to look down the abyss and discover their best selves. They will have to overcome the obstacles you speak of because of their own blood, not mine. If they can't do that then my blood is not the problem. They were rotten from the start. For each person must earn it, not be granted it, if you

302

know what I mean."

"Well, I think you miscalculated. It happens tonight and it's still happening in the future." Dionysus yawned and promptly changed the subject.

" I just had a great idea! Let me show you some old friends. It's been so long since you've been here, Osiris. We've actually grown up and you can see we are model citizens. It'll put you at ease!"

"Sure. But I'll keep close to you anyway. I can't have you fucking shit up." Dionysus's eyebrows puckered at this new expression.

"Of course. As you wish," Dionysus said smugly. "But for the interim, you both can stay close to me. I'll give you a tour." He got up from his seat and gestured beyond the doors.

"May I?" Christian glanced at Tess.

"As you wish," he said with a nod.

***

Dionysus led Tess and Christian out the door of the throne room, out the door of the temple, and down the temple steps in only what Tess would describe later as a speed tour of Olympus. Olympus was breathtakingly spacious and beautiful. Dionysus pointed out numerous divinities along the way, all in various stages of conversation or interaction with each other.

The god Zephyr appeared on a breeze. It was he who kept the calm in this realm and knew of all disturbances to the wind. He must have detected a shift in the atmosphere when he heard that the visitors whom Dionysus was parading around the city hailed from another place and were all too reserved. Zephyr looked at Christian with a worried look on his face.

"You," he pointed Christian out. "How can you be upset in such a place?" Dionysus laughed to play things down but Zephyr wasn't having it.

"What is your intention, stranger? We are at the cusp of a celebration, and I don't understand your dour presence. Nor that of your mistress." Tess looked offended.

"Concubine?" Zephyr corrected.

"Zephyr is it?" Tess cut in.

"You are correct," he lifted his chin at this query by a woman. "What gave it away?"

"The world we come from emphasizes energy. It's kind of like the pattern of wind currents, air, that sort of thing. You've picked up on our presence which was not to enjoy your celebration. We are on a different sort of mission." Zephyr's eyes puckered.

"Why would you not participate in our celebration? That is what I don't understand. Your presence signals the slightest of oppositions in the air within Olympus, and that gives me cause to worry. It is my duty to infer such matters. Dionysus, who are these people?" Dionysus again laughed dismissively.

"Zephyr, brother, you are always so astute in your discernments, and you have discerned correctly. This pair have come to warn me of what they say is an eventual misstep in our misfortunes. They come from another place, time, world, you might say, but they, mistaken as they are, mean no ill. I have vetted them. They simply need to loosen up." Zephyr's angry eyebrows abated slightly as he surveyed Christian and Tess, particularly noting Tess's curvy bust, down to her toned calves.

"You I don't know," he nodded. "But we shall get acquainted tonight." He turned his attention to Christian.

"It is you with whom I am worried. You remind me of the Egyptian. Lord of the Underworld. A friend to us Olympians. But then I wonder if it is you or one like you. For this Olympian air, how can you avoid its intoxicating properties? It should banish all injurious thought, all worry. But the sorrow is so plainly fixed in your eyes. How you can resist the atmosphere? I shall want to know the meaning of it."

Christian considered sharing with Zephyr in the presence of Dionysus the Olympian predicament, but at the mention of the Olympian aether, it suddenly clicked with Christian. Though the party was that evening, the Olympians were already drunk. Not off Dionysus, but off the very air. The air carried within it an opiate that kept them blissful, bashful, and deluded. The air was a barbiturate that made reasoning difficult if not impossible. This revelation frustrated Christian. But as long as he was with Dionysus, he felt that they still had a chance to alter the Olympian's reasoning.

***

While Christian and Tess were being given their tour of Olympus, Apollo had taken leave to the Underworld to see Hades. This mission was important to him for, while few knew this (and while it was against the rules), Apollo loved Persephone more than life itself. Because Persephone had once eaten of the fruit of the Underworld, by law she had to remain there. Because Hades could be her only suitor, marriage to him would be her sentence. At least that was the popular opinion.

But Apollo didn't care about the rules any longer. Hades wasn't happy to see him.

"Hades! You know why I have come, uncle!" Apollo greeted him.

A cloud of black ash grew tall and wide before Apollo. Hades emerged like an ember, fully armored.

"Boy, you have been huffing the air of Zephyr for far too long if you think this is the way to approach me!" Apollo, emboldened, scoffed.

"I've been down here enough to know that better sense exists outside of Olympus." Hades flared at the insult.

"So you still wish to cross me, the one feeble humans are too scared even to depict? The one Zeus Most High doesn't even dare mention? Boy, you must love a losing battle." Apollo gave Hades the "okay" sign, a visual insult equivalent to the middle finger.

"I've come for her." Hades roared.

"You've sat your lazy ass on your throne in Helicon, fatted by nectars and nymphs and now you want to be famous? Where has that man been all this time?" Apollo waved him off.

"Do you remember what you said when you kidnapped her? 'Now is the Winter?' Well, I, too, have felt no sunshine, no blooming since I lost Persephone, the only goddess I ever offered to marry."

"Marriage is a serious thing, boy. Are you ready to make a deal then for her hand? Are you ready to displace me? Are you able to displace me?" Apollo didn't hesitate.

"Yes, I am."

Suddenly, Persephone appeared. Apparently, she had been listening.

"He didn't kidnap me!" she said.

"I did not. I took her because I see the fate of all those that have died and are to die. So then tell me, if we are immortal, us Olympians, we Gods, then why do I see the fate of all of you! Something is coming!"

"It's already here. Osiris has just brought ill news. I told him that I saw no doom when he insisted, but I have been beset with images of crazed gods, fangs, and a place of learning far away," Apollo said.

"I sensed death has had him, so then I can command him to appear here! It's difficult though, he's powerful… it's like transferring myself."

The nymph's bites went down to my bones. They were going to tear me apart if Hades hadn't transferred me to the Underworld. When I arrived, I was myself again but badly wounded? Apollo caught me as I fell.

"He does not belong here," said Hades.

"He looked like he was attacked by dogs," said Persephone.

"This is a growing problem. Small acts of aggression have increased amongst us. Only I can stop it. But not now," said Apollo.

"Not now?" Persephone comforted me.

"Boy, listen to me. Whatever is about to happen you don't need to become a part of. Stay here, stay with her. You have a choice most would kill for and that is love. Take it! Don't be a savior. You don't want that kind of loneliness."

"I won't be. I'll be a part of the solution. Persephone no matter what happens, stay down here. I can't say enough that for this plan to work you must be free from what's about to take hold. And when this is all over, I will sing to you again. I love you, and if you ever miss me, just listen to the music," said Apollo.

"I don't have foresight. But I know this world is an illusion in need of people willing to fight for reality. I love you too. Leave me your lyre. And it's ok if you change your mind when you get up there and decide to come back. This doesn't have to be your fight. Our love needs a savior too. Maybe one that has more of my subtle, flowery touch?" said Persephone.

They kissed as if a hundred in a minute would not be enough. Hades, most jaded of the Gods, looks on disapprovingly and attempts to wake me up. Apollo left his lyre with Persephone and then left for an already crashing and thrashing Olympus. I awoke and was informed as to what just happened.

"He'll be forced to drink the wine by Zeus. The blood of Dionysus will consume all of them!" I screamed.

"Then it's too late. You don't strike me as normal. You have death about you, a death that hasn't happened yet has occurred. Please tell me your strangeness is a part of our solution," said Hades.

"Let him rest. The nymphs nearly killed him. You mention wine. Dionysus has been sharing a new wine for weeks now, slowly and in secret, mostly among nymphs. Your wounds are a sign of what is to come then." That was Persephone.

"Our doom. All because of the runt of the litter."

"You see that. That's it right there. I was told that this was a place of harmony, that the Zep Tepi was special because it was free from vice but all of you have the potential to be mean and self-serving. The Blood of Dionysus just clouds the conscience; it doesn't altogether ruin it. Dionysus is just a symptom of a larger problem with the gods, which

308

is a regression to a false past. You all probably don't even know that all gods are trapped anyway. That when ages end it reboots us, over and over again in a cycle, on a wheel, that we never escape. Even this saga, my battle, our fight, is but a drop of fire in a long burning sun." I said.

"That may be. And you sound like you have no hope," said Persephone.

"Then you do not know my nephew," said Hades.

"Right. You don't know Apollo. He is the good shepherd of our people, the destroyer of all evil, the balancer of the scales. If we still have him , wherever you are from, then we still have hope." Persephone said.

"If you thought you were the main character of this story, you're wrong." That was Cerberus in my mind.

"I know. I see it now. I'm just a supporting actor and that gives me the freedom to defy the narrative and be of good use for the resolution. To make a sacrifice."

"Can it be! I see what I have been sensing!You are a Furie! You sound just like they did. Search for them, bring them back to whatever world you come from! Let your kind help in kind, unite your ancestors with your future and your death won't be in vain." Persephone explained.

I began to fade out of this reality. I began to break apart like bits of soil following a breeze.

"Remember us. And forgive us for we are but children too, we know not what we do," said Persephone, wisest of the Gods, for what other season must bear the lessons of both Winter on its face and Summer on its back.

Suddenly, all went black, and Christian found himself in a box, his exact dimensions. While most of his memory failed him, he caught snatches. His detour into the past had paralyzed his memory. Before the Blood of Dionysus was the satisfying air of Zephyr, and before that?

Suddenly, the lid of his box opened, and he saw a curious Set backlit by the co-conspirators he had recognized the first semester of his senior year at Parthenon. But this time, they didn't look like students. They each were the manifestation of manic Olympians. The box suddenly shut and opened again. This time it was Tess. She was covered in sand and blood.

"It's not mine," she said as she helped him up.

"What did you see?" Christian asked, dazed, as he stumbled out.

"My father's sins... and why I have been punished for them."

She looked traumatized, her eyes fixed with the thousand-yard stare.. I wasn't going to be asking her to be more specific. I still wasn't sure how I would explain what I had seen either.

"Is that the Sphinx?" I said as I felt a terrible, trembling power from the lion-bodied, human-headed Goliath.

"Yes, just ten times bigger than the one on earth. And its face..."

"It looks like me."

"Then we are in the right place. We made it."

The sky was the same color as the black sand below. Black was an esteemed color in Ancient Egypt, the color of life bringing soil. There were so many constellations in the sky, far clearer than the sky on Earth. These constellations were easy to decipher: a lioness, a farmer, a pregnant woman, among others. The Sphinx's eyes glowed with profuse power in hues of green. Its chest opened and we walked into a corridor within a room of treasures.

But we quickly found out, beneath the veneer of gold and splendor, that there was a darker side to this corridor. On the walls were depictions of others who had gone on the Guardians' journeys. Images of Egyptian believers surviving worlds filled with daily life, many of their lives and realms of pure imagination. These were plentiful and comforting as they showed triumph and discovery. But then half those we saw we depicted failing the feather test in the Throne Room of Osiris.

The shock and despair on their faces could be felt even now thousands of years later. The final image was of many being engulfed in a black hole while the fortunate who passed the test could be seen hugging loved ones and praising who I used to be and oddly still am. There was no image of me delighting over the fate of the damned or condemning them, it all seemed so matter of fact, so transactional. The way the black hole of Ammit the Devourer made me feel was just hopeless, like I could never retrieve what falls into that pit. Could anyone ever deserve that fate, as tough as that may be to consider. I was about to find out if my grandmother did.

***

Suddenly, Tess and Christian found themselves whisked away to yet another dimension where they stood between a set of black and white pillars. Disappearing into different dimensions was no longer the surprise it had first been, so they walked along the corridor between the pillars. As they continued, the corridor began to hum with music that was barely audible but certainly present.

"Pretty advanced for whatever ancient time period we're in," Christian said lightheartedly. "I wonder what happens here." The corridor led them to a flight of steps which Tess and Christian climbed. Tess counted each step.

"52," she said as they reached the top. But Christian didn't hear. He almost couldn't believe what he was looking at. There in front of them was a wondrous scene. A much younger Sophie stood before a formidable Anubis. MA'at, the embodiment of truth and divine law, was there as well. Ammit stood in a corner and Christian's own image, Osiris, sat in the middle on a throne that shone like the sun.

"Wow. We finally caught up with Sophie," Tess was standing next to Christian now who was staring speechless at the sight.

"Yes," he said quietly. " We have." Tess nudged Christian.

"Are you okay?" While Christian struggled to find an answer, he knew that from the moment he laid eyes on this version of himself that all that had transpired in his life as a small boy who had always felt different and unwanted by parents; his early teenage years when the psychological abuse of his father Stone began and his mother became a wisp of herself, and then his early adult years when he began to give into his psychosis… and the reversal of all of that with the new but arduous path he had recently discovered with all of its missteps had to have happened for him to look at his reflection in this scene of the afterlife and recognize himself. Only someone who had been psychotic, devoted to that never-swinging pendulum, a god trapped in a hall of mirrors, a boy banished to the haunted wing of his school, a girl trapped in an age of hysteria, a seer sealed in a cave underground… and all being ripped apart by their imagination.

As if in answer to Tess's question, Christian cried out to his grandmother.

Silence! The Osiris in the scene looked directly through the vision at Christian and ordered him quiet by the squinting of his eyes, and Christian couldn't talk. Anubis stepped up to Sophie. With a flick of his wrist, he had her heart in his right hand. He placed it on the libra scale, adjacent to the feather of truth which hovered lightly for a second and then plummeted so far below the scale that the feather bobbed precariously at the sudden movement. Both Tess and Christian looked on in horror as the situation unfolded before them. Ammit snorted and awoke. Tess winced and closed her eyes. And Christian? Christian found his voice. And screamed.

The scream which reverberated with rage born of love, was clearly the acceptable kind, for it reached the throne room and gave Osiris pause. Osiris had been focused on Sophie once the feather of truth revealed her fate. But in this moment, Osiris looked through the vision at Christian. Curious he stood and came as close as the vision allowed. Both met eye-to-eye. Christian could feel memories of his grandmother being pulled through his eyes into the eyes of his reflection.

Suddenly, Osiris turned to look at Sophie. Then he looked back at Christian. Osiris's eyes welled up with tears and MA'at began to sing as Sophie's heart shuddered and then slowly rose higher and higher as the feather of truth lowered. Tess, crying, shook Christian to look: the heart had become even with the feather, and from there it would move no farther.

At this point, Osiris didn't look to Christian or Sophie,

but to Tess who slowly rose in the air with a light glowing from between her eyes. MA'at continued his quiet song that sounded like the soft return of rain after a long drought. Tess ascended. Sophie knelt. Anubis held her heart. Osiris spoke.

"To give the path bathed in the light of Atum another try, Tess has afforded you an even split with the feather of truth, Sophie. For that, Anubis will return your heart, and Ammit will return to sleep. Tess, your patience and your guidance have led you to help a loved one have the chance to give a final goodbye. Rise, Sophie."

Sophie stood.

"Judgment in this room is consistent for all who enter it. It is never opinion: only facts. And facts are like willows: they survive the storm of rebuttal. They must. They always will. Thus, Sophie, I give you now a chance to say goodbye to your grandson."

Interpreting these words as permission, Christian ran to Sophie and embraced her as if she had never been frail. Sophie, in return, held Christian tighter than she ever had before. While they held each other, now and then, shuddering with emotion, Tess slowly descended to the ground. Sophie called to her, and soon they were all embracing.

"This journey," Sophie whispered, "is not one of strangers but of a family long separated." There were yet more tears and more embracing, for none of the party wanted to let the other go. Once they did, it would be goodbye for a long time. MA'at's singing got quieter and became a hum. Suddenly, the humming stopped completely and she spoke.

"May my song live in you. Many do not hear it and many more are dead when they do. You two are living, and thus must leave now. Sophie, however, your destiny is more complicated. By sacred law you will have another chance to be lighter than the feather, but you will not see Rostau, the field of reeds. You must take a path to your most ancient ancestor, Voida." Osiris picked up the instructions.

"She has been missing for some time. And though in the past your Furie duty put you at odds with the will of the gods, you will now have alignment. Find Voida! Bring her back! And you will, I have no doubt, earn a better fate than this. I will restore you. We will be with you, for we will watch you from afar." Tess snapped back to her former self.

"No, wait. Christian saw Voida. We can find her again. Let Sophie rest." Tess demanded.

"Tess, it's alright. I want this," Sophie said soothingly. But Tess was getting irate.

"Christian? You're Osiris. Challenge him! We can save Sophie, just do something!"

Anubis, who had been quiet this entire time, interjected.

"Christian came not to change the decision, but to encourage his grandmother to believe that no matter what one must always have a rage. A rage for life, a rage for the living. A rage for those who show up for you. A rage to be understood. Perhaps if more people chose this sort of rage instead of that rage becoming their last testament, they would not see death as a sullen face with green skin. You might not like a decision, but you must always end on a good note!"

Christian nodded his head at Tess.

"Anubis is right. I wanted to come this far so that I could say goodbye. Grandma, you helped me make that happen, and for that I will always be grateful. But now, we need to escape, and Voida can help us do that. Thank you MA'at,

Anubis, and Osiris."

"Escape?" Tess asked.

"I'll explain when we are home."

"Do not forget what you have witnessed here," Osiris said in benediction. "Usually, the dead do not have mortal witnesses. Remember that there is goodness for those who choose to love rather than destroy. Anubis will walk you out, otherwise I'd fear you'd get lost. And remember, Tess and Christian, the past is only our beginning. You determine where we end up!"

Anubis gestured to Tess and Christian who hugged Sophie once more. Anubis walked them down a corridor that abruptly came to an end.

"Stop. Here is your exit in a spot you would never see coming," Anubis said.

"Will we ever see her again?" Christian asked, turning his head back to where they had come.

Anubis's eyes flickered.

"She has cheated me out of her death. I am not greedy, but I have a duty. There must be balance. Now that she will balance the scales. If she succeeds, you will see her when you yourself die and only if you are judged correctly. Or, if you take the throne of your elder version. Here is your portal. It will drop you off where you are needed," Anubis gestured for them to move forward, but then Tess turned around.

"This is bullshit. Your whole order is bullshit! You are bullshit, Anubis!"

"Tess," Christian warned, pulling her by the arm. Tess pushed Christian away.

"No, I won't go quietly. Sophie saved my life. Whatever she owed you it was because you coerced her to go against

316

her Furie nature to obey you. That doesn't make you righteous: it makes you a tyrant. Just another set of tyrant gods." Anubis's nostrils flared.

"You are strangely comfortable challenging me as if you are my equal. As if we have done this before. As if you are not you. But let me tell you something, people know my name. No one knows yours. You have no rite, no runes, no depictions on burdened stone. You are simply a passing fancy, a fad. You are youth in all its final helplessness before age. No one ever actually listens to youth. Once you have aged, you won't listen to it either and thus the cycle goes."

"Fuck you!" Tess interrupted. Anubis roared.

"You want to challenge me, insult me? Make a name for yourself and then we'll talk, Daughter of Set the Blasphemer. If I didn't know any better, I'd say you are Set incarnate, wasting his time loving his own protest so much that he thinks it actually matters. You aren't him, are you, no, because he wouldn't be so stupid as to come here and think he could escape without a terrible price for the things you have said." Anubis spun his scepter, illuminating the portal before Tess and Christian

"Now, go! You will not be given another chance."

"We're going," Christian grabbed Tess by the wrist again.

"We'll be back," Tess spat and gave Anubis the finger with her free hand.

CHAPTER 1
Three the Hard Way

Ok so, the chapter is called "Three the hard way" because there are three shape shifting tricks!

1. Zeus confronts who he thinks is christian in the music room, in fact it is actually Wep.

2. Then Zeus confronts a christian riding on a Raiju, who he fights for a while at the pantheon. This is Sysy or Loki, the female who eventually will win christians heart and reveal her true self in the coming books but for now she is shape shifting as christian while....

3. Apollo is confronted by Dionysus. By the real Dionysus is truly dead for now, this is the actual christian Belvedere shape shifted as the god of wine because christians blood is immune to the bite of the olympians and by biting him the olympians can be cured. Apollo then rages and becomes good again and says " i am not my fathers son" as he is the sun god again and he disposes of zeus.

Aftermath

Sysy reveals to Asara, perhaps right before a kiss, that she is not christian. Christian stumbles towards the two of them and reveals his elaborate plan to asara and shifts back into his osiris form to give the benediction.

Does this make sense? I think this could be a killer ending. Let me know if more clarity is needed!

"Is this really happening?" Christian said out loud as they exited the Duat into a forest so thick that they couldn't tell if it was day or night. Tess lost her footing and toppled over a tree stump into a puddle. She jumped up, cursing a streak of blue lighting.

"Are you indulging your psychosis again?" She patted the back of her pants to gauge how wet she had gotten. "You know, forget it. Real or not, we… you must act. It's the only way out of the forest," Tess huffed as she navigated a thick bramble bush that blocked their way.

Christian was quiet for a while as he followed Tess.

"Real or not? Either way, it's my reality. Huh. I hadn't thought of it that way before. Tess, you're brilliant."

"Glad to be of help," she murmured as she pushed forward. "Is it day or night? I can't tell. The branches are so thick in this forest."

"The first order of business is to see my father." Tess reeled on him.

"Are you sure you're OK? See your father? What are you talking about? What good is that going to do?" But Christian ignored her concern as he passed her on the path.

"You'll see. Hurry up, Tess, we're home." Christian had reached the edge of the wood. And pulling back an evergreen to make room for her they both stepped out of the dark and into the light.

"Why is it always the Southside of Potential Street," Tess complained. We've got our reputations to keep. Might as well hit a pub while we're here." She took a left which led to the shadier part of town but had the cheapest drinks before lunch.

"I'll see you later... hopefully," Christian grinned at her.

"You're not coming? No, don't tell me this is about your father again." Christian shrugged his shoulders.

"He's not yours. He's mine. At some point I'll have to face him. Might as well do it on the high of the journey we just took. He held out his fist for Tess to bump.

"Be safe, Christian." She looked at his fist. "It's not good-bye yet."

MAYBE BRING BACK ASARA HERE AS TESS IS GO-ING TO THE PUB.

WE NEED ANOTHER SCENE TO INDICATE THAT THIS IS WEP.

***

"So, the music building? This is where you wanted to meet me?" Stone Belvedere surveyed Christian suspicious-ly then gestured almost wistfully with a nod of his head to the performing arts center sign as they met in front of the gigantic front door.

"This is a special place. To our family," Christian put his hands in his pockets nervously. "I thought you might like to see what they've done to the place." Pulling one hand out, he reached for the handle. Stone paused for a second and looked at Christian quizzically before he stepped into the dark foyer. As Christian closed the door, his eyes swept the courtyard behind him where we had just come from. Time with Stone was a rare commodity. He needed to be sure that they wouldn't be interrupted.

"The auditorium. There's something I want to show you." Stone's quizzical look turned into a full-blown grin. Stone built that auditorium. With part of the inheritance from his parents, but it was his idea nonetheless. If there ever were an Achilles heel Stone had that was known by anyone who knew him, it was his pride in single-handedly financing almost an eighth of the new construction at Parthenon. So the smile he gave Christian was no more than evidence that Stone had no idea why Christian brought him to this building.

"After you, Christian."

Christian walked just a little bit too fast down the left hallway, fast enough to look like he was up to no good. So he intentionally slowed his breathing and pace enough for Stone to catch up.

When they entered the double doors of the music room, Christian turned the lights of the auditorium on, and all 40 halogen bulbs popped simultaneously. Light instantly flooded the room. Christian could see that Stone still wore a smile on his face which meant that he didn't assume the worst of intentions. Unsure of how to proceed, Christian walked slowly down the center aisle, beckoning Stone to follow him.

"You know, when I was around ten-years-old, I met a kid who couldn't have been more than five, who played by himself during recess," Christian looked back at Stone. "Just like me." Stone nodded his head affirmatively.

"I'm not sure why, but this kid started to look up to me. Idolize me. Maybe it was because I'd occasionally talk to him or just listen to him talk." Christian and Stone were halfway to the stage. Stone cocked his head, indicating for Christian to continue.

"I remember that he loved to sing. Man, could he sing. It was as if he was music itself." Christian and his father were now just a dozen steps or so from the stage.

"Every day, I would go to the sandbox and he would have a new song."

"What happened to him?" Stone asked with a hint of genuine curiosity.

Christian shrugged.

"I began to take him for granted, I guess. I went to the sandbox less and less and began to wander into other activities and other interests. My ignoring him like that seemed to kill his spirit. For the rest of his time at school, he never sang again." Christian turned to look Stone square in the eyes. "I killed the music, you see." Christian was maybe four more steps away from the stage. Stone stopped, and his eyebrows, once alert and curious, slit into daggers.

"I sense there's a subtext here. Either that or you're being tangential. Perhaps, you should sit down and we can call Dr. Aceso." It was a threat.

"What does a person who kills the music deserve?" Christian continued, ignoring the ominous grimace that appeared on Stone's face.

"I see. I guess I deserve the chance to explain myself then. Give me a moment." Stone unfolded his arms and just like that disappeared.

For a second, Christian thought he had imagined the entire conversation with his father to be a figment of his imagination. So he was disoriented when Stone suddenly reappeared behind him, striking him in the back of the head with a bolt of lightning.

MUSIC IS KILLED. HUGE FIGHT SCENE.

POSSIBLY HAVE PAULIE THE DEAD BROTHER OF CHRISTIAN. Have PAULIE BE GIVEN AWAY BY STONE AS A CHILD.

***

Christian must have blacked out, because the next thing he saw was Apollo, appearing out of nowhere, where the symphony of the school orchestra was the loudest.

"It's a shame. He could have been one of us. We could have been real brothers. He could have had it all." Apollo was looking at Christian in pity, lying there awkwardly, his body sprawled out on the bottom step. Stone walked into the peripheral vision of his right eye.

"Stop talking about him like it's too late. He'll see. In the world we make, the rightness of our imaginings, he will delight in what we delight in. For he is my flesh and blood in this life, and that will be all it takes in this new world." Christian shut his eyes and lay still.

"We'll use him to power the obelisks. He's the last one. But because of who he is, we'll have more power than we planned for. We can make our changes permanent for the next thousand years! Father? Father, are... are you crying?" Apollo took a step back in alarm.

"I didn't intend to sacrifice him this way. He's my heir as you are. But his parable was obvious and he has somehow figured me out. Perhaps, in the new world he'll understand my love for him..." Apollo, who had been momentarily concerned went from zero to sixty before Stone even finished his sentence

"He's your heir? This bastard son? Surely, you are of sound mind! Since when does Zeus plan on giving up his throne?"

"You misremember. I have always believed in succession. You just weren't privy to those discussions. If you wanted the power of my kingdom, then you should have been more like Augustus and less like Caligula with your Agrippina!"

"Hypocrite! You've fucked half the world and heaven. And when that wasn't enough, you sought other worlds. You have always been afraid of my power! And though you drank my brother's blood willingly, you forced me to as well. You drowned me in it yourself as a part of your own cowardly scheme! You, the Manipulator, you the Liar, you the Bad Father... you may not be as drunk as I am, but you are an alcoholic through and through." Apollo pointed at Stone with a quaking forefinger. But Stone ignored him and knelt down by Christian's side.

"At least I still have someone to love. Someone to save. Someone to fight for." Stone lifted Christian effortlessly, put him over his shoulder, abruptly turned his back to Apollo, and walked back up the aisle.

Apollo was wounded. He sat down at the grand concert piano and gave Zeus the finger. Zeus, approaching the end of the aisle at the back of the auditorium, turned around.

"Son, you should have more respect for your father if

you ever want your time to come!" In response, Apollo began to bang out a thunderous melody. With a deep inhale, Stone, rather, Zeus was gone.

***

The clouds rose and covered all light. It was pitch-black outside other than the occasional lightning strike that shook the ground continuously with shockwave after shockwave. Stone Belvedere, Zeus in the flesh, carried Christian onto the grounds of Liger where a horde of Olympians had gathered, to wait for him. Christian, having been clocked in the back of the head, was slowly coming out of his short coma. Firmly, but reverently, Stone attached Christian to the obelisk.

"That was so easy!" Christian followed the sound of the voice with eyes half opened. It was Chastity. Pointing to Liger, she yelled to everyone and no one in particular.

"Liger? Where are its defenders now?"

Stone, looking at his son placed in the form of a crucifix, nodded at Christian grimly while Christian's back arched as the convulsive power from the lighting strike on the obelisk surged through him. The pain made Christian see white and lit every neuron in his back all the way up to his brain. Almost as if on cue, the other eleven obelisks from the other eleven merry mounts rose in succession, drawing power from the god-persons attached to them. The collective screams of the writhing deities were so loud that they drowned out the thunder. Stone turned to Chastity.

"Look around you. There are now hundreds of us here. We are all gathered in one place. I have revealed myself and taken their only hope off the board. Just as polytheism conquered animism, and monotheism conquered all, a new world has no opposing force!"

The Olympic horde cheered and expanded the expression of their true forms.

"Also," Stone interjected, "Today is Christian's birthday. It's only right we have our cake!"

"He always thought 22 would be the start of the best years of his life," Chastity chortled. Suddenly, out of the blue and for no apparent reason, Christian began to guffaw.

At first, Zeus thought Christian's response was delirious. But then the tempo of Christian's guffaw turned into a laugh, a hearty laugh generated from deep within his diaphragm. But when its rhythm became irregular and the laugh turned into a cackling, Zeus went from being unnerved to rage at the disrespect.

"How dare you," Zeus started.

"How dare YOU, you fat fuck." The horde went quiet.

"What..." Zeus started to say.

"What? What what? Do you not know what, Mighty Zeus? Professional charlatan. Consummate womanizer. Eater of your own children." The tension in the air at this point was unsustainable. Christian had never before seen his father this angry, though Zeus put on an air of power under control.

"Son, you need to..." he started.

"No, bitch, you need to." Christian countered. Zeus's nostrils flared, ever so slightly. Christian had seen that before, too many times to count. He needed to drive the ugly part of his father into the light for all to see.

"Like I said, bitch, you need to." The color of Zeus's complexion changed from his sun-tanned brown to a rosy glow that flushed his cheeks.

"And what is it that I need to do?" Zeus said through gritted teeth.

"You don't know?" Christian said sarcastically. Then he went for the jugular. "To remove blood, you have to spill it."

Those were the magic words. First, they were the magic words that made Zeus crack. His face turned a bright red and his composure failed him to the point that he was unable to form words. Had he been a mortal, someone would have called 911 for fear that he was having a stroke.

Second, they were the magic words, because almost suddenly the ground began to shake slightly. Then the reverberation became a rumble. Looking at the hills that lay beyond Potential Street by about a half mile, what looked like the bursting of a dam and its downward cascade alerted the onlookers, Olympians included, that it was responsible for the rumble.

Zeus in the middle of his apoplexy-state stared befuddled. "Shit…" he murmured as it dawned on him. For Zeus, having heard the sound of many armies before, knew this sound. It was one hundred Raiju warriors charging at the Olympians who were now simpering at each other. The Raiju, who were mystical wolf gods known in Japan as mercurial and iffy in alliances, were always hungry for the most stunning of entrances. Tricksters often, but always loyal when they chose a cause.

"Who…" Zeus started. "Where…" he tried again.

"You mean how?" Christian added. But when Zeus looked to his son, he didn't see Christian but Wep in Christian's place.

"What the fuck!" Zeus yelped. Wep easily shrugged out

of his restraints, arched his back as if it were sore, and scratched his balls, looking around with a grin at the unnerved Olympians.

"Zeus, you don't even know your own kid? Why would Christian think he could convince you of anything?" Zeus, dumbfounded, spoke so fast that he spat.

"No. I won't believe it!" he said, closing his eyes.

"Believe? What does belief have to do with it? Can Christian do this?" Wep promptly produced a saxophone, playing the exaggerated opening notes of a faintly familiar song. Zeus and the Olympian horde stared on.

"I call that Stairway to the Duat. It will be a favorite. But for now, you should probably be prepared for some Japanese jiu jitsu." The Raiju were now thundering down a side street, no less than a minute away, if that.

"How could I not see through your disguise? You're not my son! Where IS Christian?" But at that moment, Wep didn't need to answer, for turning the corner on a white steed with a battle ax in his left hand was Christian, leading his warrior battalion company. And he wasn't slowing down.

Shit!" Zeus roared. But his eyes read that disappointment choked him.

At that moment the Raiju attacked the Olympians. Though outnumbered, this breed of gods weren't overpowered. Movement was everywhere and every god was engaged. Only two were not, and they stood facing each other, undistracted from the battle surrounding them.

"Father of mine!" Christian yelled above the cacophony. "The apple falls far from the fool!" Zeus's eyes were slits.

"I don't wish to fight you, but I have a temper you don't want to tempt," Zeus yelled back. But Christian, rather

328

Osiris, tempted all the same.

"You are weak! You are afraid of children! You cannot beat me!" Christian checked off the top three statements that he knew would set Zeus off. He wanted to force the serpent out of hiding. And it worked.

Zeus ran up to Osiris as Osiris dismounted his steed, slapped him on the rump, and sent him running off through the thick of the battle. Now they were face to face. With a movement faster than he could recollect, Osiris tossed Zeus into the doorway of Pithon, imploding the doors and splintering the doorframe. As if in approval, lightning struck him at that same moment while he lay inside the Pithon foyer. It looked for the moment that Osiris had changed Zeus's mind about fighting him. But Osiris was not to be fooled by Zeus's ruse of weakness, taking the opportunity to buy time.

Chastity, who had been watching this interaction, read the situation and called for the knights of Christendom. The front lawn of Pithon began to rumble, and ridges the size of bears disturbed from hibernation rose from the ground revealing a company of Crusader-clad knights, Big Grim among them.

"Christian soldiers! Surely you remember the Great Heathen Army!" Proud Odin yelled.

Big Grim unfurled Gungnir, his magic spear, sweeping it over the large mounds. From the electric coursing power emerged Vikings long dead who had been at some point in their lives called to Valhalla where they had been feasting and training, waiting for a call such as this one from their All-Father. Now here they were adjacent to and behind Big Grim. Drums and an onslaught of horns, rage from feet to helmet, swords and axes announced their resurrection and entrance onto the battlefield that was Potential Street.

Zeus, finally realizing that he was outnumbered, sprung out of the doorway with a shout and charged at Osiris. Osiris was prepared for this moment. He knew that it would come, for he knew that a snake would always prove himself a snake. Osiris gripped his battle ax and smirked at the man he had always wanted to fight.

***

During this time, Apollo, still in the music room, had been playing furiously for the past hour. Zeus had slighted him for the last time and he now was consumed with turning his power into a product. But he couldn't think straight. For centuries he had been in a fog, unable to be effective as a potential leader. He wasn't alone in this holding pattern, for none of the Olympians were able to see things clearly.

Apollo's fingers paused on the electric guitar with which he had been so engaged that the strings were hot to the touch. As he sat surveying the bulbous blister on his right thumb, he thought about his long-lost brother, Dionysus: cheerful, irresponsible, carefree. He held him in his mind's eye, and his dissatisfaction grew. Because there is no such thing as a good brother when your father favors them over you.

Apollo did not used to be this way. At one time his only passion had been music. But the Blood of Dionysus brought with it a paranoia of all possible competitors and an obsession with status. He swore in his heart that the next time that a thing or person made him feel that way, he would destroy them. But his thoughts were interrupted.

330

"Three cheers for Old Scrimshaw, and the Gods of Parthenon University! It's not what Olympus used to be but perhaps it is a good start to begin at a mortal height and then rise!" It was Dionysus. At Parthenon. In the music room. Approaching Apollo on the stage. "Rise and then drink!" Dionysus demanded.

" Impossible. Needed... but impossible!" Apollo glowered.

"No. Seems impossible is all of your friends and family feeding off of your body until you're a dry husk collecting dust in the corner of some room somewhere. Unrecognizable and unrecognized. That's impossible, brother," Dionysus said with sad eyes.

In answer, Apollo fiddled a riff on the guitar, wincing at his blisters. He stood up suddenly and slung the guitar across the stage where it crashed into the piano.

"We've become quite the rivals over the centuries in mortal philosophy. You seem to be forgetting much, like how I could drain you all again myself. You and I are pillars of personality, the doorways to ecstasy or moderation, ironically. It is ironic since I haven't felt either in a very long time." Apollo licked his fangs that slowly protruded as he spoke.

"That's tragic. Because I don't know where I've been these past four thousand-plus years. It was lonely, but not as lonely as earth must be for my family. I still had the sympathy of that which is beyond even us. That's powerful company for a victim. All the women we used to quibble over, all the times we'd race and we'd let the other win, all the things we can't remember between you and me, Far Shooter... Dionysus paused for dramatic effect. "And then all the evil that was done. The rapes, kidnappings, wars and warmongering, trials, the minotaur, and proving zealous Christendom right. All because you stole my body, you stole what gave me life. Yes, I played a stupid game, but you all didn't have to lose yourselves in it." Dionysus lifted his chin as Apollo stood up.

"You're just a requiem. A version of something we clearly underestimated." Apollo seethed a dark power. Dionysus laughed dismissively.

"No, you overestimated. The blood of mine you've had will not course through you ad finitum. Like I died, so will it. You're mortal now. And you've overstayed your welcome in this realm. It is time you left it, or..."

"Or what?" Apollo questioned as he struck out at Dionysus at the same time. Dionysus, surprisingly nimble, dodged and stood still as if teasing Apollo.

Apollo struck again and again but he missed each time. Dionysus, enjoying Apollo's frustration, got cocky when Apollo, feigning weariness, attacked him again. Dionysus blocked and repelled but would not strike Apollo. Apollo and Dionysus continued this way for the better part of a half hour until, realizing it needed to end, Dionysus struck Apollo down with a punch to the chin. Apollo lay in a heap, breathing hard.

"You look thirsty, Apollo. If only there were someone to drink," Dionysus said with a snigger.

Apollo lunged for Dionysus again, distending his fangs and latching onto Dionysus's left shoulder until he began to feel dizzy. He felt something bubbling inside his gut. Apollo detached, stumbling backwards.

"What is that?" he asked groggily. He could see Dionysus who came in and out of his blurred vision. Dionysus was smiling.

"That's guilt. Only the redeemable feel it."

Apollo fell to his knees.

"What? Something is wrong. How can this be? You are not my brother!"

"Oh, but I am your brother, and my purpose here was to save the music. Your acolyte Nike performed a miracle after she bit me which led us here to you. Sometimes gods are so easily swayed by their own temper that they can't tell the difference between Adam and the snake. Even in their own garden." A kind smile played on the corner of Dionysus's lips.

"Away with your riddles!" Apollo spat as his fangs began to fall out.

"Yes, away with them. Away with them all. Such a lazy disposition. No, I say everything can be used, anything can have a purpose or repurposing. Why would I simply tear everything around me and destroy you when a trick will bring the justice we need and that you, Apollo, so deserve." The impersonator rested his hand on Apollo's shaking shoulder.

***

Back on Potential Street chaos still reigned. The Norse Gods had picked an Olympian for themselves. Brisin, with her cloak of falcon feathers, soared around Chastity, evading her arrows.

"I never miss!" Chastity screamed in frustration. "Who are these ugly, slack-jawed deities? And where is my brother?"

Brisin caught one of Chastity's arrows, transformed it into a spear and drove it down Chastity's throat. The force knocked back other warriors into a freshly hewn crater where Chastity seizured from the blow. Brisin smiled and waited for her opponent in case she should rise again. These were, after all, gods.

Zalewski was fighting with Zeus, hammering blow after blow while Zeus in return brought the sky down on him. The sky was a frightening panoply of thunder and lightning wielded from different worlds into one sky which blinded Zalewski's vision, giving Zeus the advantage of stealth. Searching for Zeus in the resulting fog, Zalewski happened upon Will with his Spear of Justice, and Duel, with his bows made from the sacred yew tree, surrounded by twenty gods, including blood-thirsty Guerro and Athena.

The knights and Viking warriors rumbled all the while, filling in every nook and cranny available, slashing and plunging their weapons where any Olympian revealed themselves. When Zalewski finally laid eyes on Zeus again, he also noticed Osiris was facing off with him. But Zalewski, staying with his plan, raised Mjolnir and charged Zeus who countered with an ancient intuition that threw Zalewski onto his back, leaving him concussed for the better part of a moment. Ever the advantage-taker, Zeus turned back to Osiris.

Osiris could tell that Zeues was shouting something at him. But though they were no more than twenty yards apart, the din of battle muted Zeus's words. As he limped closer to Osiris, Osiris could tell that he had been wounded in the thigh by Zalewski. Finally, Zeus's words pierced the melee.

"My son! Please. I have held you in my arms, these now breaking arms. I have watched you walk away to achieve what young men do when they begin to make their way in the world, and I have swelled with pride, I have..." Osiris raised an arm above his head to order Zeus silent.

"You were creating a cabal. You used Munchhausen to enslave me in order to transform this world into a nightmare. You are lascivious and dastardly. You lie and you lie in wait for the vulnerable. My mother held me, too, for a while when I was young. You did not understand a mother's love, and you were threatened by maternal instinct as mortals call it, and that was a liability you could not stomach. And look what you did to her. I am not that emotionally-underdeveloped, pimply-faced man-child who knew nothing better than he was told by his bully of a father. And my mother is not to be the go between. It's just you and me." Osiris lowered his hand, which Zeus took as permission to speak.

"But how did you know to trick me? I could have just used Virtues Constellation with what we have if I were as evil as you say I am."

"Yes, but almighty Zeus, King of the Gods, isn't accustomed to settling, is he? How did I know? I recently took a small vacation to a time when you were quite popular."

"Ok. Riddles. So, we are doing this?"

"It's already been done." Zeus froze for a millisecond. Long enough to betray worry.

"I warn you that I have been holding back. I haven't had to fight for anything in a long time. You can ask my father, Cronus ,and the doomed Titans. I can be very hard to handle!" Electricity coursed through Zeus's body as he spoke, his voice growing like thunder clouds.

Both charged each other.

Osiris slashed with his axes across Zeus's stomach and

face. Zeus, insulted, swung back at Osiris, underestimating how strong he was. Overcompensating, Zeus landed a punch which sent Osiris through the Summit Center all the way back to the 1901 Hall. Summit, a relatively new building, was a popular destination for students. But with the veil in tatters, students and faculty members were running with no direction being clearer than any other. 1901 was a much older part of the building built in 1925. It was currently used as a dorm with its west wing now collapsed. As Osiris rallied himself, he noticed people running away through the thick dust that filled the air. A female approached him, noticeably less panicked than the others..

"Christian!" Osiris blinked his eyes, and stared back at the person in wonder at the person standing over him. It was Asara.

"Asara?" was all he could say. Asara grabbed him by the hand to help him up.

"Again, you need a better set of plans if you're going to get all of this under control."

"Trust me. Even you would be impressed by this one. Once all is revealed, that is." Christian wiped the dust out of his eyes. "Do me a favor?"

"Sure. But, Christian, it's been almost three weeks. I figured you would have tried to reach me."

"There will be time for that later."

"Well, what's the favor?"

"Run!"

From the sky as if on cue Zeus descended with a storm of lightning through the ceiling, smashing a hole in what remained. Instinctively, Osiris shielded Asara from the debris then lunged for Zeus.

"There you go again, Christian. Like I said, you need a

better plan. Take this back out on Potential Street. I'll catch up with you later and we'll talk." And with that, Asara disappeared into the dust.

***

Zeus was hunting. Losing sight of Christian in Summit, he had returned outdoors to the battle on Potential Street. He was so enraged that his skin was forming new wrinkles. Surveying the fight, he saw a deadlock. Once King of the Gods, he was now witnessing the loss of his potential paradise. He took a deep breath. Though still powerful, he was not as immortal as he used to be. But, given the occasion, he could summon just enough of his old divinity to tip the scale. Couldn't he?

"Now you face a power!" he screamed at no one in particular.

But a street over, Big Grim noticed a shift in momentum, preparing his spear Gugnir to target the source but it was too late. The ground shook and the combatants lost their footing, pausing long enough to seek out the reason for the earthquake. Suddenly, the focus on the battlefield began to be directed skyward. Zeus had grown to the size of a skyscraper.

Zeus yelled, the bass in his voice reverberating across the ground, causing the fluorescent light bulbs in the street lamps to vibrate at such a high pitch that they began popping in succession. Car alarms began to go off and the alarm buildings in the buildings across campus began beeping so loudly that students and faculty members began exiting with abandon only to be frozen right outside the doors when they saw the gigantic Olympian advancing down Potential Street. Zeus laughed at the chaos, determined that destroying everyone was just reward for his wounded pride.

"I won't let one bipolar child determine the fate of the world. I've been forgotten but no more! I am Zeus. The Father of Men, and I am all!" More lightning than an afternoon Florida thunderstorm zig-zagged across the sky.

Before Zeus could wreak the havoc he was set on unleashing, a voice much louder than his own answered him.

"I am not my father's son!" exploded like a tornado touching ground across the battlefield that had become Potential Street. Like the gasp of a hero who foresaw his own return, it was the force of sacred effort. The sacred effort of a son who had had enough! THIS IS APOLLO.

Down on the ground, several of Osiris's friends rejoined him, Asara included.

"You were right," he acknowledged her with determination in his eyes. "I needed a better plan. And now here he is!"

A furious golden light brighter than the sun descended out of nowhere, snatched up the shocked Zeus, shook him like a rag doll, enveloping his writing frame, and carried him high into the clouds."

There was a pause in the battle. No one was striking. All were in awe. Even the remaining Olympians were quiet and no longer hell bent on causing trouble, having witnessed the unfortunate ascension of their leader. The Vikings were relieved, and the Knights had their spell partially broken. Addressing the unease in the quiet, Osiris addressed the Olympians first.

"It's over."

Then he pointed at the Vikings who had more or less regrouped.

"Your duty is completed here."

Then he pointed to a group of nights.

"It is finished."

Each group in its own way understood the import of the message. There was no more cause to fight. There would be no more cause to fight, for this Apocalypse preempted by the second coming of Zeus hadn't turned out the way each had feared and anticipated for the last two thousand years. Asara touched Osiris's shoulder as he ended.

"You should formalize this," she hinted. "Don't send them away empty-handed," she nodded her head towards the knights in particular. A light came in Osiris's eyes and he smiled.

"And one more thing," he announced to the group. "A benediction." And then from the depths of Osiris's soul sprang up a prayer he had remembered since he was a young, scared child. One that his grandmother Sophie taught him.

The Lord is my shepherd; I shall not want. He maketh me to lie down in green pastures; he leadeth me beside the still waters. He restoreth my soul; he leadeth me in the paths of righteousness for his name's sake. Even though I walk through the valley of the shadow of death, I will fear no evil, for You are with me; Your rod and Your staff, they comfort me. You prepare a table before me in the presence of my enemies. You anoint my head with oil, my cup over-flows. Surely goodness and mercy shall follow me all the days of my life; and I will dwell in the house of the Lord forever.

As Osiris finished these words, he noticed that the knights had been murmuring among themselves and the tension had disappeared from their faces. Now that Zeus was gone, a song arose from the battlefield. A song that had been in the works for centuries from the black Moorish converts like Saint Maurice who fought in Spain, to Joan of Arc, the female heroine of France, to the cobbled streets of Scotland and to the Holy Land. This song erupted as long-deferred freedoms do. And with its conclusion the knights were gone to better days and restful nights, slaves to the Olympians no more.

The Olympians were stunned. By this time Christian had made it to the obelisk in front of Liger. He felt it calling to him and had the commandment ready now that he could focus and be unimpeded. The Vikings continued to hold the Greek Gods back with the help of Zalewski, Brisin, Duel, Will, and now Sysy. Dité watched from afar, calmly with many designs in her head.

Osiris touched the obelisk. It was overwhelming. Tess grabbed his hand so that he could use her strength. Wep grabbed his hand and the way opened up.

"All gods and goddesses under the influence of the Blood of Dionysus, I cast you away. Far from here be carried, to a place where your inebriation can wear off for the sake of better devices. You cannot have Olympus but you cannot be here either, I say you must go to the place you fear the most, only to escape if you have atoned! Let this commandment go unbroken." Let nothing but fate alone be able to undo it. I doubt they will undo it, for I do not hear them protesting it now even though I can hear all the verse. Say hello to darkness, your old friend, talk with it, this Erebus that we all know in the corners of our rooms. And in the sound of silence may your dreams be restless. May blunt cobblestone streets be walked without proper footwear. May your nights be split and your days with naked light confront you. For you have done great sin upon this earth and you must atone. But though you are not dead, nothing will disturb you nor the peace we will feel in this time of tribulation. So whether it is the diverse Duat or Hades, deep within Tartarus you go. You will not be the bane of the new prophets who say Hallelujah! from their knees on this redemptive day. As your evil departs this earth, we, the survivors, can finally rise for those you have killed. Be gone, be gone and atone!"

Wep stood up and happily gave some of his power to this charging command. All of those long attached to the obelisks on Potential Street felt their strength return to them. They understood the mysteries of this world, that some myths are real and some things that are real can inspire. So, they shouted and stomped these demons away. Into the sky, the defeated Olympians flew as a large hole opened and swallowed them.

Christian could swear he heard the earth itself breathe a sigh of relief as if Cronus had just lifted the heavy tyrant sky off her bosom. The obelisks freed their captives. The Norse celebrated with meade that they shared with the warriors and the rest of those who had enjoined the battle. All were overjoyed and well thirsty. Much of campus was in ruins, and Potential Street was a burning, broken heap. But, still, they would celebrate.

***

"The veil needs some of that Marvin Gaye healing," Wep crooned.

"I think I have the perfect idea," Christian countered as a bold light descended towards them.

The largest Viking Christian had ever seen, a six-foot-seven shield maiden, sauntered up to them. She looked angry, as if she had been insulted. She grabbed Wep's saxophone, inspected it like it was a waste of time, looked around at her kin, smiled, and began playing it with ease. At that moment, Christian knew what they needed for Dean Maiden.

A few hours later after some planning, Christan sat in the White cafeteria during dinner time with Asara, Tess, and Wep but disguised as Bjorn. Christian knew that Dean Maiden liked to eat in White, so he made Bjorn's presence obvious.

She liked to eat breakfast at night, so she approached their table with a tray of cereal and a glass of chocolate milk. Christian as Bjorn offered her a seat and she sat. She ate like a kid, as if she needed to be cheered up by her food.

"Quite a day today!" he said.

"I was doing paperwork off campus so I wouldn't know. What happened?" Dean Maiden lied as she concentrated on her spoonful of cereal.

"There was a fight. A brawl really. I guess you could even call it a battle. We also found something very special. Or should I say someone."

"I remember the day the music died. It carried on, but

no matter how good it was, it just was never the same." Wep took a sip of tea.

"I don't think she gets it, boys," Tess sighed. Dean Maiden stopped eating mid-bite.

"I must say I really don't."

"Perhaps, she will... in about five seconds," Christian said as he gave the signal.

"5,4,3,2,1..."

"Step one: you say we need to talk," sang a shield maiden as she sat down adjacent from them with her tray stacked with pizza. Vikings love what they've never had.

"He walks. You say sit down. It's just a talk. He smiles politely back at you,"

"You stare politely right on through," Tess and Asara sang.

"Some sort of window to your right, as he goes left and you stay right between the lines of fear and blame."

"You begin to wonder why you came," everyone in the dining room was singing now with about as many loud, eager Vikings as they could fit in along with the rest of them."

"And then.... he returns to her..."

"Where did I go wrong? I lost a friend. Somewhere along in the bitterness and I would have stayed up with you all night. Had I known how to save a life," sang Apollo, revitalized, restored, and sober of mind and spirit.

He continued the song with the rest of them, singing the accompanying melody and background track and Wep added a saxophone solo. Dean Maiden couldn't believe her eyes.

Nearly four thousand years apart, with him, her true love, lost in the vices of people who were bent on his cor-

343

ruption. When Christian figured it all out, who she was and saw their origin, he knew that no matter how significant he might seem, he was not the main thread of this story. This was their story, the story of how an embarrassed young man with a bipolar diagnosis recognized that this world needs music and music needs the Queen of Innocence and Experience.

In Greek myth there is but one source that briefly mentions the failed courtship between Apollo and Persephone. It's a love song that no one had ever really heard. Now it was Christian's purpose, and Dean Maiden didn't have to call him her ex-boyfriend anymore.

"Stop! How is this possible." She looked Christian dead in the face.

"My blood. He had some and it reversed the blood spell."

"The only way to remove blood is to spill it. I get that now. I haven't heard him sing in… I'm Persephone by the way, Christian. I know you know but now I get to be honest. I can't feel my toes. It's as if we just left each other for that final time." She struggled to stand.

"Your name means sweet song. You're the eleventh muse, the one all history now bends to place in the best of fates. Now go make your love famous," Christian was crying from eyes to mouth.

Dean Maiden stood up. The song finished. They and their love were the last of their kind, as it should be. This was justice, and Furies pursued justice rabidly. A tearful and exhausted Dean Maiden turned to Christian.

"Christian… I knew you had it in you!"

The patience of Spring and the subtlety of a flower, that's the power we need… that evil hates to face.

An hour later, Christian and his friends put Liger on tap

and celebrated. In fact, the whole street was on tap that night as people partied like they had saved the world. They drank special mead only meant for victories, and danced. Asara and Christian had a lot of catching up to do.

"You must have really done a lot of thinking about what I said during your two-week vacation," she nudged. "Minus two days."

"You sound like you want to take credit?" Christian joked.

" No." She smiled coyly.

"Now that my hero days are done, maybe…."

"Sure. I could use a boyfriend who can shapeshift. Keeps things interesting." She winked.

Sysy came dancing at the couple with a pitcher of meade.

"Maybe next time you'll do an impression of me. I think mine was Oscar worthy," Sysy said playfully.

"If there is a next time."

"Christian, there is always a next time. That is the problem." But, you still do not embrace the true vision of yourself. You were murdered, and in death you endured terrible horrors, saw unseeable things... a nightmare of magical torture empowered by pure hatred and betrayal. And now, look at you. You stand in two places with power beyond any book, spell, creed, or being because you endured a spell meant to unmake you. Maybe one day you'll see it… what Set could not, for he risked making you the Alpha and Omega, magic and counter magic, Life and Death, just to impose damnation upon you through the most powerful spell of its kind. For what was sunken, shrunken, bitten, and torn, if ever risen, undeniable, delivered, the juggernaut who will know... the Rage of Kemet!" Sysy poured mead in Christian's cup, splashed drops on his face playfully and then chugged the pitcher herself. Then Sysy disappeared.

"What does he mean by that... that they're being a next time is the problem?" Asara asked as she pulled Christian in close.

"What do you know about Buddhism? You know a good plan when you see one. Maybe you can help us with the escape one."

"Why are we escaping?"

" Because if we don't ... it'll be like none of this happened at all."

CHAPTER 1
Sacred Effort

Wep, Tess, Asara, and Christian decided to take a walk to Ye Ole Sammich' after the night of celebrating. Because the Vikings could not stay long in their realm, Big Grim sent them back to Valhalla to await Ragnarök with revelry and training. As for the Norse Gods, they had either collectively passed out or went to Summit for the last slices of pizza.

While Big Grim guarded the Liger obelisk which was still glowing, Christian and the others cared for those who had been captured and trapped on the obelisks as the veil began adjusting to their freedom. That good old Karmic Elasticity.

After they got their sandwiches (Christian got three), he decided to call his mother.

"Hello, who is this?"

"It's Christian."

"Oh, will you look at that? My phone has you in here as Christian. I must know you somehow. You sound young. Are you a friend of Francis, our babysitter?"

"No, I… I'm a close friend of Francis's. We are neighbors in fact! Francis talks about him all the time, and I'm starting a soccer league for the summer for children ages seven to ten. Would your son be in that age range?"

"My son is seven. He'd be perfect for your league. A bit clumsy at first when he tries new things, but with help he

347

gets the hang of it!"

"Ok, ma'am. Well, I actually have to take another call, but I will be in touch! I'll put you down on my list. You will be hearing from me very soon."

"Great. You know, you sound just like his father. Or like you could be his other brother."

Christian hung up disappointed. His mother had reverted back to who she had been before his father's spell. He needed to act quickly. Eventually, she was bound to discover that there was no seven-year-old Christian in the house. And when she did, how would he get her to see the real him?

He went back to the group and explained. All but Wep were perplexed.

"You've shown that with great effort you can feign another person. But for this to work, you'll need to let someone else play seven-year-old Christian. Someone who knew you when you were even younger than seven." Christian sensed a dramatic pause at the end of Wep's statement and felt too uncomfortable to let it linger.

"I'm sorry I was so harsh on you when I came back. I was angry. I'd be honored if you'd help me, old friend."

"You know that back in the day, most of the gods--even the Raiju-- saw me as a third wheel. All but you. You've accepted my faults and have chosen to appreciate the best of me, even when I got tunnel vision. So... let's do this." Wep touched Christian's shoulder as they turned to walk to the crossroad.

Christian looked at Tess. She smiled and hugged him.

Then he looked at Asara, feeling more than a little awkward. They hadn't really talked about them.

"So, doesn't the hero get to kiss the girl in the end?"

Asara prompted.

"I couldn't have done this without you telling me to get a better plan. Being a hero is what was necessary. Now I just want to be with you!"

"Well, my Halloween costume from last year came with a cape, just in case you ever need one again." She melted into Christian's arms.

As they kissed, he closed his eyes. He was finally certain that all of this was real. He could never have imagined an ending like this. With his eyes closed, he saw the image of this phrase, ▩▩▩▩ ▩▩ ▩▩▩▩.

***

"Christian, dinner time!" Mrs. Belvedere paused, listening for his footsteps.

"He's never late for food," she muttered to herself as she walked up the steps to his room.

As she got closer, she heard strains of the first song she had ever given him on cassette: Dave Koz's Together Again. She opened the door.

"Hey, you're having a party in here and didn't invite me?"

"Sorry, mom. I didn't wanna leave my room." But it was Wep. Wep did a pretty good job imitating Christian.

"Now why is that, honey?" She sat down on his bed, gesturing for who she thought was Christian to sit next to her. Wep consented.

"I had a nightmare. I lost you to a monster. A very insecure monster. In the dream, it took me a pretty long time to find out that you needed saving. A lot happened to me.

349

It was just me and the monster. For so long." Wep was in the zone.

"Well, I bet you were very brave. But you know, no child should have to go through that." She put her arm around Wep.

"Let me tell you something about monsters like that. They are more scared of you than you are of them. See, monsters feed on fear. And when you aren't afraid, they get desperate. But it's like the Stoics believed: nothing can hurt you unless you let it. If I were ever under a monster's spell, just know that I would still be me, fighting every second to get back to you."

In an instant, Christian realized that this was the moment he had been waiting for. It was time for him to make his entrance.

"That's why I need you to forgive me," Christian said softly as he opened the door to his bedroom.

Mrs. Belvedere's response was priceless. She looked at Wep, and then she looked at Christian. Understanding swept over her as she realized that, somehow, both were the same.

"Forgive you for what?" She swallowed hard as tears welled up in her eyes.

"Mom, I spent a long time being angry at you. Each time you had a chance to do what you felt was right, you capitulated to my father's will. At first, I thought it was because you loved him more than you loved me. Or that you were just a bad mom." She stiffened at this.

"Is that so? And where is this monster that casts spells now?"

"Gone. Or just too afraid of the Furie standing before you as your son."

"A Furie! It's been a long time since I have heard that word. I was never trained—blame it on my lack of concord with my mother—but I was quite the teenager. If you're the Furie, then you must be spectacular! Aren't you, my beautiful boy?"

She understood Christian's ruse, what he was really after. In one fell swoop, she hugged him more tightly than he had recalled in a long time.

"I'm feeling the weight of the time that has gone by. From now on, we face monsters together. You teach me what you know so I can never fear looking someone in the eye again."

"Mom, I will."

When Christian turned to look for Wep, he was gone.

***

The next morning, Mrs. Belvedere and Christian drove together to campus. This new start at our mother-son relationship felt exactly as he had always anticipated it would. When they arrived, she wanted to visit the library and museum.

"Let's meet for dinner in a couple of hours," she suggested. Christian agreed and set off for Liger to find Big Grim and a few other friends. The place was empty when he got there. A bright pink, sticky note was stuck to Grim's office door. Christian pulled it off and read to himself.

Because we quaked the earth, He is loose.

"What the f…" Christian's phone vibrated in his coat pocket. Pulling it out, he saw that he had at least ten missed calls from Asara. He checked his voicemails. There were three. As he listened, each was indecipherable. Then he saw the text.

You forgot to say Nymphs, too was followed by a heart and arrow emoji.

Asara never used emojis.

Christian looked around him to make sure that he was alone. Once he confirmed that to his satisfaction, he disappeared himself to the Duat for Wep and Tess. All he found was Wep.

"Where is everyone?" He sounded more agitated than he intended.

"Tess went with Rioghain to watch over the obelisks. You just missed her."

"But Asara. Where is she?"

"Why does that matter? She's forgotten you."

"She called me. Like ten times."

"What? She still remembers you? That's actually surprising now that the veil made things normal again. You sure?"

"Yes, I'm sure. I've got to find her. Let's go." And in a second they were off.

***

"So you brought me all the way over here just to thank me?" Tess asked quizzically as she searched Rioghain's eyes. The tension at the FB Waters merry mount obelisk was evident.

"No, to kiss you."

"What?"

"Who could deny that we are fated?" Rioghain leaned in.

Tess hesitated at first, but upon a second glance at Rioghain's new beauty, kissed. In a flash, a wind like the sound of an approaching train blew hard and fast. The ground shook, and everything on its surface violently shimmered.

Rioghain suddenly pulled away, pushing Tess ten feet into the street where a truck hit her solidly, snapping her back. The truck careened left, overcorrected, and then screeched to a stop on the right shoulder.

Out of the truck stepped the long-aggrieved goddess, Ix Chel of the Mayans and Goddess of the Moon in wondrous regalia. Yemaya, Yoruba Mother Goddess of the Ocean, got out on the passenger's side in full splendor. Both were shining. Both joined Rioghain by the obelisk. While it wasn't fully charged, the three had plenty of power left together to complete their mission of revenge.

Rioghain roared a poem, a prophecy that foretold everything a grim future as the obelisk bowed to former glories. She had warned long ago that this would happen. Half in Gaelic and half in English, she chanted, recharging her spirit and summoning her power that had been shuttered and gray for centuries. She held hands with her powerhouse, sister cohorts, for the catharsis was overwhelming and deserved to be shared. They had waited two thousand times an Odyssean mile.

Afraigid rig don cath
Kings arise to [meet] the battle
rucatair gruaide
Cheeks are seized

aisnethir rossa
Faces [honors] are declared
ronnatair feola,
Flesh is decimated,
fennátair enech,
Faces are flayed
ethátair catha -rruba
Things of battle are seized
segatar ratha
Ramparts are sought
radatar fleda
Feasts are given
fechatar catha,
Battles are observed
canátair natha,
Poems are recited
noatair druith
Druids are celebrated
dénaitir cuaird
Circuits are made
cuimnitir arca
Bodies are recorded
alat(-) ide
Metals cut
sennat(-) deda
Teeth mark
tennat(-) braigit
Necks break
blathnuigh[i]t(-) [cét] tufer
Hundreds cut the blossom
cluinethar eghme
Screams are heard

354

ailitir cuaird
Battalions are broken
cathitir lochtai
Hosts give battle
lúet(-)ethair
Ships are steered
snaat(-) arma
Weapons protect
Scothaitir sronai.
Noses are severed
At_ci[ú] cach ro_genair
I see all who are born
ruad_cath derg_bandach
in the blood-zealous vigorous battle,
dremnad fiach_lergai fo_eburlai.
raging [on the] raven-battlefield [with] blade-scabbards!

-Elizabeth Grey
She continued, altering her former prophecy from The Second Battle of Mag Tuired, now in a language any passerby could understand.

I have seen a world which will be dear to me.
I decry the world that comes first
Summer without blossoms.
Cattle will be without milk.
Women without modesty.
Men without valor.
Conquest without a king.
Woods without mast.

355

Sea without produce.
False judgements of old men.
False precedents of Olympians.
Every man a betrayer.
Every son a reaver.
The sun will overcome Jupiter
The Wolf will be unbound.
A hero much as his mother.
A heroine much as her Father
With futile chivalry, we will crown
But then No last names, no chaperones, no permission,
What goes 'round comes back around

The covetous spell reached far and wide. She sealed them with her last words.

Trade an evil time for a Poly rhyme.
Because a Son did deceive his father.
Justice will perceive so much farther...

Far up high, the stars rearranged themselves and the ground below shook and opened. Like objects in a tornado, the materials of the modern world vanished.

***

Cerberus had warned Christian. Was it now too late to

356

listen? Having defeated one evil, it looked like they still faced an ancient unknown.

***

It was hours later when Christian was awakened by a bright light, or so he thought. The room was dark and the only light came from the crimson beams of the moon. He blinked his eyes.

Wait. That isn't moonlight.

In the upper left window pane, Christian saw a red star which emanated a light that dwarfed the light of the moon. He blinked again, but harder this time. That star was moving. It was getting closer and brighter. Hold on. That window looked strangely familiar.

Groggily, Christian lifted his right hand to rub his eyes. It wouldn't lift any higher than a few inches before he felt resistance. He tried again, and heard the clink of metal on metal. He tried his left hand. Same problem.

Christian was cuffed to his bed. That jarred him awake, and he tried to sit up.

"Where am I?" He asked out loud, alarmed.

Someone else was in the room and stepped into one of the crimson beams.

"Asara?"

"Silly Christian. You're back!"

Dr. Aceso was looking down at him.

————THE END | To Be Continued————

About the Author

Justin Williams studied engineering at the RWTH University in Aachen, Germany and the Norwegian Institute of Techonology in Trondheim, Norway. He has held senior and executive positions with well known companies in the Energy Industry. He is the author of the book *How to Sell Engineered Products.* He lives in Houston, Texas with his wife and son.

VIRTUES CONSTELLATION